Surviving Sunday

A Chronicles of Warfare Novel

Melinda Michelle

Published By

G.M.M.E.

Global Multi Media Enterprises

Global Multi Media Enterprises (GMME)
P. O. Box 3763
Tallahassee, FL 32315
850.396.2665

GMME Results...GMME Purpose...GMME Destiny!

Visit our website at: **www.gwendolynevans.wix.com/gmme**

Email us at: **gwendolynevans21@yahoo.com**

ISBN: 978-0-9891460-1-2
LCCN: 2013940232

Cover photo courtesy of: Bigstockphoto.com
Cover creation by: GMME

Acknowledgements

I would first like to thank the one and only Almighty God for giving me this gift before the foundation of the world and for letting me finally realize I had it. I thank him for his awesome grace and unmerited favor that is shining on my life. Next, I would like to thank my editor, "Dr." Yanela Gordon, for her selflessness, tirelessness, and honesty in the editing process. You are amazing, and I hope and pray that this is a long term relationship we have. I write it, and you rip it to pieces without a red pen, and a smile on your face, LOL.

My girl, Ileana, what can I say? You have been annoyed, pestered, and forced to read my drafts and a sounding board for my random concepts, and you did it with such grace and honesty, I can't help but adore you. Thank you for being my friend ALL these years and always supporting me no matter what new idea pops up in my head at any random time in the middle of the night! You ROCK!!!

I want to thank my amazing surrogate family in Tallahassee that gave me the idea for this story. Joshua, Maleah, Sharvis, and Chantiel, and your beautiful babies are just like real family. Thank you for being absolute idiots and some of the funniest people I know. Hanging out with you guys planted an idea in my head that just took off. I appreciate y'all letting me fictionalize you all to launch my writing career. I am so excited for what God has in store for all of us. We are a dynasty waiting to happen!!!

I want to acknowledge Barbara Joe Williams and the Tallahassee Authors Network for giving me the platform and support to take this book from concept to fruition. The support and feedback you guys provide is so cool. How blessed are we to have an organization like this?

I want to thank ALL my family and friends for their love and support. Special thanks to Keisha for reading it and coming all the way to Florida just to give me feedback. Howard for "delegating" and getting me the feedback that caused a pivotal change in the book. Thanks to Elder Sharvis Whitted for answering all my Bible questions. To Michelle, thank you for turning this book into an "Eventive Impression." ☺

I want to give a shout out to the Family Worship and Praise Center (FWPC) for their support and for being the most awesome church ever. To my Pastor, Cyrus Flanagan, you are an AMAZING man, and I hope you are overwhelmed with a lifetime of blessings, love, and support. You are tireless in fighting for our destiny and the fulfillment of our lives outside of the church. We don't have to wonder if you are keeping us covered because we see it. We do not take you for granted. We know what a gift we have. May God bless you and your family with long health and happiness. Oh and thanks for letting me use your sermon! ☺

Dedication

I dedicate this book to the greatest parents in the world, Marvin and Juanita Evans. There are no words to describe how blessed I am to have such great parents. I want to thank you for the faith that you instilled in me, and thank you for always supporting my dreams. I cannot wait to bless your lives in return. No two people are more deserving.

Prologue:
Another Realm

They all stood together in a room in the recesses of a local building on the northwest side of town. The modest room was as humble as they were majestic. A faint dripping sound could be heard from one of the pipes as they waited for all to assemble. The last messenger they had been waiting for finally arrived. He whispered into the ear of the Captain of the Host. Tallis, the messenger angel, came with the information from the Lord God Almighty as to what was about to take place.

There stood waiting for instruction were sixteen angelic beings. Eight military, four messengers, and four ministering angels were present. The Captain, Valter, was just as his name meant the ruler of the army. The Scandinavian stood with the authority of the legions he had commanded through the millenniums. Having now heard the message that was sent, he began to put into place a strategy.

All the military angels stood eight-feet tall and wore their weapon like it was one of their limbs all attached to them by golden sheaths. While some weapons were visible, others were covered by their wings. Depending on their heritage, their skin shimmered in shades of gold, silver, and bronze. They were dressed for battle. Their brilliant iridescent white wings were tucked behind them in parade rest. Had they been expanded they could not all fit in the modest room. The second in command was Nero, an Italian, who was known for his wisdom. He spoke to the other angels in his firm but soothing baritone voice, "The captain has brought us here because there is a war on the horizon. We need to prepare for what's to come."

Valter, whose voice boomed deeply with authority coating every word explained, "There is a war ahead for this city that we cannot afford to lose. The Strongman of this city has been at work far too long and the saints have cried out. Homosexuality is running rampant, greed, and idolatry are taking over, and now blood is being shed by all manner of violence. We cannot allow our adversary to take over this city. There are too many generations at stake in this one place. This nation's doctors, nurses, pharmacists, lawyers, teachers, financiers, bankers, philanthropists, and politicians are all being made in this city. They have great destinies in the earth, and if they are destroyed and cut off before their purpose is manifested, then we will not only have lost this city but the generations to come."

The Native American, Ahiga, one of the military angels, stood with his hand on his weapon as if ready to draw at a moment's notice, "When do we begin?"

Nero said, "Be patient, my friend. We must go through the process, and we cannot let our adversary know that we are on the move. Right now, there are more of them than us. Trust me, your chance to fight will come soon enough. We must take a defensive posture until we get the numbers we need. It is important to remember to keep yourselves as concealed as possible and to only draw on the adversary if it is absolutely necessary. We don't want this first battle to take place until we are ready."

Ahiga asked, "Why must we be passive? We can send some of them back to the pits right now."

Valter smiled. He always loved the fight in Ahiga. They had come through many battles together and he was sure they would go through many more. "Just as Nero said, there is a process, and we are not fighting to win a battle, we are fighting to win a war," he said. "We will use might but only when the time comes."

Ahiga clenched his jaw to try and release some of his righteous indignation. Valter continued, "The first strategic attack will be on members of the Kingdom Builders Worship Center. This ministry will play a significant role in the war to come, and they need to be guarded."

Kamau, the African warrior, the quiet warrior, met his eyes. "Captain, Ahiga and I have been assigned to Kingdom Builders, and we report that there has been more activity of gossip and backbiting than normal. There is a remnant willing to pray at all times, but it's still not enough prayer to cover for us to do what we will need to do."

Valter responded. "You two keep stirring up prayer warriors; tell them to send for more help because we will soon need it. I believe the eight of us can handle this assignment but when we triumph against our adversary, he will send stronger demons and the saints will be tested like never before." The others nodded their agreement and understanding.

"The first three attacks will begin tonight," Valter said. "We have to be prepared to protect." He looked over to the ministering angels, Aidan and Gage. They stood in brilliant blue sapphire robes that glimmered as bright as their wings, each standing six-feet tall. "One of you is assigned to Seth, the minister of music, and the other his wife. They must not give in to their emotions if this battle is to be won. His gift of music is a weapon against our adversary and that adversary is on assignment to silence it."

Valter looked to the messenger angels, who stood seven-feet tall, in their sparkling emerald robes that so starkly contrasted their pearl colored wings. They each brandished a weapon of either a knife or a dagger. Valter picked out Cree. "You will go to Emma Lee, the mother of this close knit group that is being attacked. Trouble her spirit. She has the heart, and she is willing. Make sure she covers each of them by name, Seth, Sheridan, Grey, and especially Kadijah. Grey cannot afford to lose her faith, and she cannot fail this test that falls to her because it is crucial to the battles ahead." They each nodded in acceptance of their assignments.

Valter looked to Quan of Vietnam and Cheveyo of Native American lineage, "You two are assigned to Kadijah, and you are never to leave her side. She has a decision to make, and you need to make sure she makes it soon because she is the key. You two will definitely be met with opposition. We can trust that the Lord God Almighty will make a way."

Savas, of Turkey, stepped forward, "Captain, whom do I cover?"

"You cover Grey. Her greatest battle has not yet arrived, but the foundation has to be laid. She will need protection." He cried out, "Bojan," directing his attention to another military angel of Siberia. "You go with Savas just in case our adversary sends more than one after her."

Valter continued, "The rest of you messengers, Lance and Darrow, stay close to me because after the prayers go up, you will be busy with the messages sent out to bring help to the city. And you two ministers, Orion and Roman, for the time being cover the Pastor. Keep his spirit fed, there is much that is about to befall his congregation. Lastly, to my army, remember to conceal yourselves. Do not alert the enemy to your identity. Robe yourselves as ministers or messengers or even as humans. They are not to know we are in battle mode. Kamau and Ahiga, you are exempt as they already know you are the guardians of the gates at Kingdom Builders."

God's elect all gathered in a circle, Valter admonished, "We must be about the Lord's business." In unison, the angels shouted, "The Lord strong and mighty, the Lord mighty in battle." The sound their wings made collectively was harmonic, and it was thunderous. The brilliant streaks of light that shot out from them were majestic. The average human eye could not behold because it was divine and only shined but for a split second.

†††

Downtown atop the dome of the Capitol building he sat perched on his talons. He was the color of a moonless, starless sky. His yellow eyes gleamed with satisfaction at the destruction he had made sure took place in the city of Tallahassee, Florida. A huge mass of evil, his scales gleamed silvery when they caught the light of the moon. His talons were razor sharp and his wings a black silk that billowed in the slight breeze were expanded three-feet on each side. His face was that of a reptile with fangs that curved under his jaw.

Ten years ago, the media reports were so boring they could be used to put anyone to sleep but not anymore, not since his reign. Today, the news was filled with violence, murders, and robberies. Idolatry, homosexuality, greed, perversion, and so much more were running amuck. He was on his way to winning this city for his Master.

The collegiate and political city was the perfect place to take as a trophy for The Dark One because the destinies they would destroy, and the plans they would thwart would be a huge blow to the Kingdom of Heaven. He smiled just thinking about it. His sulfurous breath darted from his nostrils.

The day-to-day mayhem was unfolding beautifully in his opinion. The saints at that pestering church were starting to cry out. They were getting too much Word in them. They were starting to believe what that pastor of theirs was preaching; he was winning more and more young souls to the other side. If he got them while they were young, then they would most likely stay that way. That church was once insignificant and now it was growing with an army of praying saints. That ministry alone had so many people that could destroy his plan to take over the city for good that he had to act quickly.

He was now pacing the dome of the Capitol annoyed that his soldiers were late. He wasn't quite mad yet because he knew at the least they were out tormenting souls, but his patience was wearing thin. He had other matters to contend with. His right-hand man or better yet, the sniveling demon, Corruption, was by his side.

A dark, slimy, creepy entity, Corruption, had bat-like wings atop his shoulders. His red eyes were searching to and fro to see if he could see any of his fellow demons coming ahead. In his frustration, the Strongman back-handed Corruption and sent him hurling back, his rancid breath polluting the air when he screeched. Corruption reached out with a claw and stopped his fall against the building. He flew back up and said, "Your highness, they will be here."

Before the Strongman could strike him again, his legion began to descend upon the Capitol. They were all manner of evil and ugly. They crept, they crawled, they flew, and they slithered. The darkness they brought permeated the air with such an evil heaviness that every animal within a mile scurried.

The Strongman said after they had all settled, "I'm going to make this simple. I don't like what's going on at that church on Olive Street. I want you to do whatever your evil heart's desire to keep them from praying. Destroy their faith in God and in man. He looked over and said, "Jealousy!"

"Yes, your evilness?"

"You find someone with a jealous heart, and you use it to contaminate the congregation, because after all, no emotion can stand against you and your antics. Attack the remnant of prayer warriors. Take with you other imps of gossip, bitterness, complacency, and fear. Run rampant through the congregation with distraction. Take their focuses off our main targets."

"Corruption!" he summoned.

"Yes, your highness?"

"You are to assign warriors to take out the music in that church. You must take out the banker and the future politician." He pulled out his sword and placed it under Corruption's neck. The other demons and imps began laughing and making fun of him. Corruption hissed, but by doing so, he felt the Strongman's blade piercing his scales. The Strongman said, "If you fail, I will send you back to the pit myself. You won't even be worthy of being sent by one of God's elect."

Destroyer, a conniving ball of evil, looked on with great interest because if Corruption failed, he would be sure to rule the city while the Strongman was busy with more important things. He despised Corruption and would use this opportunity to show the Strongman that he should be in charge of keeping the city from falling back to the saints. It was Destroyer's goal to make sure that Corruption failed at his assignment with him being the one to recover all. "The attacks begin tonight, go and do not come back if you fail," the Strongman threatened.

Part One:

Opposition

Chapter 1:
A Willing Vessel

Mother Emma Lee Ellis - 10:45 P.M.

I had been tossing and turning for the last thirty minutes. Sleep was not trying to find me since I woke up in a cold sweat. I had the strangest nightmare. I don't know what it meant, but all I could see on the unfamiliar faces of the people in the dream was pain and then there was just chaos. It didn't make sense, but it felt real.

I got up and went to the kitchen to get a warm glass of milk. I sat down at the kitchen table and began sipping it. My goodness, the rain was coming down out there. "That rain is violent. It's gonna tear up my garden out there, I swear." I got up to look out of the kitchen window to assess the damage.

The thunder roared and shook the entire house and a flash of lightning lit up the sky so brightly it looked like the rapture was taking place. I jumped back. "Oh, it's time for me to sit my behind down and turn out these lights." I took a step and froze. I got this chill. It was the strangest feeling and then all of a sudden, my heart got heavy.

"Lord, is that you? Are you trying to tell me something?" I got real still and closed my eyes so I could hear God's voice. The thunder roared again and I jumped. "See, I'm trippin'," as the kids would say. "Let me take my behind to bed." It had been many, many years since a storm spooked me.

After emptying the glass in the sink, I rinsed it out, and headed to my room. As I crawled back in the bed, I looked at the clock; it was 10:58 P.M. It is so past time for my beauty rest. By the time my face hit the pillow, I felt something tugging at my heart. A loud whisper said, "Pray!"

I sat up, "Lord, I'm tired; these old bones of mine put in some work today. You know I am going to talk to you first thing in the morning, can it wait?" I think I made Him mad because my heart just got so burdened I could hardly stand it. "Ok, Lord, I'm up, I'm up." I propped myself up against the headboard and began to pray. "Dear Lord, I don't know what's going on, bu..."

I felt an urgency to get on my knees and pray. "Lord, I just don't see how that's going to make a difference. I'm not that young and so if I get down on my knees, are you gonna help me get back up?" I was cranky, it was closing in on 11:15 on a rainy night, and God was probably considering smiting me right about now. My spirit got so troubled I didn't know a woman my age could get down on the floor so quickly. "My goodness. Well, what's wrong?"

I began to pray, "Well, Lord, what is going on? Ok, Father, I surrender, forgive me for my disobedience and slothfulness. Lord, I am your vessel, use me. Open my spiritual eyes so that I can stand in the gap for whatever soul is in need." I got quiet and waited for God to show me who was in need of prayer because I had a feeling whoever it was I needed to call them out by name.

I heard, "Sunday dinner."

"Sunday dinner, Lord, this is not the time to be thinking about no plate." Okay, I needed to focus. Sunday dinner, I was puzzled. "Well, let's see, we always have Sunday dinner at Jeremiah and Mia's house. Let me start with them. "Father, look upon my dear friends. Watch over them, and protect them from all hurt harm and danger. I place a hedge of protection around their children and ask that you keep them. Lord, please give them strength as a family and strengthen them in you. Order their steps. I speak against the attack of the enemy on their lives."

My heart was getting heavier, it wasn't them. I began to pray for Nathaniel, trouble probably always followed him. "Lord, help him to be the man you have called him to be. Keep him from temptation and the destructive path the enemy is trying to set before him. Help him to make wise decisions and to surrender his will to you."

My heart got heavier. "Lord, who is it?" I asked frustrated. Kadijah's face appeared to me just as clear as day. The look on her face was horrifying, and she was scared. My heart got even heavier. "Oh, dear Jesus!"

I began to cry out, "Father, in the name of Jesus, save her, Lord. Send your angels to her aid right now, God. I come against every attack of the enemy on her life right now. Satan, I bind you and send you back to the pits of hell. You will not take her life; you will not destroy her destiny. She will be everything that God has called her to be. Jesus, I need you to send your comforting spirit to give her wisdom on how to get out of this situation. Give her your peace that surpasses all understanding. Let your angels walk with her and protect her right now. Lord, send them right now."

I began to weep for her, for her life, for her future, for her soul. "Lord, you said in your word, one can chase a thousand and two can put ten thousand to flight. Father, I come against every demonic force that is on assignment for her life, and I send them back to the pits of hell, and they shall not prevail against that precious child. God, let her know you're there; let her know you're right there with her. God, I seal it in your son Jesus' precious blood."

I continued to cry for her. My heart was so heavy for her, but I had no more words. I kneeled there for a while crying out to God and speaking in tongues on behalf of that dear child. After a while, the burden began to lift, though I didn't have complete peace yet.

I got up to go to the bathroom to get some tissue to clean my face and my nose. As I came back into the room, I still couldn't shake the feeling that someone else that I loved was in need of an intercessor. I sat down on the bed to get my bearings. It was twelve o'clock in the morning.

"Lord, Jesus, what is going on tonight?" As I closed my eyes and I began to listen to my heart, I could see my baby, Sheridan, balled up in so much pain. A mother never wants to see her child in pain.

"Oh, Lord, what's happened? Father, look upon my child right now. I don't know where she is, but you do. I can't wrap my arms around her, but you can. Lord, send your ministering angels to comfort and keep her and to let her know no matter what she is facing, you are all she needs to get through it. Help her to set her emotions aside and put you first in her life. God, help her to throw caution to the wind and trust you like she never has before. God, you didn't bring her this far to leave her, this I know. Let your Holy Spirit comfort her right now in the midst of whatever it is that she's facing, Lord."

"Hmph," I had a thought, I wondered where Seth was while my baby was in so much pain. I felt a gentle press on my heart to pray for my son-in-law.

"Oh, Lord, Jesus, what is going on in that house over yonder? Look upon my son, Lord. Let your word guide him and give him wisdom, knowledge, and understanding in this situation, Father. Send your ministering angels to his side, and I pray for his mind Lord. Give him peace, and show him how to trust you in the midst of his adversity. Let him know that in you lies all the answers he could ever need. I pray for his destiny, Lord. I know you have called him to be a mighty man of God and whatever he is facing, you will make it work for his good. I rebuke all the plans the enemy has to knock him off track. I declare that they will not stand. Help him to trust in you to see him through."

I began to feel better, like I was really making a difference in the spirit realm. I had a feeling that God was moving in a mighty way and that my prayers were being guided. I'm glad that I got up off my behind to do my part. I got back into bed and lay down. When I closed my eyes, I saw Grey's face. She was scared, too, but not like the fear that was in Kadijah's face. Well, yeah, I guess that makes sense. It just didn't seem right to go to sleep and not pray for her, too. I got out of the bed and back on my knees.

"What in the world have these kids got themselves into tonight? Father, look upon Grey right now wherever she may be. Protect her from anything the enemy may be throwing in her path. Cover her right now in your son's precious blood. Let her know that you are right there with her directing her path and ordering her steps. Let her know that you hold her destiny in your hand and that nothing is too hard or impossible for you. Lord, I know she can be a handful, but she has a good heart and most importantly, she knows you are real. Send your angels to watch over and protect her. Let her know everything will be okay. If she just puts her faith and trust in you to take care of her like your word promised you would. Father, I cover these young lives in the blood of Jesus. I seal their doorposts with the blood of the lamb and the angel of death will not come nigh. These things I pray in Jesus' name, amen."

Finally, my heart was at peace. It had been a long time since I felt God's presence like that and a burden on my heart to pray.

"Lord, I know you are working it out." I got up, and got in the bed to go to sleep. Right before I closed my eyes, I looked at the clock. 12:55 A.M. The storm was subsiding, and I drifted off into an anointed and peaceful sleep.

Chapter 2:
The Surreal Life – 11:42 P.M.

Kadijah

Blackness was everywhere. I could not comprehend what was happening around me. It was just complete nothingness, and then fear suddenly gripped me when I heard a blood curdling scream. I did not know where it was coming from.

Suddenly, my throat started burning, and I realized the scream was coming from me as I was re-entering the world of consciousness. When I finally came to, I opened my eyes and everything around me was blurry. I had no idea where I was or why my body felt like lead, and my head felt like it was about to explode.

Well, common sense kicked in, and I opted to get up and make some sense of this situation. That turned out to be a little more work than I anticipated. My body was so heavy. I placed my palms face down and tried to lift myself up, but to no avail. When I hit the ground again, I realized my body was aching because my ribs were bruised badly and a pain shot through my back that suddenly brought reality into focus.

I was fighting for my life and had no idea how I got here or how I would get out. I drew in a breath causing more pain to radiate through me as I pulled myself up on my knees. My vision was blurred, and I couldn't make out my surroundings. I finally turned myself over and propped up against a wall.

I knew I needed to get out of here, wherever here was, but I also knew I wasn't one-hundred percent. I needed to assess the damage that was done to me. The first thing I checked for was my clothes to see if they were all there. Thank God I didn't appear to have been violated.

I pressed my hand on the left side of my face, no pain. I pressed my hand on the right side of my face, and it felt like a thousand needles were stabbing me. Clearly, I had a black eye. I licked the inside of my mouth to see if all my teeth were there, and tasted copper. There was blood coming from somewhere, but my front teeth seemed to be intact.

I cupped my hand over my right eye to single my vision to try and determine where I was and what happened. I could hear that it was raining and thundering outside, and there was a dim light shining into the room.

In the darkness, I made out my purse. My keys were sprawled out on the floor. I jumped to look for my cell phone ignoring my body's not so silent cry for help. The phone was gone. Shoot! Ok, plan B. I reached for the keys. They weren't mine but at this point, I'd drive a semi-tractor trailer up out of here.

"Wait," a voice screamed inside my head, "You need a weapon." I agreed that made a lot of sense. I searched around for anything. Then, on a little table, there was a trophy. It wasn't my desired choice, but it was heavy so I grabbed it, stuffed it in my purse, and put my purse around my neck and shoulder.

I got my bearings, and I heard some rattling coming from behind me. I hesitated because my blood ran cold and stopped me in my tracks. Oh, it was time to go. I blinked out of that and ran in the opposite direction of the noise. It ain't nothing like adrenaline to fuel you past your preconceived limitations. I could see a door, and I headed for it. When I got on the other side of it, I was standing on an old rickety porch. "Where in the heck am I?" I whispered.

"Run!" the voice in my head screamed. It didn't matter once I spotted the car that looked to be a dark sedan. I was about to click the unlock button on the keys when it occurred to me that whoever was after me could hear it so I ran up and unlocked the door manually, jumped in the car, and started it. I slowly backed out of the driveway onto a dark street. I turned on the lights and took off as fast as I could.

There was no one on the road. There was nothing, just a dark road in front of me and an even darker road behind me. The rain pouring down hard outside sounded like bullets hitting the car. It was the blinding rain that made me actually grip the steering wheel at ten and two in fear for my safety.

At this point, my safety was a concern, but I would rather kill myself in a car crash than to let whoever was after me get the satisfaction of ending my life. My head was throbbing. I was so confused. The clock on the dashboard read 12:15. I couldn't tell where the rain ended and my tears began. I was so scared.

"What happened back there? Oh, God, I just need one moment of clarity." Out of nowhere, bright lights appeared behind me flashing like crazy and gaining on me. I was so scared. Was that him? Is someone trying to help me? What do I do? This fool might try to run me off the road. I was approaching a light, and it was just as red as Rudolph's nose but there was no way in hell I was stopping this car, so I punched through it. Thank God no one was coming.

This fool was still behind me, and there was a gas station coming up, though it looked like it was closed. Next thing I knew, I heard a loud boom, and the car went haywire. I think I blew a tire. I handled the car the best way I could and managed to swerve it into the station, just barely missing the pump.

I could hear the car behind me screeching to a halt. I have to get out of here, but there was nowhere to go. I began to shake because I had never been so scared in my life. Next thing I knew, I was sliding down in the seat into the fetal position because my mind was blank.

I heard tires screeching when I felt the other car crash into the driver's side of the car I was driving. I flew to the passenger side and my head hit the window. Everything got still, everything got quiet, and everything moved in slow motion. The irony of blood coming from your head because of pain is that it tickled when it ran down your face. I could feel myself slipping into unconsciousness, so I just closed my eyes.

I heard a door slam, and I jumped back awake. Wait a minute, this is my life, and I just can't go out like this. I reached for all I had left, hope. I whispered, "Dear Lord, please give me strength."

An idea came to me. I grabbed the keys out of the ignition and climbed into the back seat as quickly as I could. I pulled the latch to let the seat down and climbed into the trunk. I was closing the backseat just as I heard the driver side window breaking.

I tried to catch my breath while at the same time holding it so they couldn't hear me breathing. When I heard the person fussing and cussing, I reached in my purse and pulled out the trophy. When I heard more windows breaking, I pushed the button to pop the trunk, jumped out, and started running for my life.

I didn't know how far I would make it, but I had to try. I could hear them screaming and turned to see if they were close behind. I tripped over something and went tumbling to the ground. Dag, how could I be so typical?

I screamed out in pain because I fell on the trophy. I rolled over to keep going, but this time adrenaline wasn't enough. By the time I stood up, the person who was intent on ending my life was in my face with a gun pointed at my head.

I shrieked, "Oh, my God, it's you!" I froze. Her eyes were wild and crazy. She almost looked like somebody else, but it was definitely her. Time stood still and all I could focus on was the barrel of that gun. I couldn't make out what she was saying because I kept thinking, "So, this is how it's going to end?" Suddenly, I felt faint.

The last thing I heard her say was, "I hate you, and I am going to ruin your life just like you ruined mine." I dropped to my knees, and the only thing I could think of was P.J. always saying, he's a very present help in the time of trouble. I screamed, "Jesus!"

Chapter 3:
Don't Get Caught Slippin' – 11:48 P.M.

Seth

I just sat there thinking. The pouring rain tapping on the window was adding to my anxiety. The thunder was so loud I felt like it was God yelling at me for the mess I'd gotten myself into.

I started staring at the glass in front me not believing that I was actually about to drink some hard liquor. For the first time in my life, I took a sip of alcohol and not for pleasure, but simply to ease my pain. I gulped down as much whiskey as I could stand. It was an instant regret.

My throat and chest were on fire. I thought this was supposed to help the pain, not make it worse. I caught a distorted glimpse of myself in the mirror across the room and what I saw sickened me. Look at me with this drink in my hand, a minister, a man of God. It just didn't feel right. I pushed the drink aside. "Man, what are you doing? Has your life really come to this?"

When I came home tonight, my wife was gone along with her suitcase and some items of clothing. I have no idea where she went or when she's coming back. I called her cell about 100 times and all I got was her voicemail. I've left so many messages the box is now full.

"Lord, let her be alright." I always wondered what my lowest point would feel like, but I never anticipated this. I looked around my office, but it was blurry, and I couldn't clearly make out anything because my eyes were bloodshot red from crying out to God. I had been crying so hard I never actually got out a prayer. Although I knew the Lord understood my pain, I felt like I needed to put it in the air. So the angels could pick it up and run with it.

I got out of the chair and lay out on the floor, desperate. "Lord, I am so sorry for the mess I have gotten myself into, and I know it is downright arrogant of me to come to you now that I am up a creek without a paddle, but I need you like I have never needed you before. I could lose everything—my wife, my ministry, my future. Forgive me for being so naïve and forgive me for not listening to the still small voice you gave when there was still time to prevent this nonsense. I take full responsibility for falling for her manipulation, and I take full responsibility for letting my own past come back with a vengeance to jeopardize my future. Lord, I am no saint, but I am also far from a heathen. You know my heart and my desire to live my life according to your will. In your Word, you said, "*Ye shall know the truth and the truth will set you free.*"

"At this point, your Word and your promises are all I have to hold on to because everything I thought I had is now either gone or hanging on by a rapidly unraveling thread. My wife can't stand the sight of me; I actually make her physically sick. That's the part that truly hurts. I know that our marriage has endured some bumps and bruises on the count of this mistake I made, but the fact that she is taking her word over mine speaks volumes about where our relationship is headed. The people I thought were my friends are whispering behind my back. My integrity has been assassinated. Lord, my heart is breaking, and I mean literally. I have never experienced emotional hurt so severe. It actually hurts to breathe. God, how can this get worse? You know what, I take that back. I don't wanna know if it can get worse. I know your Word inside and out. Since I try my best to live my life by it, I know that I can trust in it. *In Romans 8:28, you said that all things work together for good to them that love God and to those that are called according to His purpose.* What I do know is that I was called to fulfill your purpose in my life, and I love you with all my heart and soul so this situation will turn around for me. However, what I feel is far from what I know, so I need your peace that passes all understanding to help me see the blessing in this situation and to increase my faith. I never knew just how much faith was needed to have faith the size of a mustard seed. I've got a big mountain I need you to move. I thank you, Lord, for your comfort, your faithfulness, and your love. These things I pray in your son Jesus' name, amen."

I began to pick myself up from the floor. I knew the average man would never admit to breaking down like this, but sometimes you had to let go of that macho crap and lay prostrate before the Lord. When a man could humble himself before the Lord and admit that he needed Him to make it through, then he had become a real man.

I got up, went to my desk, and sat in the chair so that I could get myself together. All of a sudden, I felt the most peaceful spirit fall over me. My headache began to dissipate and the heaviness on my heart began to lift. I leaned back, closed my eyes, and started worshiping God. At that very moment, I knew that His hand was on the situation. There is nothing like His comforting Holy Spirit. Just a simple heartfelt prayer, I felt so much better.

My phone rang. I glanced at the clock because I knew it was late. 12:30. Maybe it's Sheridan calling me back. Without looking at the caller ID I answered, "Sheridan?" Her voice was cocky and sinister and not my wife's.

"Oh, trouble in paradise, its darn near one o'clock in the morning, and the missus ain't in yet, huh? You know this could be so much easier if you would just stop fighting the inevitable and be with me. Your life as you know it has finally come crashing down just like I told you it would. I told you I prayed about this, and you are supposed to be with me. Now the sooner you get that through your head, the sooner you can make an honest woman out of me. Forget about what's her name, and help me raise our child. Just stop lying to everybody."

I just whispered the only name that could help me now, "Jesus."

Chapter 4:
I Plead Insanity - 12:04 A.M.

Sheridan

Have you ever plotted someone's murder? I mean like from start to finish, not leaving out any details. What if I get caught? What if I don't get caught? Can I live with myself? Hell yes! I wouldn't lose any sleep over that lying bastard.

Well, after all the plotting of scenarios, alibis, and getaways, that split second of clarity allowed for some much needed Holy Ghost conviction. He will never know how the Lord used common sense and CSI to save his life because my hair sheds like crazy, and I just know they'd find some of my DNA at the scene. That fool better be glad I'm saved.

I was driving in this horror movie rain seething at my lack of ability to murder my husband. By the time I got to the hotel, checked in, and got into my room, I was a mess, just a hot mess. My clothes were soaked from the rain, my makeup was running down my face from the tears, and I couldn't even put into words what my hair looked like.

I stared at myself in the mirror. No wonder the front desk clerk looked at me like I was a charity case. Now I understand why the look of shock spread over her face when my credit card was accepted. I look like a homeless person that just walked in off the street. You know what? I really don't care. I look just how I freakin' feel.

I looked around the room in its simplicity—a double bed, a night stand, a chair, a table, and a sad little dresser. It wasn't my home, but it was a place of refuge for my darkest hour. My God, how did I get here?

I moved the chair next to the window, sat down, and stared out. The rain usually calmed me, but this rain was scary. It was pouring so hard and thundering so loud, I felt like it was the soundtrack to my pain. It inspired the tears to start flowing again. It was like I was in competition with the window to see who could drop the most tears the fastest.

My sobs started off quiet and dismal, but the more I thought about my life in its current state, the harder they came. My tears were out of control now, and I was shaking. The pain in my heart was unbearable. I tried to tell him, but he wouldn't listen. I knew that heifa was up to no good. But I can't just fault her. He played his part too and obviously well.

A baby. A freakin' baby. How the hell? I don't even have kids from my own husband and now this trifling skank done got knocked up. At first it was like a bad dream, like even though all the evidence was against him, I just knew in my heart that she was lying, and I could trust my husband's side of the story. I was sorely mistaken.

I wanted the DNA test, and there was no way I was going to wait for the baby to arrive. I wanted to shut her up once and for all, so we paid for it. I mean that bastard swore to me it wasn't his. He said there was no way possible because he never slept with her.

Let her tell it, they made passionate love, and this child was a result of what they were always destined to be. Well, in actuality, I guess I married a liar because the test came back a positive match to my husband, that slimy excuse for a man. I cannot believe he slept with that slut, and he's supposed to be somebody's minister. He got me round here lookin' like boo-boo the fool. I'm so freakin' mad I could just choke the life out of him and that hussy!

But I always hear my momma's voice in my head saying, "You need to pray, God will see you through this. You need to talk to God, and see what he has to say about it." I know what God has to say about it. Thou shall not commit adultery. I know this is the one time I am supposed to trust in God, if I was ever going to do so. I just can't hear God right now, and maybe I don't want to hear God right now, especially if all he is going to say is that I need to forgive. Forgiveness is the last thing on my mind. It's a good thing I left my gun at the house. I think I might use it on somebody tonight.

Lord, why me? Why us? Why now? I just couldn't stop crying, and my head was throbbing. I couldn't take any more of this crap. I let out a scream from deep within my soul to try to let go of some of my frustration. It only helped to intensify the headache that was about to drive me insane. I imagined rock bottom being very near.

The phone rang. *Who could that be, no one knows I'm here?* Curiosity got the best of me. I sat down on the bed and answered it, "Hello."

"Ma'am, there was a disturbance reported from one of the adjacent rooms on your floor. I was calling to make sure everything was alright."

I let out an exasperated sigh. I knew better, but I snapped. "Yes, ma'am, everything is fine, and you can tell my nosy behind neighbors that my husband cheated on me, and I screamed to make myself feel better, and the next time they have a problem with me to come see me themselves."

I hung up. I knew I was wrong, but dang, I just wished people would let me be. Is it too much to ask to mourn and plot my husband's death in peace? Ok, Lord, I didn't mean that, I take it back, I'm sorry, I don't need no spirits trying to attach themselves to me while I'm vulnerable.

All of a sudden, I felt short of breath. My life as I knew it was spiraling down into the pits of hell. I placed my head between my legs and started taking deep breaths. This was too much. *I just need...God I just need, you. As a matter of fact I need you more than I ever have because you need to work on me. The thoughts I'm having makes me question whether I was ever saved. I just felt a burden to pray.*

Even though I didn't want to, I forced myself to at least attempt to tell God what was on my heart.

"God, at this point, I have no big words, I have no poise, and I have no agenda. I just flat out need you. I honestly don't even know how to pray about this. I have no idea what to say. I feel like I'm losing my mind. Nothing but the pain seems real. I know Seth is the man for me. Didn't you see this coming? You couldn't warn a sista? I can't be a divorcee at twenty-nine and only five years of marriage to show for it. God, I need you to do something."

I lay down on the bed and glanced at the clock. It was 12:50 when I cried out, "Jesus, help me!" Sometime later, I fell asleep.

Chapter 5:
At Wit's End – 12:29 A.M.

Grey

I had just left Brooklyn and Sydney's place, so I could head home. It had been storming for quite some time, and it finally seemed like there was a break in the storm. It usually took about twenty minutes for me to get home, but hopefully, the elements would cooperate this one time.

I know I probably shouldn't have been out tonight, but I just needed to hang out with my girls and just laugh. Life as I knew it was very complicated. I will say that I am proud of myself though, because I haven't been overly worried or stressed about it, but just continually praying and waiting for God to work it out.

Some months ago, I got behind on my house payments, and the foreclosure notices started coming. I tried to handle it on my own, but they were not returning my calls, I had stopped sending them what little payments I had because they would only accept the full amount. It's a little unnerving when your bill collector rejects your money because it isn't enough and sends it back.

When I finally talked to Pastor Josiah, he told me to ask Sheridan to help me because she worked in real estate to put herself through school. She hooked me up with a foreclosure realtor and a housing counselor, Mrs. Wyman. This old lady was a trip, but she knew her stuff. She started communicating with my mortgage company on my behalf, but they ignored her, too. I heard an ambulance siren somewhere in the background, so I prayed, "Lord, let them be okay, have mercy, and send help." You never know when you'll need to reap the prayers of a stranger, so I always tried to say a prayer if I knew someone was in need.

In the meantime, P.J. told me to save what little money I had after I paid the rest of my bills and put it in a savings account to build up a cushion, so I could make the payments when all of this got straightened out. One good thing though is that my Altima, my first car that I actually got on my own, would be paid off in three months. I was ecstatic because that would free up more money for other bills.

My faith was on point. I was patiently waiting and trusting God to make it better, that is until I got the notice for my day in court. Now, I ain't gonna lie, I won't say I failed the faith test, but I did stumble a bit because I absolutely, positively, did not want to stand before anybody's judge and have him look at me like I was a failure.

It was like a kick in the gut. Even though I knew God was going to work it out that was a part of the test I didn't want to take. Brooklyn said the court date might be a good thing because my mortgage company would finally have to communicate with me. Well, whatever, because my prayer was that I wouldn't have to see a judge.

At times it seemed overwhelming, but I knew that God was real. The way I figured it, no matter what happened, he was going to make a way. I just wished he would make a way that didn't require me going through the doors of any Leon County Courthouse. It's like setting the court date made it a reality. It made the attack official. I believed that God would turn it around long before it got to anything officially legal. Besides, if I lost my house I would hate to have to put that annoying Barrington Scottsdale up for adoption. I mean, who would want him? He was such a pain in my neck.

The rain was starting to pick up just a little as I turned on Lafayette Street. Up ahead on the opposite side of the road, there was a red Avalanche attempting to make a left turn in front of me into the Checkers. This idiot, can't he see there isn't enough time to make the turn.

I slowed down, and he looked like he had the common sense to stop making his turn. I started to relax as I got closer, and then out of nowhere, he gunned it. I realized at that moment, that I was about to hit this fool. Everything started to go in slow motion.

Lord, really, a car accident? With everything I got going on, do you really think I need this? You couldn't turn me down any other street in all your infinite power? Way to throw a curve ball God. Good looking out. I could swerve right and into the ditch or I could hit him head on. I knew I was going to hit him, and there was nothing I could do. I began to panic because I hated with a passion that sound that cars make when metal strikes metal. No, I think it's better described as a fear of the sound.

I only had a split second to decide, and I felt hitting him head on was better than going head first into the ditch that had water rushing rapidly through it. This was without a doubt going to happen. There was literally nothing I could do, so I braced myself for the impact. I simply said, "Jesus."

Everything went black.

Part Two:

Before the Flood

Chapter 6:
Believe Half of What You See. . .

The funeral was packed, and Naomi looked around confused. Her mother was dead, and the only emotion she felt was awe of the beautiful cathedral in which she stood. The sunlight shone through the stained glass windows and cast a thousand sparkles on the golden hued vaulted ceilings. The huge brass pipe organs and the statues that were placed throughout the sanctuary, made it seem like a fairy tale.

Here were all these people there to mourn a woman that she could not muster one feeling for. Not sorrow, not hurt, not joy, not hate, and least of all, love. Knowing your mother abandoned you at birth to fend for yourself in a world full of strangers because she was too selfish to abort you, tends to leave one emotionless.

She was dead. Why should she cry? She'd never met the woman. She wasn't even sure how she ended up in the box that was about to be six-feet underground, but she felt it her human obligation to be there for the time honored speech of "ashes to ashes and dust to dust."

Since she had moved to Tallahassee and given her life to Christ, the pain her mother's abandonment had left her with had begun to be bearable. She hadn't given the woman very much thought until she heard through the grapevine that she was dead.

After days of digesting the news that she would never get to meet the woman who went half on a baby with a man she had yet to identify to give her life, she decided she'd better find out if the rumors were true. It took all her will power, but she reached out to her aunt, her mother's sister, and inquired about the woman who gave her life. She confirmed, she was indeed, dead.

Naomi was in a state of confusion, she had yet to shed one single tear. She knew this could not be healthy. As she made her way down the center of the church, she noticed all the patrons looking at her probably thinking how she knew the dead woman, just like she was thinking why did so many people come to the funeral of such a horrible person. These didn't look like the crack heads and vagabonds she'd expected to see.

They all looked like honorable citizens which made the woman even more horrible in her book. She obviously got rid of her and went on to live a great life. By the size of this Catholic Church and the caliber of the mourners, the dead woman must've been a stand up citizen. She was still trying to find a tear to shed for the woman who spit her out, but it wasn't gonna happen.

About midway down the aisle, she noticed Seth nodding his support along with his wife and a few other choir members. That warmed her heart, and she found an emotion, gratitude. She was grateful that he made it his business to be there to support her in her time of bereavement, if that's what you would call it.

She knew he cared about her; after all he drove all the way down to Miami to be there for her. Well, his wife was there, but that was just a minor complication. Her feelings for him grew stronger in that moment because having both come from abandonment is what tied her and Seth together. She knew he would be there for her, and she would be sure to have plenty of need for his shoulder. As she got closer to the casket, she wondered what the woman looked like.

When she looked into the casket, would she get a glimpse into the future as to what would be staring back at her when she looked in the mirror twenty years from now? She had come to about the third row when the line to view the body came to a standstill. The woman viewing the body was determined to turn this into a ghetto black funeral even though they were in a Catholic Church.

She was screaming and hollering at the top of her lungs, "No, don't take her, don't take her, Lord, take me instead!" Naomi leaned to the side to get a better view. Now, this woman was a character. She was hollering, "Don't take her," about a woman who had been gone for days now. The loud mouth stood about five-seven, dressed in a hot pink church lady skirt suit with the matching hat that looked like it had been attacked by sequins and a neurotic bedazzler.

She had a cane that was clearly made for someone all of five-three, but yet, she was using it as a third leg. Obviously, this woman liked attention. She screamed again, "Noooooooooo! Don't leave.

I'm coming with you. I'm coming with you. How am I gonna live without my best friend?"

She finally looked like she had enough of screaming and was about to make good on her promise to climb into the casket when one of the clergymen ran up and grabbed her before she could make a complete fool of herself. Naomi had to stifle a laugh. This was hilarious.

The clergyman that kept the woman from knocking the casket over was straining to hold her big butt up; beads of perspiration were popping up all over his forehead. Naomi recognized him as one of the pastors that had visited their church in Tallahassee. If memory served her correctly, he was a friend of Pastor Josiah. Her forehead creased as she tried to recall his name, "P" something, she wondered. By now, the line was moving again, and she was almost to the casket.

She felt a knot in her stomach. Maybe she would finally feel something for this person that lie there without expression. She stepped up to the casket and looked in at the beautiful and very peaceful face of Samantha Birdwell. Time stopped, along with her brain because she couldn't remember to exhale. Once her chest started to fill with the air she wasn't letting out, she remembered to breathe, but it was too late. She had looked her mother in the face and fainted.

When Naomi came to, she could hear voices. At least one was familiar and one not so much. Her eyes fluttered, and she immediately sat up. She became dizzy from the rush of getting up and eased herself back down. "My sister, go easy there, you just experienced a myriad of emotions, and you need to pace yourself."

She didn't recognize his voice, but she did know his face. What was his name? As she cleared her throat, she looked around the small room to see Seth's wife standing by the door talking to another one of her fellow choir members, Ebony, also known as the church gossip.

She sighed thinking to herself, this was sure to be all over the church with a few twists for entertainment value. Of all people, why was Seth's wife here helping her? Why wasn't he here? He was the only one who could possibly understand what she was going through. But knowing Seth, as church etiquette, it was only logical he would send a woman to minister to another woman. Pastor Josiah was a stickler for that, a woman prays for a woman, and a man prays for a man, it won't give the enemy an opportunity to distort the purpose of the moment.

"What happened?" she managed to get out just above a whisper. Sheridan walked up to her and sat next to her, "Naomi, sweetheart, you fainted when you looked into your mother's casket. Pastor Percy brought you into this auxiliary room. The service has already started, do you want to go in and sit through the rest of it?"

She could have slapped her, with all she had going on the last thing she wanted was for *her* to be all up in her face. Through her anger, she managed to speak, "Uh, yeah, I guess we can go back inside, but can I have some water first?"

"Pastor Percy can you get her a cup of water please?"

He smiled and replied, "Sure thing, Mrs. Richards, I'll be right back."

"That's his name," Naomi said just above a whisper.

Sheridan looked down at her, "So, you do remember Pastor Percy, huh? He used to be in the prayer group with Pastor Josiah when they went to FAMU a long time ago," she said.

"Oh, yeah, now I remember, he's been to our church a few times."

"Yeah, he has his own non-denominational church down in Ft. Lauderdale," Sheridan informed her.

"Well, what is he doing here at my mother's funeral?" Naomi inquired.

Sheridan shrugged, but Ebony stepped right in, "Well, I heard that his church was in some kinda financial struggle, and he had been visiting churches all around this area speaking trying to get money. He usually only speaks at churches with a large congregation to ensure his "love offering" is a decent one. But he is here as a pall bearer today, so I don't know how that happened."

They both stared at her in disbelief. "Anyways," Sheridan said, rolling her eyes at Ebony, "it's not important why he's here, you just be glad he was there to get you up off the floor before big mama in the hot pink fell on you as she made her way back to act a fool over your mom's casket."

Naomi rolled her eyes; she could just picture the scene. Pastor Percy walked back in and handed her the water. She drank it slowly and asked, "Where is the restroom?"

Sheridan said, "I'll take you," as she helped Naomi out of the small room.

Pastor Percy looked at Ebony and said, "Well, I love to see young ministers lending a helping hand. I know it can't be easy on Sheridan to have a husband in the ministry, especially since they have only been married such a short time."

"Oh, they do just fine," Ebony let him know, "they are one of the most beautiful couples at our church."

"I didn't mean to imply anything to the contrary, just an observation. Lord knows it's hard enough to live your life right, but when you add in the responsibility of being a minister and the dedication it takes to have a successful marriage. It can be overwhelming at times. I just admire her ability to be a servant."

"Well, it's easy for her because she has the man of her dreams by her side."

"Yes, well, Seth is a lucky man for having a supportive wife in the ministry. I'm sure it isn't easy."

Ebony smirked, gushing with delight for an opportunity to drop some dirt. "It sho ain't, I think Sheridan would have a different opinion of being a servant if she knew how much in love Naomi is with her husband."

Pastor Percy just stared at her with disbelief. He regrouped, "Sister, you should not spread such vicious rumors, gossip only serves to divide the church against itself."

Ebony tisked, she knew what she was talking about, and she let him know it, "Oh, it's not gossip, its gospel, and you can take that to the bank. Naomi is head over heels in love with that woman's husband."

Pastor Percy was skeptical, "And you're telling me his wife has never noticed that?"

She let out a slight chuckle, "Oh, I have caught her looking at Naomi cross-eyed a couple of times, but Naomi hasn't done anything that would actually expose her true feelings yet," Ebony said with complete conviction.

Pastor Percy was momentarily disturbed, but he managed to say, "Well, sister, like I said, the church is no place for gossip, and if there is some validity to your story, you should just pray for all parties involved that God would intervene and help everyone involved do what's right."

She rolled her eyes, "Oh, yeah, Pastor, I'm praying."

"You should get back to the service," he said in a dismissive tone. Ebony obliged him and walked out of the room.

Pastor Percy sat down on the bench and began to let his mind wrap around the information he had just received, and he wondered how he could use it to his advantage. That little Naomi was fine, and she was also very vulnerable right now. He could do the obvious, but his marriage hadn't recovered from the last scandal, but he could take it a step further and plant some seeds to exact revenge because of what was done to him. A devilish smile spread across his face as he let his thoughts fester.

†††

At the reception after her mother's funeral, Naomi sat alone on a loveseat in the den as she absentmindedly watched all the people interacting. She was still thinking about her time at the gravesite. As they lowered her mother into the ground, one single tear dropped. It didn't even have enough power to fall off her face. It stopped mid-run on the side of her cheek. That was all she could spare for the woman who gave her life.

The half a tear wasn't because she hurt for her mother. It was because as her mom's casket made it's way into the ground, so did every explanation as to why she chose to abandon her and go on to have another life without her first born child. And the thought of not ever knowing caused more pain than the actual death should have caused.

Her aunt approached her; she seemed hesitant but decided that it was now or never. She took a seat next to her niece and waited for an invitation to speak. Naomi looked at her like she was crazy. How dare she have the gall to sit next to her? Her mother may have buried all hope of a happy childhood for her, but her aunt put the nail in the coffin.

"What do you want, Aunt Miriam?" Naomi snarled at the woman who was already nervous.

Her aunt calmed herself by tapping her finger on the edge of the loveseat. After a few deep breaths, she spoke. "Naomi, I know I am the last person you want to see, but burying my sister has put some things into perspective for me. I don't want to go on like this, and I'm sorry for the way I have treated you and for all the pain I've caused you."

Naomi's response was silence with a blank stare. Her aunt kept going, "I know you always wanted answers, but you think they were buried with your mother today. I have been holding on to most of the story for the last twenty-three years but because of my petty jealousy and some hatred toward your mother, I chose to keep it from you."

Naomi gasped, now tears found a reason to flow freely.

"Your mom was our father's favorite, she was the smart one, she was the pretty one, and she was the dark skinned one."

Naomi looked at her puzzled, "Huh?"

She had never heard of a person holding someone dark-skinned in higher regard than someone like her aunt who was high yellow and had green eyes. Not to mention her aunt was just as beautiful as her mother.

"I know that's not the normal standard among black folks but let me explain. Our father was as dark as they come, we used to joke he was so black he was purple, and we called him shadow behind his back, and everyone in his family was either dark brown or black. Our mom was not dark, but she was far from light so when I came out, there were many questions that plagued the whole family. The family rumor was that I was a result of mama's fling with some white man. Not that anybody ever came with anything concrete, but still, our father always treated me like I was a stepchild. Who understands the shades of blackness, maybe there was someone white in our bloodline, maybe a great, great grandmother was a slave and their slave master crept over to the shack to sprinkle our blood line with some shades of beige and pastel eyes, but nonetheless, still I was the black, or should I say, the white sheep of the family."

Miriam took a breath. "Even though our father treated me like a bastard child and our mom tried to overcompensate when he wasn't looking, Samantha and I were close while we were growing up. We did everything together, she was my older sister, and she protected me, even from our father's insults. Whenever I would do something to get in trouble, he would always be the one to beat me, it's like he thought beating me was beating his wife for her indiscretion, if there ever was one."

Naomi interrupted, "But you look just like my mother."

Her aunt sighed, "I know, but that didn't make one bit of a difference to him because we both looked like our mother, so all he saw was the hue of my skin. When Samantha left for college, he paid for everything, and sent her off like she was majesty. When I graduated, two years later, he made me work my way into the local community college. I ended up quitting after a little under a year and working full time at McDonald's. I worked my way up to management, and I've been there ever since. My life hasn't been bad; it's just been very mediocre and lonely. Having never married or had kids of my own to help keep my mind otherwise occupied didn't help the jealousy and anger that I let fester."

Naomi interrupted, "Aunt Miriam, what does any of this have to do with me?"

She patted Naomi's leg, "I'm getting there. I just need you to try to understand the why of what happened to you since you've already lived through the how." Naomi nodded her willingness to continue listening.

Her aunt continued, "As I was saying, after your mother finished her education, our father sent her on a trip to Paris for graduation. She had been telling him she wanted to get away and see the world. She would take a year to spend on her own and gain her independence. Since she was his favorite and probably to torture me at the same time, he agreed. She went to Paris for a year. By now, I had experienced so much secondhand love; I was practically used to it. Besides, I hadn't seen our parents in over two years; I didn't even sit with them at her graduation. As soon as she got to Paris, she met a man, and it was love at first sight, or so she said. You were a result of that little tryst."

Miriam spared a glance at Naomi. "She called me all hysterical, so I told her just to get an abortion, and come home. She said she didn't want to do that. She was scared of disappointing daddy, and if he found out she was pregnant, he would make her come home, and she would be a disgrace and out of his heart forever. She called me because she had a plan. She wanted me to take her child as my own.

Knowing that I hadn't seen our parents in over two years nor was I planning to, she thought the idea was perfect. She promised to help raise you, but she needed me to bear the brunt of this one. I don't know why I agreed, but like a fool I did, probably because she had always tried to make my childhood better by loving me despite our father's hate for me. I had no idea that your mother would walk away from me and you like we were yesterday's garbage. She actually joined in the family ridiculing me about having a bastard child." She sarcastically chuckled, "And since you were half white, her story made perfect sense."

Miriam shook her head. "Child, you came out looking more like my child than hers. But the real drama started when daddy got wind of your grey eyes, it further solidified in his mind the affair that our mother must've had. I guess he never thought I'd been with someone of another race. He had been looking for proof for many years, and he thought this was his proof. Back when I was a baby, they didn't do DNA tests. Mama's baby, poppa's maybe, it was just a question they let linger. Their marriage went downhill after that. So much so to the point that my mother came to me and begged me to submit to a DNA test to shut him up once and for all. I told her hell, no! She, of course, was stunned, but I didn't care, she let that man torture me all those years and had the nerve to ask me to bail her out to please him. I was grown and out of his house, I didn't owe him a thing. But the part I do regret now is that I knew I belonged to my father."

Naomi gave her a wide-eyed stare. She continued, "I got a sample of his DNA and sent it to a lab via the internet. My last encounter with them was the reading of the will of our maternal grandmother. After that, we went out to dinner, all the while pretending to be a family to ease my mother's pain of losing her mother. I took his straw for his sample, swabbed my cheek, and then sent it off in the mail. I actually got the results about three weeks before my mother asked me to submit for one. They stayed married but from what I understand, they were never what you would call a happy couple. That supposed betrayal was too much for him to bear. I was glad he was suffering, and I didn't want to do anything to ease his pain because he never eased mine."

Naomi sat there stunned, and her brain could not put together a full thought to save her life. When she finally came up with one, she smirked, "Well, that explains the mystery of my grey eyes."

Her aunt let out a faux laugh, "Yeah, that's it alright." She finally looked into her niece's eyes.

"I felt so betrayed by what my sister did to me that my hate for her grew towards you. I thought about putting you up for adoption or even into the foster care system, but since my family already knew about you, the last thing I needed was them berating me about not being able to take care of my own child. I couldn't give you the love you needed because I didn't have any in me to give. I never knew what it was like to be loved. My father hated me and instead of my mother doing something about it, she cared more about her marriage to that mean son of a, well, you know. I know it wasn't right, but I figured as long as you had food and shelter you would survive. That's all I ever had, and I'm still here.

There isn't much I can say to you now, but your mother was younger than fifty, and her life is gone. That made me realize that I never started living mine, but I couldn't go forward with my plans until I at least explained myself to you. My parents are dead to me, and I don't even know my sister's husband and their children. Once she turned her back on me and you, she was out of my life, too. Her husband contacted me after she died to tell me that she left me some money, guilt money I suppose, or perhaps hush money to take her secret to my grave."

Miriam took another breath. "So, I've decided to sell my house and start a life as far from here as I could think. She didn't leave anything for you because that would have been too close to right to have her precious family be privy to her twenty-three year old indiscretion. I know that I caused your life much pain, but now you know that's all I ever knew. With my apology, I wanted to give you this so you can finish school and not worry about anything while you try to make something of yourself. With your scholarship this should help."

She handed Naomi a folded piece of paper. Naomi unfolded a check written to her in the amount of $10,000. Naomi gasped.

Her aunt interrupted her response, "Before you say anything, I know this won't in the least bit compensate you for what you've been through, but maybe it can give you a start. I know it didn't come from your mother and even in her death, she didn't extend to you one gesture of love. But trust me, I have held on to unforgiveness all my life, and it made my life a living hell. Please, I beg you. Find it in your heart to forgive all who have caused you pain and move on with your life while you're young. Finish college and find something you want to do with your life. Don't get so caught up in your career and forget about love. Get married and have lots and lots of babies and give them all the love you wished was given to you. Trust me. You'll be a better person for it."

Naomi sat there completely traumatized at all the information that had just been thrown in her lap. She looked up at her aunt and she seemed to be patiently waiting for a response. "How did my mother die?"

She placed her hand gently on Naomi's knee and said softly, "Ovarian cancer."

Naomi politely moved her knee from under her aunt's touch; her aunt got the message, on every level she understood where her niece was coming from. "Where did I get my name from?"

Her aunt smiled, "I named you after the maternal grandmother I told you about, her name was Naomi, and she always loved me unconditionally, though we didn't see each other much, we talked all the time through letters. She left this house for me, and that's why I moved us out of Tennessee and to Florida."

Naomi's heart dropped as she asked, "So, all this time my mother was in Miami?"

"Actually" her aunt responded, "They lived in Ft. Lauderdale, but this is the church they got married in, and this is where her husband chose to have the ceremony. Since she was so "generous" in her dying wish to me, I agreed to have the reception here at my house. Gave me a chance to see the family I had totally left behind."

Naomi still was not satisfied, "So, why did I never see her if she was so close?"

Her aunt began shakily, "Sweetheart, she was married to a prominent man, and you were her dirty little secret so she never bothered to have you in her life once she got with him. She couldn't let him find out she had a child out of wedlock who she abandoned, and I didn't ever want to see her, so you just got the rotten end of the stick. I knew I didn't do much for you, but I didn't want you to have to hear from her own mouth that she didn't want you, so I kept you away from her. I was contemplating whether to call you when she died, but then you called me. I never lied to you about who she was, but I always discouraged you from ever finding her. That's why I never gave you her whereabouts. I knew it would hurt you more to be rejected by her than to hear it from me. Her husband thinks you're his niece. He always tried to get her to reconcile our relationship, but she couldn't risk me exposing her, and I never wanted to see her face again. He even called me a couple times to make the first move; I hung up in his face both times."

Miriam rolled her eyes. "She was too busy being the perfect socialite, wife, and mother to grace us with her presence."

Naomi had one last question, "Where are my grandparents?"

Miriam looked down at her feet as she answered, "Your grandfather is dead, but your grandmother is in a nursing home somewhere in Orlando, she suffers from Alzheimer's."

Naomi fixed her face to be as serious and no nonsense as possible. "Aunt Miriam, thank you so much for the money. At my church, Pastor Josiah talks all the time about forgiveness and how it frees us. I know God can't forgive me until I forgive you and my mother, but today that's just a risk I have to take."

She got up and walked to the bathroom to clean her face. Her aunt sat there digesting her words, though it pained her to know her niece's bitterness went beyond the capacity to forgive, she hoped Naomi would learn from the life she'd led for all those years. As she stood up to finish hosting, she noticed Pastor Percy leaning on the door frame closest to where they had been sitting. She rolled her eyes when he made eye contact with her, she couldn't stand the snake.

Chapter 7:
This Message Will Self-Destruct...

Once Naomi closed the bathroom door, she sat down on the toilet and cried her heart out. She cried for the love she didn't have for her mother. She cried for the love she should have for her mother. She cried over the fact that her mother never wanted her and chose to move on with her life without her. She cried for the father she would never know. She cried for the two brothers that she had that would never know her. She cried because there was no one in the world she knew who could prove she was her mother's child.

Her father may as well have been a ghost because he only existed to her mother, and she took all her DNA with her. She cried for hate and unforgiveness. She just couldn't let go of the negative feelings she had for her mother and aunt. She cried for all the pain that her aunt experienced because even though it was the reason her life was miserable, she understood exactly how her aunt felt. She cried because even though she couldn't forgive her aunt, she sympathized with her because she had been dealt a jacked up hand, too. She hated herself for showing any compassion for that woman.

Naomi cried for the love she never had from anyone and that she so desperately wanted from the only man who had reached out to her and tried to understand and help her with her pain. She cried because the one person she ever felt able to open up to was happily married to another woman. If she didn't have to hate Sheridan, she would actually adore her because of the great person she was, and this thought made her cry even harder. Now her tears were tears of confusion. She cried for all the tears she had never shed.

There was a knock at the door. Her tears had become sobs. She was barely audible. "Just a minute."

"Naomi, this is Pastor Percy, I just wanted to make sure you were okay."

She sighed, exasperated, "I'm okay. I will just be a few minutes."

"You don't sound okay," he managed to say in his most sincere voice.

Percy stood five-ten and was the color of a brown paper bag. His brown eyes appeared sincere against his average face. He said, "When you come out, I'd like to pray with you. I didn't mean to eavesdrop on your aunt's confession, but it was hard not to. I felt like I was at the right place at the right time because you would need a friend, an ally while you are dealing with all of this."

She hesitated, "What do you mean?"

He knew he had her now, "I mean that right now, I am the only person here for you, and that's no coincidence. I know your friends had to leave, and I believe this is a divine intervention. Take your time, get yourself together, and then come and find me on the porch."

Naomi was confused, but they always said God worked in mysterious ways. It couldn't get any more mysterious than this. After all, she was there all alone. The only person she knew there was her aunt, and she had enough of talking to her for a lifetime. "Pastor Percy, you still there?"

"Yes, my child. I am here."

She felt better, "I will be out shortly."

Naomi got off the seat and blew her nose. She washed and dried her face. The reflection staring back at her was monstrous. Her make-up was randomly placed all over her face and her eyes were more than puffy. She didn't care. She didn't know anybody there anyways, and she had a gaping hole in her heart.

She quietly left out of the bathroom trying to avoid her aunt and made her way to the porch. She closed the door behind her, and she saw Pastor Percy sitting on the porch swing seemingly deep in thought. She walked up to him and whispered, "Pastor Percy."

He seemed startled. "Oh, Naomi, I'm sorry. I was just meditating while the spirit was speaking to me. Please have a seat."

Naomi apprehensively sat in the rocking chair next to the swing. Pastor Percy let out a chuckle, "You know I don't bite."

Naomi let out a small laugh and began to relax just a bit. She stood up and sat on the swing next to him and said, "So, what do we do now?"

He placed his hand gently on her shoulder. "If you want to talk about anything, you can go ahead."

She shook her head. "I don't have anything to say."

He placed his hands in his lap and folded them to make her more comfortable. He began to take on a fatherly tone. "Naomi, I know that you have unforgiveness in your heart, but that's no way to live your life."

She didn't respond, so he continued, "I know you feel like your pain is unbearable, but remember God will never put more on you than you can bear. Whatever you go through, it is to prepare you for where you're going. Your life is going to be a testimony to many others. I know you feel that no one loves you, but that's not true either. You're at that point where you feel like you're ready to be in a relationship and move your life to the level that only a companion can take it to, right?"

She hesitantly nodded. "God has a man for you that is going to love you and treasure you like the queen you are. Before you walked up, I was praying for you and asking for guidance on what to say to you. I felt in my spirit to tell you this."

Naomi perked up, hoping for one thing to go right in her life. Pastor Percy continued, "There is a man in your life that you feel you have a special connection with because of what you've been through. He has a presence about him that makes you feel comfortable opening up to him."

Naomi could not believe what she was hearing. Could he really be talking about Seth? She just stared at him blankly, praying he would continue. Pastor Percy saw the excitement in her eyes, and he had to check himself to keep from laughing in her face.

He continued, "In short, this is the man for you. Now you just need to put your trust in the man upstairs and watch it unfold before your eyes."

Naomi's mouth was agape. Her voice was trembling. "Pastor Percy, you are describing a man in my life so perfectly, but this can't be right, because he's, he's..."

Pastor Percy cut her off. "Naomi, don't talk like that, remember life and death are in the power of the tongue. What does the word say about impossibilities? With him all things are..." he gestured for her to finish the Scripture.

"She smiled and said, "Possible."

He smiled, "That's right, and don't you forget it. Now you just watch and wait for the opportunity to present itself."

Naomi was really confused, she wished that Seth was the man for her, but he was married to somebody else. Was he trying to tell her that their marriage would end and he would marry her, what in the heck was going on? She quickly blurted out, "But Pastor Percy, he's..."

"Stop." He cut her off again by throwing his hands up, palms out. Pastor Percy saw the confusion in her eyes, and he knew he had to sell this once and for all. He pondered on which Scriptures he could put out there that, if not rightly divided, could be a little misleading. He also considered those that no matter what the situation, they would work to his need of them at this moment. He reached out and grabbed both her hands.

"Darling, I know this is a confusing time for you with everything you've got going on, but remember how Job got double for his suffering. Trust me when I say this is about to turn around for you. What does the Scripture say, all things work..."

She smiled, "Together for the good of those who love God and are called according to his purpose."

He rubbed her hands. "That's right. I know you love God, and you know he's got a purpose for you. Remember, his ways are not our ways, and his thoughts are not our thoughts. This is one of those instances where you need to follow your heart. Hold on to that hope you have and let no one take it from you. He is the man for you, you trust that, and you move on it."

She was still hesitant, "But I thought it said *he* who finds a wife?"

He chuckled, okay, she was a babe in Christ, but she had some knowledge of the Bible. He had the strongest urge to say "touché" but he passed. "You are absolutely right, but remember the book of Ruth?"

She shook her head. "I'm not that familiar with it."

There's one born every minute, he thought to himself. "Well Ruth, upon her mother-in-law, Naomi's instructions, placed herself right in Boaz's path. He could not help but see her, and he married her."

Naomi looked at him trying to figure out if he was serious. "Her mother-in-law's name was Naomi?"

He laughed, "Yeah, it was, but it just goes to show that yes he found her, but she had to be in his path because how can one find something that they never get a chance to see? Look, Naomi, I know your head must be spinning because the information you just got from your aunt was soul shattering, but you never know when your life is going to turn around. Just go rejoice in what God is gonna do in your life."

For the first time since he'd seen her, she flashed a genuine smile, and he knew the seeds were planted. She reached out and hugged him, "Thank you Pastor Percy, for everything."

As he embraced her, he said, "I'm just allowing the spirit to lead me where he sees fit. Go in the peace of God and hold on to his words for your life no matter what the situation looks like."

Naomi got up to go back into the house; she was indeed ready to leave. She waved back as the door closed behind her.

Pastor Percy sat there with the smug look on his face letting his mind wander about the kind of drama that was sure to transpire when Naomi dug her claws into Seth, and Sheridan dug her claws into Naomi. He couldn't help it. He laughed all the way to his car as did the little black yellow eyed imp, named Jealousy that lived with him daily and had him bound.

Chapter 8:
There Is Hope after Failure

Kingdom Builders Worship Center was a unique ministry where the heart of the pastor was reflected in everything that took place. He had a heart for people, all kinds of people, no matter their walk of life. Pastor Josiah Stone, who was affectionately known as P.J., was the founder of the church.

He was from deep down in the Mississippi Delta. At age fifty, he did his best to instill in his very young congregants, of mostly thirty and under with some "seasoned" members sprinkled throughout, that they should always have a servant's heart, and they should always care about people.

He taught them titles were never who they were, just a position in life, but they were to always be willing to dig their hands in and do the work of the ministry whether it be cleaning the pews or preaching the word. Kingdom Builders had been established for only eleven years, yet God had grown the ministry by leaps and bounds. For a young church, they had many ministries and had made their mark on the city of Tallahassee.

As the choir stood in the choir loft with the baptismal pool as its backdrop, the soft white walls trimmed in black made the church appear open, even though they were in desperate need of more room. They had only occupied the building for about six years, and the membership was bursting at the seams. It wasn't what you would call a megachurch. The membership was less than a thousand people, but it had a mega heart for people.

Next to the choir was the band—drums, two keyboards, an organ, bongos, and a trombone player. The three sections of pews framed the altar where the glass podium that displayed Kingdom Builders Worship Center stood. The podium had an emblem of a shield with a dove that also looked like fire on one side. The Word of God was on the other.

As the choir ministered one of Seth's powerful songs, the anointing could be felt throughout the building. It was like a heavy blanket fell over and coated the congregation. Even the non-believers felt it. They didn't know exactly what it was, but they knew something in the atmosphere had changed.

The praise and worship leader, Gyselle, began to go into another level of praise when her sultry, anointed voice set the place ablaze and sparked another wave of worship. There were a few stragglers and visitors in the congregation that hadn't exactly realized what the power of praise could do. They stood there looking around not knowing they could change their atmosphere simply by lifting their hands and saying, "Lord, I thank you."

As the worship began to settle, Jeremiah, the pastor's Armor Bearer, took his Bible and notes to the podium and returned to his seat. The congregation stood as Pastor Josiah advanced to the podium so they could approach the throne of grace united.

Unseen to the human eye, the Angels, Orion and Roman, flanked the pastor's sides and were there ready to minister. They nodded to Ahiga and Kamau who stood at the doors in the back of the church. The little demons and imps that had made it into the sanctuary took notice that there were new angelic beings in the sanctuary. It didn't worry them though because they were invited by their human hosts whom they had bound.

Josiah was a solid man with a cappuccino complexion. He stood about six-two and had dark gray eyes that could bear into your soul. He had a low haircut with sprinkles of gray at the sides and a streak slightly off center that gave him a distinguished look. He stood for a moment, bowed his head, and began to pray silently. Shouts of praise could be heard in scatters throughout the congregation.

He began aloud, "Hallelujah! Father, we praise you for your presence in this place. Thank you for the Holy Ghost that's in the midst of us, on the inside of us, giving us life, giving us hope, and vision. We thank you, Lord Jesus, that your word is among us, your hand is on us, your eyes are upon us, your ears are tuned to this place, and our voice. Your blessings are flowing right now. We thank you, Lord, that the gifts of the spirit are operating—the word of knowledge, the word of wisdom, the word of insight, the gift of discerning, the gift of healing, and miracles in the name of Jesus Christ. Release your angels, God, to minister, I pray. Let them bring gifts of healing, gifts of salvation, the gift of joy, peace, and finances, in the name of Jesus I pray. Let the Holy Ghost be active. I pray in the name of Jesus Christ. Adjust our attitudes. Adjust our attitude to one of great joy, great excitement, and great participation. We thank you, Lord Jesus, that there's life in this place, there's hope in this place, there's help in this place. Now release your word, release your voice upon your people God. We thank you for it in the name of Jesus Christ. And the saints of God said, amen."

A chorus of amen's followed. He said, "Shout Hallelujah! You may have your seats."

"What a wonderful service, what a wonderful spirit in this place. We can have an alter call right there." Amen's could be heard. "I said, we can have an alter call right there." More amen's, some stood, and shouted, and waved.

"I'm already full. Anytime people are blessed, I'm already full. My life has been about helping people; my calling has been about helping people. It's the greatest joy to give someone hope, to say I'm with you, I got you. I'm here to support your dreams and goals. We have to establish people to take their position in the world and perform at their maximum potential with integrity. So they can operate in the world system and still be governed by the Holy Spirit. There is nothing like that kind of witness for God."

"This morning I have a thought to share with you, and I'm not going to be long before you. I know time has been spent with the presentation of scholarships, but I'm not a long-winded preacher. The message is there is hope after failure." There was a chorus of amen's.

"I wrestled with this because I can talk about hope all day long, but if you don't understand what hope is, then you can't overcome failure. So my task is to break it down for you to understand what hope looks like, what it sounds like, and how it acts. I want you to be able to identify hope, and know how to apply it, and how to receive the hope that is already inside of you. Now remember, you're gonna have some failures, so it says, there is hope after failure. So whenever something comes up short, they foreclosed your home, when your financial aid in school didn't come through, when you feel like you're a failure because of your past, after failure there's always hope. Now remember that hope is an attitude.

The Bible says in Job 14:7, for there is hope of a tree."

He repeated, "There is hope of a tree, if it be cut down that it will sprout again. Now the Bible has likened us as trees saying you shall be like a tree. Let's look at what failure looks like. A tree normally has bark, branches, leaves, and fruit that you can see. When failure comes, it cuts down the visible part. Nothing remains that looks like you're alive. All that's left is a stump of what your life used to look like. Yet, there is hope for you. When you can't even see it, you can't even put your hand on it. When there is nothing left of your future, of your marriage, of your faith, yet there is hope in your life. The word says it shall sprout again. That means a tree has an attitude that you can cut me down, but guess what? I'm coming back again. That's what hope looks like. There's always hope. There is always hope after failure. If a tree that has no eyes, no sense to hear, to touch, to smell, to see, and whatever the other one is."

There was laughter from the congregation, "If it knows it's gonna sprout again, then you should certainly know the same. How does it know it's going to sprout again? Because there is hope in the tree. God has placed something in it to hope again. You are greater than a tree, so no matter what you face in life in relation to failure, there is always hope for you. There is no such thing as a hopeless situation. *I like what Paul said in I Corinthians 13. He said now these three abide faith, hope, and charity. The greatest of these is charity or love.* So, now we see that God has put a value on hope."

He deviated and pointed to a young man sleeping in the crowd, "Stay with me. You with me?" A neighbor tapped the parishioner that was now embarrassed. He shook his head, "Focus. Don't be coming here falling asleep. I know I ain't that boring. Shoot, I work too hard praying and fasting for y'all to be falling asleep on me." More laughter, some amen's, a few ooh's.

He continued on with the rest of the sermon as the congregation began to regain their composure and the laughter died down. Orion and Roman watched with great care as the words of the message began to free some of the parishioners. They could see which ones accepted it, which ones rejected it and which ones that would have to fight to keep it. A young lady that had come in with a demon of complacency had just made up in her mind to be free.

Ahiga walked down the aisle to her, pulled out his weapon and said, "Go." Complacency looked around to see if there were any imps or demons willing to help, but he found none. He reluctantly released his hold on her and when he did, Ahiga struck him. His loud wail of pain could only be heard by the spiritual beings as he vanished in a cloud of yellow smoke.

The angels focused back on Pastor Josiah's message. "Hope is the right response to failure. Know how to respond to failure. Hope can take a problematic past and make it a promising future. For some of you, your life has been one problem after another, whether it was you or your brother, your sister, your mama, or your daddy or whatever, but hope will change it to a promising future because it adjusts your attitude to how you see things. And I know you're out there this morning. God is saying do not base your journey on your past. Base your journey on hope because your future has a great promise in God. He's on your side, He's working for you. This God of hope gives you peace and joy in believing that you abound and overflow in hope. You don't need a prophecy to have hope. You don't need hands to be laid on you to have hope. You can have hope right there in your bed of despair, right there while you're getting the bad news, even in the midst of being told no. Your mind is saying there's a yes somewhere. He has a plan for your life; adjust your attitude based on what you know about God."

"Hope is like a thermostat. Thermometers just check the temperature. Problems are thermometers. They show you how many problems you got and how hot it's getting. It can only record your problems, but hope is a thermostat. Yeah, you know them thermostats got two components on it, it's got a built in thermometer, but it also has another apparatus that when it judges where you are, it will kick in, and cool it down for you. Amen! Glory be to God. It will say hey, hey, hey, too hot, cool it down. That's what hope is. It will adjust your life."

The inflection in his voice began to change with intensity on the parts he really wanted to hammer home. Some people stood to their feet. He continued, "That's how the Holy Spirit works. If it's too hot, he'll cool it down; if it's too cold, he will warm it up for ya. That's the power of hope. If they cut you down to a stump, you gotta dream again. Hope is your regulator. You choose to be happy, you choose to rejoice. That's why God told Joshua, you shout now because when you shout, the walls are going to come down. Hallelujah!"

He paused to wipe the sweat from his face with the handkerchief that lay on the podium. Shouts all over erupted. He began to speak in tongues, and the congregation stood. "If you're dealing with any situation, be it legal, financial, your education, come up here when I open the altar because God is gonna work it out. You catch hold of hope, and hope catches hold of you."

Some of the demons and imps began to feel their grip slipping as people were being changed by the anointing in the building. "I want you to come now. Do not let the devil stop you from getting what God has for you."

Slowly people began to make their way towards the altar. The first lady, Darcy Stone, was a statuesque woman of café au lait complexion and honey brown eyes. She directed each person who came for prayer to an alter worker who prayed with them individually. She looked over at Grey as she pointed to a straggler that was the last to come up.

The altar was full that day. Sheridan, Jeremiah, and Mia were among the altar workers pulled from the congregation. The altar workers began to touch and agree with the individuals and offered them the prayer of salvation, if they didn't know God as their personal Lord and Savior.

As they were praying for those that sought some help in their walk, Pastor Josiah began to share members' testimonies, and the faith of those attending was increased. Many of those members were going to need to pull on that anointing and those testimonies for weeks to come as their lives began to be challenged.

Chapter 9:
Protect and Defend

Seth

Sheridan and I were leaving our house headed to Sunday dinner. I was definitely ready to eat, so I hoped Jeremiah was done cooking. "Baby, did you remember to get the dessert out the fridge?" Sheridan asked.

"Oops." I said, "Oh, my bad, baby girl. I'll go get it."

She rolled her eyes, "Boy, what did you do before I came along to keep your life in order?"

I smirked, "You get a lot of credit, baby, but let's not get greedy."

She stuck her tongue out and made me laugh. When I got back, she was in the car belted in and on the phone. When I slid in, she hung up, "Who was that, babe?"

"Mia, talking trash making sure we weren't going to be late because they are waiting on us to start."

"Whateva, we get there when we get there. Next time, tell her they need to allow me time to feel you up."

She slapped my arm, "Boy, hush!"

"Make me!"

She laughed as I reached for her hand to kiss it. I looked at my beautiful wife. She had beautiful light gold skin that was set off by soft brown eyes and full pink lips. I leaned over to kiss her. She asked, "What was that for?"

I smiled, "Just for being you, baby girl."

She blushed, and it felt good to know that after five years of marriage, I could still get that reaction from her. I kissed her nose, put the car in reverse to back out, and be on our way. They lived about five minutes away if all the lights cooperated.

I was headed up highway twenty-seven, and I turned right on Fred George Road. Sheridan was running her finger up my hand on the gearshift trying to get some stuff started. She was trying to make me turn this car around and hold up dinner for real. As I stopped at the light at Old Bainbridge and Fred George, a situation caught my eye.

I pointed towards it, "Look, baby, something ain't right about that."

"What, baby? Oh, no, look he just took a cooler out of one truck and put it in the other." It was three white men and a black woman at the gas station. There was damage to what seemed like her car and a few scratches on one of their trucks.

I said to my wife, "Now, baby, you know I'm gonna have to stop because ain't no way I'm just gonna let three white men be all up in a sista's face like that, and she's by herself."

She said, "Yeah, baby, I know, do ya thang."

As I went through the light, I turned left into the gas station and undid my seat belt.

I looked my wife dead in the eye, "Sheridan, stay your butt in the car, do you understand?"

She sucked her teeth. "I'm not playing, baby, I'm going to make sure this woman is okay, but you are my wife, and I need to know that you're okay. Stay in the car."

She rolled her eyes, "Okay, baby."

At this point, they were arguing about who was at fault. It was a honey colored petite sista with a red and dark blonde afro, and I could tell she was a little scared. She seemed like a scared cat backed into a corner and ready to strike if she had to. The aggressor was tall, blonde, and lean. The others were a tall skinny one with red hair and one shorter with a medium build and black hair.

I walked up behind the sister and asked, "Gentlemen, what seems to be the problem?"

She looked over at me and for a moment, she was confused. I gave her a nod, and she seemed to catch on pretty quickly and stepped back so that I was now in between them.

The blonde one said, "Dude, who the hell are you? Do you even know her?" I checked my temper. After all, I was poking my nose in other folk's business, but this was just not about to go down like he thought it was.

"It doesn't matter who I am, but since I'm here, why don't I just stand here with her," I pointed at the sister, "until the authorities get here, and the issue is resolved."

Just then, Sheridan yelled from the passenger side through the driver's side window, "You okay, girl?"

The sista gave a timid smile and nodded her head. I knew my wife, she was genuinely concerned about her welfare, but she also wanted to let her know that I was off limits. You just gotta love her. I gave Sheridan a look that said don't you even think about getting out.

I turned back and asked, "Has anyone called the police yet?"

The sista spoke up and said, "Not yet." She pointed to the blonde. "He just got out and got all up in my face yelling at me like he was crazy. He hit my car."

He moved closer to say something, but I put my hand up, "That's as far as you gonna go today, buddy, so let's just everybody chill out." His face turned red, and I thought, *Okay, Lord, you know I don't do violence, but if I have to, I will swing on this cat.*

He said, "This stupid bi..."

I cut him off, "Homie, you better buy another vowel and quick because you will not disrespect this young lady like that. I don't care if it's her fault or not."

He raised his voice, but he didn't come any closer. "Dude, whatever, you don't know what happened, the light was green, and she slammed on the brakes."

"Like I said, you need to find a different way to express yourself. You will not call this woman out of her name."

Dark hair spoke up, "Come on dude, chill. It's not that serious. Let's just wait for the cops and be on our way."

I said, "Now, that sounds like a plan."

I assessed my opponents. The blonde was hot and ready to fight. He was about six-three with a solid lean build. The dark haired one, who seemed nervous and remorseful, stood at about five-ten with a husky build. The last one seemed a little confused. He was about six-one and scrawny as a bean pole as he stood there with his hands in his pockets just looking around anywhere and everywhere but at me. He was clearly drunk.

I decided if I had to, I would hit blondie in the mouth, dark hair in the gut, and even if I couldn't get to the third one by that time, Sheridan's violent behind would be out the car with Boomer in hand, and we did not want this to go there. I needed to keep everybody calm and with their hands to themselves.

I positioned my body to completely shield the sista and yelled for Sheridan to call the police. She said, "I already did. Don't worry, I got you, boo."

I leaned back against the sista's car, and she followed suit. They were now talking amongst themselves. I couldn't hear much but a cuss word here and there. As long as words that started with a "B" or an "N" were not uttered, we wouldn't have any problems.

I could hear sirens in the distance and shortly after, their disco lights flashed as they pulled up to the scene. One officer was black, and the other was white. The black officer got out first and observed the situation. The white officer was right behind him.

The white officer zeroed in on me and asked me, "What seems to be the problem, sir?"

I shrugged my shoulders, "To be honest, officer, I really couldn't tell you. I'm just here to make sure this young lady was okay until you guys arrived. You would have to ask the parties involved." I pointed to both sides at blondie, and the pretty sista without a name.

He had a puzzled look on his face because he couldn't quite understand what I was doing here. The brother made eye contact and gave me the universal nod as if to say he understood, and he appreciated it. Blondie jumped in, "She was in the wrong because the light was green, and she slammed on the brakes for no reason."

She yelled, "I had a reason."

The brother said, "Okay, relax. Step over here." He pointed away from us, "And you give me your statement. You two," he pointed to dark hair and red and said, "You two come on let me get your statements, too."

The white officer approached the sista and said, "Ma'am, you wanna give me your account of what happened?"

She still looked a little shaken, so I walked up to her and placed my hand on her shoulder so she could relax. "Ma'am, do you feel safe now?"

She nodded slowly, "Thank you for stopping. Everything just happened so fast, and I had three men in my face, and I was so scared. I really appreciate it."

I reached for her hand to help steady it. "No problem. I really hate to leave you, but we're already late. I just couldn't let this situation play out like that."

She wiped the perspiration from her brow and said, "No, you go ahead, thank you. Thank you so much and your wife."

She turned and waved at Sheridan. I looked at the officer and said, "You have a nice day."

As I walked past him, he made a gesture for me to stop, and he looked me in the eye and said, "I'm just curious, sir, really, why did you stop?"

Well, he did ask, so I decided to tell him straight up. "Officer, I saw a scared black woman, and a white man in her face, and right or wrong, that just did not sit well with me. In order for me to go on with the rest of my day, I had to know for sure she was going to be okay, and stopping was the only way to do that."

He stared for a long moment, and then he shook my hand and said, "Okay. Thanks for satisfying my curiosity."

I told him, "Don't believe the hype. We protect and defend what's ours."

He nodded and I walked back to the car. Hopefully, I changed any negative stereotype he had about a black man.

Sheridan said, "So, you know, I had done pulled Boomer from the glove compartment and was down for whatever."

I looked down in her lap, "Baby, please put the gun back up."

She obliged. "Why you acting all scared? I got my papers on Boomer."

I shook my head. She said, "I'm just saying, babe, I was ready."

Lord, why did I ever give this nut a weapon?

Chapter 10:
Sunday Dinner I

The Justice house was in motion. The kids were playing, and Jeremiah was in the kitchen preparing the meal for people he had come to think of as his family away from home. Mia, his wife of six years, was in the office checking her Facebook page. Mia was a petite woman with a round face the shade of cocoa with long jet black hair that she prided.

As she sat at the computer, she scanned her page with her brown eyes. Their three-year-old daughter, Madison, approached from behind and studied what her mom was seeing. Mia had clicked on her mother's page because one of her mother's friends caught her attention. It was a man, she thought she was sure, but he was dressed like one very ugly woman.

Madison looked at it with great interest. In her raspy voice with an almost imperceptible lisp, she asked, "Who is that nigga person standing there dressed like a girl?"

Mia turned around abruptly as she stared in shock. She managed to say, "Baby, what you just asked me?"

Madison looked puzzled because she thought her mother was behaving very strangely, and she didn't think she said anything wrong. Madison repeated the question.

Mia shook her head as she walked into the kitchen and told Jeremiah what his daughter asked her. His round brown face registered disbelief. He shook his head and blamed it all on his wife. Madison walked into the kitchen and stared at them like they had lost their minds. She was more upset because no one answered her question.

Jeremiah stooped down low to meet Madison's brown eyes and said, "Princess, tell daddy where you learned how to use that word?"

She innocently asked, "What word, daddy?"

Mia joined in and said, "The word nigga."

Madison's brows furrowed and her three-year-old brain thought hard to remember where she learned it. She shrugged her shoulders and said, "Probably one of y'all," and walked out of the kitchen to go play with her brother.

Jeremiah shook his head and said, "Stop using racial slurs around my kid."

She chuckled. "You're right. It sounds really offensive when it comes out of the mouth of a three-year-old. We have to do better." Jeremiah was making his strawberry glaze for the salmon he had just taken off the grill. He stood about six-two and looked like what Mia would affectionately call her teddy bear.

Mia said, "You need to watch your language around your children."

"Uh-uh, Mia, that be you with the bad words."

"Nope, don't blame me for your kids. In any case, we need to guard our tongues very carefully and have a talk with her about rude words."

Jeremiah shook his head as he continued sautéing the fresh green beans. He checked the rest of his pots as the doorbell rang. Mia didn't move immediately, so he asked, "You gonna get that?"

She smiled mischievously, "Maybe I will if you give me a kiss first." He obliged, and she sashayed to the door.

It was her nephew by marriage, Nathaniel. Nathanial was deep brown and stood at six-three. His body was lean and muscular, and his features fit his face perfectly. His close cropped black hair elegantly framed his face. He strolled in carrying juices and sodas with his comedic overly proper voice. "Hello, hello, black people. How are you doing on this fine Sunday afternoon?"

She laughed, and thought, *What did I marry into?*

She gestured for him to come on in. He strolled into the kitchen, traded pleasantries with Jeremiah, and put the drinks into the refrigerator. He went to pick the seat he, Grey, and Seth fought over religiously every Sunday, the cream colored reclining leather chair. The chair was accompanied by a matching sofa with two reclining seats and a tan suede loveseat.

There was a fire place with a mantle and a forty-inch flat screen TV that played football. The beautiful sky lights boasted amazing light that made Mia's newly cleaned tile floors glisten. As he marked his territory by plopping down in the chair, the kids came running out to greet their cousin.

The oldest, a five-year-old named, Jeremiah Junior or Lil Jay screamed, "Cousin Nate, guess what? I was good in school all week!"

Nathaniel said, "Well, son, that's what you're 'posed to do, so I can only reward you with a high five."

Lil Jay thought he would accept the high five, but he would try his story out on his Aunt Grey to see if she would do better than a high five.

Just then, the bell rang again, and Lil Jay rushed to get it, "Who is it?" he asked.

"It's Grey," she responded, and he opened the door.

Lil Jay and Madison screamed, "Auntie," in unison and rushed into Grey's open arms. She put kisses all over both of them and then reached back for her bag full of paper plates, cups, and utensils. Nate got up to help Grey with her bags, and when he returned, his gratitude came in the form of Grey smiling a triumphant smirk as she sat in the coveted leather recliner. He just shook his head at her and said, "This is not over, Grey."

Grey yelled her pleasantries at Mia and Jeremiah because there was no way she was giving up her chair. She would find another time to hug and greet them.

Mia poked her god-sister in the neck, "What's up, big head?"

"Nothing man. I've been meaning to ask you have you had any luck finding Yolanda."

"Girl, no."

"Well, the reason I asked is because I saw her in traffic not two days after we were talking about her, but by the time I realized it was her, she had pulled off."

Mia said, "She's just been on my mind, and so I'll just keep praying for her."

"I asked to be her friend on Facebook, but that was months ago, and she clearly denied me. When I checked it again, her page was shut down."

"Well, all we can do is pray for her."

Yolanda had been Grey's roommate and a part of their crew when they were back in college. They knew she was always a sneaky broad, but once she and Grey became roommates, she showed her natural butt to the point where the falling out was monumental.

Grey had written her a nine-page letter because she honestly believed she really had no clue why her life was so messed up. She wanted to show her what character flaws she possessed that were holding her back in life. That was three years ago and none of them had heard or seen her, but they believed she was still there. God had recently placed her on the hearts of Mia and Grey.

Madison climbed into Grey's lap and started playing with her necklace as Lil Jay came to her to report on his good behavior. Jeremiah entered and said, "Hey, y'all, the food almost ready, but you know who we waiting on. Kadijah said she's on her way, but I haven't heard from the Richards's, they should have been here a while ago."

Nate asked, "Well, what else is new? They are probably somewhere being nasty anyways."

Grey rolled her eyes. "Well, I ain't mad at them because whenever I get married, I will always be late."

She laughed at herself, and Mia said, "When you get married, I will stop coming to your house!"

They both laughed as Nate and Jeremiah rolled their eyes and focused on the football game playing on the TV.

Kadijah walked in with more drinks and exchanged pleasantries. She was the only dinner patron that never played the recliner game. Nate took her bags and put them in the kitchen as she sat to watch the game. She was fairly new to the clan and had been invited to Sunday dinner by Mia after they met on the dance team.

Kadijah didn't know it, but she was still under observation because the "council" took the members of their family dinners very seriously, and not everyone fit in with the closely knit group of friends. The kids, out of politeness, hugged her. She hadn't quite mastered the banter with them, but she had great potential in their eyes. If she played her cards right, by offering toys or candy, she would be in with no problem.

Though Kadijah had yet to be saved, she had joined their church. It's not something they discussed openly, but all were praying fervently for her salvation. They were determined to win her for the Kingdom no matter how long it took, even if she didn't stick around for Sunday dinners.

Jeremiah returned. "Well, the food is done, but of course, we are still waiting on Sheridan and Seth."

There was a collective groan, and Mia said, "Now, y'all know we wait for everyone to get here so just chill out."

Everyone went about their business as they waited for the last of the crew to arrive. After about fifteen minutes, the Richards's graced them with their presence, and the trash talking began.

Sheridan said, "Okay, before y'all start this time, we have a really good excuse. Y'all ain't gone believe what happened."

Seth came in towering over Sheridan's five-foot-six frame at six-two carrying more desserts. Seth was the color of dark chocolate with heavily lashed brown eyes. He wore his hair in a short, neat afro. "Yep, we had an unexpected stop to make that couldn't be helped."

Nate chimed in, "Well, that sounds interesting and all but can we talk about it after we've done grace and everyone has a plate?"

They unanimously concurred. Jeremiah said, "Ok, let's pray."

Lil Jay asked excitedly, "Can I pray? Can I pray?"

Jeremiah cut his eyes as he was about to protest because he knew he was only doing it to get attention, but Mia beat him to the punch and said, "Sure baby."

He began. "God is grace; God is good, netusthankhim for our food. Amen. Eat now!"

They laughed and said, "Amen."

As always, the ladies went first. One by one they washed their hands and prepared their plates of grilled salmon, wild rice, fresh green beans, and corn bread. The men followed, and Mia got the kids situated as the grown-ups headed back to the living room. For the first ten minutes nothing except the TV could be heard, and Nate broke the silence. "So, now why is it that we had to wait to eat all this good food?"

Seth swallowed and said, "Ah, man, because we ran up on a car accident, and it was this sista and three white dudes was in her face. So, you know, I had to stop and see just what the deal was?"

Kadijah had a puzzled look on her face. "Okay, and so why did you have to stop for a stranger in a car accident? Was she hurt or something?"

Nate said, "That don't matter. Ain't no black man gonna stand around and let a white man be all up in a sista face, just not gonna happen."

Grey asked, "So, do all y'all feel like that?"

There was a collective, "Yep."

She said, "Well, that's something I've never heard before but very interesting."

Seth continued, "Anyway, so she wasn't hurt, but she did look scared, so I just pulled over and got out to stand with her to let them know she wasn't there by herself. I calmed the situation down and told Sheridan to call the police."

Sheridan said, "But you know I was already on it. And I made sure to wave and let my presence be known so she didn't think this was going to be no fairy tale ending or nothing like that."

The women laughed, and Mia gave Sheridan a high five. The men shook their heads.

"Anyways," she continued, "I also got Boomer out just in case something serious jumped off."

Kadijah was the only person who didn't know who Boomer was. "Who is Boomer?"

Sheridan said, "Oh, that's my Colt .38, baby."

Kadijah was shocked, "Oh, my God, you have a gun?"

Grey, Mia, and Sheridan all looked at her like she was slow and Sheridan said, "Uh, yeah, and I have it with me most of the time."

Grey said, "I got one, too. Sometimes I leave it at the house, but I do have a permit to carry it with me. Mine is a Walther 380 PPKS. It will get the job done."

Kadijah was a little uneasy, and she looked at Mia, "Well, do you have one?"

Mia laughed, "Yeah, actually, I do have a revolver because my hands are kinda small. But since I had my kids, I don't carry it on me or in my car anymore. Now we keep it locked away safely out of reach. They don't even know it's here. But one day, we will teach them how to use one."

Kadijah was very confused, "Okay, why do y'all all have guns? Do y'all know how to shoot them?"

Grey said, "Okay, I see we gone have to school you. We go to the range at least twice a month together, but we've had them for years. We ain't them ignorant folk that just wanna turn it to the side to try and look cool when we shooting and can't hit nothing. We practice because if you pull it out, you better be ready to use it. I got mine back in college because this guy I dated started showing stalker tendencies when I ended it. I am not now, nor will I ever be, a statistic. I wasn't trying to wait for him to do something stupid."

Mia said, "And because we were roommates at the time, I had to get one too because if he acted a fool at the house, we both had to be prepared."

Kadijah looked at Sheridan, but Seth spoke. "I got her one because when she used to sell real estate, she was always traveling to remote places, and I especially didn't like her out by herself in Monticello and Wakulla. You know they still shut down at noon on Thursdays in Monticello like they used to do so the people can come out and watch the hangings."

Kadijah gasped, "Are you serious?"

Jeremiah said, "Uh, yeah, you ain't at the bottom now. This is the top of Florida which is basically South Georgia. It's a little different up here."

Nate said, "Thanks for the commercial break, but, uh, can you finish the story?"

They laughed as Seth continued. "So, yeah, man, that was basically it. We waited with her 'til the police got there, and the black officer already knew what time it was so he just nodded at me when he got the gist of the situation, but the white cop was like okay, seriously, why are you here? So, I told him the truth, and I basically said, don't believe the hype about black men. We protect our own."

Sheridan jumped in, "She had the cutest blonde and red afro that almost made me want to go natural."

All the men took this as the opportunity to go back to watching the game, as the women continued discussing hair and whether they would ever take the plunge and go natural. Like so many Sundays before, one-by-one, they slowly dozed off to take a nap before the second round of eating began.

About two hours later, the kids started to surface, and then the party was back on. Everyone started to stretch and recover and get ready for plate number two and the ice cream and cherry pie that Seth brought. They ate, laughed, argued, and talked about politics, religion, interracial dating, and the all too popular topic—submission in a marriage. Jeremiah wanted to play Monopoly, but Mia still had them on punishment from the last time he, Nate, Seth, and Grey played. It was a game where friendships were almost ruined and morals were questioned. They opted for karaoke instead.

Kadijah dipped before the start of the bad singing saying she had homework to get to. Mia went about getting the kids all cleaned up and ready for the next day. She made cameos for her favorite songs as the others sang karaoke.

After they got tired of pretending to be famous singers, they opted for a movie and Mia opted for bed. She awoke about two hours later when she realized Jeremiah was not next to her. She peeped out into the living room and saw Jeremiah asleep on the floor with Madison asleep on his back. Little Jay was curled up with his Aunt Grey in the recliner, so she must've won the final battle for that coveted spot.

Seth and Sheridan were asleep on the love seat, her feet curled in his lap and her head on one arm as his was cocked back on the top of the sofa with his mouth wide open.

Nate was stretched out on the sofa with his hands folded atop his chest like he was casket ready. She knew the ridiculous snoring was coming from her husband. Mia just laughed and got sheets and blankets to cover them all. She wouldn't wake them, she knew they would sporadically find their way home since they all lived within five miles of each other. She made a pallet and lay on the floor next to her husband and daughter. She hated sleeping without him.

Chapter 11:
Death and Life Are in the Power...

Grey

I was sprawled out on my very comfy, very plush bed with pillows galore when I knew my state of blissful slumber was over due to my alarm clock ranting and raving about getting up. I hit the snooze button, and then I felt around for my cell phone because I knew my weather text was only seconds away. I wanted to shut that up before it got a chance to start.

I heard the bane of my existence walking around the house. He knew I did not want to be disturbed, but did he care? No, he did not because he was selfish. I was tired of supporting the little ingrate. He had taken over my house, and it was all I could do not to put his pathetic butt out on the streets. He was the man in my life as those who knew me often referred to him, but they did so just to annoy me because they knew how much I despised him. I would get rid of him, but I just couldn't. I'm obligated to let his arrogant, self-centered, snobbish behind continue to live off me.

I felt him jump on the bed, but I refused to make eye contact. I felt Barrington's cold nose sniffing at my hand. *My cat,* I thought cynically. I use the word "my" very loosely and to irritate him, I called him Barry. I don't abuse him as not to offend the pet lover or a card carrying member of PETA. Well, not physically anyway, maybe emotionally and mentally.

He eats well, sometimes better than me and the evidence is his fat lazy butt that plopped down on my bed. However, in my defense, he abuses me emotionally and mentally and every now and then, physically. The only reason I allow him to dwell in my domain is because my neighbor, Ms. Charmaine, left him to me in her will.

This little old lady was like a thousand years old; she passed a few months back. I used to sit with her on her porch and chat for the two years I have been here. She was the sweetest lady, and she made the best homemade lemonade and sweet potato pies. For some reason, she was oblivious to see that Barry and I never cordially interacted, but whatever.

He was the love of her old age, and she left specific instructions for him to be with me. I loved Ms. Charmaine, but she was so old you couldn't even be mad she made her trip to the pearly gates. Now, because of my love for her, and my respect for her last wishes, this raggedy cat was a resident here with me. I turned my head and looked into his cold green eyes. I stuck my tongue out, and he did the same. I had to laugh because I think I taught him that because for the first month, I did it every single time he got in my face.

There was hope for our relationship until he chewed up my favorite bedroom slipper. From that moment on, we have been sworn enemies. I sat up and rolled my eyes at him and in his usual disrespectful manner, he traipsed his tan furry butt right across my lap and hopped down to head to the kitchen as if to summon me to fill his bowls. I obliged, but only because I didn't wanna go to jail for neglect.

After feeding that ingrate, I decided to shower and get dressed, might as well. I mean, why be stuck at home on a Saturday arguing with Barry all day. But when I actually thought about it, I didn't have anywhere to go that I could justify spending any money. What to do? What to do? Ignore Barry. Check. Roll my eyes at Barry. Check. Okay, that was the norm, so I decided that I would relax in the rocking chair on my porch and pick a book off the shelf I had been meaning to read.

I picked up, *House*, by Frank Peretti and Ted Dekker. I thought it would be a little scary, so I wanted to start early so I had time to forget it before bed. I mean, I'm no punk, but I do live by myself in a heavily wooded area with Barry's lazy behind as the only man to protect me. Lake Jackson has creatures that haven't even been discovered yet.

Before I went outside, I put *The Nanny* on the DVD player because for some reason, Barry liked to watch it. That would keep him from bothering me for a while. I told him, "You know, you're on punishment from coming outside right? The last time I let you out, you brought a half dead snake in my house and almost caused me to shoot a hole through you, it, and my hardwood floors. So, if you want some fresh air, I suggest you go play around in the garage."

Surviving Sunday   - 69 -

He responded by lifting up his leg and licking. I couldn't stand him. I went out the front door and placed my book and some juice in a wine glass on the wrought iron table that was on my porch. I needed to bring my trashcan back to the house before I had to hear my next door neighbor talking noise about it. Who thinks about a trashcan like that? I mean most days I get home, and it's dark. I'm not going out there to bring in a trashcan, please.

When I pulled my trashcan up to the garage, my neighbor was outside with his dogs. I waved, "Hey, Lawrence, you doing alright today?"

Lawrence was a character. Every other word out of his mouth was profane, but he had a heart of gold. He was very handsome for an older dude. Well, not that much older, he was eight or ten years older. He stood about six feet and wore his hair closely cropped. His complexion was the same caramel as mine, and while I had light brown eyes, his were hazel. I had this game going in my head to see if I could apply the cussing censor at the right time. I was actually getting pretty good at it.

He threw his hand up and said, "Girl, where you been wit yo crazy bleep?"

I rolled my eyes, "How's your wife and kids Lawrence?"

"Bleep, they good, they in the house. We barbecuing today so come on over and get a plate."

Just then, his wife, Sierra, came outside and said, "Hey, Grey," as she waved.

She was beautiful and what you would call an Amazon. She was about five-eleven. I should work out with her like she always asks, but that's just too close to right. Her skin was the color of over creamed coffee and her shoulder length red hair was in a swinging tail. Lawrence looked back at her and said, "Boo, tell Grey that her bleep need to quit playing and let me introduce her to cuz."

She rolled her eyes, "Larry, stop all that and leave that girl alone."

He grinned at her and said, "I can't be nobody but me, babe, take it for better or worse."

I laughed as I checked my mail. My neighbors were very entertaining. As I headed for the front door she said, "Grey, please come over later and get a plate."

I said I would, and then Lawrence yelled, "And tell that ugly bleep cat of yours, he can't have none of my food."

I laughed and went back in the house to get my cell phone.

I came in and Barry rolled his eyes at me, his usual greeting, and I returned the favor. I walked into the kitchen to get a snack and brought it back in the living room as I stared at the notice still on my coffee table. The legal documents said they were going to foreclose on my house.

I sat down on the sofa. For a fleeting moment, I wanted to give in to the fear of losing my house, but I quickly recovered. I knew God gave me this house, and I knew He would make a way. I also knew He wanted me at my current job even though they stiffed me the $7,000 more they offered in the interview, but since it was still five more than I was making, I took it with a hope and a prayer that God would work it out. And He did. After a year of working there, they finally paid it, but by then, I had so many bills that were behind.

My insurance and property taxes were never included in the payment, so I had to pay those. All my bills just seemed to increase, and my mortgage hadn't been paid in months. Life was crazy. At this point, it was a waiting game because Sheridan got me involved with a housing counselor, and we got the ball rolling since the mortgage company was refusing to return any of my calls.

When I first moved in, it seemed every month the Lord made a way out of no way. I received a check for $2,500 from the sellers, which covered two months. The HR rep at the new job offered me a sign-on bonus. After taxes, it ended up being the exact amount of my mortgage payment. Somehow, someway, it got paid month after month, and I never missed a meal.

Then one day, it's like God just decided, okay, it's time for you to learn faith. But I already cried about this once, and that was all. I am leaving it in God's hands; He is going to make a way because I love my house and after all, He gave it to me. Barrington jumped in my lap. I scratched his head and told him, "Okay, Barry, you better do your part and pray, too."

He closed his eyes like he was really praying as I continued to scratch his head. I laughed and shook my head and spoke as I did every day since the first notice, "I will not lose my house!"

I got up to get the oil, and I anointed every door post as I prayed and covered my home. This was not of my doing, and it was out of my control, so I began to do what was in my control. Speak life over a very dead situation. I heard my cell ringing, it was my mom. "Hey, Denise, what's up?"

"What did I tell your butt about calling me by my name miss missy?"

"What up, crazy lady, how are you?"

"Well, I just wanted to call and mess with you. I hoped I would wake you up."

"Ah, ha, that's why I was already up. Nah. Why would you want to wake me up?"

"Girl, cause I had to tell you about this psycho next door to me."

I rolled my eyes. My mom's favorite neighbor, turned friend, had recently turned psycho over the fact that my mom's lawn man cut off a part of one of her plants that hung over my mom's side of the fence. My mom refused to fire him. It went from her neighbor not speaking anymore to shooting birds and the like.

I tuned back in, "So her estranged son came and knocked on the door to say hey to me. Then, Ms. Anders came out and went to cussing me and called me all kinda whores and liars, saying I was gossiping about her. Girl, you know God has done a work on me cause I just stood there just as calm as I could be. I told her that this situation wasn't that serious and that I was praying for her cause I really didn't know what she was talkin' bout. Girl that set her off, she told me I needed to pray for myself. And then this hussy said if she catches me talking to any one of her family members again, she gonna come to my house and beat my "A" and that was the last straw."

I gasped, "For real? Y'all old behinds round there bout to beat each other down bout a weed?"

She laughed, "Girl, I don't know what that woman is going through, but something is not right. I think she's trying to put roots on me."

I fell out laughing, my mother was so dramatic. "I politely told her that if she ever come knocking on my door. They will change the name of this street to "Beat Ms. Anders Down Avenue.""

I snorted, "Okay, thug misses, on that note, I'm getting off this phone to read my book, cause y'all got too much going on down in Central Florida for me."

"Bye, baby, love you."

"Love you, bye, ma." I went back outside and got comfy in my rocker and prepared to read my book. Barry thought he was slick and that I wasn't paying attention to him sneaking out. I told him, "You better not leave this porch, or I will not let you back in my house."

He must've understood because he came, got in my lap, and did what his lazy butt does best, closed his eyes to go to sleep. Now, finally, I could read in peace, chapter one. Then, my phone signaled a text message. "Ugh! What now?"

It was a text from Viviana. Viviana was my classmate in undergrad, and we were practically inseparable. We had every class together once we got into our major, and I swear I parked on her couch for a whole semester just because I didn't wanna drive back to my side of town just to get up and end up right back at her place. I graduated, decided to stay here, and work in banking, and then I pursued my master's degree. She opted to go to work for the IRS right out of undergrad, and she moved back down to South Florida. I really missed my friend. It read:

Hey neener (lol). I need to talk to you about something that's very important. Its work related so I need you to call me on Monday at my office. ~Viv~

I laughed at the stupid nickname she gave me back in college and for the life of me, I could not remember why, my goodness, it's been almost ten years. I replied:

Hey squeak! Um, why you sounding all cryptic and stuff? LOL. Ok will do, let me read my book in peace. *Grey*

Chapter 12:
What About Your Friends

Kadijah

I was on my way to hook up with my girls from the dance team at church. I've never really been the type of chick to keep a lot of females around, but so far, so good. The dance team was how I met Mia, and her crazy family. We were getting ready for a big production, so we spent a lot of time together whether we wanted to or not, so we had better like each other.

I pulled in front of Tiara's house behind Constance's car. I had known Tiara longer, but Constance was a new edition to our little gang. Me and Tiara were pretty close, but I could tell me and Constance were really gonna hit it off. She just kinda drifted toward me when she joined the team. But Tiara was my dawg; I had known her for almost a year, we did everything together. She was a little shy, but sometimes she could be the polar opposite. It was my first set of Christian friends, and they seemed to really be doing their best to live their lives for Christ, not like the hypocrites I was used to.

I got out and rung the bell. Constance opened the door and said all loud and ghetto, "What up, chick, took you long enough. We ready to watch the movie."

I rolled my eyes, "Whateva, learn some patience bout ya'self young one."

She laughed. She was about two years younger than me, and Tiara was a year older than me, which made her twenty-six. This was her first time hanging out with us officially outside of dance team. I resigned myself to know I was probably staying over because I just got there and already didn't feel like driving back to the other side of town. Glad I always kept a packed bag in my trunk, a habit from my days of partying hard in Miami.

That's where I'm from, we should be called the city that never sleeps or as they would say in Miami, *la ciudad que nunca duerme.*

I'm not fluent in Spanish but living down there, you pick up quite a few languages, well, at least, partially that is.

Constance was from Atlanta, and Tiara was from Orangeburg, South Carolina. So, it was always interesting to be around them. Constance took the bags I had brought with me into the kitchen. She was long and lanky with a short hair cut. She and Tiara both had the same reddish brown color, whereas, I was what you would call on the yellow side.

In contrast to me, Tiara was thick and curvy and while I wasn't as poor as Constance, you could say I'd be in-between. She brought all the food into the living room and started placing it down on the wide open space of the floor. There was pizza, chicken wings, gummy bears, popcorn, and sodas galore. Our dance team coach would have a hissy fit if she saw this. Tiara threw out three floor pillows and put in the DVD, *The Princess and the Frog.* Even though I was too grown to admit it, I loved this movie.

Constance asked me, "So, Kadijah, Tiara said you had a man. So, tell me about him. How long y'all been together, is he here? You know, what's the deal?"

I really wasn't big on dishing the man details, especially since we weren't exactly on the same page these days. We had been arguing ridiculously, and his attitude was really starting to disturb me. But in the interest of sisterhood, I would give the basics.

"Well, we've been together for about a year, and he is doing rotations back in Miami, he's a pharmacy major at FAMU, and I can't wait for him to get back up here."

She gave me a look like, is that all? I politely replied back with a look that said, yep, it is. Tiara said, "Don't feel slighted, she doesn't dish out very much about her boo and to be honest, I can't blame her. Females can be downright trifling, including the ones in the church."

I smiled at Constance and said, "No offense."

"None taken," she said, though the look on her face definitely said otherwise.

I said, "Well, alrighty then, subject change."

"Agreed."

I asked Constance, "So, what made you come to Tallahassee?"

She replied, "Let's just say I have some unfinished business and decided to get an education while I was at it."

Okay, could that answer have been any creepier? I gave Tiara a look that said, say something, now.

She just burst out laughing. Heifa, I couldn't do anything but laugh, too. Constance looked at us like we were crazy. She was oblivious to our shared thoughts.

Then, Constance asked, "How bout we play, truth or dare?"

Tiara agreed, but I was hesitant. Oh, well, if I didn't wanna answer the question, I would just take the dare.

I said, "Okay, fine, your idea so you can go first."

She asked Tiara, "At what age did you lose your virginity?"

"Wow, you go right for the jugular don't you?"

She smirked, "Saves time so we can get to the movie sooner rather than later."

Tiara rolled her eyes, "I was sixteen."

Tiara asked her, "What is the one thing you have done that you don't want anyone to know about?"

Constance looked away for a minute and then said with a straight face, "I used to practice witch craft."

I choked on my popcorn, and Tiara spit out her soda. Then, Constance kinda just laughed it off and said, "I'm just playing, no, seriously, I stole a pack of Nerds once from the corner store."

Tiara and I kinda gave each other a look that said we better sleep with one eye open.

I wasn't letting this go. I asked her, "Why in the world would you say that, even if you were playing?"

She rolled her eyes, "It's no biggie. I just wanted to say something to grab you guys' attention. That's all. Don't be so sensitive. What does Pastor Stone say all the time, fear not, right? I mean, don't worry, I won't cast a spell on you in your sleep, and I didn't put any kind of potion in the food I brought."

We both spit out everything, and Constance fell out on the floor and laughed 'til she cried. She said when she got her bearings, "Y'all should have seen the look on your faces, God, y'all are so scary, relax. I don't know the first thing about witch craft. My field is more in the expertise of voodoo."

Tiara said, "Okay, that's it, you gots to get the hell up out of here.

She blinked, "Are you serious?"

I said, "As a freakin' heart attack, bounce lil mama."

Her face got red, and she started mumbling under her breath as she gathered her belongings. Before she could reach to pick up the food she brought, Tiara was already headed to the trash with it. Constance was putting on her shoes and she said, "Oh, my God, I can't believe you guys are overreacting to a joke, this is ridiculous. I was just playing."

Tiara and I fell out laughing and said "Gotcha!"

She looked dumbfounded, face now red with embarrassment. She rolled her eyes extra hard and said, "Y'all make me sick!"

We laughed some more. She said, "I promise, I will get you two back for that. Y'all are awfully good at practical jokes seeing as how you threw perfectly good food away."

Tiara smiled, "Oh, that was real just in case you are crazy, and we just too naïve to believe you."

That made me snort. We ended up cooking some breakfast food to eat while we watched the movie.

†††

After the movie, it was still pretty early, and so we just sorta stretched out and prepared for the inevitable girl talk. Constance got up to go to the restroom and Tiara said, "Sleep with one eye open just in case."

I snickered but thought, *She did have a point.*

When Constance came over, she asked me, "Are you real close to your parents?"

"What are we back to playing truth or dare?"

She laughed, "No, the movie just got me to thinking. Charlotte had her daddy to spoil her even though Tiana was poor, her mom still loved her unconditionally, and the only reason she didn't give her the world is because she didn't have it to give."

I said, "Wow, life lessons from a Disney movie."

She chuckled. I answered, "Well, my parents were great, my mom isn't my real mom, my real mom died, and my step mom raised me since I was about four or five when my dad got remarried. I don't know. I have the kind of parents who always loved and supported me. I talk to my moms almost every day and my pops maybe once a week. He's not a big talker, but I know it's just who he is and not a reflection of his love for me. He's the one that got me interested in politics, and that's why I'm a political science major now. I'm thinking about law school afterwards."

I looked over at Tiara, and she had a tear running down her cheek. I asked, "What's wrong?"

She sniffed and said, "Let's just say, I didn't have that growing up. I never knew my mom, and I didn't meet my dad 'til later in life. I have some issues with it, but since I started going to Kingdom Builders, I've been trying to move forward and not hold any resentment in my heart. I'm really glad I came here."

She looked at me and said, "I know what motivated me to come here, but when I got here, it wasn't what I expected. There are many things in my past I've tried to run from, but eventually, I know I'll have to deal with them if I ever want to be a whole person and move forward."

Constance hugged her and said, "It's going to be alright, just take it one day at a time."

She said, "Thanks, I'm so glad I found y'all."

I said, "Okay, enough of this. Let's have some fun."

"Agreed."

We did karaoke badly and played cards. We watched, *The Beyonce Experience*, and almost broke our necks trying to mimic all the moves. I hadn't laughed that much or that hard in a while. After that, we fell out on the floor. Before I closed my eyes, I felt something. I don't know how to describe it, but something in this room just wasn't right. I was too tired not to fall asleep.

Part Three:

Spiritual Warfare

Chapter 13:
Luck Is For Those Without Skill...

Naomi was walking with her girl, Tameka, at The Regency Mall in Jacksonville, Florida, pretending to listen to her best friend rant and rave about her newest relationship, but Naomi's mind was elsewhere. It was where it always was, on Seth. She was specifically thinking about how to get him in her life permanently, how to get rid of his wife, and how to do it as quickly as possible. "Naomi, Naomi! Are you listening to me?" Tameka whined.

"Huh? Oh, yeah, of course, I'm listening. You were talking about you and Sylvester's date the other night."

Tameka tisked, "No, I was talking about me and Jimmy. I told you I broke up with Sylvester last week, and I'm through with him, but Jimmy is my soul mate."

Naomi rolled her eyes, "Oh, yeah, of course, he is. Do you realize that you change soul mates every month, Tameka?"

"Whatever, Nay, I may change men like I change underwear, but at least I am not running around fantasizing and plotting about a married man who does not want me or has the least bit of desire to leave his wife for me. So, you don't judge me, and I won't judge you!"

Naomi glared at her, but she thought for a moment and even though she wanted to slap the piss out of Tameka, the girl did have a slight point. It didn't seem like Seth wanted her, and he and his wife seemed to be more in love than they were when she started crushin' on him.

She mumbled, "You're right, Tameka."

She hated admitting defeat where Seth was concerned. She was determined to help bring that word to past that the pastor gave her at her mother's funeral. She was actually contemplating giving up because all of the things she had done had not worked and only served to make his wife more suspicious of her not-so-Christ-like activities.

As if it were a sign from God not to give up, she looked into the food court and spotted Seth. Her heart began to beat so hard and loud, she thought he could hear it from the ten-feet or so he was away from her. She decided, in that moment, she would seize this opportunity for all it was worth.

"Tameka, look, there's Seth."

"Where?"

"Right there, next to the pizza place. This is fate, and I am going to walk right up to him and lay it on the line."

"Girl, are you crazy? If he's right there, his wife has got to be around somewhere," Tameka said looking around for Sheridan.

"Well, she ain't there now, and plus, I got you for lookout right?"

Tameka hesitated, this did not feel right, and she just knew whichever way this went, something very bad would come from it.

She saw the determined look in her girl's eye and reluctantly confessed, "I got your back, Nay."

"Thanks, girl, just keep an eye out for his wife, and I'll find out if he's here alone or not. This is fate girl, what are the odds of him being here in Jacksonville on the same weekend I am here?"

"Ok, Naomi, but isn't his wife from Jacksonville?" Tameka reminded her.

"So, if I have any luck out there, she is somewhere with her family, and he is here by himself," Naomi boasted triumphantly.

Naomi began to walk towards him. She couldn't believe her luck or was it her destiny, to be here with him. She and Tameka traveled to Jacksonville to get away from Tallahassee for the long weekend for some shopping and maybe one of the day boat cruises. As she got closer, she noticed he had a very rugged air about him. She had seen him outside of church clothes before but never in street clothes. He sported a sky blue Sean Jean sweat suit with the shirt open exposing the definition of his chest through the white wife beater. She could swear she saw the top of a tattoo on the right side of his chest. He accented it with a pair of baby blue timberlands and a baby blue New York Yankees fitted cap cocked to the side.

Naomi was instantly turned on. Her body started to tingle in places it probably should not have. This man was sexy. Maybe he really let go whenever he was out of town. As she approached him, she noticed him staring at her with what she could swear was absolute desire in his eyes. She said a silent prayer that he wanted her as much as she wanted him.

As Naomi approached him, he did a double take. She was absolutely breathtaking. Here was this olive complexioned honey with jet black hair that flowed past her shoulders, grey eyes, and the sexiest pouty lips he had ever seen. Her make-up was done to perfection, she was wearing some very fitted skinny jeans and a hooker red v-neck blouse that didn't expose her cleavage, but it let you know she definitely had some.

With the hips she carried, he already knew what she looked like from behind. The four-inch pumps she sported had his mind all the way in the gutter. She was approaching him like she was on a mission to make him hers. Because looking at her instantly turned him on, he was more than ready to finish whatever she started.

Naomi walked right up to him. Because he was more than a foot taller, she sassily looked up into his eyes and said a sexy, "Hey, Seth."

He looked down at her and smiled naughtily, "Hey yourself, pretty lady."

She could not believe he was actually flirting with her. "Why are you looking at me like you've never seen me before?" she asked.

He hesitated, "Um, I have never seen you looking like this." He paused for dramatic effect and looked her up and down like she was something good to eat.

Naomi didn't expect this response from him, and it made her a little nervous. She quickly regrouped because it was the moment she had been praying for. She was going to make the most of it.

"So, what are you doing here?" she asked.

"Oh I just needed to get away for a few days, you know, regroup."

"I feel that, so where is your wife?" The expression on his face was unreadable, but his right eyebrow shot up and another wicked smile spread across his lips.

"Not here," he simply said.

Naomi was grateful and before she could get another word out, he put his finger on her lips and bent down to whisper in her ear, "You wanna get out of here?"

She stepped back in shock and looked him in his eyes. All she saw was how much he wanted her. She ignored all her common sense and every bell and whistle that was going off in her head. She scooted back up to him and grabbed the bottom of his jacket, leaned up on her tip toes until her lips were seconds from his and said, "Absolutely!"

Naomi turned back to see if she could see Tameka anywhere. He asked, "You here with somebody?"

"Uh, yeah, my girl, Tameka, but she drove so I just need to tell her I'll catch up with her later."

She spotted her and quickly made a motion for her girl to "shoo" when she started towards her. She put her thumb and pinkie to her ear and mouthed to signal she would call her. Tameka just stood there with her mouth wide open staring in disbelief. Her girl had officially lost her mind. But she was grown, and Tameka didn't have time for the drama. Before she turned to leave, she held up her phone as if to say, "Call me, if you need me."

After that, she told herself, "Hear no evil, speak no evil, and see no evil." Tameka headed to her car, hoping she wouldn't have to get her friend out of some awful situation.

Naomi gladly placed her hand in his as he reached for her and started toward the exit. She had butterflies in her stomach but quickly suppressed the nervousness to put into motion her plan to seal this deal once and for all. She was fully prepared to sleep with him, that wasn't even a question. She just wanted to make sure if this was the only encounter, he was stuck with her for life and wifey would just have to deal. As they walked out to his car, she began to ponder scenarios about how to make this situation work to her advantage. They approached a car she didn't recognize, a fire red Dodge Charger. Seth drove a black Nissan Pathfinder.

"You got a new car or something?"

He had a strange look on his face, but recovered and said, "It's a rental."

"Seth, you rented a car to drive from Tallahassee to Jacksonville?"

He laughed, "Hey, sweetie, sometimes you just have to do it big even in a short distance."

She shrugged, "I guess."

He let her hand go and walked around to the driver's side. She stood there a little disappointed and stunned that he didn't open her door for her like he does for his wife on every occasion. Then, she thought she was here and his wife wasn't, so she opened her own door and climbed in.

By the time she got in, he had already changed the CD to an old school mix that you would hear on any quiet storm. She put on her seatbelt and relaxed a little, closed her eyes, and let Maxwell take her exactly where she wanted to be because she was indeed "fortunate" to be in this moment. As they pulled away from the mall, she asked, "So, where are we going?"

"My hotel."

Her heart thudded in her chest. "I thought your wife had family here, and you're staying in a hotel?"

He looked a little irked, and she thought, *Maybe I'd had better stay off the wife topic.*

Besides, why did she keep reminding him of the woman she wanted him to forget? He gave her a sly glance and said, "I told you, she wasn't here, and how about we keep the conversation focused on us? Whatever's in Tallahassee stays in Tallahassee, and whatever happens here, stays here, understood?"

She nodded, "Uh, I need to stop at a drug store or something."

He knew exactly what she wanted to stop for, but he already had a few of those with him. He almost told her so, but then thought that it might bring up questions he didn't want to answer about why a married man was carrying around prophylactics. After all, he was about to take her to his hotel and get some much needed release of unwanted tension he had been carrying around. There was no sense in putting his business on Front Street by allowing her to believe this wasn't an isolated incident.

"Sure, there's like a Walgreen's on every corner in this city," he replied.

He decided the less conversation they had, the better. He reached to turn the volume up and began to relax, hoping she would follow suit. They were headed down Atlantic Boulevard on their way toward the beach. As Maxwell gave way to Shirley Murdock's "As We Lay" he grinned, enjoying the soundtrack to his little unexpected escapade.

She seemed to be a little uneasy so he placed his hand on her thigh and gently began to massage it. She instantly released her tension, and she seemed to melt from his touch. He smirked and mentally stroked his ego. This would be too easy. He pulled into the Walgreen's on the corner of Atlantic and Kernan and quickly took a spot in the front that another car was exiting. She looked at him and said, "Be right back."

Naomi headed toward the store and walked through the automatic doors. Her mind was racing a thousand miles a minute. Her advantage in this situation was the protection would be hers because it was unlikely he would have any. Knowing this, she had come to three conclusions, don't use one, poke holes in it or keep the condom and insert the baby juice when she got back to her hotel. The flaws with these options were, as a married man, he would probably insist on a condom, and she didn't want that to put an end to her transaction by not having one.

She would have to find a way to pierce it without him being the wiser. She could not squander this opportunity, and he may be one of those men who prefer to flush his own bodily fluids. If she did get to dispose of it, how long would it keep, and how long before she would be ovulating. Hell, for all she knew, she could be ovulating right then, but at twenty-three years of age, she never decided to understand the timing of ovulation. She never thought she would ever need to know how long sperm would last before it was ineffective. Dang, she needed to make a decision and quick. She went to the appropriate aisle.

She picked up a three pack of Trojans and some lubricant. She needed to make sure he got turned out because if all else failed, there was always the possibility that he would be sprung, and this wouldn't be an isolated incident. She was headed to the front counter when she realized she didn't have anything to puncture the condoms with. She did an about face and went down the aisle to get a pack of safety pins. She then went down another aisle to find some super glue. She got them and headed back to the front counter to pay. She paid the cashier and asked, "Where's your restroom?"

The clerk pointed toward the back of the store, "It's right next to the pharmacy, ma'am."

"Thanks."

Naomi couldn't help but smile as her plan began to unfold in her mind. She quickly hurried to the bathroom and went into the handicapped stall. Once inside, she dropped the box of condoms on the floor and stepped on it. She picked it up and carefully opened it. She then took out all three condoms, the safety pins, and poked five holes in the center of each condom; squishing each of them to be sure the lubricant wasn't seeping out. She was good. She then put them back in the box and took out the super glue. She glued the box back together and examined it. She was impressed with her ability to think on her toes. The box would simply look like it had gotten smashed in her purse, and he would be none the wiser that the box had been previously opened.

She trashed the pins and the glue, put the condoms back in the bag, and put it at the bottom of her purse. She then refreshed her make-up and headed straight for the front door. Thinking to herself, "Sheridan better watch out for me. Who needs luck when I got skill?"

She had a Cheshire cat grin on her pretty face all the way through the front doors.

Chapter 14:
Hell Hath No Fury...

Naomi was riding on the passenger side of Tameka's car. She was seething. She had never felt so disrespected and used as she did at this very moment. As a matter of fact, let's add embarrassment to that because she didn't even want to face her friend. Naomi was grateful that her friend loved her enough to come all the way from Orange Park to Jacksonville Beach to pick her up from what she was now seeing as a one-night stand.

She wondered if it was a one-night stand if you already knew the person. She prayed that she could forget the night before and how she set herself up for emotional suicide. She was almost on some slit-your-wrists type devastation and not horizontally like they do on TV, she was thinking straight up and down with the blade! A tear rolled down her cheek as she thought back to the night before.

They got to his hotel, and she just knew she was in for the most romantic night of her life. Maybe he would order room service and get some strawberries and champagne like Richard Gere did in "Pretty Woman." Ok, maybe comparing herself to a prostitute's story was not a good precedent. This was already adultery.

A pang of conviction hit her; she brushed it to the side because she was determined to live in this moment. Maybe there would be a massage or something she hadn't even thought of that would make it more special. She wished she had some sexy lingerie to put on, but she was grateful she always took her aunt's advice and wore matching underwear.

As they got on the elevator, she felt the need to be closer to him so she put her arm in his and placed her head on his chest. He didn't embrace her like she hoped but remembered he was a married man. This made her look down at his ring finger, and she didn't see his wedding band.

She wondered when he had taken it off, but then again, she was glad because she could do without it crossing her line of sight. This would be a night to rival all nights from her past and would set the standard for all nights in her future. Nothing would ruin this moment for them and the beginning of their great love.

As they stepped off the elevator, she was taken aback when he released her arm from his and basically just walked out. Because common sense told her to, she followed him. Once inside his hotel room, he tossed the key onto the nightstand, and she stood at the door waiting for his direction. The room was simple and didn't look extravagant.

It had two double beds with tacky Hawaiian print covers, a table and two chairs by the window, a dresser and the nightstand between the beds. His silence was starting to bother her so she asked, "So, what are we going to do tonight?"

He turned and looked at her with a crooked grin. "Oh, I guess you think this is about to be some wine and dine type foolishness, baby girl, huh?"

She gasped, though she tried to hide it, "Well, exactly what is it gonna be then?" she asked with a hint of testiness.

She was not about to let him control this situation since she didn't like the direction he was taking it in. His face took on a serious tone.

"Look, we are both adults, and you knew exactly why I asked you here. I am not here to force myself on you, so if this is not what you want, then by all means, there's the door," he said, as he pointed towards it.

He walked up to her with a very determined gaze in his eyes and used his body to pin her up against the door. She immediately looked down because his gaze was doing something to her she had never felt before. He lifted her face up so that she could look him in his eyes. He gently brushed his thumb across her lips, and he grinned at the way she trembled under his authoritative touch.

"I know what I want, and I'm a hundred percent sure it's what you want too, which is why you approached me the way you did in the mall today. Now, either you are the woman you behave like or you're not. No sweat off my back, sweetheart. Remember, I got a wife at home."

She swallowed hard, and he could literally see her thoughts racing to and fro through her eyes. He knew she was putty in his hands, and he enjoyed every minute of watching her squirm. He knew if he pushed her, she would rise to the occasion. If he was going to risk this, he wanted it to be worth his while. Her body was trembling both from being turned on by his apparent ability to control a situation and a little scared because she really didn't know exactly what she had gotten herself into. This was a side of him she had never seen, but she realized that this man was older than her, and if she wanted to beat out her competition, she had to show him that she was indeed a grown woman.

She pushed her chest into his and licked her lips, "Even if your wife was in this room, she couldn't give you the pleasure that I could, so why don't you get your mind right."

She pushed him off of her and gave him a naughty smirk as she walked into the bathroom and closed the door.

She took several deep breaths as her hands were shaking, and she realized she had better get it together now or walk away now. She was so nervous she had to steady herself to keep from vomiting. She had a pang of a conviction. *What am I doing? I cannot sleep with this married minister. This is crazy, Naomi. Get a grip. You worked so hard to get your life together and get away from your past. What are you doing? Just walk away right now!*

She almost walked away because she knew deep down what she was doing was wrong. Even if he was meant to be her husband, there had to be another way. She had a different reason to feel sick to her stomach now, it wasn't nervousness, it was disappointment in who she'd become. She looked at herself in the mirror and had the urge to turn away from her reflection because she didn't like who she had become.

Was this an obsession? Wait a minute. She would have plenty of time to apologize for her sins later. It was a two-and-a-half hour drive back to Tallahassee. She was not about to squander her one chance at happiness. She couldn't walk away, she had been praying for an opportunity like this, and she couldn't let it slip through her fingers.

She turned on the water and washed her face. She started to calm down and realized she was too nervous to do this the way she wanted to. In that instant, she decided she would become somebody else, just to seal the deal and give her true self a chance to process these thoughts. She thought of the sluttiest girl she knew,

Cathandrea Slater, from high school. This girl was the epitome of a tramp, but she was beautiful and confident. Everywhere she went, a man's eyes followed.

She closed her eyes and tried to remember everything about the way Cathandrea carried herself. "Now, what would Cathandrea do in this situation?" she whispered to herself.

It only took her a few minutes to get into character. She smiled as she started to reapply her make-up. She was about to give the performance that would rival any Oscar winning actress. She gargled with some mouth wash and stripped down to her underwear, but she put her shoes back on. She took the box of condoms out of her purse and stepped out into the room to take control of her destiny.

He was sitting on the bed wearing nothing but his boxer briefs. She licked her lips. This man was gorgeous, and her heart began racing. She was so in love with him, and now she was finally going to show him what he meant to her. With a smirk, she thought, to hell with right or wrong and definitely to hell with Sheridan. She wanted to remember everything about the way he looked in that moment. This opportunity was one for the money.

His stare said he wanted her as his eyes roamed her body from head to stiletto heel. She all of a sudden felt self-conscience and then remembered she was not Naomi Walker, she was Cathandrea Slater. Her eyes did a once over, and she was turned on to the Nth degree. There was something about the way he looked at her. She noticed his tattoo again and that was sexy as hell to her, like there was once a little bad boy in him.

On his right peck, there were two clown masks; one was crying and one was laughing. There were words under it, but she couldn't quite make them out from where she was standing. Well, she was determined to bring the bad boy out of him tonight, or at least Cathandrea was, she laughed to herself.

She did a slow, seductive walk, and climbed onto the bed. His voice was raspy, "Well, I guess you ain't shy no more."

"Shy, who me? I was never shy, baby, maybe demure, but never shy," she said. "Come to mama, and let me show you what you've been missing."

She waved the box of condoms in his face and placed them on the nightstand. She smiled as she said, "You got three tries to satisfy me. If the third time is not your charm, you will never get this opportunity again."

He laughed, mildly amused, and very turned on by her sassiness and her challenge. He replied, "I only need one time, and let's not forget, baby girl, by the lust in your eyes for me, the opportunity has always been mine for the taking."

She wanted to deny it, but she was sure her love for him was written all over her face. He reached out and pulled her close to him. When his lips touched hers, she thought she would melt on the spot. With every touch, she trembled in his arms. She knew she had to give this her all, if she ever wanted to keep his heart tied to hers.

✝✝✝

Naomi was absolutely exhausted after the third round. She was glad she only bought a package of three because she didn't think she could have gone another round. This man had an insatiable appetite. His wife was more of a prude than she'd thought; he was obviously deprived of some good lovin'.

She gently stroked his face as he slept. She took her finger and traced all the contours of his face trying to remember every curve and every detail that was the face of the man she loved with all her heart. She smirked, remembering how she made him scream. She just knew he would be coming back for more. Her body was tired, but her mind was racing. What would the next day bring? She snuggled up to him and put her hand on his chest. That's when she finally read what his tattoo said, "Laugh now. Cry later."

It startled her just a bit because it felt like a premonition, the writing on the wall warning her. It would be ironic if that was how this affair ended. She was definitely laughing now, she had successfully played his wife for the fool, but later would she be crying because she was the fool? She hoped by some miracle there was a straight shooter in the bunch and just maybe, she was pregnant as she drifted off to sleep wrapped around the man of her dreams.

She awoke to find herself in the bed alone the next morning. It took her a minute to adjust and remember where she was and what she was doing there. She felt very vulnerable lying in the strange bed in her birthday suit. She heard the shower running and suddenly had an idea. She climbed out of bed and headed to the shower to join her man. She opened the door and peeked inside the shower curtain, the man was fine. She was just about to climb in when he turned to face her.

"Girl, what are you doing?"

She was taken aback by his animosity. "I'm joining you for a shower, baby, is that not okay?"

"Baby? Oh, naw, I would prefer you wait your turn," he pulled the shower curtain closed.

Oh, that hurt, but she was even more pissed off at the moment. She snatched the shower curtain open. "Excuse me, how you gonna try to play me like that? Oh, I'm good enough to screw, but I can't shower with you? You don't know who you messing with, Seth. I'm not playing games with you."

He raised his voice, and his tone was downright disrespectful. "Girl, take your behind back in that room, and wait 'til I'm done. You know what, as a matter of fact, why don't you call a cab to take you back to wherever it is you came from. Oh, and wait for it in the lobby!" He snatched the curtain shut, "Now, open it again and see what happens?"

She was crushed. There was nothing she could do to stop the hot tears from cascading down her pretty face. She just stood there unable to speak and unable to move. This could not be happening to her. Did he really just use her to get his rocks off, and now he was acting like she was some tramp he just met? He didn't even have the decency to take her back to her hotel. His voice boomed from behind the curtain,

"I know your silly behind ain't still in this bathroom. You need to step, and I would like you out of my room by the time I'm finished. If you noticed, I put all your belongings on the floor by the bed."

He could hear her sobs now. He started to feel a little guilty for his harshness, so he did the best he could to make her feel better but not to give her any hope of more than he was willing to give. "If it makes you feel any better, I didn't once think about my wife while I was wrapped around you. So, thanks for the entertainment. I left a dub on the nightstand that should get you back to wherever it is that you're going."

He let out a laugh that shattered the last pieces of her heart, and she walked out the bathroom and slammed the door. *Well, so much for her feelings*, he thought, very pleased with himself.

†††

"Naomi! Naomi!" Tameka shouted. "Girl, are you okay?" Naomi didn't respond, "That's it, I'm pulling over."

By the time Tameka pulled into the gas station, Naomi was hysterically in tears. "Girl, what happened? What did he do to you," Tameka asked nervously.

Naomi cried, "I hate him, I hate him. I can't believe he did me like that. Then, he had the nerve to leave twenty dollars on the nightstand like I really would have taken it. I felt so cheap and used."

After a few moments, her breathing began to calm, "But you know what, I am not gonna sit up here in tears over his simple behind. I am not some whore that he can have and toss to the side. What he doesn't know is that I play for keeps, I don't play games. I got something for him. Not only did I tamper with all three condoms to ensure his baby juice was free to do what it was made to do, but I now know details about him that his wife will be thrilled to have me describe to her. He thinks he's going try me like some two dollar ho. Oh, hell, naw! I got something for him. I can't wait to take a pregnancy test, and if I'm not, then I'm telling his wife about his extracurricular sextivities, and she's gonna leave him, and he will have no choice but to come to the only arms who's willing to love him! He is going to be mine one way or another, and I really don't give a dern which way it is!"

Tameka had to remind herself to close her mouth as she realized she was about to drool because her mouth had been hanging open for so long. She had no words. Naomi had lost her ever loving mind and she was scared of the girl. *So, this must be what crazy looks like*, she thought. She wished she had done more to stop Naomi's obsession with their married minister. She knew all she could do was pray for her friend and all the people who would be torn apart from this web of lies and deceit. "Lord, Jesus, help me," she silently prayed.

Chapter 15:
Round One...Ding!

Sheridan

I was on my way to the church to pick up the checkbook from Seth. I really hate when he forgets to leave it at home in the office. I knew he was at choir rehearsal, however, it was almost 3:30, and it should be about over now. I pulled into the church parking lot to find a parking space. We really needed better parking because I did not want to scratch the new pearl white 300 my husband just bought me. I decided to park on the street behind the church. The walk would do me good.

When I reached the sanctuary, I could hear many conversations so I knew rehearsal was over. I walked in, but I didn't see Seth. He must've been in his office on the other side of the sanctuary. I waved to all the choir members I passed by. When I got to Naomi and Tameka, Naomi looked at me and rolled her eyes. What in the heck was this chick's problem? She had taken her little crush on my husband too far. She didn't know me. I wasn't the one. I decided to let her foolishness slide for now because I was in the sanctuary of a church.

I knocked on Seth's door. "Come in."

I closed the door behind me, "Hey, baby. How are you?"

He walked around the desk and gave me a hug and a kiss. Then, he slapped my butt. "Now, you know you were wrong for that, Seth."

"What you talking about. We married. Ain't nothing about that wrong."

I laughed, "Whatever. How was rehearsal?"

"It was good. They are ready to do the newest song I wrote. We'll sing it tomorrow at the 11:00 A.M. service." I loved that one partially because I helped write it.

"Okay, well, I can't wait to hear them sing it. So, you got the checkbook."

"Yeah, baby, it's in my bag over by the desk."

I moved to look through the bag and found the checkbook. "Oh, baby, while I'm thinking about it, you better get your little girlfriend before she gets dealt with."

He laughed, "What are you talking about?"

"Don't play stupid, Seth. You know, I done told you several times about Naomi, and when I walked in the sanctuary, she rolled her eyes at me. So, now I know for sure she's after you because all I did was walk by and speak. You better get her before I do."

He shook his head, "Baby girl, please, don't act a fool in this church. She can like me all she wants but ain't nothing ever gonna be done about it. It's pointless to acknowledge. I even postponed our next duet since you have been on this tirade about her having feelings for me."

I rolled my eyes. "She don't care nothing about that, and I'm not worried about y'all singing together for the Lord because your voices do harmonize well together, but she trying to do more than sing with you on a song. She trying to make beautiful music with you, and I'm going to make a war cry before it's all said and done."

He laughed, "Girl, you crazy. Look, baby, let me wrap up here, and I'll meet you at the house. Are you going home now?"

"Yeah, as soon as I drop this payment off, I'm heading to the house."

He walked over, kissed me, and then hit my butt again, "Can't wait to get home then."

I laughed as I walked out of his office. "You so nasty."

Everyone had cleared out of the sanctuary. I was thankful for that because I wouldn't be tempted to chop Naomi in her throat. I walked out into the foyer on the side of the sanctuary to stop by the restroom before I left. When I looked up, I saw Naomi and two of her friends standing by the bathroom. Well, looks like I spoke too soon. *Okay, Sheridan, you can do this, just don't say anything and just go to your car. You can hold it.*

I was almost to the door when Naomi looked up at me and said, "Now that you're gone, let me go and have that conversation with Seth in his office I've been meaning to have."

That stopped me from walking out the door. "Excuse you?"

She looked at me like she didn't understand and said, "Oh, honey, it's not the first meeting alone in his office, and it certainly won't be the last."

Before I knew it, I was in her face. "Look, you little lying heifa, I don't know who you think you're talking to, and I know you don't know who you messin' with. You ain't had no meeting alone in his office because he doesn't get down like that. Don't let the cross round my neck or the soft curls in my hair fool you. I'm from Duval County, baby, and I will slap you just as hard as I will pray for your salvation. You need to watch your mouth, and you better stay the hell away from my husband."

She smirked, "Oh, his office is the last place you need to worry about me being in. You need to be checking his pockets for hotel room receipts."

Okay, it's official. She was literally begging me to slap her, and I didn't want to be rude and deny her what she so desperately needed.

"Look, whore, I know what you're up to, but it's not gonna work. He's married to me, and I am not playing games with you. All these lies you letting fly out your mouth ain't fooling me. Now, this is the last time I'm going to tell you to stay away from my husband. He don't want your scandalous behind."

I guess she must've wanted to show out for her little friends because she stuck her D-cups in my face and said, "Who you calling a whore?"

I looked at both her friends to assess the situation just in case I had to take all three of them out. It was obvious they didn't want any part of this. I put my finger in her face. "Well, obviously, I'm talking to you because only a whore would throw herself at a married minister with no regard for her self-respect or dignity."

I think I struck a nerve because she backed down a little bit and said, "Oh, don't get so high and mighty talking about he a minister, because even though he's supposed to be a "man of God" he is still a man. Now, look at you and look at me. Physically, I got this on lock, you stuck up, heifa. He gots to get tired of your bony behind, which is why he's been sniffin' behind all this thickness."

She pushed her chest in my face again for emphasis. I laughed because Seth, like most Black men, could care less about some

Surviving Sunday   - 97 -

breasts. I had plenty of what my husband preferred. Okay, I'm done with this, and I told her so.

"You got one more time to try me, Naomi. I'm done repeating myself. Consider yourself warned."

It sounded like somebody was walking out of the sanctuary. It must have been Seth. I was about to walk away when she put her hand out to stop me and said, "Or what?"

I looked down at her hand on my arm and then looked at her like she had lost the good sense God gave her. Okay, well, since I'm a woman of my word, I calmly backed up, placed my left hand behind my back, and rotated my two karat diamond ring solitaire to the inside of my hand. As I looked her dead in the eye, I gave her the sweetest most sincere smile I could muster.

I said a quick silent prayer, "Lord, forgive me for allowing the devil to use me like this so close to your sanctuary."

I whipped my hand from behind my back and slapped the taste out of her mouth. It took her head a whole three seconds to snap back and face me. I saw blood running from her mouth, and that was with my left hand. This working out stuff is paying off. But I was about to pop her one with my right, and that would lay her butt out.

I heard Seth scream, "Sheridan! Are you crazy?"

He came and grabbed me so fast I didn't have time to hit her again, this time with a closed fist. He was squeezing me tight as he pulled me out into the breezeway. I almost couldn't breathe. "Let me go, Seth," I yelled as I tried to squirm free.

He was too hot with me. "Girl, what is wrong with you? Are you really playing the role of a jealous female? You had no business putting your hands on that girl."

No this Negro was not defending that little heifa. "Negro, please."

He carried me to his truck, opened the door, and put me in. "Sheridan, I cannot believe you stooped that low. You ain't have no business hittin' that girl. She could press charges on you."

"Seth, I don't give a dern about her, and if you sit up here and defend this girl to my face, we are going to have a problem."

"Sheridan, calm down, I'm going to see if the girl is okay. You stay right here and don't move."

Oh, no, he did not. "Negro, who you talking to? Have you lost your mind, and now you going to see if she okay?"

He cut me a look that said I was overstepping my boundaries. Then, he said, "That's right, I'm going to see if she okay because if she's not, I can't just leave her here seeing as you are the reason she's hurt. Stay here."

He walked away. Oh, this fool must think I'm stupid. What kinda mess is this? He was about to turn the corner when Naomi and her two friends came walking toward him. Seth asked, "Naomi, are you okay?"

She was holding her mouth, and there was blood on her shirt. She stopped and looked at me, then looked at Seth. "Tell your wife you will both regret this."

She walked to her car. They got in and drove off. I could tell by his body language that Seth was pissed. But I was too mad to care. How dare he run off to see if *she* was okay? When he got to the car, I jumped down his throat.

"How in the hell you gonna go running to her making sure she's okay. I'm your wife. You don't even know what happened before you showed up, but you siding with her."

"That's right, Sheridan, you are my wife, and you are the one I'm trying to protect. You always letting your emotions dictate your actions and because of that, you could end up in jail. If that girl decides to press charges on you, then what are you gonna do?"

I guess that never really crossed my mind. "Well, that doesn't explain you running to her side, Seth."

He looked at me like I was speaking Portuguese. "Sheridan, what are you talking about? I am concerned about you, my wife. I am trying to protect you, my wife. I couldn't just leave the girl here bleeding all over the church, now could I? I'm sure she said something, and you felt the need to respond with your hands, but you better learn how to walk away. I don't have time for this foolishness. How did you bust her lip with just your hand?"

I didn't want to tell him. "Sheridan," he asked again, "How did you do that?"

I mumbled, "I hit her with the diamond in my ring."

He couldn't hear me, "What did you say."

I blew out a long breath, "I hit her in the mouth with my diamond." He looked at me with his mouth agape.

I looked at him like he was crazy, "What?" He just shook his head at me.

"Sheridan, your behind is crazy."

I wanted to slap the piss out of him and even though my adrenaline was rushing, Seth was over six-feet tall. I knew he was usually meek, but I could tell I was pushing him out of the element of his personality. "Look, Seth, I'm done with this conversation. If she presses charges, she presses charges. I bet you she will think a little harder the next time she decides to open her mouth to disrespect me. Now, could you please just drive me to my car so I can go?"

He cut his eyes at me and started the car. "You need to stop being petty and jealous, Sheridan."

It took everything in me not to slap him, but common sense reigned in this time. Slapping Naomi was one thing, but slapping Seth was not an option. Contrary to what he thinks, I ain't crazy. "I'm not jealous, however, if you would have dealt with this when I first warned you, we wouldn't be in this situation now."

"Oh, my God, why do we keep having this same discussion Sheridan, dang? Yes, I was the person she reached out to when she got in the choir because I know what it's like to be abandoned and move on. Yes, I tried to minister to the girl on how to deal with what she's been through. I have never been alone with the girl, nor have I ever done or said anything to make her think this was something else. You really need to let this go."

Ugh, why are men so freakin' naïve? "I wish I could, Seth, I really wish I could."

✝✝✝

When I got back to the house, I was so mad my head was hurting. This had gone too far, and it was time I nipped it in the bud. He was going to deal with this foolishness one way or the other. I thought this Naomi situation was far from over, but I would just take this one issue at a time. I heard Seth come into the garage. I knew he would be in my face in a few moments.

"Sheridan," he called, "Where are you?"

I rolled my eyes. "In the bedroom."

I heard him messing around in the kitchen, and then, he opened the bedroom door. "Have you calmed down yet?"

I had to catch myself because a flip comment was on my tongue. "No, not quite."

"Baby, what is the deal with you and her? Do you just not hear me when I say I ain't paying that girl any attention?"

I let out a long sigh. *He just doesn't get it.*

"Seth, I am going to tell you this one last time. That little girl wants you. She doesn't like me. I'm not sure why, but for whatever reason, she sees that there is something between you two. She is very capable of tryin' to manipulate some foolishness, and you just refuse to see it. Something is not right about this girl's crush on you." He walked over, sat on the bed next to me and grabbed my hand.

"Baby, I just think you're overreacting. Now, she might have a crush on me, but she knows I'm married and that I love you. She can't possibly think that I would leave you for her or engage in an affair with her. Do us all a favor and just keep your distance until she gets over this and finds a nice young guy to keep her attention."

This man was going to drive me insane. I pulled my hand away from his and said, "I'm going for a walk *by myself.*"

I walked out of the room and out of the front door.

When I got to the edge of the driveway, I pulled my cell phone out of my pocket and called my mother-in-law. She answered on the third ring, "Hey, mama, this is Sheridan."

"Well, hey, sweetie. What a nice surprise. How are you?"

"I'm fine, just going for a walk."

"Oh, I need to follow your example and work on this little pudge that just popped up out of nowhere."

I laughed, "Ma, my call isn't as casual as I'm making it seem."

I thought I may as well get to the point, "I really need to talk to you about something."

"Is everything alright dear? Is Seth okay?"

"In a matter of speaking everything is fine, but I do need to talk to you about your son."

"Go ahead, baby, I'm listening."

I took a breath, "Well, as you know, Seth never talks much about his birth parents and even though he says he has forgiven them, he still harbors some bitterness about this situation. Without going into too much detail, there are some areas in our marriage that cannot progress until he deals with this. I was wondering what information you had to see if we could locate his birth mother." There was silence.

I knew this was a gamble, but I was tired of just sitting back and doing nothing, I was starting to feel like I was losing my mind and my husband.

"Well, Sheridan, that was unexpected. Excuse me for being caught off guard."

"I know it was out of the blue, I was just trying to get straight to the point and let me apologize now for my attitude. It's been one of those days."

"Well, honey, I have had many of those in my lifetime." She let out a sigh, "I can't say I wasn't expecting this day to come, I just thought I would be hearing it from Seth, not his wife."

"Ma, I know he wants to deal with this, but he's been dragging his feet. He just needs a little push."

"Sheridan, if he's not ready, you shouldn't push him. Sometimes you just have to leave well enough alone."

I sighed. "I understand what you're saying, but you're forgetting I'm a psychologist, and I counsel married people. I have done my best to get Seth to go ahead and reconcile his past and now it has caused a problem in our marriage. I do not want to lose him, but we can't go on like this, trust me. Marriage is about teamwork and where he is weak, I have to be strong. Whatever he finds out, I will be there for him. You have my word that I will be by his side to help him get through whatever we may uncover."

"Sheridan, I know that he needs to know where he came from, but there are some things surrounding his adoption that have the potential to really cause some very deep pain. There are things that I have kept from him since the day we brought him home, and I have dreaded every day having to explain them to him. The only reason I am going to give you the information I have is because I had a dream three nights ago about him calling me and asking me to help him find his birth mother. I have been preparing myself to open this can of worms ever since. When you asked, it shocked me because I had been expecting a call from him. I guess this was just God's way of letting me know it was time."

I let out a sigh of relief. "Thank you so much, ma, you don't know how much this means to me."

"Well, before you get all excited, you are going to have your work cut out for you. All I have is her name, Monet Grayson. I don't know where she could possibly be. She signed over all her rights. What I can give you is the lawyer's name who arranged the adoption. Let me warn you right now this lawyer may not be so cooperative. He is much higher on the food chain now than when we adopted Seth. He has much more to lose."

That piqued my interest. "Why not?"

"Honey, all will come out in due time. I will give you all the information I have, but it will be up to you and Seth to take it from there."

I asked, "What's the lawyer's name?"

"His name is Logan Randall of Randall and Associates, and the last time I saw him, he was in Dallas, Texas. I don't have a number, sweetie. That was twenty-seven years ago."

I stopped walking and leaned up against a telephone poll.

"Well, I guess I have my work cut out for me, don't I?"

"Yes, you do darling. Do me a favor, don't expect too much. The circumstances surrounding his adoption were pretty dire."

She really had my curiosity now. "Well, thanks again, ma."

"Not a problem. Sheridan, if you can't find anything I will not tell you all the details surrounding his adoption. If it comes from me, Seth will have to be the one to ask, agreed?"

"Yes, ma'am, agreed."

"I love you, baby, and I'm praying for you young married folk. Whatever is going on, trust me; this is the first of many battles. So, grow some thick skin darling. You're gonna need it."

"Yes, ma'am. I love you, too."

I disconnected the call. Now my head was spinning. What did she mean by dire circumstances, and what was up with this lawyer? So, his mom's name is Monet Grayson, very pretty name. Lord, Jesus, what am I about to get myself into? Mama Richards makes it sound like it's some kinda tangled web of drama. *Well, Sheridan, it's time to see what you are made of. You had the guts to call and ask his mama for the information, ain't no point in backing out now. Now how exactly do I get to Dallas without lying to my husband about why I'm going?* That's when I had an idea.

I turned back toward the house. I needed some time to get some information together. I would go back, get the car, and go pay this bill that I almost forgot about foolin' round with that simple behind girl. When I got back in the house, Seth was laying on the couch reading. I grabbed my keys off the counter and said, "I'll be right back. I'm going to pay a bill."

I was out of the house before he had a chance to respond. Thank God for the Internet on the cell phone. One call to four-one-one and a search on Google should do the trick.

✝✝✝

After I returned and walked back in the house, it was quiet. I knew he couldn't be sleeping. Napping was my thing, not his. I called out, "Baby, where are you?"

He yelled back, "I'm in the office."

I walked down the hall to the office. He was sitting at his oak desk looking so handsome. Oh, he had on some navy blue sweatpants, and a wife beater. Dang, he was sexy. I didn't know what it was about men in sweatpants, but it was an instant turn on. After I convinced him we needed a vacation, we were definitely going to be making up. I walked over to him and sat down on his lap. He looked at me like he knew I was up to something. I hated the way he could talk without ever saying a word. It was so annoying. I kissed him on his forehead, then on his cheek, then on his nose, then on his lips. He wrapped his arms around me and pulled me closer to him.

He broke our kiss. "So, I take it you've calmed down?"

I smiled, "For now."

He laughed, "Okay, Sheridan, what are you up to?"

There was no reason to be coy. He knows me too well.

"On my walk, I had a thought."

"Oh, yeah, and what was that?"

"We need to get away. We need to take a few days and just go relax and maybe do something crazy and maybe," I gave him a wicked smile, "practice making some babies." He laughed.

"Well, I can definitely get down with that."

He kissed me. "So, where exactly do you plan on going to get away, relax, do something crazy, and practice making babies?"

I smiled. "Well, I'm glad you asked, because I was thinking Dallas."

His eyebrow shot up, "Dallas, as in Texas?"

"Yeah, do you know of any other Dallas?"

"I'm sure there is another one, but I'm not aware of it. Why did you pick Dallas, baby girl?"

"Well, we've never been, it's far from Florida and Naomi, and they have a really cool attraction."

"Really, what's that?"

"They have mystery dinner theatre."

"What?"

"You know, those dinners where there is an unexpected murder, and you're all suspects, and you have to find out who the killer actually was."

He looked at me skeptically. I had to really work hard to sell this one. He still looked unsure.

"Okay, baby girl, that is real random, a mystery dinner theatre?"

"Yes, baby, why is that so random? I think it would be a lot of fun, and you know how I am always looking for something new to do."

"How in the heck did you find out about this dinner theatre?"

"I heard a colleague mention it, and then, well, Google of course?" I had to remember to repent for that lie.

He leaned back and studied my face.

"Okay, Sheridan, I will go along with whatever you're up to. I don't care where we go as long as there are no phones, no interruptions, and you are wearing no clothes."

I kissed him and said, "Done, done, and done." He lifted me up and put me on top of the desk and kissed me passionately. Oh, how I loved this man.

Chapter 16:
Revenge Is Best Served Cold....

Tameka was driving Naomi's car trying to forget the last scene she had just witnessed. They'd just dropped Keisha off and were heading to her house. She could not believe Seth's wife hit Naomi in the face and actually drew blood. It was becoming clear to her that you really couldn't judge a book by its cover. Unlike Naomi, Tameka didn't think that Sheridan was stuck up. She always thought her to be very classy and very conservative, but she let the hood out of her today. She thought Naomi just pushed her too far. She wondered what Naomi was going to do.

"Hey, are you okay?"

Naomi sucked her teeth. "Hell, naw. I'm not okay. That heifa hit me."

"Well, Naomi, you can't exactly say you didn't provoke it. What in the world made you say something to her in the first place?"

"Girl, I don't know. I just felt a surge of hatred toward her, and I wanted to do something to let her know she really don't have that man on lock like she thinks she does. She walk around that church like her mess don't stink, and she needed to be taken down a peg or two."

Tameka shot a quick look at Naomi and then focused back on the road. "Naomi, you are tripping. Sheridan is one of the sweetest people at that church, and she ain't never done anything to you until she saw how you were flirting with her husband. As a matter of fact, didn't you tell me she was by your side when you passed out at your mom's funeral?"

Naomi was pissed, "Exactly whose side are you on, Tameka?"

Tameka rolled her eyes. She was fed up with Naomi's little attitude lately, "Don't try to play the victim over there okay and don't put me in the middle of this mess. I am just trying to make some sense out of this. Ever since you spent that night with Seth, you have not been yourself. You've been moody, vindictive, and manipulative. Ain't nobody put a gun to your head and told you to sleep with that married man. Now you wanna get all 'woe is me' when he treated you like the ho you presented yourself to be."

Naomi started to cry. For a moment Tameka felt bad, but she knew she was speaking the truth, and obviously, Naomi needed to hear it. She asked, "Naomi, what's wrong?"

Naomi sniffled, "I'm pregnant."

Tameka slammed on the brakes, "WHAT?"

Naomi was taken aback by the sudden stopping of the car, and she clinched her chest. Tameka realized what she had done and looked in the rearview mirror to make sure they were not about to get in an accident. Thankfully, there was no one on the road, and she pulled over into a nearby parking lot.

Tameka put the car in park. "Naomi, what did you just say?"

Her friend looked at her with fear, regret, and guilt in her eyes. She said, "I'm pregnant, Tameka, with Seth's baby."

Tameka thought she would have a panic attack. She put her head down on the steering wheel and took a few deep breaths. After a few minutes, she calmed down. She asked, "Why didn't you tell me?"

Naomi sniffled. "I was going to have an abortion."

"No, Naomi," Tameka's eyes began to fill with tears. "Please don't."

Naomi wiped her tears with the back of her hand. "Seth has been very distant since this happened. He has been avoiding me like the plague, and I started thinking, even if I do have this baby, he isn't going to leave his wife. So, why put myself through all of it?"

Tameka shook her head. "So, that means you're about eight weeks, huh?"

Naomi nodded, "Yep. I just keep thinking about what Pastor Percy told me. He's supposed to be with me. When is it gonna happen?"

Tameka rolled her eyes, "Naomi, I think you are foolish for believing that man. I bet if you told Pastor Josiah what he said to you, he would start rebuking both of y'all. Just because he's a pastor doesn't mean he can't be foul."

"Whatever, Tameka, how could he possibly know about Seth to describe our relationship to me like that? How could he possibly know that I had feelings for him? And why would God tell me that when I was at my lowest point ever. Now, that's just cruel."

Tameka reached for her hand. "Sweetie, I think you are equating Pastor Percy with God. Just because he said God said it, doesn't mean he was being truthful with you. Now, why would he do it, I have no idea. We may never know, but I think you need to let that go. God would not tell you that a married man is the one for you."

Naomi rolled her eyes. "He is the only good thing I have in my life, so excuse me for grabbing on to some hope."

Tameka had had enough. "You know what, you sound stupid as hell. You don't have him. He's married to somebody else. Have you ever stopped to think about what this is going to do to his position at church? Have you thought about his ministry? He writes some powerful songs, and he is purposed to do great things, but you were too selfish to think about anybody but yourself. Did you ever stop to think how much this is going to hurt his wife, and their marriage, our church?"

Naomi wanted to slap her. "What are you talking about? I didn't make this baby by myself, and I don't care how many songs he wrote, he fornicated right along with me. He wasn't trying to minister to me that night."

Tameka cut her eyes at her. "You are the one who trapped the man into impregnating you. You walked up to the man with every intent on sleeping with him. Of course, he was wrong, but tell me this, why would you want a man with such low integrity that would sacrifice his marriage, his ministry, and his position in the church for a one night stand? If he is such a bad person, why do you want to be with him?"

Naomi was quiet. She had no response. Tameka continued. "Yeah, that's what I thought. You ain't got nothing to say. You manipulated this whole mess on some foolishness I told you not to believe in the first place. You were so selfish, you couldn't see past what you wanted. Pastor Percy was a wolf in sheep's clothing and look at how your life has gone downhill ever since you heard that *prophe-lie*."

Naomi put her head down and spoke. "You know, I can't blame Sheridan for hitting me because if I were her, I would have slapped the mess out of me, too. However, she is just too cocky, and she walking round here like she got the perfect marriage, and she so stuck up."

Tameka sighed. She didn't think Sheridan was stuck up, but there was no point in going on with that argument. "So, what are you going to do, press charges?"

Naomi was not one to just turn and tuck tail, she was a formidable opponent. A crooked smile crept up on Naomi's face, and Tameka immediately felt sick to her stomach. "Nope, I'm not going to press charges. After all, she doesn't even know I'm pregnant, well, at least, not yet. If I press charges, she will only get probation or something because I know she ain't never been in no trouble. I am going to get her for putting her hands on me, for looking down on me, and for judging me. I will be in her husband's life for the next eighteen years."

Naomi looked down and touched her belly, "You hear that, little one. You can thank your step mama for not being able to control her temper because she just saved your life. She just gave me the motivation to let you live."

Tameka stared at her friend in disbelief. Her girl was really out there this time. How could she be so nonchalant about this child's life? She didn't agree with how it got here, but its life should not be determined by its mother's desire for revenge on a day-to-day basis. Tameka knew then, even if she didn't want to be, she was caught up in this foolishness because she, after all, was the only person who saw them together. She didn't agree with what Naomi did, but she wouldn't tell a lie to protect Seth either.

She decided then for her part, she would tell what she saw with her own eyes, and the rest would be up to science. I mean, if the baby was his, a blood test would prove it. She couldn't say she knew for a fact they slept together, just that they walked out of the mall hand-in-hand. The other thing she would do is be there for Naomi because she would obviously need a voice of reason, and she would pray her behind off because all hell was about to break loose.

Chapter 17:
Killing Two Birds with One Plane Ride

Sheridan

I was standing there biting my lip because my mind was racing a thousand miles a minute. If I said I was nervous, that would be an understatement. Through some obviously convincing scheming, I got Seth to agree to this trip not under completely false pretenses, but I may have kinda, sorta, maybe led him to believe something other than my real intentions. I let out a deep breath. Lord was this our marriage now? Manipulation, mistrust, possible mistresses, that made me sick to my stomach.

We were waiting in line at the car rental place in the Dallas Fort Worth International Airport. Seth was so excited about us getting away and that made me feel even worse. I asked him to get the car while I ran to the restroom. I looked at myself in the mirror and really didn't like what was looking back at me. Yes, my intentions were pure, but my methods were far from it.

How in the heck am I going to get away from Seth long enough to go see Logan Randall? I took another deep breath. *Okay, Sheridan it is time for some creative thinking. Well, I could just tell him the truth, duh. Yeah, I guess I could, but that's not exactly creative now is it, genius?*

I massaged my temples because I could feel a headache coming on. *Think, Sheridan, think! Okay, let's see, today is Saturday, and we are leaving out of here Tuesday morning. I have an appointment with Mr. Randall at 3:00 P.M. on Monday afternoon. We are supposed to go to the mystery dinner theatre tonight, so that gives me about—I looked at my watch. It was almost one in the afternoon. Okay, so that gives me about fifty hours to come up with something brilliant that is close enough to the truth not to be a lie. Come on imagination, don't fail me now.*

After I got myself together, I headed out the restroom towards the car rental counter. All the noise and the hustle and bustle of this airport were beyond annoying me. My phone about gave me a heart attack when I felt it vibrate. I was too high strung.

I answered, "Hey, baby."

Seth sounded happy, "Hey, where are you?"

"I'm headed back to the car rental."

"Okay, I got the keys, and I can't wait to get you to the hotel."

"Bye, nasty," I hung up.

The drive was nice; I was so paranoid about Seth reading my troubled spirit, I was like a kid on a road trip. I kept my face glued to the window marveling at all the beauty passing me by—the skylines, the buildings, and the culture of this foreign city I was in. I could hear the navigation system give Seth directions, but I chose to focus on any and everything outside of that car. By the time we got into the hotel room, Seth could barely keep his hands off me.

I decided to use this opportunity for my pleasure and my purpose. I love making love to my husband, but right now I needed to put his butt to sleep so that I could brainstorm. It took me two rounds and almost two hours, but he was sleeping peacefully, and I could barely keep my eyes open. I had to do what I had to do.

I sat up on my elbows, yawned, and then I got out of the bed, went to unpack my robe, and my laptop. Seth had me so distracted; I barely got a glimpse of the room.

Looking at it now, I realized I picked a good room. The king size bed, while unmade, was still very inviting and comfortable. The room had a small lounge section with two plush lazy boys and a table in between. The TV was a thirty-two-inch HD flat screen mounted on a gorgeous cherry wood stand. The nightstands were the same deep cherry wood and then I peeked at the bathroom. Oh, I could not wait to soak in that beautiful spa tub. There were wall-to-wall floor length mirrors and two sinks with a standing only shower.

I realized I had been wasting valuable time, so I decided to see what was going on in the world, and maybe something would come to me. I was careful to be quiet. I don't know why because Seth was snoring so ridiculously loud, he was disturbing my thoughts. I got situated at the desk and booted up the computer. After a few moments, I put in my password, and decided to check my email first.

My box was full of messages from Facebook, so I decided what the heck, let me log on. Before we left, I had posted that I was on my way to Dallas for much needed relaxation so it was probably comments from that. I was reading through the comments when I finally got my way out of this mess. I had a comment on my status from a classmate from college, Vanessa Davis. I hadn't seen her in years.

It said, "Hey, Sher, how the heck are you? I couldn't help but reach out when I saw you were going to be in Dallas. You know I've been here for about two years, and I would love to see you. How's Monday for lunch?"

I would call this a miracle, but I'm pretty sure God was not condoning my behavior at this point. Maybe, just maybe, all things were working together for my good. Well, whatever it was, I was taking it. I quickly posted a comment and told her, "Girl, yes, I will be there with bells on. You have no idea how perfect your timing is."

I told her I could meet her for a late lunch at 1:30. I left my cell number for her to text me to make sure we would be able to meet at the time I needed. I also quickly found a restaurant online in the vicinity of Logan's office and told her to meet me there because I had an appointment downtown that I needed to be on time for. Then, I deleted the message I just sent in case of some strange bizarre twist Seth logged into my account to figure me out.

I felt such a relief off my shoulders. Now, I just wanted to relax, enjoy my husband, and my vacation, and leave the drama for Monday afternoon. I climbed back into the bed and cuddled up next to the man I loved more than life itself.

†††

My baby and I had a wonderful weekend here in the Lone Star State and because we had such a good time, it made me feel even guiltier. Now, Vanessa was making me feel guilty because I knew that I could have had a much better time catching up with her if my stomach wasn't in knots, and I was actually paying attention. Though I must admit, she looked absolutely amazing.

I felt like in one respect, I was betraying my husband with every minute that got closer to three o'clock, but then on the other hand, I felt I was on the verge of solving one of the greatest mysteries known to man. I really was happy that she got married and had beautiful kids, but you know, some things just don't compare to lying to your husband and going behind his back to find the woman who abandoned him. I promised to keep in touch, paid my bill, kissed her cheek, and started on my way to the law firm. I was such a horrible person today.

The law firm of Randall and Associates was in one word—interesting. As I walked through the huge tinted glass doors, the foyer was beautiful. It was decorated with paintings that looked very expensive. There was a beautiful marble fountain in the middle of the foyer and the running water immediately made me feel calm.

I noticed the décor was contemporary. Judging by the eclectic collection and positioning of the artwork, statues, and furniture, I concluded that this man's closing arguments were very abstract. Okay, how did I connect those two things? Maybe there was some weird childhood parallel between coloring things the wrong universally accepted color and successfully arguing the law. I chuckled to myself at that thought.

Here I was on the verge of doing some serious damage to my union, and I was trying to make intelligent jokes about some random man I didn't know, who probably paid someone else to decorate his office.

I sighed and whispered, "Jesus, deliver me from myself!" I realized that I needed to focus. I had obtained this appointment by giving the impression I was in need of a defense attorney. So, what exactly was my game plan to pull the rug from under him and get him to confess to me intimate pieces of a shady deal he'd done almost thirty years ago? Well, at least, I think it was shady.

Ok, Sheridan, you can do this. You counsel for a living. Look around and gather some information that will help you understand something, anything about how this man's mind works.

I glanced at my watch. I still had about fifteen minutes before the start of my appointment. I turned on my psychologist switch and hit the ground running. Between the elevators there were several magazine covers framed of Mr. Randall. He was indeed a very handsome man, well, for a white man, because Lord knows one of the most beautiful things he ever created was a black man!

His skin was creamy white but with enough color for him not to be pale. His teeth were perfectly white, and his features were perfectly sculpted. He had overly arrogant son-of-a-not-so-nice-word written all over him. On each cover, he wore some variation of a blue or gray suit and red power tie that hung very well against his obviously chiseled body. For all appearances, he looked like a man that had it all together, but I was not a woman fooled by appearance.

I used my education, my instincts, and my training to look for insight and then saw it. It was right there plain as day in his eyes. In all of the pictures, his smiles were confident and bright, but they never quite reached his eyes. His eyes held a shadow of some sort, maybe pain, maybe guilt, maybe regret. The eyes never lied. One thing I knew for sure, this man for all his accolades, was not as happy as a person would assume.

Something was not right about the unhappiness that screamed through those sad eyes despite all the polishing. The elevator ding brought me back into reality, and I stepped in as an attractive couple elegantly stepped out. I tried to get my mind in counseling mode so that I could get under his skin if need be. His arrogance would only intrigue me to put him in his place. I'm sure he was used to intimidating people he encountered, but not this black woman. I was on a mission.

Exiting the elevator, I strolled through the corridors. I found Logan's office suite and walked in. His secretary, or the politically correct title, his executive assistant, looked up from her desk and smiled at me. She looked like somebody's grandma except her eyes were sharp, and she had perfected a sincere smile.

I walked up to her desk and told her, "My name is Sheridan Richards, and I have a three o'clock appointment with Mr. Randall."

She smiled. "Oh, yes, Mrs. Richards. He is on a call right at the moment, but I will let him know you are here. Please, have a seat and help yourself to a pastry or a beverage, or both."

I nodded and thanked her while I went to take a seat on the very plush red suede sofa. I looked over at the pastries and while they did look tasty, I didn't know how long they had been out, so I had to go with, nada. Besides, the knots in my stomach had returned, and there was no way food could compete with them.

The longer I waited, the more nervous I became, and I didn't know why. In my profession, I encountered all sorts of people. I was so afraid about what information I might find out that my heart started beating just a little too hard and a little too fast. I was excited to finally get this issue underway. I was also feeling uncertainty about what this would do to my marriage.

Suddenly, I got a jolt of energy to get this over with, and I was ready for the cat and mouse game to begin so that I could get the information I needed to get what I wanted. The thought of a mind game about to be played with a formidable opponent had me pumped; my adrenaline was so high I had the munchies!

I realized that my emotions were all over the place. I was like a spider monkey hopped-up on Mountain Dew. I needed to pick a feeling and stick with it. *My goodness Sheridan get yourself together.*

I said a quick prayer to try and reign in calmness. "Lord, I know this is probably not the best situation I have found myself in but just let some good come out of this please. Amen."

His assistant picked up when her phone rang. She nodded an okay before she hung up. "Mrs. Richards," she called. "Mr. Randall will see you now."

I rose, smoothed down my skirt, ran a hand to make sure my sophisticated bun was still in place, and put my game face on. She walked toward a glass door and opened it to let me in. He stood and came around the desk with his hand extended, wearing a dark gray suit with a blue shirt, and a paisley tie that brought the colors together. I took his hand, and I could see he was impressed with my firm handshake.

He flashed that million dollar grin and said with that good ole boy drawl, "Mrs. Richards, it's a pleasure to meet you. Please, have a seat. Can I get you a cup of coffee or a beverage?"

"No, thank you. I'm fine."

"Well, okay, then. Let's get started."

He took his seat. "As my assistant said when you called, I had a cancellation so you really lucked up on this appointment. I have been very busy these last few months with several open cases so I hope I can accommodate you with your current matter. If not, I can recommend some other attorneys in the area who tend to be more affordable and more available."

Oh, no, this arrogant prick did not just try me. I know I'm not dripping with diamonds, but I'm far from a homeless woman on the streets.

I felt the Duval County rising to the surface, and I had to suppress it and remember that I was a professional, but now I had no qualms about blackmailing this over-indulgent, self-absorbed, assumptive snake. I put on my sweetest smile and said, "Mr. Randall, I don't consider this luck by any means. Let's just say it was meant to be."

His left eyebrow lifted. "So, are you saying that because this is fate, I will lower my rates to take my place in destiny," he smirked.

Oh, I was so going to enjoy watching his pretty butt squirm. I stood up, walked around to the other side of his desk, leaned back against it, and crossed my feet at the ankles. His shock at my boldness was just what I needed to throw him off balance.

I said, "No, Mr. Randall. Your billable hours were never a factor, but since you decided to show me the obvious lack of character you possess, I will get straight to my point. I didn't come here for your legal services, I came here for information, and you are going to give it to me freely. So you can go ahead and tell your accountant not to record this hour as it will be pro bono."

He chuckled sarcastically, and his eyes sparkled with the threat of the challenge I was bringing. He smiled as he looked me up and down and said, "Is that so?"

I returned the smile, "Oh, yes, it is indeed so." I leaned a little bit closer. "You see, I know that you haven't always been a man that operated on the up-and-up, and I know you dabbled in other things that were not just getting off murderers and cheats!"

I didn't know the exact details of the adoption although I deduced it was pretty shady by the way Mama Richards relayed the information. I was praying my threat gave me even the slightest advantage to dig my entire foot all the way up his behind instead of just my freshly manicured toes! It worked. For a moment I saw a flicker of panic flash in his eyes, but then he regrouped.

He cleared his throat. "Mrs. Richards, I'm afraid you aren't old enough to have been privy to any indiscretions that are in my past, if there were any to speak of."

I challenged him. "Is that the best you can do to defend your character, Mr. Million Dollar Defense Attorney? That was weak and even the untrained eye can see I struck a nerve. Let me tell you who you are dealing with. I'm a psychologist, Mr. Big Shot Attorney, and I have been profiling you since I walked through your big, over-compensating lobby doors, and I know your arrogance is just a façade. I see the sadness in your eyes. Tell me; is it guilt, pain, or regret? You are much too confident a man for it to be rejection."

He shifted in his seat, so I went for the jugular. "I know the smiles you have plastered on your face twenty-four-seven are just a mirage you use to invoke confidence to your potential client, but I'm not a client. I am a woman on a mission. I tell you what, if that sadness gets too much for you to handle, you can come see me at my office for an hour, and we will consider this a quid pro quo, your information for my services to let you unburden your heart."

His face flushed red with anger and embarrassment. "Now, you listen here you two dollar shrink."

I cut him off before he said something that I would have to slap him for. "No, you listen here. You arranged the adoption of my husband twenty-seven years ago, and I know you arranged it illegally. All I want is the mother's name and any information you have on where I may find her. If you don't give me this information, and if you think of insulting me one more time while I am in your presence, I will have you disbarred so fast, you'll have whiplash and this two-bit shrink will haunt your dreams every single night. You can hate me forever while your reputation disappears out the door. I don't have the time, or the patience, to play games with you, Mr. Randall."

I gave him my very best do-not-mess-with-this-black-woman face as I folded my arms across my chest and sucked my teeth for good measure to let him marinate on my threat that could easily turn into a promise. I wanted to laugh because I was probably giving him a complex about black women from here on out. I would apologize to my sistas another time for playing into the angry black woman stereotype, but right now, my hood was showing, and I was powerless to stop it. In my defense, it did suit the situation.

I watched several emotions spread across his face. It went from anger to confusion, to recollection, to fear, and then unexpectedly, to remorse. He sighed heavily and gestured for me to take my seat on the other side of the desk. I looked at him like 'I'll move when I'm good and ready.'

He sighed again, "Please, Mrs. Richards."

Well, since he said please, I obliged, especially since the psychologist in me ached to get to the bottom of the obvious pain that was now etched on his face. He cleared his throat and spoke.

"Ok, Sheridan, may I call you that?"

I smirked. He went on, "Because clearly we have reached a much more intimate place than client and lawyer."

I relaxed a little bit, "Clearly."

He looked up at his door and waved his assistant away. I guess her nosy butt could see this was not the typical first-time client meeting.

I rolled my eyes at her. *Oh, Lord, help me. I am behaving so far from Christ-like today I feel like I need to do a Hail Mary, and I'm not even Catholic.* I focused my attention back to Logan. He began in a very relaxed voice. "You know, you're right. It isn't luck that brought you here. It is fate, and if there is a God, he has a very interesting sense of humor."

I perked up with interest. This was a man itching to unburden his soul.

He went on. "The reason I was so insulting to you is because your last name unnerved me. When my assistant informed me of a potential client named Richards, I was intrigued because I have had some dealings with a Richards' in the past that has recently resurfaced in my life. I thought this must be a coincidence, and my curiosity got the best of me, so I told her to accept the appointment. Then, when you walked in, and you were an African-American woman with an obvious agenda, I got nervous thinking this may not have been such a good idea. That is why I insulted you. Hoping you would storm out and this would once again be swept under the rug."

Clearly, he didn't know who he was dealing with. I was running out of patience so I cleared my throat. "Logan, I can appreciate you are at some sort of crossroads, and you are seeking some sort of penance, but can you please get to the point because my life is at a crossroads, too, and I need this information so I can decide where to go next. I apologize for my attitude. I'm usually quite a lovely person; however, you caught me on the wrong side of my emotions today."

He smiled sincerely for the first time since I arrived in his office. "Well, Sheridan, I can appreciate your urgency so I will give you the Cliff's Notes version. Yes, I arranged for Mr. and Mrs. Richards's to adopt your husband. I was young, greedy, and angry. Looking back, I realize my actions were loathsome."

I folded my arms impatiently, but he did have my interest.

He continued, "You see, my stepsister, Cassia, accused my father of molestation and abuse. Then, she stole money and ran away from home with her best friend. Neither I, nor her mother, believed her. My father was an upstanding citizen, and I hated her for the shadow she cast on his reputation. The hatred I had accumulated for her ran deep. That's why when her friend, Monet Grayson, came to me pregnant and desperate because Cassia was in some sort of legal trouble, I pounced on the opportunity to exploit both of them."

I perked up when I heard his mother's name. This story was getting too twisted for a Monday afternoon. He went on. "Reece and Shayla Richards contacted me about helping expedite the adoption process. I told them I could do one better. That's when I hired a private investigator to find Monet and bring her back, seeing as how I had dismissed her out right the first time she came to me. I explained a couple desperately wanted a baby. I told Monet if she signed over her parental rights, I would get Cassia off. What I didn't tell her was that I would be charging them $30,000 for her unborn child; though I'm sure she suspected something was in it for me. She was a very smart girl."

My eyes practically bugged out of my head. "You did what?"

He held up his hands, "Wait, there's more. Some several years after, my father got very ill and on his death bed, he confessed to my stepmother that he had in fact abused and molested Cassia and that he didn't want to die with that on his conscience. I was standing in the doorway during the confession, and I cannot even begin to explain to you the range of emotions that took place within me at that moment. My stepmother, however, was very adamant about how she felt. She was in shock momentarily and then damned him to hell. She told him he had better hope her child was still alive and that she could find her and try to make up for choosing to love a man over her own flesh and blood. She said if he died before she could find her, she would bring him back from the dead just to make sure she was the one that personally sent him to hell. That night, he had a stroke and slipped into a coma. My stepmom and I grieved heavily, not because we were losing him, but because he was not the man we thought he was. She asked me to find my stepsister. I promised her I would. The next day she told the doctors to pull the plug, and she never looked back."

All I could do was let out a whistle. This guy and his issues would keep me employed for life. I asked, "So, did you ever find your sister?"

He rubbed his hand over his face as if he was worn out. "Yeah, I did, and I gave the information to her mother. Their relationship was too damaged by then. Cassia was not willing to listen. Lately, I have had this burden on my heart to find her and beg for her forgiveness. My actions played a role in pushing her into the life she had to lead once she ran away from home because it was no longer the safe place it should have been for her. That is my guilt and my regret, Sheridan. The sadness you so skillfully pointed out to me is for the father that was not who he portrayed himself to be, and therefore, my whole childhood was a lie. I have just been dragging my feet. You being here and bringing all this to surface is like a kick in the nuts from the universe saying, it's time to get it right."

I laughed at his brashness, but my heart ached for this man—really and genuinely ached for what his family had to go through because of lies and secrets. I went around to his desk and hugged him. He squeezed me very tightly and whispered, "Thank you" in my ear.

As I stepped back, I wiped a tear from my eye and smiled. "Well, I'm sorry I had to get all in your face, but from your bio, I figured you were a shallow, self-absorbed man. If I knew you were just a big ole teddy bear, I would have gone about this a lot differently."

He laughed and said, "Wow, I feel like for the first time ever, my burdens are starting to be lifted. Listen, I don't know where Monet is, but I do know where to find Cassia, and I'm one-hundred percent sure they are still as thick as thieves. One breathes in and the other exhales. I'll give you her numbers and would you let her know to expect a call from me sooner rather than later?"

I smiled. "I sure will."

He wrote the information, and I gave him my business card. I told him if he needed it, my couch was always available for him and that I would have to charge him because he clearly already got his free hour. He laughed, walked me to the door, and thanked me again for stomping into his life and getting all "up in his face."

We hugged again, and I whispered to him, "By the way, there is a God, and He is in control of everything. Before the foundation of the world, he decided that you and I would meet on this very day to begin a healing process for so many people."

He pushed me away at arm's length and looked me in my eyes very puzzled and said, "You know, you said that with so much conviction and sincerity that I'm inclined to believe you."

I smiled. "Give God a try. I promise you won't regret it. You and your family's healing will be in my prayers."

As I walked out, the assistant shot me the most confused look I had ever seen on a face. I smiled, and as I left, I saw her running into Logan's office full of questions. Somehow, a burden had been lifted from my heart. I still felt bad for the deceit I planted into my marriage, but I also knew that I was supposed to be right where I was today. "God, you are so amazing indeed."

Chapter 18:
Baby, Trust Me

Sheridan

"I cannot believe you went behind my back and did this? So, that whole trip was just one big manipulation, huh? It didn't have a doggone thing to do with you wanting to spend time with your husband, did it?"

I stared at Seth blankly. "You went too far. You just kept pushing, and I told you I wasn't ready, and now I'm sitting here holding this letter from some woman that claims to be my birth mother? What in the world possessed you to do something like this?"

Seth pointed his finger in my face, "You know, what we need to work on is our communication because you obviously didn't understand me when I told you no. We are going to handle this today, believe that. How dare you go behind my back and ask my mother to give you this information? This borders on some serious trust issues, Sheridan. This is my business, and you had no right to interfere!" Seth pretty much screamed that last part at me.

I gave him a very cold and calculated look. He sat down on the couch and folded his arms. I stood in front of him. "Are you finished with your little tirade now? Can you stop talking, and let me tell you why I did what I did?"

"Whatever, Sheridan, I'm done talking so you go right ahead."

I rolled my eyes so hard my head hurt. In my calmest voice, I began to explain because I knew I was wrong on some level.

"First of all, you act like I don't know you well enough to know that you would have been upset about this? Obviously, it was a risk I was willing to take. I can take your little nasty attitude and your short sightedness for a little while if it would finally get to the root of this issue. I have been telling you to deal with your past for I don't know how long. Seth, I don't care what that letter says or reveals. I plan to be right here with you to help you through whatever pain, embarrassment, or healing process that is necessary. I know you say you have forgiven your birth parents, but you still carry around bitterness for being abandoned by them, even though you had *two* loving parents who took care of you and afforded you all the opportunities they could possibly give you. By the way, I think you need to see it from the point-of-view of a person who didn't have parents at all or who grew up abused and mistreated. You were fortunate, and you need to acknowledge that. It's time for you to let go of your abandonment issues because it has officially started drama in this marriage. I got so tired of you pushing this off to the side. Because you refuse to deal with it, we got problems with this little tramp, Naomi, at the church."

He interrupted me, "Oh, here you go with that again."

I butted right back in and stuck my finger in his face. "Oh, no, playa, remember you were done talking. You need to listen to what I'm saying. I don't know why men are so doggone naïve. I'm telling you that little skank wants you, and she has been using the connection between your similar issues to play on your sympathy and get closer to you. Because you are so bitter, you can't even see the enemy using your bitterness to come up in our relationship and wreak havoc. I had to do what I had to do. This is not about jealously on my part. This is about me being able to see something you cannot. You think just because you're a minister, you got this on lock, huh? Just because God is blessing you, does not mean you got it all together."

He interrupted me again. "I know that, Sheridan, but I really think you are making too much out of this Naomi thing. I don't have any kinda feelings for that girl."

I put my hand up. "Stop interrupting me, Seth. You allowed your arrogance to forfeit your time to talk. Now, I'm talking, and I'm not finished."

He cut me a nasty look, and I knew I was treading on thin ice. I continued anyway.

"Yes, I called your mother and yes, she gave me the name of the lawyer who handled the adoption. Yes, I went to see him and yes, I got your birth mother's information. I called her, and she already knew who I was. How, I don't know. I gave her our number and our address. That was two weeks ago. When I checked the mail today, I

Surviving Sunday   - 123 -

saw the letter. I did it because this baggage is affecting our marriage. I am no longer going to sit back and watch it turn you into something you were never meant to be. I love you too much for that. Now, you can be mad at me for however long you need to be, but today we are reading this letter and today, we are dealing with this issue before it allows the enemy to bring us more drama than it already has."

He just stared at me with an unreadable look. I could see he was hurt, scared, and mad. I wanted to reach out to him and hold him, but I was determined to stand my ground. This had gone on too long. I saw a single tear drop from his eye. He wiped it almost as quickly as it formed. My heart was breaking for my baby. I know this had to be hard. I wish I didn't have to force him to do this. He didn't understand, Naomi vexed my spirit, and I knew she was up to no good. He just kept giving her the green light even though he was too clueless to realize he was doing it.

He spoke barely above a whisper in a shaky voice. "Baby, I don't think I can read it, but you're right, I do need to hear it, and it is past time to deal with this. I know you're right, but that does not excuse the way you went about doing it."

He handed me the letter and I replied. "I love you, Seth, and I'm sorry. You're right, my methods were manipulative and maybe errant, but you gotta know my intentions were pure."

"I know, baby. Let's just get this over with," he sighed.

I opened the very thick letter and pulled out several pages. It was hand written in a very feminine, elegant cursive writing. It looked like she put a lot of love into it. I sure hope so. I just asked her to tell him the truth and no games. She said she would, let's hope she did. I cleared my throat and began to read:

My Dearest Seth,

I know you must've wondered about me and your father many a night. I know you always came up clueless because your parents never had a clue as to what or why you ended up in their arms. I promised your wife that I would hand you the truth and even though this affects other people, like your parents, I owe you the truth, and I hope you can handle it.

I chose to write instead of call because I didn't want you to interrupt me, and I didn't want to shy away from giving you the information you needed to begin your healing process. I am a very blunt woman, and that's the only way I know how to be. My heart is full of secrets, but I will give you what you need to know. What I don't tell you in this letter, I hope to one day say to your face, it would be better that way, and maybe selfishly, I am holding some things from you in hopes that you will allow me to see your handsome face.

Let's start with how I knew your wife before I ever heard her voice. I have followed your life since you were about ten years old. I have pictures from every achievement, school recital, graduation, and your wedding day. The private investigator I keep on my payroll kept tabs on you so I could see my precious baby grow into the man you are today. It takes a special kind of woman to do what your wife did for you, so if you're angry with her, please don't be. Her reaching out to me served to heal an ache in my heart that I have had for almost three decades.

I know you're thinking if I knew where you were, why didn't I come for you and take you home. Sweetie, I've lived a very, let's call it, an interesting life and when I realized the type of parents you had and the stable life you were given, I did not want to cause you trouble or confusion because the life I led was only going to hurt you. So, I chose for once not to be selfish. I had peace because I felt like that was where you belonged; like that path was part of your destiny. I was a little disturbed knowing you were being raised by white parents, but when I found out about the older black couple, The Redding's, that lived next door to you that helped to show you who you are, and where you came from, I once again found my peace. They and your parents have my deepest gratitude. Plus, I remembered my best friend, Cassia, is white, and she is closer to me than my own blood. I remembered color doesn't matter as long as the love is pure.

Let's start where you began, with your father. He's dead. Sorry, I told you I was blunt. Take a deep breath son, here goes. When I was twenty, I got pregnant with you, and I killed him. He was beating the hell out of me, and I had, had enough. He was a pimp, a drug dealer, and Cassia and I were his prostitutes. I wasn't tricking anymore because I was pregnant with you, and I had gotten myself clean off drugs because I thought you were a little miracle. This was the first and only time either of us had ever gotten pregnant which was unusual. We figured this was a miracle indeed.

I jumped in between a fight between him and Cassia. He was accusing her of keeping money from him. He went from beating the hell out of her, to beating the hell out of me. I was so tired of him hitting on her. That was the first time he had ever hit me, but he beat Cassia every chance he got. I think it was because he sensed she was used to a man abusing her, and she wouldn't fight back. I got away from his grip when Cassia hit him to get him off of me. I got the gun from under my pillow, and I blew his brains out.

You should know I have no regrets, and I would do it again without flinching. That was the first and last time a man would ever put his hands on me. That man caused me more pain and drama than you could ever imagine. When the cops came, Cassia took the blame because of you. She wiped my prints off and put hers on the gun. When they arrested her, I couldn't handle it. How could I face the world without my best friend? She was my sister. We had both gotten each other out of many sticky situations since we were little girls, but this truly showed me how much she loved me. I couldn't let my friend take the fall for me, seeing as how I had no regrets about doing it. Cassia had a stepbrother, who didn't like her very much, but he was a very good defense attorney, and I sought him out to help her. He, of course, looked at me like I was an orphan begging for bread and dismissed me immediately.

Cassia had been in jail a week, and I was shocked when Logan sent for me. There was something different about him this time. He looked like a man on a mission. I was about eight months pregnant. He said he was glad I was willing to come back, which was foolishness, seeing as how he summoned me. He had a couple that wanted to buy a baby on the black market, I later found out. They were desperate to have a child. Good people just unable to have kids. He told me if I let him have my baby, he would represent Cassia and get her off on self-defense because there were plenty of witnesses to say your father had been frequently abusing her. His slimy butt just wanted the payoff for you. I'm not sure how much they paid, and I never saw a dime of it. I was mortified, and I left feeling very trapped between a rock and Satan. I went to visit Cassia and told her. We cried together, and she told me not to do it. She was willing to take the fall and do the time, but we had to protect our little miracle. She said I had given up my life to be there for her when we ran away all those years ago, and it was her turn to make a sacrifice for me. She told me she loved me, and they took her back to her cell.

That night, I cried, and cried, and tried to pray. I realized as much as I loved you, I couldn't offer you much of anything. Cassia was all I knew. Sure, I had my parents, but I was so ashamed of the life I had lived that I couldn't face them. I had not seen them in six years. I sent them a postcard at every holiday, with no return address, to let them know I was still breathing and that Cassia and I were doing okay. I called them at least twice a year so as not to seem like an ungrateful child. I thought about what Cassia said—protect you at all costs and that's what I did. I chose to be the answered prayer to a family so desperate to love a child that they would buy one. I can't explain it, but that night I had such a peace about my decision that I knew someday it would all work out. The next day, I met with Logan and signed the papers. I held you once and kissed you goodbye moments after you were born. I never wanted to meet your parents because at the time, I never planned on you hearing how it all came to be. I knew in my heart that you would be okay.

I cannot tell you how much I love my best friend. According to the good book, if I was David, she would be my Jonathan. Ha, I can hear Cassia now saying, it's my ego that made me David and her Jonathan. Oh, don't be shocked. Just because I lived a sinful life don't mean I don't know the Word son. How do you think I still have my sanity? It's because God was always there, even though I haven't been His best child, I know He was always there, otherwise, there is no way me and Cassia would still be here.

After Cassia's charges were dropped and everything was over, she came back, and I was ecstatic because I couldn't wait to tell her about the stash I had found. One night, I stumbled onto a safe your father had hidden in the closet floor. Since he wasn't the brightest crayon in the box, it didn't take me long to crack it. In it, I found close to a million dollars. I knew right then that this was a turning point for us. When Cassia got out, I put her in a drug rehab program, and I went back to school, got my GED, and went to community college, and on to a university to get my degree in business administration. Cassia took the same path, except she got a degree in accounting and finance. We were never idiots, just took a long detour through purgatory for a few years. We decided to take advantage of the city we lived in, and the money we had acquired. There were so many young girls and guys on the streets of Vegas. My philosophy was, if you're going to be a ho, have something to show for it. We opened up an escort service, a very high end escort service. It started out with only four escorts, three girls, and one guy. You would be surprised how much rich women pay for affection. I didn't want them on the streets forever, so we gave it a purpose.

Our escorts had to sign a contract. They could only stay in the business for a maximum of five years. If they wanted to leave before then, they were welcomed to. They were subject to random drug testing, and they had to go to school and get a degree in something. If they wanted to go to graduate school, or law school, we would foot half the bill as long as they maintained at least a 3.5 GPA. If they tested positive for any drug, they were out. I would pay for the stint in rehab, but there were no exceptions. I put them in etiquette classes to make sure they knew how to be ladies and gentlemen. They had to agree to save twenty percent of their income because I believe in the principles of the Bible. If it worked for Joseph, it would work for us.

They also had to agree to give ten percent away to a charity or a church. I believe in tithing. I didn't make them give it to a church if they didn't believe in that, but they had to give it away to someone that was trying to help people. They had medical exams every three months, and all the girls were put on birth control, and the men were snipped. Upon completion of the program, our escorts would have a degree, a sizeable bank account, a nice investment portfolio, and they would own a piece of property in some other state. They also had to take a financial course on how to manage money taught by Cassia so as not to squander their hard-earned money. They would move on with their lives and never look back. Eventually, we bought a hotel with forty rooms and used it as our place of business. Our escorts were provided security detail, and they were given panic buttons. Our security guards were instructed to beat a man within three-inches of his life, if he laid a hand on one of our girls.

I am proud of all my girls and the few guys that picked themselves up and made something out of their lives. Through hard work and discipline some bad choices they made didn't punish them forever. Now, this is probably the most bizarre story you have ever heard, but it's true. This is the life that I have lived. Cassia wanted to finally find a man, settle down, and have a normal life. I understood because I wanted out, too. We stopped accepting escorts, and when the last one finished, we shut it down. That was five years ago. Now, we run a halfway *house. We still get them off the streets, but without the sex for money part, get them on their feet, and educated.*

Since you're a man of God, I know you know better than to judge me but still my decisions have affected your life and for that, I apologize. I love you, Seth, with all my heart and while I regret the pain I've caused you, I don't regret my decision to give you up because looking at your life, I know now this was the path you were always supposed to take. Even though I was financially stable, it didn't make sense to me to rip you out of that life to bring you into my very strange one. I'm proud of the life you live, and I even like the church where you minister. I had my investigator check out that pastor of yours, and he turned out to be just what he portrays himself to be. I think it's safe to say that I made the right decision. It was my intention to wait until your thirtieth birthday to finally reach out to you, but your wife found me first. In everything, give thanks for this is the will of God in Christ Jesus concerning you, and that is according to First Thessalonians 5:18. Whenever it's comfortable for you, give me a call, and hopefully, one day soon, I can rest my eyes on you and hold you in a mother's embrace. Enclosed are all my numbers and my address.

With all my love,
Monet Grayson

The only word that came to mind was, "WOW!"

Tears were flowing down my eyes halfway through this biography so I was almost hesitant to look at Seth. I wondered if Logan ever reached out to his sister and if he knew what we now knew. He may be calling me for a session. When I looked up, I saw that Seth's eyes were red and yes, the tears were flowing. What could I say? There was nothing to say. This was crazy and we needed some time to let it sink in.

I folded the letter, put it back in the envelope, and laid it on the table. Seth was still quiet so I climbed onto his lap, laid his head on my chest, and let him cry. I cried with him because I didn't like for anyone to cry alone in my presence. With all this information, a person would have to be soulless not to come to tears. Seth very rarely shed tears. After all, this was a twenty-seven-year old wound that had been exposed and reopened. We just sat there crying together.

I don't know how much time passed. My tears had stopped flowing, but Seth still had a few left. Before they were free falling, and now they were coming few and far between. I wanted to laugh because his tears were so slow, now they started to tickle as they fell down the inside of my shirt. I'm not big on quiet for long periods of time, and I'm not big on crying for long periods of time, so I felt the silliness rise up in me. It was time to try and make him laugh.

I kissed my baby on the forehead and whispered, "Seth?"

He let out a soft chuckle. I let one out too and asked, "What's funny?"

He chuckled again and said, "You. Because I know you are about to try and make me laugh."

I smiled. He knew me so well. "There is something I've wanted to say for a while now."

He laughed and said, "Go ahead, baby girl. Get it out of your system."

I let out a laugh and said, "Baby, your moms is a righteous gangsta'!"

He laughed, so I continued. "I'm for real. She 'round here packin' pistols under her pillow, she runnin' hos, she got body guards and stuff, and she got people scared of her. We should call her escorts the untouchables since she told her guards to beat a Negro within inches of their life! Who even says stuff like that? I'ma have to call her Professor Pimp! She done upgraded the oldest profession known to man. She schooled those kids on advanced placement for streetwalkers. Or better yet, prostitution honors." He burst out laughing.

I was too tickled now, so I kept going. "She got private investigators 'round here spying on people and stuff, and she even had Pastor Josiah checked out. She probably would have had him taken out if he was one of those fake pastors!" He was doubled over laughing now. I continued, "Wait. Let's talk about how she pulling pistols to say bring me back a 3.5 GPA, or I will take you out." I laughed.

"She got these people in this halfway house scared as hell. She is scaring folk into the straight and narrow."

He laughed harder, "But wait, baby, wait, yo mama so ig'nant, she 'round here with a gun to yo head talkin' bout pay your tithes? How you a Bible totin' madam and make your escorts pay they tithes? So, when they turn it in they be like, well, it got a lil sin on it, but you know it's the right thing to do."

We were both on the floor now, this was hysterical. "Oh, and don't get me started on this here best friend of hers."

"We can call her Cassia Capone." I laughed out loud, "Yeah, hopefully, she making sure their taxes is paid on time. What kinda mess they got going? Ebony and Ivory running round playing Captain Save a ho!"

We were both in tears now but from laughing this time. My stomach hurt so badly from laughing at his mama and her friend. These broads were really on some other stuff. We laughed until our faces hurt. Once we finally got all our giggles out, we both got quiet again because while there was humor, there was still reality. Seth lay down on the floor and pulled me on top of him.

He grabbed my face and got serious on me. "I love you, baby girl. Thank you for making me do what I needed to do. I am so sorry for all the foolishness and what you had to put up with because of my bitterness. I promise I am going to deal with this prayerfully, and eventually, I will reach out to my mother because she seems to be an interesting person to know."

Interesting was an understatement. He continued, "Don't let me get complacent in this, baby. Stay on me to meet with her and be there to pray me through this."

He made my heart smile. I told him, "Baby, I am here. I love you, and we're going to get through this. As a matter of fact, I believe we can get through anything."

I kissed him passionately and laid my head on his chest. We both lay there on the floor quiet for a while. I asked, "What are you thinking about?"

He responded, "What information is she keeping from me? What was my father's name? How much money did my parents pay for me? How did they end up so desperate for a child that they had to go that route? I could probably think of a million more."

I stroked his head. "All in due time, baby, let's just relax for a while, and let it all sink in."

I said a silent prayer for my husband, his mother, her friend, Cassia, and Logan. "Lord, work this out and heal all their hearts. Bring them together as the family they were always meant to be."

I chuckled softly because I could just see that family reunion now. I had a thought. "Baby?"

"Huh?" he responded.

"So, you know Jeremiah and Grey are going to clown the mess out of you when they hear about your mama right?"

He laughed. "Yeah, they are going to ride on me from now 'til eternity."

I laughed as I snuggled as close to my husband as I could physically get and drifted off to sleep.

Chapter 19:
And Then All Hell Broke Loose

Seth

I jerked awake to the sound of the phone ringing. I was a little disoriented, and I realized Sheridan was still lying on top of me.

Ring. I gently nudged her, and she stirred. She was so crazy when she was sleeping. "Baby, wake up. I gotta get the phone."

Ring. She moaned, "Huh? What? Leave me alone."

Oh, here we go. "Sheridan, baby, wake up." I shook her again.

Ring. She stirred, lifted her head, and lay down again on the other side of her face. I couldn't help but laugh, "Girl, get your butt up."

Ring. She mumbled, "You can't have my ice cream."

This time I laughed and sat up with her. "Girl, you trippin' wake your behind up!"

She finally opened her eyes. "Baby, why you being so loud?"

Ring. I gently lifted her onto the sofa. Waking her up was harder than getting a Republican to side with Obama.

Ring. I went to get the phone off the kitchen counter and looked at the caller ID. It was my parent's number.

Okay, Lord, I can take the hint, no time like the present. "Hello." I knew it was my mama.

"Hey, sweetie, how are you?"

I could tell in her voice she wanted to know if we had heard from my real mother. "I'm fine, ma. How are you?"

"I'm fine, baby. Just, you know, wondering what was new with you."

I laughed. She wasn't going to ask. "Ma, what's new with me is I received a letter from my birth mother."

I heard her let out a gasp. She asked a shaky, "And what did she have to say?"

I let out a sigh, "Ma, she had a lot to say, but we can get into that later. Why don't you start with why you bought me on the black market?"

She let out a short scream, "I can't believe she told you that."

"Ma, calm down, she only told me because she wanted me to know the truth. She didn't do it with intentions to hurt you."

"Seth, I can't believe you're already defending her. You don't even know her," she whined.

"Ma, will you calm down, please. This is not a contest between you two. I'm not mad at you and dad. I just want to know the truth. I am finally trying to deal with all of this so I can move on."

She sounded irritated, "What do you mean so you can move on?"

I was getting frustrated and impatient. I mean, I had waited twenty-seven years, and she was still avoiding it. "Okay, look, ma, you need to calm down. I understand this is not how you intended for me to find out, but the truth is out now so can you please just get over it, and tell me what the hell happened."

She had her voice back now. "Now wait a minute, Seth. I don't know who you think you are talking to. You may be grown, but I am still your mother. Yes, I owe you an explanation, but you owe me some respect so you watch your mouth, or I swear, I will get in my car and drive to Tallahassee and beat the black off you. Do you understand me?"

She was right. It wasn't like me to be disrespectful. I let some of the bass out of my voice since she decided to use the same phrase on me that got Mrs. Redding the desired effect. "Yes, ma'am, I'm sorry."

She began, "I'll tell you the short version because this is a time of my life I don't like to talk about."

She took a deep breath. "When your father and I first got married, we wanted to have children right away. We tried for a year with no results. After that, we went to the doctors. One said it was me, another said it was your father. It was confusing and frustrating. We just continued to pray and try. After another year of trying, I got pregnant. Of course, we were ecstatic and very excited. Our prayers had been answered. But I miscarried after a month. You can't imagine how devastated we were. Your father, bless his heart, was a rock for me and he wouldn't let me give up hope. After about six months, we tried again and got pregnant. We were a little nervous, but once we made it to three months, we began to get excited again. But I miscarried again. This time we were both devastated and at this point, started to doubt and blame God. It caused a strain between your father and I because I stopped wanting to try. We started having problems in our life that we never had before."

She sighed, "In retrospect, I now know it was the enemy distracting us from trusting God. I became so depressed; I pushed your father away. He ended up having a one-night stand with another woman. He came home and told me about it the very next day, but I was so upset about not being able to conceive, I didn't even care. I began hoping she may have gotten pregnant because at least then, one of us would have a child. As sick and twisted as that was, I was out there like that. I started blaming God and behaving all 'woe is me.' I was pathetic. Your father threw himself into his work and so did I; we needed something else to focus on. The next year on our anniversary, we decided to scratch a much needed itch, and I got pregnant again. We were so nervous. We walked around on eggshells for weeks. This time, the baby came prematurely at seven months and was stillborn. I can't even begin to describe this pain to you."

Her voice began to crack, and I could hear her crying. Tears started to flow from my eyes again. I said, "Ma, if this is too hard, I understand. You don't have to tell me."

She gathered herself, "No, it's okay. I need to get this out." She cleared her throat. "I almost went insane. I had so much anger and bitterness toward God because I could not understand how he could continue to torture me. I was done. I was done trying because I refused to torture myself anymore. We looked into adoption, of course, but it was going to take much longer than we'd thought, and I think your father was more concerned about my sanity than anything else. He got in contact with a classmate of his from undergrad, Logan Randall, to see if there was anything that could be done legally to speed up the process. That's when this got interesting."

I felt for my mother, but I knew I shouldn't interrupt again so I sat down on the couch to hear the rest. Sheridan curled up next to me as soon as she felt my weight next to her. She asked, "Seth, you still there?"

"Yes, ma'am."

She continued after a deep breath. "So, Logan told your father that he may have a solution to our problem, but it would cost us. He told us he knew of a young woman that was due any day, and she really didn't have the means to take care of a child. For the right price, she might be willing to give up the baby. When your father told me this, for a split second, my conscience bothered me about doing it. I didn't know what this young woman's situation was, and I was in no position to judge her. All I knew was I wanted a baby and someone may be giving me the opportunity to have one. I told your father to find out how much. Logan told him $30,000. We had that at our disposal because your father's parents left him a trust fund that he came into when he turned twenty-five. He didn't want to do it because of the legalities, but I begged him. In my mind, my rationale was that we had so much love to give to a little baby that it didn't matter how we came to love him, just that we loved him."

She let out a breath, "After about a week, I convinced your father, and we got on a flight from Houston to Dallas and met with Logan. When we got there, Logan told us that the mother had agreed and was willing to sign over all rights. We could pick up the child the day it was delivered. He then told us that you were African American. We, of course, were a little taken aback because of our naïve assumptions, but when your father looked me in my eyes for my answer, he knew I didn't care if you were plaid. I was already in love with you. We paid him half that day and would give him the other half the day we picked you up. I never met your mother. You were delivered by a midwife in Logan's home or so I was told, and we came and picked you up the next day. He gave us all the paperwork we needed, and we brought you home. How you doing, baby, you okay, you want me to go on?"

I cleared my throat and said, "Go on, ma."

She continued, "We loved you, you brought us so much joy, and we could not have been happier. I realized how much your father loved me, what he had done to make me happy, and I felt very lucky to have him in my life. Our families didn't take so well to our new addition. The only one who took to you was my mother.

She was just as happy for us as I was, and she spoiled you every chance she got. We caught a lot of hell from people we thought were our friends. They couldn't see past your color."

She went on, "When you were five, we finally decided to leave Texas. Your father got a job down in Florida, and we moved. I quit my job to stay home with you, but I became a teacher once we got to Deland. Shortly, after we moved, I got pregnant and nine months later, your sister arrived. I was so afraid that we would lose her too, that I put myself on bed rest. That's how we met the Redding's. I would always see Mrs. Redding on her porch in the afternoons and one day, we began to talk. She wanted to know how you came to be our son. I told her we adopted you because we tried unsuccessfully for years to have a child. She was the sweetest old lady, but she was blunt. She told me that her husband wanted to know if he could visit with you and take you down to the barber shop to get your hair cut because the way we had it looked a mess. I laughed, and we became fast friends. They were twice our age and taught you and Renet all kinds of stuff about black history and many other cultures. They were a blessing. Renet probably knows more about black history than other black people because she was always stuck up under you, and you both loved to go and visit the Redding's. I was grateful that color was never an issue for you and her and that you guys have a great relationship. I love you both so much, and I thank God daily for both my babies."

I laughed, "Ma, we're not babies anymore."

"Son, to me, you two will always be my babies."

I cleared my throat, "Ma, I know this was hard for you, and I appreciate you telling me all of this. I know I was blessed with wonderful parents, and I don't wish my life would have been any different. We can never understand God's plan, but it all works itself out."

"You are so right baby. I had to see that God took me through all that to be desperate enough to be your mother so that your destiny could be fulfilled. I'm glad that you are finally dealing with this. I always thought it unhealthy that you never asked about your real parents, but then I just assumed since you had the Redding's, maybe they filled that void. Are you going to contact your real mother?"

I thought about it for a moment. "Yes, ma'am. I plan on calling, but I don't know when. I plan on meeting her but not just yet. I need some time to digest all of this and definitely some time to pray about it."

Sheridan was starting to wake up. She yawned and got off the couch to get a drink. My mother got my attention again, "Your dad said he loves you and if you need to talk, his ear is available. He also said don't be afraid to cry if the need arises."

I laughed, "Ma, trust me, I shed enough tears today to last me the rest of my life."

I heard the doorbell ring, and I wondered who that could be, it was almost nine o'clock at night. My mom was still talking, "Seth, I just want to apologize, and please, don't think ill of me and your father. The way you came into our life was wrong, this I know, but we loved you then, and we love you now. We will be here to help you get through this."

Before I could respond, I heard Sheridan yell out, "What in the hell are you doing at my house?"

I looked up, but I couldn't see who she was talking to. I got up and headed toward the door. There were two conversations going on, but the one I was focused on was in front of me. I heard Sheridan yell again, "Why in the hell would I care if you're pregnant or not?"

Who in the world is she talking to? "Ma, I gotta go. I'll call you right back."

I hung up before she could say anything and when I got to the door, Sheridan was giving Naomi the evilest look. *What in the world is going on?* I tried to defuse the situation.

"Naomi, what are you doing here?"

Sheridan jumped back into the conversation, "She about to get stumped into the ground is what's about to happen."

I stood in between them and held Sheridan back, "Baby, calm down."

Naomi interrupted, "Look, don't be threatening me, heifa. If you touch me this time, you're going to jail because I am with child, and the reason that I am here at this moment is to tell you that I am with your child." She pointed at me.

That one threw me for a loop, "Come again?"

"You heard me, Seth; I'm pregnant with your baby."

I laughed because there was no other response. She couldn't possibly be serious, and I started to look around for hidden cameras because I had to be getting punk'd. Just that quick, Sheridan came from behind me and before I even saw what she was trying to do, I grabbed her with one arm, and pulled her back into the house. One thing I knew about my wife was that she could be ghetto as hell. *Lord, what was she like pre-salvation?* That was a scary thought because she would swing first and ask questions later as it is now.

"Lord, help my wife keep her hands to herself." I silently prayed, "And Lord, let me wake up from this nightmare."

I was body blocking Sheridan when I let out a long sigh as I pinched the bridge of my nose. "Naomi, what are you talking about? Why are you here for real?"

She rolled her eyes, "Negro, is your skull too thick? Are you listening? I'm here because you knocked me up Martin Luther King, Jr. Day weekend while we were in Jacksonville together. Don't act like you don't remember. If you recall, you commended me on my performance that night. You told me that while you were wrapped around me, you didn't think about your wife once."

I was stunned; I could not believe what I was hearing. Then, Sheridan screamed, "Negro, what the hell? You were supposed to be ministering in Jacksonville that weekend for Pastor Josiah. You mean to tell me that you were screwing this tramp?"

I looked at my wife like she was crazy. "I was there to minister, I didn't see this girl in Jacksonville, and I didn't even know she was there."

Sheridan looked like she was about to cut me and kill Naomi. I could not believe this drama that was unfolding in front of me. Lord, Jesus, help me. Naomi turned around toward her car and motioned for someone to come to the porch. I looked over at Sheridan. Her face was bloodshot red. This had gone too far.

"Look, Naomi," I began, "I don't know what kind of sick joke you playing, but this isn't funny, and you need to take your little behind home and quit playing with me and stop disrespecting my wife on her own property."

Just then, Tameka walked up to my porch. "Look, Seth, I'm not trying to cause no drama. I'm just here to tell the truth. Now, I saw you leave hand-in-hand with Naomi from the mall while we were in Jacksonville, and you saw me too, so don't lie. Now, Naomi is pregnant, and you need to do the right thing by her, and just so you know, she's willing to do a DNA test."

I was livid, "Girl, what the hell are you talking about? I don't know what kinda scheme y'all done cooked up, but you ain't seen me at no mall leaving with no female. Get off my property with this foolishness."

Naomi gave me a smirk, "Don't get cocky, playa, thinking this can't possibly be your baby because of the three...," she shot Sheridan a look and gestured by holding up three fingers, "yes, I said three condoms we used, but I would just like you and your wife to know that I poked holes in all of them," she smirked. I was about to close the door in her face because this was some sick bull crap, but Sheridan stopped me. She had a new sense of calm as she stepped in front of me. *Uh-oh, she's calm, this can't be good.*

She got in Naomi's face and said, "Look, obviously, you're pregnant, this I can see. You want my husband, this I can see. You are a trifling wench to throw yourself at a married man and trick him into impregnating you, this I can see. What I can't see is why my husband would sleep with your trivial behind. Obviously, somebody is lying. I want a DNA test. You make yourself available first thing Monday morning and after the doctor tells me what a liar you are, you got until that baby drops to anticipate the beat down I'm gonna put on your immoral behind! And I'ma do it, not just for me but for every other married woman you got the potential to try. When I get finished with you, you are going to run every time you come in contact with a man wearing any kind of ring on his left hand!"

With that said, she slammed the door in their faces. When she turned around, the look she gave me almost broke my heart. Before she could say anything I put my hands up. "Baby girl, I do not know what they are talking about. I ain't never touched that girl and when I was in Jacksonville, I went to help the minister of music at the House of Hope, and that is all I did." She shot me daggers with her eyes.

"I'm sitting here thinking about what we just went through not more than a few hours ago, and it is blowing my mind that I am now listening to you defend yourself against that tramp I been warning you about for months."

I interrupted her, "Baby girl, listen."

She shot back, "Shut up, Seth. In my heart I want to believe that she's lying, as a matter of fact, I know she's quite capable of it, but to get Tameka in on the lie along with a specific time and place in the same city you were conveniently "ministering" in. It's all too trifling and confusing for me. I cannot believe this mess, Seth. How could you be so stupid?"

Now, I was hot, "Sheridan, what are you talking about. Don't you see me standing here telling you I never touched that girl? Please, get a DNA test because that will exonerate me. I have never touched that girl. First of all, I have no desire to touch her, and please don't forget you're my wife. What I look like cheating on you? Let's just forget for a moment that I'm married. I'm a minister, and she sings in my choir. I can't even believe you would think that I would risk that. You know me better than that. You're really, actually starting to piss me off believing this chick over me."

She rolled her eyes. "Save that self-righteous crap for somebody with boo-boo the fool written across their forehead, okay, Seth. I don't need a lecture on your holiness, and I dern sho don't need a lecture in your faithfulness either because the truth is, the odds are not in your favor on this one, homie. You're right, you have never given me a reason to not trust you and so for the next two days, you get the benefit of the doubt. Monday morning this will all be behind us, and we can move on from there. But the one thing that's really got my head messed up is why would she be so confident that a DNA test is going to prove you're the parent, if she knows you never touched her?"

I shrugged, "I don't know because she's crazy."

She rolled her eyes, "I agree she is crazy, but she seems awfully confident that you're the father of her baby. If she wasn't confident, she wouldn't be willing to submit to a DNA test before the baby is even born. That's the part that's breaking my heart, Seth. A woman would not admit to trapping you if she never even slept with you. So, I tell you what, I'm going to get in the bed. How about you take the guest bedroom tonight?"

She walked away before I could respond and slammed our bedroom door. Where was I, in the twilight zone? I don't care what Sheridan said, there is no way Naomi could prove that I slept with her and been stupid enough to knock her up. I don't care how confident she is. I did not sleep with that girl. That's my story, and I'm sticking to it. The phone rang, scaring the crap out of me because I forgot it was still in my hand. I answered without checking the caller ID.

The caller seemed a little nervous, "Seth, are you okay, baby? You got off the phone so suddenly, and I thought I heard Sheridan fussing in the background."

It was my mother; I tried to calm her nerves. "Ma, I'm okay, but I just got a whole other set of problems to deal with."

She responded, "Seth, what kind of problems? Is everything okay up there? What can I do?"

"Nothing, ma, just don't worry about it. I got myself in this mess, and I will find a way to get myself out of it. I love you ma, good night."

I hung up before she could respond. As I headed to the guest bedroom, I wondered how in the world I could have been so stupid and not seen this coming. One thing I couldn't do was lie to myself. This mess was my fault and that much I knew to be fact.

Chapter 20:
The Twilight Zone

Sheridan

These past two days have been dreadful. I didn't know I had the capacity to ignore my husband. I refused to speak to him, and I refused to listen to him. I can't explain how mad I have been waiting for Monday to get here. I cannot believe this is my life. How did we go from finally resolving the issues with his birth mother to being closer than we've ever been before, and end up with some woman accusing my husband of fathering her bastard child?

I just don't know what to say or do or even how to feel. I, of course, want to side with my husband. I have never known Seth to lie about anything. This tramp is throwing me for a loop because she is so confident that she opted for the DNA test, and she says she slept with him while in Jacksonville on the same weekend I know for a fact, he was there. Then, when you add in Tameka as an eye witness that they were indeed together, what the heck am I supposed to think?

But then, if he did sleep with her, why would he be so adamant in saying he didn't do it. I mean, he looked me dead in my eye and said he never touched the girl. I can't believe he would look me in my face and lie like that, especially after she admitted to poking holes in the condoms. This whole mess is insane; I feel like I'm living in a crazy TV drama of some kind. This cannot be my life.

I had to get myself together. We had an appointment with my doctor in an hour. I couldn't wait to find out what we could do to resolve this issue as soon as possible. No matter the outcome, I was still going to have problems. If it turned out Seth was telling the truth, then he was going to hate me for taking her word over his and if it turned out that Naomi was telling the truth, well, let's just say we won't make any plans for our anniversary next year because I am out of here.

I felt a pang of conviction. Here I was not sure of anything and already deciding on divorce. Didn't I just tell my husband the other night that we could get through anything? Did I really mean it? At the time, I thought I did. Now, I'm not so sure. I love that man with all my heart, but this is something I never thought I would have to deal with being with Seth. He had always been a man of integrity, always trying to do the right thing. He was always the voice of reason and always the level-headed one. How could he be so stupid? I tried to pray, but I couldn't because my heart had too much malice and anger in it to even approach God. My prayers wouldn't reach the front door let alone heaven.

I threw on some jeans and a t-shirt. There was no point in make-up because I had been crying for two days, and I looked a hot mess. I slicked my hair back into a ponytail and threw on a baseball cap. I had to prepare myself to utter the first words I'd said to my husband in two days. I was just going to assume he got the note I left him telling him we were going to meet at the doctor's office at 11:00 this morning.

I took a deep breath and walked to the guest bedroom. I knocked on the door. I cannot believe my marriage had been reduced to me knocking on a door to speak to my husband. This was sick. He called from behind the door, "Yeah?"

I asked, "You ready?"

There was a beat of silence. "I'll meet you in the car in two minutes."

I sighed and said, "Okay."

I walked to the garage and got in the car wearing wrinkled jeans and a t-shirt. Shortly, after I started the car, Seth walked into the garage. I pushed the button to let the garage door up and looked at my husband. It gave me some comfort to know he looked a hot mess, too. His eyes were bloodshot red, and he looked like he hadn't slept the last two days either. When he got in the car, I spoke, "Good morning."

He shot me a nasty look, put on his seatbelt, leaned his head back on the seat, and closed his eyes. I sucked my teeth loud, but I guess I deserved that. I wouldn't even let him talk to me all weekend, and I guess he was close to his breaking point because I was dern sho close to mine. I put on my shades and backed out of the garage.

The car ride was silent, not one peep from either of us. I was so glad when I pulled into Dr. Kincaid's office because it was time to have some kind of communication with another human being. As we walked in silence toward the door, Naomi was walking across the parking lot. We made eye contact; she smirked at me and patted her belly. My blood pressure shot up, and I was about to turn towards her and slap the piss out of her, but Seth grabbed my arm quickly and guided me toward the door. The fact that he knew me so well both comforted and pissed me off at the same time. I should have beat her behind that day at the church and got it out of my system. "Lord, Jesus, help me with my violent streak," I silently prayed. "Help me not let the devil use me to act a fool today."

Seth gently pushed me toward the seating area and shot me a look that basically said sit down and shut up. I rolled my eyes. He went to the receptionist and filled out the sign-in sheet and came and sat down next to me. I knew he was angry with me, but I appreciated him sitting next to me to let that heifa know that we were a team in this together, and I was thankful he was still by my side. Naomi and Tameka came and sat right across from us. I guess Seth felt the heat radiate from my body because he reached over and held my hand. He looked at me with a very reassuring look and whispered, "It's gonna be okay."

I don't know why, but I believed him. In that moment, I had a sense of peace, and I had hoped that this nightmare would be over soon, and we could go back to our normal lives.

After about fifteen minutes, the nurse called my name. We all followed her back to Dr. Kincaid's conference room. I loved my doctor, but I never thought I would be in her office with two other women and my husband seeking paternity testing. She had a bright smile on her pretty brown face and said, "Good morning everyone."

She got no response, so she continued. "Okay, then. Well, why don't you all have a seat, and tell me what's going on."

Seth and I took a seat on the right side of the table, and Naomi and Tameka sat on the left side, leaving the head of the table for Dr. Kincaid.

"Well, let's not everyone talk at once now," she chuckled.

I let out a sigh because this mess was not funny. I was ready to get this over with so I told her what was going on. "Look, Dr. Kincaid, this is what's going on. This tramp...,"

Seth shot me a look, I rolled my eyes. "This young lady is accusing my husband of fathering her child. My husband says that he never touched her. Under normal circumstances, I would believe my husband and tell her to go to hell in some gasoline draws, but it seems that they were both out of town in the same city on the same weekend, and her friend here, said she saw them together that weekend. She said she would submit to a DNA test because she is very confident it will not prove her a liar. She claims that condoms were used, but she tampered with them to ensure her impregnation. There is no way in hell I am going to sit around and wait for her to have this baby to find out which one of them is lying to me because somebody has got to be lying. I know they can test for paternity while you are still pregnant. Let me know what it costs. I will write you a check today, and then tell me how long I gotta wait to hear the results."

The look of shock on Dr. Kincaid's face was noticeable, but I understood because this was some foolishness. She cleared her throat, "Well, Sheridan, it's not exactly that simple. There are two procedures that can be performed but both depend on how far she is, and there are risks involved. I can tell by the look on your face you are serious about not waiting so I will give the recommendation to have it done, but first, you all need to understand the options. It may just not be feasible."

That pissed me off because there was a possibility we would have to wait this out. I sighed, "Well, doc, what are the options, and how much risk is involved?"

She turned to face Naomi and said, "There are two possible procedures, one is called amniocentesis and the other is Chorionic Villus Sampling or CVS. The timing of the DNA testing during pregnancy is vital. There are two precise windows of time in which the test can be done. The first window is between the eighth and thirteenth week of pregnancy. At this time, a CVS can be done. The gynecologist will insert a needle into your vagina, through your cervix. They are trying to obtain little finger-like pieces of tissue that are attached to the uterine wall. These are known as chorionic villi.

Your doctor will also use an ultrasound to help guide the needle. The chorionic villi comes from the same fertilized egg that your baby comes from, and therefore, has the same DNA as your baby. There is, of course, with any invasive procedure, risk of miscarriage, bleeding, and cramping, and also infection."

She paused and looked at me for a moment. I rolled my eyes, and then she continued, "The opportunity for the second procedure, amniocentesis, is between the fourteenth and the twentieth week of your pregnancy. With an amniocentesis, your doctor will use an ultrasound machine to guide a thin needle into your uterus, through your abdomen. The needle draws out a little bit of amniotic fluid. The amniotic fluid is then tested for DNA. However, there are risks with amniocentesis as well. These risks include a chance of harm to the baby and also a chance of miscarriage. There is also the chance that you may also experience cramping, vaginal bleeding, or leaking of amniotic fluid."

When I heard about the risks of the procedures, I felt bad for insisting on this. I was pissed, but I wasn't heartless, and this was an innocent baby's life at stake. If given the chance, I would gladly slap Naomi at any given moment, but I couldn't say that I would want her to risk her life to satisfy my curiosity. I mean, I didn't want her dead; I just wanted to serve her up a good old-fashioned beat down.

Dr. Kincaid interrupted my thoughts, "What is your name, darling?" she asked Naomi.

Naomi cleared her throat and replied, "Naomi Walker."

Naomi looked scared as hell. The doctor spoke again, "How far along are you, Naomi?"

"I just turned twelve weeks on Saturday."

She qualified for the first procedure; this was up to her now because I wouldn't push it if it could hurt her or the baby. Dr. Kincaid asked her, "Naomi, you can have the CVS procedure done, and the accuracy is 99.9%. Is this something you want to do of your own free will?"

I started to speak to tell her she didn't have to do it, "Look, Naomi..."

She cut me off as she smirked at me, "Yes, doctor, it is because I can't wait to wipe that smug look off of Sheridan's face. Right now, this DNA test is the single most important thing on my To Do list."

Oh, no, this ho did not just try me. I was about to stand up when Seth grabbed my elbow very strongly and said a very low, "Don't." It startled me because this was the first reaction Seth had shown. He had been stoic the entire conversation.

I rolled my eyes, "Okay, doc, if this is what she wants then that's fine with me. When can we schedule this because as you can see, it's urgent, and my patience is wearing thin?"

Dr. Kincaid turned to me, "Now, we need to talk about the cost of this procedure."

I told her, "I don't care, tell me now, and I will write you a check because it don't make me none. Either way, I'm coming out of pocket. I can give you the money or it's going to the clerk of the court for my bail because I hit a pregnant woman."

I cut Naomi a look to let her know she was treading on thin ice. Dr. Kincaid tried to stifle a laugh and said, "The procedure is fifteen hundred."

I said, "Done. Not a problem."

Dr. Kincaid stood up, "Okay, well, we will get you in immediately. Seth, we will take your sample today, and Naomi, see my nurse on your way out to schedule the procedure. Once the procedure is done, it will take about seven days to receive the results. Sheridan, I will call you and let you know when they schedule her appointment. To keep the playing field neutral, I will schedule the reading of the results for all of you to be here, and I ask that you keep your emotions in check while you are in my office, please. Seth, come with me," She motioned with her hand.

"You all try to enjoy the rest of your day. I will work to get this issue resolved as quickly as possible. If you'll excuse me, I must get to my next appointment."

She waited for Seth, but he reached back and grabbed my hand. I knew he was thinking there was no way he was leaving me unsupervised with only Tameka to protect Naomi. We walked out of the door.

A nurse took us into an examination room. She swabbed Seth's mouth. I could tell he was humiliated. I didn't care, I needed the truth because until then, I was in marital limbo, and I couldn't stay there for another six months. After the nurse left, he just looked at me with such disappointment in his face that it almost broke my heart. I didn't know what to say, "Seth, I'm sorry, but I have to know, and this is the only way."

He cut his eyes at me and grabbed the door knob. "No, it's not the only way. You could trust in the man you married, a man that has never lied to you or given you any reason to believe I would ever do such a thing to you or to us. I cannot believe you are taking that girl's word over mine. I have always been there for you, and the first time we are hit with a challenge, you show just how little faith you actually have in me. Well, so much for getting through anything, huh?"

I opened my mouth to defend myself, but he cut me off. "Let's go home, Sheridan. I'm done talking about this."

I grabbed my purse and walked out behind him. I didn't even know what I was feeling, anger, hurt, guilt, betrayal, just pain. I prayed, "Lord, Jesus, help me, guide me, and point me toward the truth. I am not going to make it through these next few days without you. Amen."

When we got to the car, Seth didn't even open my door. That hurt. I got in on the passenger side and looked out the window as a whole new set of tears flowed down my face.

Chapter 21:
Don't Push Me

Seth

I was living in the equivalent of purgatory. For the last week, there was no peace in my house. Sure, it was quiet, but definitely no peace. How could you live with somebody and not talk to them? Seriously, not one word between us. Well, I did try to talk to her a few times, and she just looked at me like I was stupid. She made me feel like I was being disrespectful because I had the audacity to open my mouth and talk in her direction. Not to mention, I was going crazy to tell somebody about how I came to be adopted.

I was going through the worse thing I had ever been through, and my wife had handed me a cold shoulder. I could not wait for the results to get here so we could put this nonsense behind us and move on. Though, I wondered how exactly I was going to move on with a wife who apparently did not trust me. I couldn't even explain how bad it hurt to know that she took this woman's word over mine. I mean, I was standing there looking her in her eyes, and I told her I didn't sleep with her, and she still humiliated me at that doctor's office. I was so pissed, I was afraid that if I opened my mouth, I would cuss Sheridan slap out. On top of everything else, we were out $1,500 for this nonsense.

For the past week, I had just been talking to God. It's a good thing I worked at the church and had uninterrupted access to that altar. I discovered that Ebony found out about the baby, and I was pretty sure it would be all around the church at any given moment. This was a nightmare.

After Pastor Josiah saw me laid out on the altar for three days straight, he wanted to know what was up. I told him about everything, about my mother, her strange life, and then this nonsense about knocking Naomi up. He just looked me in my eye and asked me if I slept with her. I looked him dead in his eye and told him I didn't sleep with her. He looked at me for a long moment. I'm pretty sure he was praying, and then he told me he believed me. He told me he had a feeling this would get a lot worse before it got better, but even Jesus was persecuted. He said that he would be on my side until the truth exonerated me. He told me that he always admired me as a minister because of my integrity. He said the reason why I was the minister he put the most responsibility on, was because I had his same heart for people and for God. He told me that he knew God chose me to minister in that church in music and in teaching, and there was never a doubt in his mind that I was called to be there.

One thing was strange though, when he left me in the sanctuary that day, he came back and said, "Just because something is a fact does not mean it's the truth. Son, your answer is in God. Trust him with your life."

And then, he walked away. Now, that had my head spinning. *Oh, Lord, what was about to go down?* I just continued to stay in prayer because of the cryptic words P.J. gave me. I knew I was in for an all out spiritual battle.

I prayed for my strength, Sheridan's understanding and forgiveness, and Naomi's deliverance and for the truth. Physically, I was garbage, but spiritually, I was on point, and I was ready for whatever mess the enemy had. Even though my wife was not my favorite person, I still loved her with all my heart, and I was not about to lose her over a deranged chick. I was just about to read my Word when there was a knock at the bedroom door. I walked to the door and opened it.

Sheridan was standing there looking as bad as I felt. It gave me some solace to know she was hurting, too. Before she could say anything, tears started flowing from her pretty eyes. I went to reach for her, but she backed up. That stung. "Sheridan, what's wrong?"

She wiped her face and cleared her throat, "Dr. Kincaid called, and she wants us to be at her office in an hour."

I didn't know whether to be happy or sad, "Okay, I'll drive," I replied. I gently closed the door and lay across the bed. Lord, what awaits us at the doctor's office?

When we arrived at the doctor's office, she had a straight face, and I could not tell what she was about to say. Naomi was late which had Sheridan livid. She was shaking her leg and biting her nails, which is something I have never seen her do. I bowed my head and prayed silently, "Oh, God, can this just be over already?"

Sheridan spoke first, "Look, Dr. Kincaid, can you just tell us the results now."

"I'm sorry, Sheridan. I gave my word that I would be neutral so we will wait for Naomi to arrive."

Sheridan let out a frustrated sigh. Just then, Naomi walked in. *Oh, brother, here we go.*

Dr. Kincaid gestured for Naomi to have a seat. I didn't like that she was in Sheridan's reach. I had to be ready to hold her back at any given moment. Dr. Kincaid opened the envelope on her desk and pulled out the documents inside. She looked at each one of us. Then, she looked at me with disgust and said, "The test results came back, and I need to inform you all that they show that Seth is indeed the father of Naomi's child."

What the, how in the, who did what? This can't be happening to me. My first thought was to reach for Sheridan; she snatched her hand away and got up. Naomi stood up, looked at Sheridan and said, "That's right, you siddity heifa, your man is the father of my baby. Deal with it."

Sheridan ran out of the office, and I was on her heels. When I got outside the office, she was bent over throwing up into a nearby trashcan. Naomi walked by and laughed as she said, "I'll be in touch, baby daddy."

I felt my hate for that woman rising. I went to Sheridan, "Baby, look, I don't know what is going on, but I did not..." she cut me off.

"Shut up, shut up, you lying bastard. I cannot believe you gonna sit up here and keep lying to my face. You've been trying to convince me you were so innocent. You've been making me feel bad for wanting the test like I was betraying you and all the while, you knew you slept with that girl. You looked me dead in my face and lied to me. I hate you!"

I was stunned. Did she just say she hated me? She walked away and grabbed a paper towel to clean up. She walked back toward me and the pain I saw in her face broke my heart, but I didn't know what to do. That's when I saw it in her eyes. She was about to hit me. She tried to slap me with her right hand, I grabbed her wrist. She tried to slap me with her left hand, I grabbed her other wrist.

She was really mad now, and then she did the unthinkable. This woman spit in my face. I felt my blood pressure rise. She had gone too far. I never had the desire to hit a woman but at this moment, I wanted to knock her lips down her throat. I tightened my grips on her wrists and yanked her toward me. I could see the fear in her eyes. She was afraid of me. I never wanted her to look at me like that again, but this would be the last time she ever tried me like this.

I could feel my nose flare as I spoke through clenched teeth, "Have you lost your freakin' mind, girl? I am not now, nor have I ever been anybody's bastard. Now, I understand that you are in pain, but the disrespect stops here. Don't you ever in your life try me like this again. Do. You. Understand?"

She didn't open her mouth. She just shot me daggers with her eyes. Now, I had a death grip on her wrists and she winced, so I repeated, "Do. You. Understand. Me?"

She said a shaky, "Yes."

I began to relax my grip just a little bit and said, "This is the last time I am going to say this, I did not sleep with Naomi Walker, and there is no way in hell that child is mine. This conversation is finished."

I released my grip on her and wiped my face as I walked out the door. I turned back to her and said, "You take the car, I'll find another way home."

I saw Dr. Kincaid rushing to her side as I headed toward the exit.

Part Four:

Redemption

Chapter 22:
Under the Shadow of the Almighty

Grey

When I opened my eyes, I couldn't see anything but smoke, and I began to choke hysterically. I was trying to make sense of where I was and what happened. There was a chemical smell and my lungs began to fill with thick white smoke. My right hand was stinging like it had been burned. I realized that both of my airbags had been deployed, and I opened the door so I could breathe.

As I opened the door, I got a quick glimpse of the red truck that hit me backing up and driving off like a bat out of hell. I kept choking and trying to fumble with my phone to dial nine-one-one, but between my screaming and shaking, it was virtually impossible. A man in a car passing by slowed to ask if I was okay and I yelled, "No!"

He drove off. I mean, what was the freaking point? I tried to dial again, but my phone kept asking was I sure I wanted to dial emergency.

I was shaking uncontrollably and disoriented. This was ridiculous. Just then, two men ran from across the street. I could barely make out their faces because I was hysterical. The rain was now just an annoying mist, and the tall one asked if I was okay. I screamed, "He just left. I can't believe he just left. He didn't even stay to see if I was alive. I can't believe he just left."

The man tried to calm me down, "I know, ma'am. We saw him drive off, but we couldn't get the entire tag because he drove off so fast. Have you called the police?"

I tried to calm myself, but I couldn't. I just shook my head. He took my phone and pulled me away from the street and into the parking lot of Checkers. There was a car with two women in it, and they came to get me. The younger one put me in the passenger seat, trying to calm me down. It was so hard to breathe; I could taste the powder from the airbags in my mouth. She rubbed my arm and asked, "Are you okay?"

I was crying now and said, "I can't believe he left me. How could he just leave and not know if I was alive or dead?"

I looked over at my car and the front end was pretty much missing. She said, "But, look at how many people came to your side to help you. It's okay, don't worry about that person. They don't even matter right now. What matters is you're okay."

I knew she was right, but I couldn't stop crying, not out of pain, but out of anger. The tall guy came back with my phone and asked me my name, I said, "Grey."

He smiled and said, "Grey, the police are on their way. It's going to be okay."

I shook my head, and he and his friend walked off. The sister in front of me was the color of honey, and she had a beautiful afro that was shades of red and dark blonde. I thought it was odd to notice that at the moment, but she was right in my face.

She asked, "Are you hurt anywhere?"

I looked down at my hand that was stinging. Other than that, just right above my left knee there was a dull throb. I think I hit it on the steering wheel, and I must have burned my hand on the airbag when I braced for the crash. "No, nothing major, as a matter of fact, other than being disturbed and scared, I think I'm pretty much okay."

She smiled, "Well, tomorrow you're going to have whiplash so enjoy the shock of it now."

The woman in the back seat looked like an older version of the woman in front of me and she asked, "Is there anyone you would like us to call?"

The only number I could think of was Brooklyn's. "Um, yes, my friend, Brooklyn."

She took out her phone and asked for the number, I obliged. Thank God, Brook answered. She told her I had been in an accident, but I was okay, and then she told her my location. The paramedics arrived and rushed over to me. Everything was a blur and happened so fast. There was an oxygen mask because my lungs were still filled with airbag smoke, but I didn't like that. It felt very unnatural. I remember declining the ambulance ride and then the Sheriff pulled up. By then, I was beginning to calm down. I explained to the Sheriff as best I could what I remembered, and then he took statements from the pretty sista with the afro and her mother. The tall man and his friend walked back across the street gave their statements, and then I saw Brooklyn and Sydney pull up.

Brooklyn stood by her truck in blue jeans and a white t-shirt observing everything. She was tall with a pretty mocha face. Sydney was wearing sweats and asked the officer if she could hug me now. He laughed and told her yes. Her hazel eyes sparkled against her light brown skin. I hugged my friend, and then Brooklyn said, "Girl, your wig a lil crooked. You may want to fluff that thing out, what if you end up on the news, and that paramedic was cute!"

I laughed, "Uh, I had been just a little preoccupied, but please do fix it."

She laughed and began to fluff out my wild curls. The paramedic walked up to me to ask if I was sure I didn't want to go to the hospital. I shook my head. "You may want to consider getting that exact same car because it just saved your life."

I looked him in his eyes and said, "I love my car, but trust me when I tell you, it was Jesus that just saved my life."

He nodded and walked off. Brooklyn said, "What happened?"

"Girl, it was crazy, but what I do know is that when I knew I was going to hit that truck, I called on Jesus, and then I blacked out. When I woke up, it was all over. I didn't feel the crash. I didn't hear the crash and really, the only thing I feel is a little stinging from the airbag on my hand."

I was amazed because I knew that Jesus had protected me to the point that I didn't even feel any of it. Brooklyn said, "Well, amen, girl. God is too good."

Then, she hugged me. The young sister with the afro walked up to me and said, "I'm so glad you're okay. I was in a little fender bender a few weeks back so I know all too well how scary it can be."

Her mother said, "She was blessed because this young man and his wife showed up and protected my baby from those drunken nuts. Ain't no telling what would have happened had they not shown up?"

The young lady smiled and said, "I never knew his name, but I'm just glad I was able to return the favor to someone else."

My mouth dropped open, "Oh, my God, I know the man that helped you."

She looked at me strange and said, "How do you know you know him?"

"Because he came to dinner and told us about it. His name is Seth. He is like a brother to me. And then, I remembered his wife describing your hair. It was a Sunday afternoon, right, at the gas station on Fred George? I guess it is a small world after all."

She looked at me stunned and said, "Oh, my God. Well, I have been hoping to run into them again so that I could formally thank him and his wife because at the time, I just wasn't thinking straight. I was in awe of how that brother just stood up for me without knowing a thing about me."

I said, "Yep, that's my Seth. What is your name?"

She stuck out her hand, "My name is Yvonne, and this is my mother, Gracie."

"It's so nice to meet you two and you know what, y'all should come to Kingdom Builders Worship Center one Sunday, that way, you can thank Seth and Sheridan in person."

She smiled and said, "I will definitely do that."

Brooklyn said, "Let me get you a card."

Because she was the church's administrator, she always had Kingdom Builders info on her ready to hand out. I hugged Yvonne and her mother and thanked them for everything. And then, I heard someone call my name.

I looked up, and I'll be darned if it wasn't Yolanda. Okay, God, you are really on some other stuff tonight. She walked up to me and hugged me like we were the best of friends. She asked, "Are you okay?"

I was still in shock, and I just nodded. She continued, "Girl, I was just passing by, and I saw your tag, and I said that's Grey's car. I had to see if you were okay." I was speechless.

She looked over at my car, let out an expletive, and then she said, "God is good, girl; it's amazing you walked out of that car."

I just shook my head. A cuss word and praise in the same sentence, "Yeah, it is."

She hugged me again and said, "I'm glad you're okay, and it was so good to see you."

And just like that, she was gone. Brooklyn returned from pulling her car up to mine so that they could take everything out and looked at me crazy and asked, "Tell me that was not your old roommate?"

"Girl, yes, it was. Me and Mia were just talking about her not that long ago and wondering if she was okay."

"It's been years since you've seen her, right? Well, what did she say?"

"Nothing really, just that she saw my car and wanted to see if I was okay. She just hugged me and left as fast as she came up."

Brooklyn said, "Okay, yeah, now that was random."

I looked skyward and just shook my head, "Lord, what are you up to?"

Brooklyn and I helped Sydney transfer the contents of my car as they clowned me about the chicken wings sprawled all over the floor and all the other contents in my car when the tow truck pulled up. It was a very sad state of affairs as the chick scraped up the front parts of my car off the ground with a shovel and dumped them in the back seat. She hooked it up to the tow truck and dragged it away as Sydney documented it all on her iPhone. I was so hurt, I loved my Altima. God, really, three more payments, really? Dang! Oh, well, it is what it is. I'm alive and well, thank you, Jesus.

Brooklyn insisted I go to the emergency room because the pain tomorrow would definitely require some prescription meds. I got in the car and obliged as I rested my head. Brooklyn called my mom and my sister, Mia, to let them know what happened and that I was okay, while Sydney called Sheree and told her to meet us at my house in about an hour.

†††

After the E.R., we filled my prescriptions for pain meds at the twenty-four-hour pharmacy and headed to my house. It was almost two in the morning. Sheree stood there in her pink pajamas fussing about what took us so long because now my Epson salt bath was lukewarm, and she would have to run new water. She was genuinely upset because her pretty brown face had a slight red tint to it. We just looked at her and laughed as Barry weaved through everybody's legs. He, for once, didn't cut his eyes at me, and I didn't have the strength to lick my tongue at him.

Once he was bored with our presence, he went back to his resting place and proceeded to go back to sleep. Brooklyn made plans to stay with me for the next two days to get all my insurance claims and rental car in order. Gotta love my friends, even though I could do all of this myself, it was nice to be taken care of. Sheree sent me to soak in the tub, and I gratefully obliged as she and Sydney prepared to leave because their schedules were not as flexible as Brooklyn's. They would definitely be hurting at work tomorrow; I was so blessed to have them.

I was about to undress and get in the tub when I noticed what I was wearing. I had on a black sleeveless blouse and black slacks with a thin red belt, red shoes, red necklace, and red earrings. I smiled because it made me think of the blood on the doorpost and how that was the symbol to let the death angel know to keep it moving. I closed my eyes for a silent prayer, and I received a vision. In my mind, I could see an aerial view of me in my car driving right before the accident. I couldn't see a face, but I could see wings wrapped around me, and they were blocking me from all harm. I opened my eyes, and felt goose bumps all over. "God, you are so incredible."

As I soaked in the tub, I thanked God for keeping me safely under his shadow.

Chapter 23:
A Very Present Help. . .

Kadijah

I heard the gun click. It sounded like it was either stuck or the safety was on. Well, at least, that's what I think it meant. It didn't matter, though. I was just ecstatic to be able to take another breath. I looked up at her, and she was getting frustrated with the gun because it wouldn't shoot. The craziest thing happened; I heard a whisper in my ear say, "Take the gun."

I knew there was nobody out here but me and crazy horse. What's even crazier is that I felt like there was someone next to me. Her focus was split, and I snatched the gun. Even though I had never held one before, I began to release the clip, and I also popped out the bullet in the chamber. How in the world did I know how to do that? It was like something was guiding my hands, and it all happened so fast. She looked at me, screamed obscenities, and I could see her hatred for me dripping like venom off her teeth, but she never touched me.

Then, I heard the whisper again in my ear, "Run, left."

Okay, now this was just crazy, but so was this nut in front of me so I took off. The rain was beginning to become a mist. I could only imagine what time it was, but I kept running. I had been running for at least ten minutes in the cold, dark, drizzle of this insane rain. There was a house coming into view. I was tired, in pain, and I needed to rest.

I slowed down because this was definitely some scary movie type foolishness. I was not about to go to that house. I didn't care how bad I felt. Then, I saw a light come on through the window. Oh, God, my heart couldn't take this kind of pressure. I was bent over trying to catch my breath when the door opened. I wanted to run, but my body was not trying to take one for the team. The silhouette of a curvy woman showed through the lit open door as she began to come toward me slowly. I stood about five-feet away from her when I had this peace just flood me.

I heard the whisper again, "It's okay."

The woman slowly approached me, and she called out and asked, "Is your name Kadijah?"

Oh, my God, what in the world is happening to me right now? I took a deep breath and said, "Yes, ma'am."

She clutched at her heart in what seemed like relief and let out a breath. "Honey, somebody somewhere is praying for you. I declare the Lord woke me up from a dream about you, and he told me to hide you in the house and take care of you."

I was stunned speechless, and I just blinked at her. She was now in my face, and she reached for me, but I hesitated. Then, I heard the whisper in my ear again, "Go with her."

This was freaking me out, but what other choice did I have. I took her hand and she said, "Come now, honey, I know this is strange, but it's okay. I'm a nurse, and you look like you could use some patching up."

I started to walk with her towards the house. She stopped suddenly, stared toward the end of the driveway, and smiled a smile I had never seen on anyone before. It was a smile that was amazed and reverent, but I looked back, and I didn't see anything. Then, she started walking again.

I was in so much pain and so tired. I could care less whether this woman was crazy. I just knew she was a godsend. When we crossed the threshold of the front door, she turned back. She looked up as if she was looking in the eyes of someone really tall, and she nodded her head. Okay, I couldn't help it. I finally found my voice, "Miss, what in the heck are you looking at?"

She had tears in her eyes and said, "If you could only see what I see. There are two angels guarding this door. They are protecting me and you."

I looked up and all I saw was a dark sky, and then I looked at her like she was on that pipe. She smiled and said, "There are two of them. They stand about eight-feet tall each with beautiful wings. One is carrying a sword and the other a weapon, I'm not quite sure what it is, but it does look scary. They stand fierce, dressed for battle, and in control. We don't have a thing to worry about." I just looked at her puzzled.

She closed the door and said, "Honey, the enemy tried to take you out tonight, but somebody was praying for your protection. They sent out for some warrior angels, and they are here to do the spiritual part of protecting you while I do the human part of helping you get well."

This woman had to be every bit of sixty-years old and her home was full of random pieces of furniture that didn't go together but somehow made sense. There were pictures everywhere, all in different frames. She led me to a flowery sofa. Thank God, there was no plastic on it. After she spread towels over it and gave me a couple, I sat down on it, and I swear, I melted into it.

My body was very much appreciative of the opportunity to just rest and know that at any given moment, I wouldn't have to flee for my life. The woman walked away for a while, and I just relaxed and tried to make sense of the past hour or so of my life. Why was that girl trying to kill me? I thought we were friends or at least civil associates. She came back with first aid supplies and more towels.

She said, "My name is Ms. Ruth, and I'm going to do my best to patch you up with what I have here and first thing tomorrow morning, we will go to the emergency room. Are you hungry, sugar? I can make you some nice chicken soup in no time?"

Even though it hurt my bottom lip to do so, I smiled, and said that I wasn't hungry. She looked at me the way all mothers do that says, I know best.

After Ms. Ruth bandaged up my open cuts and gave me some pain medicine, she told me that she was going to fix the soup anyway, just in case. I heard her clacking around, but about ten seconds later, I was out like a light.

Chapter 24:
For God So Loved the World...

Kadijah

When I woke up the next morning, my body was sore, and some parts tender, but I had a blanket up to my neck. I was tucked in so tight; I thought I would pee on myself before I could get out of the cocoon. Ms. Ruth appeared out of nowhere and said, "Let me help you, sugar," and undid her swaddle of blanket.

I slowly walked back to the bathroom. My face with its array of bruises and apparent battle scars was too much to bear this early, so I went to relieve myself. She knocked on the door and said, "I got up early and went and got you something to put on from the Wal-Mart. I believe it's your right size. So, when you come out, it will be sitting on the table in the hallway with a towel, a wash rag, and a toothbrush. Then, you can have some breakfast, and we can take you to see a doctor. Leave the bandages on, I will redress them before you eat something, and you are going to eat something."

I rolled my eyes, but I was also in no position to be defiant. I got the stuff she bought for me, some simple gray sweats, and some plain white underwear. I knew it would be a struggle, but I went ahead and proceeded to shower and changed.

After I finished, I actually felt better. I didn't look much better, but I did feel almost human again. I walked into her little kitchen that was cozy, and quaint, and sat in one of the four chairs at the little wooden table. It smelled like grits, eggs, and bacon. My stomach started to signal that I was indeed hungry. She set everything out on plates and poured me orange juice, but left it at the counter as she came to redress my wounds.

I asked, "Do you live here by yourself?"

Her eyes misted slightly as she said, "Yes, dear, now that my love has gone on to glory."

I felt sad for such a nice person and said, "I'm so sorry to hear that."

She said, "Oh, don't fret for me none. We had a good life, and one day, I will see him again."

She finished the bandages, washed her hands, and got the plates. She placed mine in front of me and said, "Let's pray."

✝✝✝

The ride to the E.R. was awfully quiet. I was in my own head, and she just kept humming "Amazing Grace." I couldn't figure out what was going on, and I also couldn't figure out this pull or tug on my heart. I mean, here was this woman who appeared out of nowhere, these angels she claims she saw, which by the way, she swore they were sitting on the roof of the car. Because in my mind, if they got wings, why don't they fly next to the car instead of being lazy and sitting on the roof. They must be low on their frequent flyer miles. That made me chuckle out loud.

She asked, "You okay?"

"Yes, ma'am." The left side of my brain was telling me this woman was a loony, but my heart was telling me that maybe all that stuff Pastor Josiah had been talking about was actually real. I'd been going to that church faithfully for two years. I'd completed my membership classes, and I actively served in the dance ministry, but I had never accepted Jesus Christ as my personal Lord and Savior. After every service, they made the request and recently, I had been feeling the same tug that I felt right now, but I refused to take the step. I think everyone there just assumed I was already saved.

I had been around so called "saved folk" all my life, and I swore they were the biggest bunch of self-centered, self-important hypocrites, I had ever known. *So, why should I be saved? I think I'm doing alright just being a good person.* Then, I heard some of Seth's teaching echo through me. He'd once said, "Being good is not enough to enter into the Kingdom of Heaven because God is holy, and there were a lot of "good people" that would bust hell wide open. The only way we will ever be good enough to be with God is to be covered by his son's blood. Only then, will we have reached a status worthy enough to enter into Heaven."

Ugh, I don't wanna hear all this right now. Ms. Ruth was parking the car. She was around the car and at my door by the time I got it

Surviving Sunday

open. She was fast for sixty. I said, "Thank you," as she helped me inside.

The E.R. wasn't very crowded with its white walls and ugly blue chairs. She helped me sit down in the area where no one else was, and I was grateful for that. There were news reports on the TV as she went to check me in. There was some story on about a woman losing eighty-pounds and beating diabetes after she had been hypnotized into believing she had a gastric band. Now, that made me snort, and it made my bruised ribs scream. Ms. Ruth came back with a clipboard full of papers for me to fill out.

I said, "Um, I don't have any ID or insurance information on me, but I do know my driver license number by heart."

"Oh, honey, don't worry about that. I'll be paying cash for your visit."

I looked at her blankly. She just smiled like she was happy to do it. "Okay, lady, you don't even know me, why are you doing all this? This is crazy."

Her brow furrowed, but only for a flash. "Well, sweetie, what would you have me to do except be obedient to what the Holy Spirit is instructing me to do? I don't have to know you. I know God, and I know that He sent you to me to get some help and that's what I'm going to do."

Again, I just stared blankly at her, but my resistance to her did begin to melt just a little bit. I was usually a prideful person when it came to receiving help, but I was in such desperate need of it right now, what could I do?

She went on, "Now, I was praying last night about what God would have me impart in your life before we go our separate ways, and there's a couple things I need to do, but first, finish your paper work so we won't be distracted, hun."

I obediently did what I was told, and she took them back the desk. When she came back, she had a determined look in her coal black eyes that made me squirm in my seat.

She sat, grabbed my hand, and said, "I know that you have been running from salvation for quite some time now, but it's time to stop running, Kadijah. God has shown Himself to be very real in your life in the last twenty-four hours and even the most devout atheist would have to agree with me had they been a witness. The whispers that led you out of that situation and to my house, those were the angels that somebody sent to you. The tug you feel in your spirit right now is God speaking to your heart. I know you haven't always seen the most productive Christians in your life, but that has absolutely no bearing on you and your relationship with Christ. God has placed you in a ministry and among peers that will help you grow in Christ. Don't squander your divine purpose because you're stubborn or too intellectual for your own good. Now, will you let me lead you in the prayer of salvation?"

At that point, I barely noticed the tears that trailed down my face, but I did notice the warm sensation in my chest. It was like heartburn but in a good way. I was astonished by how much this stranger knew about my life and my personal feelings. I asked, "But why, why would any angel or God go to all that trouble?"

She smiled, "Besides the fact that He loves you so much, you have a powerful ministry inside of you. It is so great, and it will be the starting point of so much change in the earth that the enemy has been trying to take you out for years, but every attempt failed."

I nodded my head in understanding. She continued, "Okay, now one more thing. Did you know the person who attacked you?" I nodded again.

"Okay, I feel like you're supposed to give your Pastor all the information you have, and he will know how to get to the bottom of this. It's going to be alright, and I don't want you to fear her ever again. God's got you covered, love." She bowed her head and said, "Repeat after me."

Chapter 25:
That Still, Small Voice

Josiah

I was just a little confused because I was on my way to the church and found myself taking an alternate route. Why am I headed downtown? Then, I heard it again, "ABC."

Ok, this was like the third time I had heard those letters today. And then, I not only heard it, I saw it. The ABC Lounge was a part of the Shannon Hotel. Okay, Lord, this is weird, but then I felt a strong need to stop. It's too early in the morning for this, but I'm also too old to be hardheaded when God sends me on a random mission so I obliged. I put on my blinker, turned in, and found a parking space.

I walked into the lobby and headed straight to the service desk. The clerk was a pretty petite blonde woman with a welcoming smile, and there seemed to be a light around her like she was the person I was there to see. I smiled and decided on the honest approach, "Hello, I am not exactly sure why I'm here, but maybe you can help me. I think I may be looking for someone, but I'm not sure who."

She gasped audibly and said, "Oh, my God, this is crazy. You look familiar, aren't you the pastor of Kingdom Builders?"

Okay, God you are indeed in control. I replied, "Yes, I am and you are?"

She grinned, "I am a frequent visitor. I haven't joined yet, but I will be on Sunday because you just confirmed to me that God is not only very real, but He definitely has heard my prayer, and His spirit definitely resides in you."

I wasn't quite sure, so I asked, "Would you care to explain why I'm here?"

She took a deep breath, "Okay, I had to work the late shift the night before last, and I checked one of your members into a room. She looked like she was hanging on by a tiny piece of thread. I wanted to ask was she okay, but she looked like she would claw my eyes out if I didn't hurry and put her in a room."

I stood there amazed and asked, "Who did you check in?"

"Her name is Sheridan. I believe she is the wife of your music minister. I started praying for her the night she checked in. When I came back to work, I looked her up to see if she was still here, and she was. So then, I asked God to please send someone to help her because whatever she is going through, it's pretty bad."

Okay, God, I hear you, I gave her my best reassuring smile as I read her name tag, "Kelly, it's going to be okay. Kingdom Builders would be grateful to have another prayer warrior on the team. Thanks for doing your part and don't worry, God is clearly in control, and this too shall pass."

She looked relieved and said, "Thank you, Jesus! Now, I'm not supposed to give out this information, but I know this is God so she is staying in Room 222."

I nodded as she pointed to the elevators. I began to walk away, but she grabbed my hand. I looked back and saw the sincere plea in her blue eyes. She said, "She hasn't ordered room service, and this is going on her third day."

I squeezed her hand, "Not to worry, I'll take care of it." I headed for the elevator praying and asking God for words of wisdom.

I got off on the second floor and after reading the sign in front of me, I headed left. I got to Room 222, saw the do not disturb sign but knocked anyway. No answer, so I knocked again and waited. Okay, Holy Spirit, I can't do what you are sending me to do if you won't convince her to answer the door. I knocked again, "Sheridan, its Josiah, open the door."

I heard footsteps, and then the locks began to disengage. She opened the door, and I was almost frightened at what I saw. She needed some tough love and a comb, "Girl, what in the Sam Hill is wrong with you? You look like somebody beat you down with an ugly stick, and then kicked you with the ugliest shoe they could find!"

She rolled her eyes and walked away, but left the door open. I stepped in and closed the door. The room was all dark and gloomy. The spirits of depression and discouragement were so thick I could feel it. Happiness did not dwell there. It was time to rebuke this mess. Even though she was fully dressed, including shoes with clothes that wrinkled would be too kind of a word to describe. She climbed right back in the bed and drew the covers over her head.

Okay, this would be a challenge; I let her have her moment of defiance as I went to open every curtain in the room and then picked up the phone on the nightstand. Some light needed to come in and expose all this darkness. I dialed room service. The perky voice of a woman answered, "Good morning, how may we be of service to you?"

"Yes, this is Room 222, and I would like to place a breakfast order of apple cinnamon oatmeal with sugar and milk on the side, a side of fruit, and orange juice."

"Yes, sir, would you like any coffee with that?"

I looked around the room and saw that Sheridan had taken full advantage of the in-room coffee pot and said, "Absolutely no coffee!"

"Yes, sir, we will get this right up."

I thanked her and hung up. I pulled up a chair to the side of the bed so I could get in Sheridan's face.

I began, "I know you can hear me so you may as well make this easy on yourself. I raised four daughters so I fear no crying woman with an attitude, okay."

Without lifting the covers, she said, "What do you want P.J.? What? And I am not eating no oatmeal!"

"First off, you are going to eat, even if I had to shove it down your throat. I know you haven't eaten since you got here two nights ago."

That got her attention; I bet she was trying to figure out how I knew that. "Don't look so shocked. God sent me here, and He saw fit to give me details along the way." She rolled her eyes and pulled the covers back over her head.

"Girl, look here now, this was an interruption to my plans just like it's one to yours, but you know I'm gonna do what God says do. Now, you need to take a good look at yourself. Your hair runnin' all ova yo head like roaches that just scattered in the light. You got shadows under your eyes that are darker than a moonless sky. A crack head has more style and class than you right now, and all you done consumed in two days is coffee, and you know yo lil' scrawny self cannot afford to spare a meal. As a matter of fact, if Jesus had a list of people who didn't have to fast because they couldn't afford to miss a meal, you would be third on it."

That made her laugh, but she kept laughing, she laughed so hard I considered changing careers for a split second, and then in a flash, she was crying and crying hard like fresh sorrow just entered her heart. Before I could react, someone knocked at the door, and I heard, "Room service." I rose to open the door.

A fresh faced, young man was there smiling. I took the tray from his hands and walked it over to the little table. I pulled a five from my pocket and handed it to him as I closed the door. Sheridan had been reduced to sobs now, but this pity party was officially over. I put on my authoritative voice just like I did with my daughters when enough was enough.

"Sheridan, get up and go wash your face so you can eat." She didn't move fast enough. "I mean now!"

She got up and dragged her little self to that bathroom. *Lord, these kids, these kids...why didn't you send me to the boy, they are so much easier to deal with?* She looked three steps down from presentable when she came out, but it was better. "Sit down, Sheridan, say your grace, and eat." She obeyed with only a slight roll of her eyes. Ah, progress. I pulled my chair back over to the table and sat down.

"Sheridan, you need to know that God has heard your prayers, He sees your tears, and He's saying it's time to dry them up. Running away from your problems doesn't make them disappear; it just leaves a trail for them to follow." She was pushing her oatmeal around and not eating it.

"Sheridan, I was not playing about shoving the food down your throat, stop playing with it, and eat." She rolled her eyes and put a spoon full in her mouth.

"Girl, I know I'm your pastor, but I am also old enough to be your father. If you roll your eyes at me one more time, I am going to call your mother and hand her my belt when she gets here."

She gave a little laugh, but she didn't roll her eyes. "I am aware of what's going on because Seth told me, and I want you to know something, I believe him. There is not one doubt in my mind."

She snapped, "Oh, really, you do because I believed him, too, but that was until the DNA test came back 99.9% positive that he was the father of that slut's baby."

I blew out a breath. *Whew, okay, didn't know that.* I ain't gonna lie, it caught me off guard, but then the Holy Spirit brought something back to my memory, just because something is a fact does not mean it is the truth. However, Sheridan was not trying to hear that so I knew I needed a different tactic. I took a deep breath and prayed. Okay, Lord, I need some wisdom now.

"Okay, Sheridan, that's hard. I'm not going to sit here and pretend that it isn't, and I'm not going to ask you to do it either." Then, I felt the Holy Spirit kick in. "But truth be told, the reason you are falling apart right now is because you want to walk out on your marriage, and you know God is telling you to stay. Your pain and frustration is coming from the fight within you to do your will and what you know is right." Fresh tears began to fall silently.

"The Bible never told us that surrendering to God's will was going to be easy, but you have known God long enough to know that His will is the best for us. So, in the end when this is all said and done, you will still be better off being obedient because it's better than sacrifice."

She spoke, "It's not fair. He cheated, my life is falling apart, and you sitting here telling me to stop crying, to stay in this sham of a marriage with this bastard who cheated on me with a little slut in the choir at *our church* where he is a minister. This is some straight up garbage and according to the Bible, I *can* walk away from my marriage because my husband broke his vows to me by lying down with that whore."

I knew I was about to piss her off, but I had to make it plain, "Would it have been better if he was a janitor and cheated with one of the teachers at a school you were not affiliated with?"

Her eyes flashed so hot that all her tears seemed like they turned into steam. I held up my hand before she could speak, "Sheridan, this is not about Seth or Naomi, this is about you and your obedience to the will of God for your life. You know that God is telling you to stay and that's why you are so angry. Even with the information you just gave me, in my spirit, I have strong convictions to stand behind Seth. I understand that you feel you can't trust your husband so what you need to do is trust God. If He is telling you to stay in your marriage, then He can see what you can't see and you know that He knows best. I promise you God is going to work this thing out and you know that God will never put more on you than you can bear. His strength is made perfect in your weakness so don't be afraid to admit to being weak in this particular area for this particular moment. God can restore your marriage and heal every pain you are feeling, but you have to be willing to surrender to Him and let Him."

She sniffed, "P.J., I hear what you're saying, and yes, God is working my nerves because I know He is telling me to stay, but I don't want to do that. Every time I say no to God, my spirit is vexed and on top of that, my heart is being ripped apart every time I remember that smug look on Naomi's face when the doctor said Seth was her child's father. This is too much for me."

I cut her off, "You're right, it is too much for you, but not too much for God. You have trusted God with your life for many years and now that you have made it to the big leagues, you can't tuck tail and run the other way. If God is presenting this challenge to you now, He has a reason. If you seek Him first, He will order your every step and bring you out on the other side strong, full of mercy and faith, and a happily married woman. Just think how you will be able to help your clients from a very personal place instead of just an intellectual place. God is in control, and He is sovereign. Since He knows what tomorrow will bring, you have to look to Him and stop fighting Him. The sooner you give up your will, the sooner the process can start."

She pushed around her last piece of fruit and without even realizing it, she had finished her food. Poor thang was probably famished. "Okay, Mr. Preacher man, since you got all the answers, where do I begin?" I stood, grabbed her hand, pulled her out of her seat, and walked to the door.

I turned to her, grabbed her shoulders, looked her in her eyes, and said, "Even though it doesn't feel like it to you, this is child's play compared to what Christ had to face when He gave up His will. So, what you need to do is say, Lord, not my will, but thy will be done, and then try some praise. Praise breaks the yokes, and you need to break the yoke of your fear, your disobedience, and your depression. When I walk out of this room, you are going to open your mouth, and you are going to give God praise for everything. Then, you're gonna do something with yourself because you look a lil' crackish. You're gonna go home to your husband and start the process of putting your marriage back together so you all can put up a united front to the enemy. I know he is probably going insane with worry. Remember, one can chase a thousand, but two can put ten thousand to flight. Together y'all are ten times more powerful than alone. God is able to do exceedingly and abundantly above all you can ask or think according to the power that works in you. Tap into the power of your praise and watch and see God inhabit it."

She tried hard to give me a smile, but it came off as a contorted smirk. I chuckled to myself, hugged her, and whispered, "It is well with your soul." I opened the door and walked out praying as I walked to the elevator. "Lord, I did my part, now you do yours." Something wasn't right about this situation. Something bigger had to be happening. This one had too much at stake. I needed my better half so I took out my phone and dialed her.

She picked up on the second ring, "Good morning sweetheart."

"Hey, honey, listen, I just left Sheridan's hotel room and..."

She cut me off, "Now, Josiah, if I were less of a woman, that statement alone could get me your house, your car, your kids, your pulpit, and all your money."

I laughed, and it felt good because I definitely needed it. "Girl, hush, you know better than that."

She laughed too and said, "Okay, baby, why is Sheridan in a hotel room?"

See, that's why I loved her, "I'll get to that part but, baby, my spirit is vexed. I'm telling you something else is going on. We need to fast and pray for some guidance on the drama and gossip that is about to hit our congregation."

She said, "Lord, Jesus, please have mercy."

I echoed, "Exactly!" Then, I began to tell her the twisted tale.

Chapter 26:
Praise Is What I Do

Sheridan

When P.J. closed the door behind him, I just leaned against it, and closed my eyes because I didn't know if I was grown enough to handle the task that was before me. But I guess I would have to do like Mia always said and take a big girl pill, suck it up, and just do it. The thought of it, though, made my knees go weak, and I just slid down the door as I fell to my knees, and cried out, "Jesus, I need you, right now!"

I hit the floor, and the tears exploded all over again. Why couldn't I stop crying? How was it possible that I even still had tears left? Then, I heard the words of a song that I hadn't heard in a really long time, "Praise is what I do even when I'm going through." *Okay, Lord, I hear you. I give up because I don't have the energy to keep fighting you.* I knew it was a losing battle when I started it. "Lord, not my will, but your will be done." I decided right then and there, that I would praise my way back home. I began to open my mouth and give God praise.

"Lord, I thank you for who you are. You said you are the God of all flesh and that includes mine, my husband's, and Naomi's. Lord, you said you would never leave me nor forsake me and in my heart, I know those words to be true. I also know you will never put more on me than I can bear. Even if I don't know it yet, this I can bear. I thank you, Lord, for whatever you did to get Pastor Josiah here to get me off my behind. I thank you for the strength you are going to give me in my weakness. I praise you now for the restoration of my marriage. I won't lie and say I trust my husband, but I do trust you, and I know I can trust your plan for my life. Forgive me, Lord, for my disobedience and unbelief. You are the God of all creation. You are the God of heaven and earth, the God that spoke this world into existence; so surely, you can speak life into a dead situation. You are the great I am, El Shaddai, God

Almighty. You are, Jehovah Shalom, my God of peace. Thank you, Lord, for giving me your peace that passes all my understanding. Hallelujah, Jesus, my savior, my comforter, and my redeemer. I give glory to your name, God, because you are more than worthy. I need you now more than I ever thought I could. I need you in all of your infinite wisdom. I need your grace that you promised was sufficient for me. Thank you for renewing my mercy everyday because I know I haven't been worthy of it. You are so worthy, Father, thank you for loving me and blessing me even when I didn't deserve it. Thank you for sending your angels to minister to me when I fell short and walked by sight and not by faith. I'm sorry for falling so deep away from what I knew to be true. I'm sorry for being selfish, and I'm sorry for presuming to know better than you do. I know it won't be easy, but if you promise to be with me every step, Lord, I promise to go back to my marriage until you tell me otherwise. I love you, Lord. I praise your name, Jesus. I thank you, Father."

As I continued to give God praise, I felt a presence fall all around me. It was so comforting and warm. The burden on my heart began to lift little by little, and I just lay there prostrate under the beautiful presence of the Lord that held me close and brought me back home. Before I knew it, I fell asleep.

When I woke up, I felt amazing. I wondered how long I had been asleep. I hadn't had a good night's sleep in weeks it seemed, and I felt refreshed and rejuvenated. There's nothing like anointed slumber. I got up and saw that it was three in the afternoon. Wow! I slept almost seven hours, but I wasn't mad because I needed it. As I walked in the bathroom, I realized I felt great, but I looked like the ghost of Kwanzaa past. Lawd, have mercy. Okay, where to start, where to start? Well, obviously, I needed a shower. Good thing I took my mom's advice and always carried a pair of underwear and a toothbrush in my purse. Then, I came to my senses and realized I did have enough wits about me to pack a suitcase.

I hadn't seen my husband in three days, and the last time I saw him, I spit in his face. I shuddered. I was so disgusted with myself. He didn't get a pass for his part, but neither should I. I had no idea what to expect when I got home, but I didn't want to add to it by looking homeless and needy when I finally did walk into my house.

After my shower, I decided to tackle my hair. I didn't know about scattering roaches, but a bird's nest came to mind. I took a comb and brush out of my bag and prayed there was a ponytail holder somewhere at the bottom of my purse. One of Grey's wigs would be ideal right now; fabulous on the go was what I needed. When I finished, I still looked a hot mess because my eyes were swollen from days of crying. The shadows under my eyes looked like death, and my skin was blotchy. I knew I didn't even have the strength to try to cover it with make-up. Oh, well, here goes, I threw all my stuff in the bag and headed to check out.

"Lord, you still there? I mean, I'm crunk right now, but I have yet to lay my eyes on the man who promised to love me and then broke my heart into a million tiny pieces, and then kicked those pieces off a cliff. I'm willing, but I know I can't do this alone. Help me, Lord, please help me, Jesus."

Chapter 27:
Patience Is a Virtue

Seth

I realized that I had just been sitting there staring into space when I heard the garage door open. My heart thumped in anticipation of finally laying my eyes on my wife. The TV was on mostly so that it would feel like someone else was in the house with me, but I had no idea what it was even talking about. This was the third day that I had not seen nor heard from my wife.

That night, I hit rock bottom. After all my calls went unanswered, I decided to pray and meditate. God told me just be still. Now, to be honest, that kinda pissed me off. Was I really to sit there and do nothing while I had no idea where my wife was or if she was okay? I knew I didn't like her right now, but I mean, I'm her priest, her protector, her provider, and He was asking me not to do what came natural.

So, after many harsh words in defiance to God, I gave up, and decided that if I was ever gonna trust him completely, now was the time. The time alone gave me some more time to fast and pray for direction. I didn't know how or why that test could possibly say I was somebody's baby daddy. Now, there was a sentence I never thought would be used to describe myself. I missed my wife something terrible, but I also didn't wanna see her either. My heart was confused.

I wanted her back in my arms, but I didn't know if I wanted my heart back in her hands. Right now, I just didn't trust her with it. She had mishandled my most prized possession, but mostly, I was hurting because she left me to deal with the aftermath of my mom and all that we found out by myself. How do we even begin to talk this out? I have no proof except my word which is normally iron clad, but even I must admit the evidence against me is a bit more than circumstantial. In any event, I was about to find out. I heard the door opening.

I turned around to face the kitchen so that I could see her when she came through it. My heart sank as I took her in. She looked exhausted. Her hair was in a ponytail, if that's what you could call it, and the shadows under her eyes looked like they had been permanently tattooed.

Her voice cracked and she tried a weak, "Hi."

I rose to go to her, but she put her hand up, "No, please stay there and sit back down."

I obliged, for now. She came over, sat down, and the familiar scent of her perfume took me back to memories that just minutes ago, seemed a million miles away. I asked, "Are you alright?"

She looked up at the ceiling as if it held all the answers and said, "Pastor Josiah came to see me today."

That threw me for a loop. *Okay, God, he could find her, but I couldn't. Okay, fine, whatever.* "Okay," I said.

"Yeah, he basically came to give me a spiritual butt whooping, and he clowned me about my appearance so bad I realized it was time to stop running from my life, and get on with this grown up situation we have gotten ourselves into."

The ice around my heart began to melt just a little at the "we." She continued, "I won't sit here and pretend like we are just going to be alright, and I'm not going to pretend that I trust you one-hundred percent, right now, but I do trust God one-hundred percent, and it's time I proved it. I know He is telling me to stay in my marriage. I made a vow to God, and the least I can do is put in some work to honor it." I started to speak, but she put her hand up.

"Seth, I have had the worst few days of my life, and I can't imagine yours was any better, but if you would please give me 'til the morning, I promise we will start this dialogue. I will participate with an open mind and a compassionate heart with as little attitude as I can stand."

She grabbed my hand and squeezed really tight, but she still had yet to look me in the face. She rose and went to the room and closed the door, but this time, I didn't hear the door lock. Hmmm, progress? Good thing she didn't give me a time because as soon as the sun rose, I would be back in our bedroom.

The next morning came too slow for me, but thank God it was finally there. The sun was barely up so she could get me on a technicality, but I couldn't stand living like this one way or the other. I was ready to fight or fail. I gently turned the knob to our bedroom door and was relieved to see it was still unlocked.

Our bedroom was spacious and wasn't overly male or female with black bedroom furniture and mirrors. She chose to decorate it in rich gold and blue tones. Sheridan was sprawled out in the middle of our king sized bed all tangled in the sheets. It looked like sometime through the night she and the sheets had a long fought battle and seeing as how she now had a part of it in a choke hold, I guess she won.

Looks like she did something to her hair last night because there was an explosion of curls covering her face so that I couldn't tell whether she was facing me or not. She had on her favorite night shirt, my FSU sweatshirt that she had cut out the neck and sleeves to make it so it was unbelievably girly that I wouldn't wear it anymore. That gave me the confidence that there still may be some hope for us yet.

She reached back to scratch her butt. I couldn't help but chuckle and why, but why, did that just make me fall in love with this woman all over again. I walked around to the far side of the bed and lay down behind her. I simply put my arm around her and pulled her close. She stirred and resisted. I pulled her tighter. She resisted some more. We were not going there this morning. My arms ached to hold her, and she was not about to deny me this basic need.

I said, "Don't fight this," as I pulled her against me one last time, and before I could react, she turned into me and grabbed me so tight I could barely breathe. I felt her body shake as she began to sob. "Shhh, baby girl, it's okay. Everything is going to be okay." I brushed her hair back so I could see that beautiful face I loved and knew as well as I knew my own.

Through her tears, she whispered desperately, "Seth, just hold me for a little while, okay? Just hold me like I'm the only woman who ever mattered to you."

Well, that was an easy request because that's exactly who she was. I gathered her with both arms now and let her cry on my shoulder until she was ready to let go.

A few moments went by before she began to pull back, and she finally looked into my eyes. At that moment, I realized that I needed to put that gleam of light I loved back in her eyes. I needed to remove all the shadows, pain, and sorrow from those big beautiful brown bedroom eyes that I adored.

She cleared her throat and said, "Seth, I'm just going to ask you this one last time and whatever the answer is, we are going to deal with it like adults. I'm not going to run away so, please, don't lie to me. Whatever the answer is, I'm going to work through this." I knew what she was about to ask me, and it took great restraint to keep annoyance off my face, but I was willing to meet her halfway.

After a deep breath she began, "Have you ever slept with Naomi Walker or any other woman for that matter?"

Okay, that last part pissed me off, and I had to count to three in my head to calm down. I pushed her up to a sitting position, and I followed. I grabbed her shoulders and looked her dead in the eyes.

"Sheridan, I have never slept with any other woman but you, you were my first, and I want you to be the last. I have no need to seek anything from any woman, especially not a woman in our own church. I would never disrespect or humiliate you like that. There would be absolutely nothing for me to gain. I have no idea how those tests came out the way they did, but I will do my very best to find out. However, at the moment, that isn't what concerns me. I have missed you more than I want to admit these past couple of weeks, and I want and need our life back. I can't deal with all this without you by my side. I need to know you believe in me and in this marriage."

Her face went through several emotions, first she looked angry and defiant, then she looked regretful and resistant, and now she just looked confused and tired. "Ok, baby girl, what just went through your head?" I asked.

"Baby," she began, "I don't have much to give you right now, but everything I have, I am going to give it to you. I said I would accept your answer, and I do, but I can't say with absolute conviction that I believe it. You need me to trust you, I know this, but it's going to take some time. What I can tell you, is that I trust God, and that He knows what's best for me and for us. The thought of another woman carrying your seed literally makes me want to vomit as you can recall I already did. I'm so confused because I have never ever known you to lie to me or anyone else for that matter. I can't imagine what you could possibly gain from continuing a charade that can so easily be exposed. In one breath, I miss you so much it actually physically hurts, but then in the next one, I want you as far away from me as humanly possible. So, what I am saying to you is that I am going to make the effort to put this marriage back together, but the strong emotions that you are looking for are just not there yet. I can't just snap my finger and make them return. You have to be willing to understand that but know that I am trying."

I cleared my throat because it was burning and there was no way I was about to shed tears. It just was not about to happen. "Sheridan, I understand exactly how this hurts you because the thought of you and another man drives me insane, but what I don't think you realize is the pain that I'm going through as well. From my point of view, I'm standing here as innocent as anyone ever could be, and the woman I love is taking the word of some delusional person over mine. Granted her delusions at the moment have scientific evidence, but our relationship has evidence, too, and it's solid. We have years of proof of our love and dedication to each other. What reason would I possibly have to ruin what has to be the most precious thing to me. There are no secrets or manipulations between us. There never has been. I have been the best husband I know how to be to you, and the thought of you not trusting my word is as painful as you being with another man, and on top of all that, I didn't have my best friend around to help me sort out and deal with all the revelations my birth mother brought into my life like she promised she would be. I have had to lean on my friendship with Jeremiah more than I ever thought I would or needed to."

She looked confused for a minute like she had completely forgotten about what happened only hours before Naomi came to the house, and our lives began to fall apart.

"Oh, my God, Seth, I'm so sorry, I'm so sorry. I completely let that slip my mind because I couldn't see past my own pain. Seth, you have to know that I would never willingly leave you to deal with that all on your own."

"But you did," I said soberly.

She got defensive, "Now, wait a minute, baby, don't act like my distraction was unreasonable. You have a child on the way, and I'm not carrying it." I wanted to snap back, but what was the point. More flies with honey as my mother would say, right?

"Baby girl, I'm sure you may not see it this way, but finding out about my birth mother and everything she had to say is at the top of my priority list. I just found out that my mother killed the man who is responsible for my being here, and I will never get to meet him. I never knew I wanted to, but now that I know I can't, that stirred up pains and emotions I didn't know I possessed. To me, Naomi and this foolishness is exactly what you called it, a distraction. It's not real to me because I know it can't possibly be. You say you want me to have faith and know that you would never willingly leave me hanging like that, but when I asked you to have faith in my word, you looked the other way."

Her shoulders sank, but I continued, "I just told you that I didn't sleep with her and here you are saying that she's carrying my child."

"Seth, look, I will admit I have never ever thought of you as a person who would lie to me or hurt me like this, but you have behaved contrary to what I know during this ordeal. That day in the hospital, you scared the crap out of me. I really thought you were going to put your hands on me so don't tell me about what I know to be true because you never know what you will do until you are put in that situation." That stung. The look on her face that day had haunted my thoughts since then, and I hated myself for putting her through that.

"Sheridan, you spit in my face. Of course, I wanted to pop you one, but there is no way in the world I would ever put my hands on you. Now, the spitting was disrespectful, but what hurt me the most was you calling me a bastard. After everything we had just found out, you threw that in my face. That was low, and that hurt. I never thought you would kick me when I was down, but you did and anger or not, I couldn't handle that. You also did something I never thought you would. You disappeared on me for three days, you didn't even have the decency to call me and say kiss my behind, and by the way, baby, I'm still breathing. Do you know what kind of torture that was for me? Neither of us should be proud of our behavior during the course of these last few weeks, but what we should have realized is that we are both human, and there are some things we need to work on."

She sighed and shook her head, "You're right, baby, you're so right. But understand this, I can't say for sure what I believe about you and that baby, but what I can say is that either way, I am going to stay in this marriage which is probably why I keep going back and forth because I have decided to accept it. I realized that still makes you feel like I don't have your back, and I'm sorry for that, but this is all I have to offer at the moment."

Boy, she was slinging daggers at a brother's heart today for real, but I wasn't exactly guilt-free so I knew this was going to be a process, and we needed to start somewhere. I lay back down on the bed and pulled her to my chest.

"Baby girl, I ain't gonna lie, that hurts more than you know, but if you're willing to stay no matter what, then I guess I need to be willing to work at this regardless of if you believe me or not. In my heart I know the truth, and it will make us free. What we need to do first is pray together. We clearly need God to step in and be a referee because we both have the right to feel the way we feel, but that's not going to put this marriage back on track. We have quite a few challenges ahead of us that we clearly need some spiritual guidance to get to the bottom of. We also need to be on one accord so we can be most effective in these spiritual things. You agree?"

"Yes, I do."

"Okay, we gonna do it our regular way where we tag team or do you just want me to pray?"

"You take this one, baby, and I'll be ready for the next round."

"Okay, let's take it to the floor." We climbed down on the floor, got on our knees, bowed our heads, and I began to pray.

"Father, have mercy on us and this marriage. Please, forgive us of the sins we have committed against you and against each other. Lord, we want this to work, and we need you make it so. Please, mend our hearts back together and help us to remember the love and bond we once shared. Help us to truly surrender to your will for our lives and to submit ourselves to each other in every way. Restore the love that we have for each other and make it stronger and deeper than it ever was before. Guide us on how to find out the truths that eludes us and help us to see the lesson that we are to learn and take with us from the trial we have found ourselves in. Lord, we thank and praise you for all these things in your son's precious blood, amen."

"Amen."

Sheridan looked up at me and said, "Now what?"

"Well, if it's okay with you, I would like to hold you a little while longer."

"Yeah, that's okay." We got off our knees and lay back down in the bed, and I pulled her into me. I began to play in her hair because she loved for me to do it. I kissed her on the forehead and said, "I love you, Sheridan."

She squeezed me tighter. I kissed her cheeks, and then her nose, and then the little mole she has on her chin. How could she even believe another woman would ever satisfy me? I looked into her bedroom eyes and just observed her face. I loved it, the angles of it, but especially the small beauty mark she had on the left side of her chin. She hated it, and I loved it. I smiled thinking about how what you see as a flaw can have the greatest admiration from your lover.

As I ran my finger over it and felt the slight raise of it on my fingertip, I marveled at my chocolate skin against her butterscotch skin and realized it was just one more thing I loved about us, the contrast was appealing. Then, I traced my fingers over her lips, those sexy heart shaped lips that had a natural line around them and whenever she put that clear glossy stuff on them, it made a brother stop and take notice.

They were glossless now, but not less appealing because I wanted and needed to kiss her, though, I wasn't sure she would receive me. A kiss was so much more intimate than sex, but I needed to know that I was still trusted with that vulnerable part of her. I replaced my finger with my lips and pressed them very softly against hers. She hesitated, but only for a moment, and she slowly invited me in as the kiss began to go deeper. I was relieved, but still I pulled back. It wasn't wise to tempt a starving man with a crumb.

She shifted slightly, placed her hand on my cheek, and said, "That kiss made me dizzy."

I smirked as she continued, "But, baby, I'm not ready just yet to make love."

"That was not my intention; sorry, I just missed you. That's all."

She laughed, "Well, did you give that public service announcement to your southern parts 'cause I don't think it got the message."

I chuckled, "Well, that part I can't help. That's just a natural reaction to the woman I love who I haven't had the pleasure of holding in quite some time. Relax, baby girl, that won't happen until we are both ready and willing."

She curled into me like she had done a thousand times before, and it finally felt like home again.

It was barely audible but I heard her murmur, "I love you, too, Seth." The dull pain in my heart began to ease away.

Chapter 28:
Child Please

Grey

I was walking around the bookstore at Kingdom Builders getting ready to close it down for the day. Both the eight and eleven o'clock services were awesome, as usual. I was tired, ready to go home, get out of these church clothes, and these fabulously painful heels. I checked and organized all the books on the left side, the sale items, Bibles, and reference books. I wandered across the store to make sure that the youth materials and Christian growth sections were in order and that I didn't need to restock or reorder any of my hot sellers. I picked up the remote to shut down the DVD of one of Pastor Josiah's sermons and turned off the TV.

As I walked around the counter to shut down the cash register, I looked up and saw my girl, Sheridan, strolling in. There was only one word to describe her today, and that was fierce. She had on a dove gray and pink wide leg pinstripe suit with four strands of gray and pink pearls lying on top of a lacy pink camisole. I couldn't see her shoes because the pants were all the way to the floor so it made her look like she was floating down a runway. Her make-up was flawless, and her hair was dancing on her shoulders with soft curls framing her face. She was absolutely glowing; it had been a long time since I'd seen her look this at peace with herself.

"Well, hey, there lil' mama, what's got you all glamorous and sassy," I asked?

She grinned wickedly and said, "Giiiiirrrrrrrrrllllllllll, I got me some twice this morning!"

I couldn't help it. I laughed and said, "Um, okay, that was random and even though it was way too much information for a Sunday afternoon, I guess I am happy for you because y'all had to get up at the crack of dawn for all that seeing as how Seth was at eight o'clock service!"

She laughed, "Yes, we did, and it was so good I nominated my man for an Oscar for best performance in a makeup scene! The votes are in, that Negro won by a landslide!"

This time, I choked from laughing, "Oh, my God, Sheri, you are crazy!"

"I'm sorry, I didn't mean to blurt that out, but it's been so long. Me and my baby are finally getting back on track, girl. At this point, I would tell that to a bum on the street, if he gave me the opportunity."

Now, that made me snort. "You know what, you stupid! But I am so happy for you."

"Girl, I know, right, but even though it's been a few months and this crazy situation hasn't exactly been resolved, she's still claiming it's his, and he's still denying, but we've been praying together and working on our relationship for the last few months. For some reason, I'm just at peace with the whole thing. I've been in my Word, he's been in his, sometimes we study together, and God has just been doing his thing all up and through our marriage, girl. It's like I can't even be mad about it. I know some way God is gonna work it all out, and the undisputed truth is on its way, I just know it."

"So, do you finally believe him?"

She paused and studied my face and asked, "Let me ask you something, do you believe him?"

That was unexpected, but it was also easy to answer, "Of course, I believe him."

Her face was puzzled, "Why is that so easy for you to say?"

"Oh, that's easy, sweetie, because it's Seth."

She studied my face again and said, "So, just like that, just because it's him."

I began to understand her point-of-view and that this was no laughing matter to her so I said, "Look, you know me and Seth are like this." I demonstrated by crossing two fingers. "I just can't see him lying once let alone repeatedly, and you know, my head is always in a fiction book so I've seen stuff stranger than this explained. Until some undisputed truth comes out, I'm going to stick with my brotha on this one. Just like the old folks say, if it don't make sense, it must be a lie in there somewhere. And this doesn't make a lick of sense. But then again, I'm not his wife. To be honest, the way I've seen God come through in my life recently, I learned that it's best we not question his methods just trust him and praise him along the way."

She asked, "What do you mean?"

I said, "Well, you of all people know the situation with my house, and then the court date. Well, while all that was bearing down on me, here comes my car accident. Now, at the time, I couldn't see it, but I realized God allowed that to happen to free me from that bill a lot sooner than the three or four months I had left to pay on it. Of course, He didn't cause it, but He also didn't steer me from it because it would work out for my good. Not only that, He blessed me with a car that is not only sexy, but paid for, honey. That court date I was paranoid about, well, God led me on a fast one week before it was to happen. The Saturday before that dreaded Wednesday, I received a notice in the mail stating that the court date was cancelled. Then, about two weeks later, I got my loan modification in the mail that not only gave me an affordable payment; it also included my taxes and insurance. Now, I have money in the bank and less bills."

I had to take a breath to keep from shouting and crying. Then, I said, "Girl, this situation has taught me that my ways are not his ways, and my thoughts are not his thoughts. I know God gave me that house, and I know God told me to take that job so it was on Him to provide for me. Now I know you know God gave Seth to you so all you need to do is watch Him work this out for you guys and bring you out on the other side better than when you went in."

She thought about it for a moment and said, "I can't really say I do completely, but the more time I spend with Seth, and the more time I think about the Seth I knew prior to it, this just doesn't make sense. Still, there is a tiny part of me that says the proof is on the paper. I do believe God is going to reveal all things in His time, and I will know for sure one way or the other. If He can work your situation out, then He can definitely work out ours. Besides, I have already forgiven him, and I have forgiven her."

"Well, honey, I am glad to hear it."

I raised an eyebrow, "Now, I know you forgave her, but how are you getting along with Ms. Walker these days?"

Her face scrunched up, "You know, when you forgive someone, there is a level of tolerance you start with and have to overcome it. I'm trying to be an adult these days and not put my hands on that little girl. She still goes out of her way to make snide comments anytime the mood strikes her. That's just the Duval County in me, telling the Jesus in me to turn the other cheek while I handle this lightweight." I fell out laughing; I loved my sweet little violent friend.

She continued, "She was pretty pissed about being asked to step down from the choir, you know, the whole unwed mother thing."

"Yeah, I bet, I can't imagine that went down her prideful pipe very easily," I said.

"Oh, no, it didn't. I mean, I don't know what the big deal is because P.J. had Seth step down as well. That really hurt him, but he understood about perception. He knows Pastor Josiah believes him, but he also knows it's P.J.'s job to keep the peace in the ministry, especially after one of the mother's came to him and acted a fool about Seth being allowed to sit as a minister when his 'house was not in order.' So, we continue to pray for God to reveal the truth of the matter so all can be right with the world again."

My heart ached for all that were involved in this situation. This was some mess you read about, not something you actually knew the people that experienced it. I was about to respond when I saw movement over her shoulder, and I'll be doggoned if it wasn't Naomi, and her side kick, Tameka. Seeing as how I knew my friend so well, and I was sure Naomi would say something to provoke her, in anticipation, I got ready to grab Sheridan. I didn't know how well I could hold her with the glass counter between us. Before I could warn her, Naomi made her presence known.

"Well, lookie here, if it isn't Lil Miss Oops I let my husband knock somebody else up."

Oh, this chick was off the glass. I saw that Sheri recognized the voice by her body language and as she turned around to face them, I grabbed the back of her suit jacket in an attempt to stop her from hopping on this silly child. I apparently was right about her intentions of trying to tear her face off because her resistance almost broke my nails. "Sheri, don't. She's not even worth the effort."

I felt her relax a little, but I was hesitant about letting her go. This little girl needed a hard lesson in politeness. I was starting to get the sensation to slap her myself, but I digressed. I tried to bring some calm to the situation that could so easily get out of control. I said, "Look, Tameka, why don't you take your friend and go on back in the sanctuary. The bookstore is closed, anyway." I saw the flash of temper in Naomi's eyes and realized that I was gonna have to put this little girl in her place one good time on the house.

She bared her teeth and said, "I was not talking to you, Ms. I'm Named after a Crayon. If it's okay for Ms. Goody Two Shoes to be in here, then it's okay for us. You better recognize who you talking to."

Okay, it was official. This chick was out of bounds. Lord, forgive me, even though I know what I am about to do. I released Sheridan because she was no longer the one who would need to be restrained. It's a good thing there was two-feet of glass counter between us. I hoped she could see the flash of vicious restraint in my eyes. As calm as I could, I said, "Okay, look young one, you do not know me, and I promise you that you do not want to get to know the old me that is contemplating the best way to put my foot in your behind without messing up my fresh pedicure."

She threw her hand up and tried to speak, but I cut her off, "Shut up! Don't you come up in here being disrespectful to me and my fam like you ain't got the sense God gave a gnat. You lucky you got a life growing inside you, otherwise, I would hop across this counter and stomp you like it was my man, calmly call you a paramedic, and then repent at the altar." I pointed toward the sanctuary for emphasis.

I continued, "You need to get some decorum about yourself and quickly because you gonna end up in a lot of pain because you clearly had nobody to teach you when to shut that orifice you use so often to speak out of turn. We," I pointed to myself and Sheridan, "Are grown women. We do not have time for your little playground pranks and your non SAT approved grammar. You're running around here trying to be all that and don't have the common decency to have some shame about yourself for the foolishness you started because you are selfish, supercilious, injudicious, manipulative, malicious, and just plain old tacky. Grow the hell up, Naomi, and deal with your situation like the adult you think you are. As a matter of fact, get some rest because you look exhausted like you haven't had any peace in your life in a while. Fast and wrong living will be your ticket to the nether regions if you don't do something about it. You are about to be somebody's mother. Is this really the example you want to set for your child?"

She looked like she was ready to spit nails, but I was not done. She needed to know it was time for her foolishness to come to an end. "Furthermore, you need to really step back from your pride and look at reality. You have to be delusional if you can't see that after all of your fabrications, and all of the conniving ideas you concocted to come between them, all you did was to set in motion a situation to bring them closer together. I mean look at her, she's glowing!"

I pointed to Sheri. "Give it up for your sake and the sake of your unborn child. Stop playing in your fairytale land and realize you are wasting who you were meant to be by trying to make the world bend to your will instead of letting your will bend to God's. Grow up, little girl, and get some substance about yourself. It's the best decision you will ever make." I couldn't really read her expression. It was something between anger, shock, and guilt. Hopefully, something got through to her. It was time for them to bounce.

I reigned in my temper and said, "Now, Tameka, you need to take your little friend out of this store. If she needs me to define any of the words used in this oral assault, I will be happy to provide her with a dictionary at my earliest convenience, or she can purchase one here at her leisure. Goodbye!"

I turned away from her and put my focus back on Sheri to let her know she was dismissed. Tameka muttered in a huff, "Girl, come on let's go. I told you we shouldn't have come in here in the first place!"

Sheridan decided to be just as tacky and started laughing before they were all the way out the door, but I was still hot. Through her gasps for air, Sheri said, "You told that girl her grammar was not SAT approved, girl, you stupid! Then, you offered the poor child a dictionary so she could understand how badly you insulted her."

She was doubled over now. Her laugh had become contagious, and my temper was starting to weaken. I couldn't help but laugh at her silly behind and said, "Girl, I'm glad you were listening because

I can't even begin to tell you everything I said to her. She made me so mad."

Sheri was wiping away tears now, "Girl, you done messed up my make-up, and I think I lost at least a pound laughing at your dumb behind. I know I got at least one ab."

I laughed, "Girl, hush, before you give me a headache. I've wanted to go off on her, but maybe that was just a tad bit mean."

I gathered my purse and locked down the register. "Come on, Sheri, before another unwelcomed customer graces us with their presence."

"It was truthful, not mean. Maybe ruthless but not mean. It was like you cussed her out without actually using profanity. Now, that's a handy skill to have."

I rolled my eyes, "Girl, you crazy."

She laughed and said, "Let me get home and change. I'll see you at the Justice house for Sunday dinner."

I looked up as she walked out the door, "Okay, see you there." I was a few steps behind her when I turned out the lights and locked the door. I headed out to go check up on the thorn in my side and get on over to my sister's house for dinner. Just in case I was wrong, I asked God to forgive me for showing out, and the next time I saw Naomi I would apologize.

Chapter 29:
Sunday Dinner II

After they had chowed down on some good old-fashioned barbecue ribs, chicken, macaroni and cheese, baked beans, and cornbread, the men turned on the Wii. Mia had warned the men that when the women got back from the store, they were indeed going to help them put together Lil Jay's costume for school tomorrow. They left the men playing the game as they ventured out to find materials to make him an African prince or warrior costume. Of course, Grey fussed at her for procrastinating, but Mia simply said, "Why would I do it by myself, when I knew all you Negroes would be here today?" Grey could do nothing but laugh.

††††

When the women came back in the house all loud and chattering, they walked in front of the TV like they could care less that the men were playing video games. They began to talk trash and Mia said, "Aww, whatever. Y'all are going to turn it off in a few minutes anyways to help with this costume."

There was a collective groan, and she just shot them all that look that all men knew whether they were married or not. They opted to enjoy the last few minutes of freedom with no more complaints. As Kadijah, Sheridan, and Grey began to clear the table and unload the supplies, Madison left to play in her room. Mia took this moment to go to the bathroom as she prayed that her cycle would be there when she got there. She was about three days late and traumatized. She had a cycle that you could set your watch by. So, one day late was enough time to panic.

When she returned, she went to the table where Jeremiah was inspecting the supplies they had to work with. She walked up to him and said quietly, "Baby, it's still not here."

He said loudly, "Oh, Lawd, don't do it to me," and put his head down on the table to pout.

Everybody turned and looked at him as Sheridan asked, "And what is ailing you now? It's just one costume. Don't be so dramatic."

He shook his head, "No, I'm being dramatic because through no fault of my own, it appears my wife may be knocked up again. Again, I reiterate through no fault of my own."

Grey and Kadijah just laughed at him. He was infamous for saying his first child was immaculately conceived, and his wife took advantage of him with the second child. They wondered what would be the reason if there was indeed a new baby on the way.

Kadijah asked, "Well, what's the big deal? Y'all make beautiful kids, and they are a blessing."

Jeremiah pointed at her, "You don't get to participate in this conversation until you have your own children and know what it is like to have kids."

Grey piped in, "Well, you Negroes should stop free balling and get something snipped or tied, it's a miracle it took this long."

Sheridan laughed. Mia said, "Now, don't get us wrong, we love and adore our babies, but two kids is a lot of work. Can you imagine another Justice running around here acting crazy like their daddy? Not to mention how expensive they are."

Jeremiah shook his head, "I know exactly when it happened, too. I slipped, got caught up, and didn't do what I was supposed to. I went straight in the bathroom and prayed, Lord, please don't let her be pregnant. I'm sorry, I won't get caught up anymore, I promise. I don't think He was trying to look out for a brother that day."

He put his head back down and began to shake it. They laughed. Sheridan said, "Okay, stop being so dramatic. Let's just find out." She called out, "Nate!"

His head jerked over from the game, "Huh?"

"Go to the store and get a pregnancy test, please. Bring me my purse, and I'll give you the money. Bring back an EPT or something that cost at least ten dollars. This isn't something you should be frugal with."

At the sound of his wife's voice and pregnancy together, Seth looked at her like she was crazy. He and Nate had not been paying attention to the conversation that had just taken place.

Nate asked, referring to all of the large handbags, "Which one of these suitcases belongs to you?"

She said, "The silver one."

Seth said, "May I ask why you need a pregnancy test, and why are you doing so in a public forum?"

"It's not for me, babe, it's for Mia." She handed Nate the money and said, "Hurry back because baby or not, we still gotta make this costume."

Nate just shook his head. Seth went ahead and turned off the game because reality seemed to be much more interesting.

As they waited for Nate to return, Grey gave out assignments. They decided that Lil Jay would be an African prince who was also a warrior. She put Kadijah and Mia on the jewels in shades of red, gold, blue, purple, and silver that had to be glued while she and Sheridan cut out the breastplate and tried to figure out how to make a scepter out of the black poster boards and a round silver and gold ornament.

She put the men on the crown because she figured even with three of them it would take them longer to do that one thing. Everybody was busy with their parts. They gave Madison all the other color jewels and the scrap paper, and she made little sparkly pieces of nothing while Lil Jay was shoved back and forth between the two groups to be measured and fussed over. He just thought all the adults in his life were nuts because all he wanted to do was go play in his room.

Nate finally got back and Mia asked, "What took you so long to get one pregnancy test?"

"Oh, I just thought I would take my time to increase the suspense and aggravation."

She snatched the bag from him as she rolled her eyes. She had been drinking water nonstop so she would be able to go as soon as he came back. Her bladder was about to explode. She went to take the test.

Grey said, "Okay, Nate, please help them nuts with the crown because all they have managed to do is staple two pieces of nothing together."

Mia came back and everybody stared at her. "What? We gotta wait ten minutes."

Everyone went back to work and got so caught up in their projects that they forgot about the test. They didn't realize how much fun they would have trying to make a child's costume or how challenging glue, poster board, and cloth could be to put together. With all of the education that was in the room, one child's costume had them feeling a little inadequate. The men could be heard discussing what a crown should look like and how could they get it to look like a real crown because they had no satin like material to put under it. Grey yelled out to them, "Use cotton balls."

All of them were mad they didn't think of it first. Jeremiah had an idea so he sent Lil Jay to get one of his baseball caps and cotton balls. When he came back he said, "Daddy will buy you another one, okay."

He just shrugged like he could care less. Jeremiah cut the bill off, and they glued the hat part to the inside of the poster board crown which was a cylinder with a point at the top. Then, they glued cotton balls around the rim of the inside and outside to complete the look and make it comfortable to sit atop Lil Jay's head. Seth and Nate worked on the layout of the jewels that would adorn the crown. The women were busy trying to figure out how to make the ornamental ball stay atop the rolled piece of poster board for the scepter.

Nate yelled out, "Use some yarn, pull it through the ornament, run it down the inside of the rolled paper, and pull it through the bottom to be taped or stapled to the outside."

There was a collective, "Oooh."

Kadijah and Mia were just about done with the jewels on the breastplate while Sheridan and Grey were putting the ivory table runners turned robe on Lil Jay for its final measure. They were all having fun and laughing and picking at each other's creations as they added on the finishing touches.

They were interrupted by a series of beeps and ringing and sounds that signaled all their cell phones had a text message. Grey was the first to reach hers and said, "It's a text from Pastor Josiah. He says Brother Williams has been diagnosed with cancer and for us to start praying. It also says that he wants us to fast tomorrow because Brother Williams is having surgery to remove the cancerous mass."

By now everyone had looked at their phones and was reading along with her. She said, "Well, Seth, there goes our lunch plans."

He said, "I know, right."

Mia looked at both of them, "Well, y'all n-words didn't have to invite me to lunch since we all work on the same side of town."

Seth raised his brow, "Uh, anyways, we do invite you, and you always forget and leave us hanging so we just don't invite you anymore."

She laughed because he was so right. Sheridan said, "Well, I guess I'll have barbecue for dinner and not lunch. They all laughed and knew they would all fast from something the next day to do their part to protect one of their own.

Jeremiah said, "Alright, y'all, let's pray. They all got up and stood in a circle and held hands, even the kids, and then Jeremiah began to call on the name of Jesus. All hearts and minds were in agreement, and there wasn't a single doubt among the believers that it would be done. When they were done, Seth hopped in the recliner before Nathanial could realize he had just lost his bid for the infamous chair. Everybody laughed. Even Nate had to laugh because he got caught slipping.

Lil Jay said, "Mommy, I thought you were taking a test? Did you pass?"

Everybody burst out laughing again and Mia said, "Oh, my God, I completely forgot about it." She went to check while everybody stopped to wait for her return.

When she came back she said, "No, baby, mommy failed this test."

Jeremiah dramatically fell out on the floor and faux cried while everyone except for Mia laughed. Madison and Lil Jay looked at each other for understanding, but none was reciprocated. Lil Jay asked her, "You wanna go play?"

She said, "Okay," as they headed back to Lil Jay's room.

Chapter 30:
An Answered Prayer

It was late Sunday evening; Valter, Nero, Ahiga, Orion, Roman, Lance, Darrow, Cree, and Tallis were assembled in the meager room that had become their meeting headquarters. They were waiting on the answer for the prayers countless saints had sent up for Seth's issue to be resolved. Having the wisdom of one who had commanded for millenniums, Valter knew that this message would set so many free that whoever was sent with it had to be enduring great resistance.

They knew the time was drawing near and so any of their small contingent that was not on specific assignment was there waiting to receive their fellow angel. Ahiga, who had been pulled from his post at the church asked, "Captain, do you think we will finally get word tonight?"

Valter responded, "I hope so because this scandal has caused members to be displaced and walk away from their spiritual covering. They have no idea how much they truly will need to be covered by this shepherd in the days ahead."

Nero in his vast wisdom said, "Captain, if the answer has taken this long, surely the battle to get it here was great. Which means it is not likely the message can just be easily handed to the vessel that the Lord chooses. Our adversary will not let that be."

Valter nodded, "Your wisdom has once again steered you in the right direction. I, too, have come to the same conclusion."

Ahiga said, "Our numbers are so few, and we cannot pull others off their assignment. We will need specific prayer cover during the course of the battle."

Nero joined in, "Captain, you cannot go out during this battle. It is too early to alert the dark forces that you are here. If they find out you are here, they will know how truly important this war is."

Valter had already come to these same conclusions. He needed to make quick decisions and a strategy. He looked around at his fleet. He had two warriors, four messengers, and two ministering angels. The ministering angels did not carry weapons because their function was simply to usher in the anointing of God so they could not assist in the fight. Therefore, he needed an armed angel to accompany them.

Valter commanded, "When the message arrives, Lance, you go to Emma Lee Ellis and trouble her to pray. That will likely not be enough prayer cover, and she may get weary if this battle is long. Therefore, Darrow, I want you to go and trouble Ms. Ruth, the one that helped Kadijah. They are seasoned saints and always have a willing heart to pray. They are a part of the remnant that has been faithfully praying for this city for years." They each nodded at their assignment.

He continued, "Nero and Ahiga, you must accompany whatever messenger is sent to deliver the answer. Orion and Roman, you will also accompany them just in case the answer comes in the form of a dream and it needs to be interpreted, you will stay there to minister and provide wisdom. I want us to be prepared for all possibilities and not delay this any longer than necessary."

Just then, a messenger angel dropped through the ceiling, and he landed hard on the floor. They all turned to face the new addition. His emerald robe was tattered, and they could tell he had indeed been in a fight. He clutched his katara dagger tightly in his hand. It was a push dagger that was eighteen inches long. It had an H-shaped horizontal hand grip designed for his knuckles to be above the short, wide, triangular blade. In labored breaths, he managed, "My name is Saban, and I have been sent to give Josiah an important message. I need prayer cover immediately. The enemy knows I'm here, we don't have much time."

Valter looked at Lance and Darrow. They nodded as their wings expanded. Valter said, "Keep them praying for at least an hour in earth time. Be aware, you may encounter opposition, and I don't have a warrior to spare." They nodded their acceptance of the challenge. Valter had complete trust that they would do their part for this fight.

Nero helped Saban to his feet. "Tell us what we're up against." Saban had gashes and cuts on his arms, legs, face, and one of his wings were tattered. There was no blood, just the shimmering watery substance that came from their kind.

Saban said, "I have fought to bring this message on six of the seven continents. Every place where Seth's music has the potential to reach the reigning prince of that region sent an attack. They kept forcing me to places that had little or no prayer cover all over the world but the, Lord, God Almighty was always with me. I've been battling for months. Michael stepped in and sent warriors to fight with me, and that's why I'm here tonight."

Valter knew that the message was locked inside of Saban and no other angel could deliver it for him. They would have to wait for the prayer cover to began and move out as quickly as possible. He wished he could make the saints of God understand how important it was for them to pray without ceasing and not be distracted by life and the tricks of the enemy. Their human minds could not fathom just how powerful a child of God actually was or the authority given to them. He needed them to realize that angels were sent to help them and that the prayers of the saints were vital. Angels sat waiting for God's instructions so that they could carry out His plans in the lives of the saints. He hoped Josiah would be the kind of shepherd to instill this knowledge in his congregation. They could not afford to give their adversary any advantages.

Valter said, "I'm assuming that because of the hour, this message will be delivered to Josiah in a dream."

Saban nodded, "Yes, this will be a dream and will require an interpretation."

Valter replied, "I have already assigned ministers to aid you."

Suddenly, Saban began to feel strength return to his body. His wounds began to heal themselves and his breathing normalized. Nero said, "The prayer cover has begun. Captain, we must make haste."

With one word Valter commanded them, "Go!"

Ahiga and Nero's eyes turned into blue flames. They expanded their wings and pulled their weapons. Saban stood with renewed purpose and expanded his wings. His emerald robe had been returned to its former glory. Roman and Orion expanded their wings and glorified. Their blue sapphire light coated all those around them. Their exit was majestic, and Valter never tired of seeing God's army head into a battle. He wished he could witness it, but he knew his presence could not be made known. For the time being, he, Cree, and Tallis would remain there steadfast waiting for their fellow angels to return with good news.

†††

In another part of town, Corruption was awaiting confirmation of some angelic activity he saw on the horizon. He was pacing the small confines of the room they were in. Destroyer just watched and took his time studying every move Corruption made so that he could sense an opportunity of weakness to destroy him. A slimy imp came in his sulfurous breath preceding him. "Your Highness," Corruption turned to face the imp. "We have confirmation that two messengers were dispatched to those two prayer warriors that gave them the prayer cover to stop the first attacks."

Corruption was seething; there was nothing else to kick so he kicked the imp who had just delivered the bad news. The imp let out a yelp. He turned to face the demons that were assembled. "The answer must be here. We need to find out who the answer is going to."

The imp that had taken the kick was picking himself up as he said, "Sir, the answer is for Josiah."

"Are you certain? And how do you know this?"

"The Strongman sent word, and it was delivered to the spies that you have watching the church. There is only one guardian at the gates of the church. I was told to bring you word so that you can get into position."

Corruption began to pace, getting more upset by the minute that the Strongman sent word to a messenger and not directly to him. He got the message loud and clear that his authority was being challenged because his first attacks failed. He also realized that his enemy was definitely shorthanded, if there was only one guardian at the gate to the church. He would use it to his advantage. His right-hand man, Deception, said, "Commander, we must go at once."

Corruption nodded and pointed to a demon with green eyes and obtrusive fangs, "You go after the messenger sent to Emma Lee."

He pointed to the demon next to him that looked like black smoke with red eyes. "You go stop the one that is assigned to Ms.

Ruth. If you do not stop the prayer cover, do not bother returning because I will have your heads." With the dismissal they took flight to execute their assigned tasks.

Corruption said, "Destroyer and Deception, you're with me. Let's go."

Destroyer smiled on the inside. The first opportunity he got he would sabotage this battle. What did he care if Josiah got an answer to this prayer? He already had plenty of ways to silence Seth and his music, all he needed now was the control. They all took flight headed towards Josiah's house.

†††

Corruption, Destroyer, and Deception arrived at Josiah's house first. There was no evidence that there had been any angelic activity anywhere in the vicinity. The gray, black, and white house sat atop a hill in the quiet neighborhood. It was a two-story home with lots of windows and a perfectly manicured lawn. Corruption commanded, "Deception, you take the front entrance. Destroyer, you take the back entrance, and I will lie in wait."

The Angelic Hosts came barreling into the neighborhood ready for whatever their adversary might have for them. They dropped down out of the sky to stand in front of the house. Deception stood at the front entrance, his fangs bared, and his sword ready.

Ahiga glorified and the white light he emitted made the dark street look like daylight. The pike he pulled out, a long pole weapon that stretched out sixteen-feet and had a gleaming spear at the tip, quickly coated with a blue flame. Nero followed suit, his spatha, a long straight sword that was three-and-a-half-feet long, coated with the same blue flame. Saban stood behind them, his wings expanded, and his katara gripped tightly in his hand.

Orion and Roman glorified emitting a gorgeous blue sapphire light that complimented the white light of the warriors. Deception began to salivate at the opportunity to send one of God's elect into retreat. Saban decided to force their hand, he flew towards the house and as he'd suspected, they pounced. Deception was heading straight for Saban, but Ahiga was lightning fast. He got between them and thrust his pike at Deception's weapon arm. Deception avoided the strike and was temporarily thrown off balance.

††††

Miles away, Lance had done his part and Emma Lee was now pacing the confines of her room in earnest prayer. He was working to guide her prayer when he felt the demonic force surround the house. He quickly burdened her heart so she would continue to pray as he did what needed to be done. He knew her prayers had to have already healed Saban. The demon arrived and stood across the room. His green eyes met Lance's gold ones. They ran toward each other clashing in mid-air as they began to fight.

†††

Across town, Darrow was met with opposition as well. It took him a little longer to stir Ms. Ruth out of her bed when he was interrupted by a snarling red-eyed demon. The demon did not wait but immediately attacked. Oblivious to what was going on, Ms. Ruth began to stir in her bed. Darrow kept fighting but yelled, "Pray! Now!"

The demon took a swipe at his face, but Darrow blocked it. Ms. Ruth felt the burden on her heart to pray though she wasn't quite sure what she was praying for. She just called out, "Jesus."

At the sound of that name, the demon began to scream and cover his ears. Darrow didn't hesitate, he plunged his cinquedea, a fifteen-inch dagger, into the demons neck. When he ripped the knife out, all that was left was black smoke, and then nothing. He went and knelt by Ruth's bed and began to guide her prayer.

†††

Corruption decided it was time to join the fight. With Ahiga's back turned to him, he ran toward Ahiga with his sword above his head ready to come down. As he began to strike, Nero's sword met his with a deafening clang. Shocked, Corruption took a swipe at Nero with his sharp talons and caught him in the arm. Nero grunted, and the wound closed right back up. He knew now that they had the prayer cover needed. With renewed strength, he spun in a circle bringing his spatha down hard, severing Corruption's arm. He howled.

Cats and dogs all over the neighborhood began to make their presence known as they could sense something amiss in their community. A few people were awakened by the incessant barking and loud screeches, but when they came to their doors and windows to check it out, they found all was well in their neighborhood.

Ahiga yelled to Saban, "Go!"

Roman and Orion immediately flanked Saban as he flew towards the house. They were almost to the door when Corruption avoided another swipe and yelled, "Destroyer!"

Destroyer flew towards the front of the house, but instead of blocking Saban's entrance, he kept flying toward the other side of the street. He stared hard at Corruption and said, "I'll be sure to let the Strongman know you couldn't handle the assignment."

Temporarily caught off guard by the betrayal, Corruption gave Nero the opportunity he had been waiting for. In one strong swing, Nero beheaded Corruption. His body dropped heavily to the ground. It burst into black ashes as did his head that was a few feet from Nero's feet. Moments later, there was nothing left of the fallen demon.

†††

Lance knew his fellow angels were depending on him so he had to end this now and guide Emma Lee's prayers. He kicked the demon hard in the chest to get him to back off and give him enough room to deliver the final blow. Lance slashed his anelace, a long dagger about eighteen-inches, across the demons face while he was trying to gain his footing. The demon howled but avoided the death blow Lance tried to deliver. Lance was shocked to see the demon run in retreat. The demon hissed, "This isn't over," as he flew back out of the house. Lance quickly got back to his assignment and continued to guide Emma Lee's prayers.

†††

Deception continued to be a worthy adversary for Ahiga. His rage at the betrayal he had just witnessed renewed his determination. He took a strong swipe at Ahiga, but he only caught his shoulder. Ahiga grinned. He loved to fight and welcomed the temporary pain. Ahiga decided to take the battle to sky. As his shoulder began to heal, he drew his opponent away from the house while Saban, Orion, and Roman headed into the house.

Deception was completely focused on his opponent as he chased Ahiga all over the neighborhood. Ahiga was enjoying toying with him but enough was enough. He hovered in the air and allowed Deception to come straight for him. Sword first, Deception was aiming for Ahiga's chest. Ahiga waited and just before the sword connected with his body, he dropped down so fast and came up behind Deception. Before Deception knew what happened, his head was separated from his body, and his ashes rained down all over Josiah's yard, and then evaporated. Ahiga grinned.

†††

Inside the house, Saban was standing over Josiah and Darcy as they were peacefully sleeping and blissfully unaware of what had just taken place right outside their home. He laid his hand on Josiah's head and glorified, casting an emerald light all around them. Josiah began to stir and the dream was transferred to him, but he never woke. Roman said, "This one is a praying man, and when he wakes up, I'm certain the first thing he will do is pray for an interpretation."

Orion agreed, "We will stay here and minister to him as God reveals what is necessary."

Roman looked at Saban, "I know you have traveled a great distance, but will you stay to join our forces and see this through?"

Saban smiled, "I am here to lend a hand and join the fight."

Roman replied, "Good because we are going to need it."

Chapter 31:
Stranger Than Fiction

Sheridan

I was exhausted. The past week had been a restless one. Seth was going through hell because he was not ready to deal with his mother and clearly, the Holy Spirit was telling him it was time. I don't know why he was being so hardheaded, but he said he didn't want to add more mess on to our already crowded plates. While I completely understood that, I thought we both had learned our lessons about not moving when God was pushing us to. I promised him that I would not meddle in his and his mother's affairs anymore so my hands were tied. All I could do was be there to hold him and to encourage him when he needed it. I had just been praying that God would work this out despite Seth being so stubborn.

Naomi was just about six months pregnant. Seth had not been over the music ministry in almost three months, and those people at my job were driving me crazy. On top of all that, I got a call from Pastor Josiah today and he wanted me, Seth, and Naomi to meet him at his office today at five. I had to rearrange some sessions, and my patients were none too thrilled, but it was the tone in his voice that said it was urgent, and we needed to make it happen. I really prayed that a resolution was about to happen because Seth was so hurt about losing his position in the ministry. Knowing that it was temporary did not comfort him in the least. I didn't think I was in the mood for another disappointment. I'm sure I could handle it, but I just simply did not want to.

"Lord, make it alright, just please make it alright."

I pulled into the parking lot and saw that Seth was already there, but I didn't see Naomi's car. I parked and got out. To my surprise, Seth got out of his truck. I hadn't noticed he was still inside. "Hey, baby."

I walked over and gave him a hug. He kissed my forehead, "Hey, baby girl. How was your day?"

I inhaled his sexy scent and said, "Ugh, don't ask."

He laughed, "That good, huh?"

"Yes, indeed. It was so lovely I wanted to pull my hair out strand by strand. Was yours as lovely as mine?"

"Why, yes, it was dear. I ran over a little kitten for sport and took the tennis balls off Ms. Luella's walker. You know our elderly neighbor down the street."

I laughed hard and playfully hit his arm, "Baby, you so dumb!"

He laughed, "Nah, my day was cool. Come on, let's go see what this is about so I can get you home, and you can vent about your rough day. If it was really bad, maybe you might get a foot massage."

I smiled, "Well, in that case, let me start thinking of believable extras I can throw in to make sure I earn it." He chuckled and grabbed my hand as we walked into the administration wing of the church and knocked on P.J.'s door.

As we waited, Seth looked into my eyes and kissed my hand, his way of telling me not to worry about what was about to happen. God, I loved this man. Pastor Josiah opened the door and said in his deep voice, "Come on in. Sorry, my wife couldn't make it on such short notice."

We traded pleasantries as we walked in. I was shocked to see Naomi already sitting on one of the sofa's in his office. I looked at my watch, and it was just now five. That girl was never on time. She looked a mess like she hadn't slept in weeks. She had shadows under her eyes, and they looked puffy from crying. Poor thang, I hoped she'd find peace real soon.

P.J.'s office was very masculine and unpretentious. It was filled with comfy leather furniture in shades of deep earth tones. We took a seat on the sofa across from the one Naomi was on, and P.J. took a seat in the leather chair between the two. The area with his desk was behind us separated by closed double doors.

P.J. steeped his hands together and said, "I've asked you all here because I had a dream last night, and I had it three times. I prayed about it all day. I believe that God was trying to show me something about this situation."

Oh, this had me on the edge of my seat now. I asked, "What was the dream?"

He cleared his throat, "I was the referee at a street basketball game, and it was shirts against skins. There were six players, three on each team, but Seth, you were on both teams. You in the shirt looked just like you do now, but you on the skins were a little different. Your hair was shorter, and you had a tattoo on your chest. I couldn't make out what the tattoo was, but it was clear there was a tattoo on your chest."

He placed his hand over his chest to show where the tattoo was. Naomi had a gleam in her eye and jumped right in, "Oh, I can tell you exactly what that tattoo says and you two," she pointed at me and Seth, "can finally apologize to me. I can't believe I didn't think of this before."

We looked at each other and then looked at her as she continued, "It's a tattoo of two clown masks, one is crying and one is laughing, and written under it is, laugh now, cry later. How else would I know that seeing as how I would have no other opportunity to see him with his shirt off?"

She looked at me with so much smugness, I couldn't wait to slap that smirk right off her face, but before I could, Seth jumped in and pissed me off 'cause I wanted to be the one to crush her world. I rolled my eyes.

He said, "But, Naomi, I don't have a tattoo on my chest. As a matter of fact, I don't have a tattoo at all."

The look on that heifa's face was priceless. I started to pull out my phone to snap it so it could go into my archives of moments to remember because I was so sick of her trying me. Vindication was so sweet! She stood up with so much force I thought she would tip over. She screamed, "You're lying. Do not sit here and lie like that. You are caught red-handed. It's over!"

I finally put in my two cents, "You're right, Naomi, it is over, and my husband does not have a tattoo."

She snapped back, "Well, I don't believe you, show me!"

Okay, that's it. I stood up "Oh, no, honey, he is not showing you a dern thing. I said he has no tattoo, and that's a done deal."

Pastor Josiah's voice boomed and said, "Okay, everybody, let's just calm down. Naomi, please sit down before you make yourself go into premature labor. Sheridan, you sit down, too."

He gave Seth a look like, please, get your wife. I relaxed a bit, sat down, smoothed my skirt, and crossed my legs. When I looked at Seth, he had the most puzzled look on his face. I realized this situation just got even more confusing than it already was. I said, "Okay, what does all this mean?"

"That's what I would like to know," Naomi interrupted, "and don't think I'm going to sit here and just believe that Seth doesn't have a tattoo on his chest just because you say."

Before I could get a word in P.J. spoke up, "Naomi, I have actually seen Seth play ball before and as a skin. He doesn't have a tattoo, sweetie, I'm sorry."

All the color drained from her cheeks, and she fell back into the cushions of the leather sofa. Her voice was very low, "But I don't understand. I was with him. Tameka saw us together. You even said he was there that weekend, so I don't understand."

Then, it looked as though a light bulb clicked on above her head, her face lit up, but not in a good way. She raked her hands through her hair violently and in a low voice said, "That's why he never said my name, that's why the car was different, and that's why he didn't have a tan line where his ring should have been. I didn't notice any of it before. I mean, who else would it be?"

It looked to me like she just figured out that hindsight was 20/20.

"Oh, my God!" she screamed, "Who was it?"

Seth and I both looked at her like her guess was as good as ours, and then I heard Seth whisper, "Oh, my God."

He stood up abruptly and started pacing the floor. "There can't be another man out there that looks like me unless..."

I cut him off, "Unless it's your brother."

Pastor Josiah stood up, "Unless it's your twin brother?"

I gasped.

The look on Pastor Josiah's face told me he knew that from the dream. He just wanted all of us to come to the same conclusion on our own. Naomi let out a wail that could make a corpse sit up and speak. In that moment, I was shocked at how much pity I felt for her, and then it hit me, the conviction to go and comfort her. I all but threw a silent temper tantrum in my mind that could rival any five-year old brat determined to get their way until the conviction got stronger. I went to her and held her as she cried her poor little heart out.

Her pain hit me like it was my own. It took all my strength not to cry with her. As I stroked her hair, I told her everything was going to be okay. My goodness, when I woke up this morning, you couldn't have told me that at this time, I would be holding Naomi in my arms and comforting her because she finally figured out that my husband was not the father of her child. God, you really do have a disturbing sense of humor. What a difference a day makes, huh? I could literally feel the Holy Spirit nudging me to let her know I had forgiven her and let this all go. After all, it was just phantom, a smoke screen, not real.

My pride wanted to fight it, but what was the point? I had already forgiven her and laid this at Jesus' feet. Now, it was time for me to walk in it. Maybe she needed to hear it to free her so I surrendered and whispered in her ear, "I'm sorry, Naomi, for everything, and I forgive you for everything. Please, forgive me for everything so we can handle the new situation in front of us."

She all but collapsed on my lap as her sobs turned into tremors and shutters. Okay, didn't see that reaction coming. I was very confused.

"Shhh, Naomi, it's gonna be okay. Don't upset yourself. Think about the baby."

She wailed, and it scared the crap out of me. Okay, seriously, what's the real deal here? I looked up into my husband's still puzzled face, and then it hit me. The guilt of me not having faith in the man that always had faith in me. The realization of it burned my throat, and it cut through my heart like fire through unsuspecting wax. He could have had a smug look on his face because I could tell he realized the guilt in mine, but that just was not his style. He would never punish me like that.

The look on his face showed compassion and understanding. It only served to make my guilt consume me. It was so thick now I could barely breathe. All this time, I thought he betrayed me, and it turns out, I betrayed him. I didn't have his back when he needed it the most. Naomi was still crying in my lap. Seth finally took a seat, and P.J. just looked like he was taking it all in.

I just closed my eyes and let the tears come. I cried because of my lack of faith in my husband. I cried because I was walking by sight, not by faith. I knew that was a disappointment to God because I should have been more mature than that. I cried because the worst of this burden was over, and I cried because the man I married was always the man he said he was. The tears continued because through it all God was good. His grace truly was sufficient. Now comes the after math, the clean up.

I managed to pull myself together. After all, I was supposed to be comforting Naomi, not falling apart. I wanted to go to my husband and beg his forgiveness and comfort him because he had to be going through it for real. Naomi continued to sob on my lap, and I continued to stroke her back and whisper words of comfort in her ear to let her know she would not be alone in this.

Wait, did I just say she wouldn't be alone in this? Wow, God, you really are working on a sister. I actually meant it because in reality, this child was related to me. Wow, this is some talk show mess for real. Not my stepson but my nephew. P.J. turned to Seth and said, "How can we know for sure that you have a twin brother out there?"

Seth cleared his throat, "By asking my birth mother, I guess."

"Do you have a way to contact her?" P.J. asked.

"Yeah, I do, actually. I have felt pressure for a week to get in contact with her, but I just wouldn't. It's funny how God had my answer hidden in the one thing I was avoiding. If I do have a twin brother, why would he pretend to be me and of all things, sleep with someone as me? If he knew enough to pretend to be me, he had to know I was married and a minister. I mean, does he hate me or something?"

I was silent because I couldn't speak over the guilt lodged in my throat, and my heart was breaking for my baby.

P.J. said, "There's only one way to find out, son, contact your mom."

Seth pulled out his wallet, and then he pulled out a piece of paper. As he unfolded it, I recognized it as the part of the letter his mom sent with her contact information. It said something to me that he carried that around in his wallet. There was a longing in his heart to know his family. It looked like he was about to get to know them whether he was ready or not. Naomi was still crying, but silently now. I stroked her back as I contemplated how in the heck I was going to make this up to my husband.

Seth was staring at the paper when he asked, "Why didn't she tell me I had a brother even after everything else she told me? She felt this wasn't what I needed to know? Did she know that my brother was here impersonating me and ruining my life?"

I had to clear my throat a few times before I could speak, "Baby, she said there were some things she held back in order to get you to see her face-to-face."

He snapped, "Well, that shouldn't have been the thing to selfishly keep to herself, especially since he apparently has my exact face!"

Oh, my, he was heated for real. It was such a rare thing to see Seth angry and not in control of his emotions, but I guess still waters really do run deep. "Well, baby, there is no point in us speculating. Just call so we can deal with this once and for all."

With his face contorted in deep frustration, he pulled out his cell phone, dialed the number, and put the phone on speaker. Naomi had given up her tears and was now staring at Seth's phone as her body jerked sporadically from the aftermath of crying. I guess she needed answers just as much as Seth did seeing as how the mystery man of the hour was her child's father.

Someone picked up after the third ring, and a woman's voice floated into the room, "Hello."

Seth cleared his throat, "Yes, hello, may I speak to Monet Grayson."

"This is she. May I ask whose calling?"

"This is Seth." Pregnant pause.

"Well, hello, Seth. I had given up on ever hearing from you. It's been months since I mailed the..."

He cut her off, "Yeah, I don't mean to be rude, but this call isn't exactly social. I just need you to clear something up for me."

She let out an audible gasp. I didn't think she was a woman that could be caught off guard. "Uh, sure. If I can, I would be happy to."

"Do I have a twin brother that you so conveniently forgot to mention to me?"

She stammered, "Uh, well. Oh, uh, how did you, where did you, uh, hear that?"

He raised his voice, "It is a simple yes or no question, Ms. Grayson."

She cleared her throat, "Yes, uh, yes, actually there's a twin, but might I ask how you came to know that information?"

The scowl on his face was a bit scary, "I know because he impersonated me, got a woman at my church pregnant, and caused a mess for me, and my family, and our church. That's how I came to know that," he said barely holding onto restraint.

Her voice sprang out finally with the fierceness I imagined it would have. She was back in control, "He did what? Wait, when did this happen?"

Seth said, "Apparently, Martin Luther King Jr. Day Weekend."

She said, "That's impossible because I know exactly where my..." She paused like something just occurred to her. Her voice came out in shock, "Oh, my God," then in anger, "Oh, my God! Seth, I have to go. I'm sorry, but I have to go now. I will contact you soon." Click.

Seth hung up the phone and dialed her back, but it went straight to her voicemail. He repeated that three more times with the same result. I could tell he was pissed, but what was there to say? We had one puzzle figured out and another one just revealed itself. This one would be a little tougher seeing as how we didn't exactly know where the pieces existed. I didn't think she had any left, but Naomi began to sob again and Pastor Josiah sat back in his chair and said, "Well, ain't this stranger than fiction."

Chapter 32:
These Are My Confessions

Naomi

Tameka had picked me up when I called her from Pastor Josiah's office. I was lying down in her bed facing her and dreading all the stuff I needed to finally get off my chest. The events that had recently taken place in my life had left me numb and speechless. How did it get this far? On top of everything else, God was kicking my behind. For the last two days, I had been having random crying fits, but no matter how bad I felt, I knew I had to tell the truth, the whole truth and soon.

Suddenly, the veil had been lifted from my eyes, and I could see all that I was and all that I wasn't. It did not make a pretty picture. I was so grateful for Tameka letting me stay with her for a few days. I was thankful that she was allowing me to unburden my heart. Simple me. This lie had a time limit and either I told it now or it would be revealed in a matter of time.

The guilt and conviction was crawling up my spine and choking me with a vengeance. I had to tell her, but I knew if I told her she might decide that she didn't want to be my friend anymore. At this point in my life, I was already thousands of feet past rock bottom, and my heart couldn't take rejection from the only real friend I ever had.

I took a deep breath. "Tameka," I said, "You have been an unbelievably true friend. For the mess I brought you into and the embarrassment you had to have faced by remaining by my side. I am so sorry for everything I put you through, and I am so ashamed."

She rubbed my arm and said, "It's, okay, Nay. It's okay."

I closed my eyes and sighed, "Tam, before you go there and say, it's okay, I have one more thing to confess to you."

She backed off from me just a little bit, and my heart began to ache. I felt like I would throw up. My stomach felt like it had been knotted up by Boy Scouts overdosed on Red Bull. I closed my eyes and said, "Tameka, I'm not pregnant."

She blinked rapidly and stuttered, Wh...wh...what?"

She looked at my protruding stomach, and her eyes bugged out. I could only imagine what she was thinking. Well, the dam had a crack in it. I may as well let the flood out. I sat up, pulled up my shirt, and began to remove the prosthetic belly. Tameka screamed and fell off the bed. Oddly enough I wanted to laugh, and I probably should because I would probably be crying for the rest of my life after this hit the fan.

She got up on her knees and said, "Naomi, what the hell is going on? How could you have faked your pregnancy? What about the paternity test? How did you get the doctor to lie?"

I cut her off, "I didn't lie about being pregnant. I lied about still being pregnant."

Her face wrinkled up in confusion and she asked, "Naomi, what in the world are you talking about? You sound like a crazy person. I'm starting to think you may be bipolar or something because..."

Her voice trailed off and the wheels of her brain started turning. She gasped, "Oh, my God. Nay, when did you lose the baby?"

I finished pulling off this faux baby incubator and said, "I lost the baby about four weeks after we found out the paternity."

Her eyes began to tear up, "Why didn't you say something?"

I shrugged, "I don't know. I mean, it just happened. I started feeling pressure and cramping, and I had been spotting for a couple of days. I was standing in my shower, and I felt something leave my body."

My eyes began to water up remembering that moment. "I screamed bloody murder, of course. When I turned off the shower, and stared at it, I knew I was looking at my unborn child. I saw it, and I can't explain to you what I saw or what it felt like to see the baby like that. I just sat there stunned and scared. It was so small and bloody. It was about the size of a dollar bill, and I could make out all of its little features. I mean eyes, nose, mouth, hands, and feet. I sat there, and I cried because I didn't know what to do. After a while, I cleaned up and drove myself to the emergency room."

I looked at Tameka, and she had lost all her color on her caramel face. Barely audible, she asked in a way that told me she was creeped out, "What did you do with the baby."

I shook my head because this was the part that still haunted me. I put the baby in a towel, put it in a plastic container, and took it with me to the emergency room. I gave it to the nurse." She went even paler.

I said, "Yeah, and I have been skiddish around all plastic Tupperware like products since. I spent the rest of that night and most of the morning in the hospital having the tissue removed and making sure there were no more complications. As I sat there recovering, I never cried again or anything. The one thing I did know, was that my chance of getting Seth to leave his wife was now gone. To be honest, I hate myself right now because how selfish is that? That's all I could think about, and that's when I made the decision to carry on with the pregnancy. I figured once he was mine, our bond would be stronger once I pretended to lose the baby."

Tameka sat back on the bed with her mouth gaped open and stared at me like I was the most horrible person she had ever had the displeasure of knowing. I said, "Wait, there's more. My child has been haunting me ever since I started lying about it."

Tameka said, "That's why you have looked so exhausted for months now. Do you think the DNA test caused you to lose the baby?"

I shook my head, "No, I was perfectly fine after that procedure and besides, nothing would have stopped me from getting that test. Yes, that's exactly why I've been so tired. I always see the baby like it was in the shower and even though the lips don't move, I can hear him saying, tell the truth mommy so I can go home."

The tears began to fall and I said, "Tameka, I don't want to be this horrible person I have become. I promise I don't. I want to stop being haunted by my dead child, but it was like this obsession I had. I mean, it went from being a slight crush to this avalanche of feelings ever since Pastor Percy told me he was mine. I know that I was stupid to believe it, still, somehow I did."

She started to cry. The look in her eyes had not been a good one. I continued, "I hate myself, and I know God took my baby because I didn't deserve it. I'm haunted by the guilt of wanting to abort the baby, and then I ended up having one anyways. My baby is dead because I am selfish. Then, I found out Seth wasn't even the father. I just lost it. Not only was all chance of getting him gone, I had been faking a pregnancy from a man I didn't even know, and the one who suffered was my innocent child."

She handed me tissues off the nightstand, "Naomi, how could you possibly think this was all going to work? Did it ever occur to you that God would never have part in a situation that was so full of lies and manipulation?"

I whined, "How can you say that to me? How dare you judge me? Did you not just hear me tell you I've been suffering all this time?"

I saw the fury in her brown eyes, "You know what, you selfish heifa, I am so sick of all the games you play. How dare you sit here and try to play the victim when you brought all this on yourself? Don't you even try to turn this mess around on me. Now I am so sorry you lost the baby. I didn't for one second wish death on this child, even though I didn't agree with how it came to be, but I have been nothing but a good friend to you despite the fact that you don't deserve it. So, back off before you lose the only friend you have."

I swallowed hard. She was right. I couldn't believe that even in my confession, I was still trying to lie, manipulate, and take the offense off me. I got off the bed and walked off. I turned to face her and said, "I have caused so much drama in the lives of innocent people. Now, they're looking for Seth's twin in order to tell him he's going to be a father only for me to tell him that he's not? I'm sure that will thrill him, but it's going to make me look like one very evil person to a complete stranger."

She walked over to me, "Nay, God is sovereign, and He knows best so we just have to trust that He is in control even in all of this chaos. I think you should come clean about everything. You need to tell the whole truth including the part Pastor Percy played in this because I never liked that man. Pastor Josiah needs to know what his friend has been up to." I shuddered at the thought of my truth coming out.

"Tameka, I'm scared. I'm scared of what I've done. I'm scared of whom I've become, and I'm scared that I am never going to be any better than I am now."

"Naomi, don't think like that. God will forgive you no matter what you've done. You just need to make it right with all the people that you have done wrong, and then pray that God heals and restores all the lives involved."

I shook my head, "No, listen, it's hard enough for me to admit this to you, but the truth is, I only wanted this baby to solidify a relationship with Seth. When I first found out I was pregnant, I got scared and wanted to abort it. I just couldn't resist getting under Sheridan's skin. Now God is punishing me. I am so getting the hell out of Dodge as soon as I can."

Tameka said, "Running is not the answer. Your demons are going to follow you. You need to come clean with the people that you hurt, and then you need to focus on getting your life right with God. Stop blaming God for your misfortune. You probably lost the baby because of the all the stress of keeping up with all your lies and deception."

My life is so jacked up. I have no one to blame but myself. I wish I could blame Pastor Percy, but he just planted the seed. I watered it and let it grow.

Tameka asked as if she was reading my mind, "Did you ever tell anyone else about Pastor Percy?" I shook my head.

"Well, maybe you should because I have been thinking there has to be a reason why he did what he did. I think he was up to no good."

I sighed, "Girl, that doesn't even matter now. You know, when Grey went off on me, her words were kinda brutal, but they made sense. It hurt to know someone else thought of me like that."

She nodded in agreement, "I think so, too. That look in her eye was just a tad on the scary side."

We laughed. "You know what surprised me most of all," I began. "Sheridan."

Tameka asked, "Why?"

"Because here is a woman I had done unspeakable things to. I mean, I insulted her in every way possible, but when it all fell apart, she was the one holding me and comforting me. On top of that, she said she forgave me and told me that I wouldn't be alone in this."

Tameka squeezed my hand, "Well, now see that doesn't shock me because that's the kinda person I always perceived her to be.

What did shock me about her is how hood she got when you tried her. Forgiveness is a powerful thing, Naomi. You could tell she had been spending time with God. I mean, she had to be to stay sane in her marriage. If you think about it, even though it would not have been her stepchild, this child would still have been related to her. That probably helped her to reconcile the situation."

I hadn't thought of that. I guess she was right. The baby would've been her niece or her nephew. We were silent for a little while, and then I said, "Well, Sheridan said they would contact me when they got all the details. We would all sit down and see what was what and where to go from here. The real scary part is will God ever forgive me for this?"

"Naomi, how could you ask that? Of course, He will. If you already asked for it, then He already has."

"Why would He? My actions could have destroyed a whole church. I mean, didn't some people leave because of it?"

She said, "Yeah, some people did. Now you have to leave it all in God's hands, Naomi. You have to let this go and start living your life as right as you possibly can. Like Grey said, you need to give up your will and accept His because in the end, you will see it's better for you."

She was right. It was time to start practicing what I heard preached to me every week. I asked, "How do I start?"

She sat up and said, "Let's get on our knees and approach the throne of God.

"First, you talk to God about everything you're feeling. Ask for forgiveness. Then, I'll say a prayer, too. Let me take you to dinner and a funny movie because you could use a laugh."

I smiled and said, "Okay."

I was so nervous about this prayer. I felt Tameka grab my hand so I began, "Uh, dear, uh, Jesus, I'm so sorry for all the trouble I caused. I finally see how I was wrong. I'm kinda at a loss for direction in my life. I know you have other crises to work on, but I'm kinda having a personal one now. Even though I caused it, I need you to do whatever you see fit to fix it or to make it work out for my good like it says in the Bible."

I cleared my throat, "Please, forgive me and come back into my heart. I don't want to be this person. I don't want the hurt that I had all my life to hold me down for the rest of my life. I wanna let go of all my mama issues, all my daddy issues, all my auntie issues, and all my abandonment issues. I don't want those issues to hold me back anymore. Please, fix the mess I made. In your name..."

Tameka began, "Father, you see us down here at a crossroads, and you know every person and every heart that was affected. Lord, I ask right now that you begin to heal and mend. Restore every life back to its rightful place in your perfect will. Lord, strengthen our church and our members. Let something good come from all this. Give us the strength to face all the consequences. We love you, we thank you, and we praise you in Jesus name. Amen."

"Amen."

Chapter 33:
Face Off

Monet Grayson

I had just hung up with my son on a phone call I had been praying to receive, but this was not at all how I saw this moment turning out. What in the hell was going on? How could they possibly know about each other when I never told either one? *Ugh, Monet, how did you not see this happening?* Well, somebody was about to give me answers because Monet Grayson was not to be trifled with. I was hot! Son of a, Lord, forgive me. I am not that person anymore. I had to call Cassia. Maybe she could tell me how my intel leaked.

She picked up on the second ring, "Hey, Monie. What's up? I thought we were meeting in like an hour for lunch. Are you calling to change our plans because I actually don't feel like going anywhere at the moment? The velvet dragon is breathing fire and these cramps are kickin' my well-tanned behind. I just feel so ick right now. So, can we do this another day or better yet, can you bring me Blue Bell Ice Cream. It will make me feel better? Ooh..."

I cut her off, "Cassia, chill out. We got bigger problems than your monthly stalker. I just got a call from Seth."

She squealed, "Oh, my God, that's amazing. Is he going to meet you? When are we leaving? Oh, wow, this is so exciting. Wait, I have to pick out an 'I'm gonna be such a great auntie outfit.' How much time do I have? What color do you think it should be? A power color. Yes, definitely a power color that says I am in control, but I am going to spoil you rotten. I'm thinking red. What do you think?"

This woman was going to drive me insane, "Cassia! He's almost thirty. You can't spoil him now, and stop cutting me off. We are not meeting with him because apparently, his brother decided to beat us to the punch. He impersonated Seth and got some lil tramp knocked up. I'm pretty sure Seth believes I knew about it, and he hates me because he believes that I have caused his once pristine reputation some hard knocks."

I literally heard the wind blow out of her sails as she stammered, "How, but I don't, but wait, when did. Ok, look this doesn't make any sense."

I knew my friend too well, and she knew something. "Cassia spit it out right now—every minute detail."

"Monie, it's not what you think."

I could feel my blood pressure rise, "Oh, it is exactly what I think. How could you let this information out without informing me of your intentions? You know, this is the kind of delicate situation that has to be handled in a way that is well thought out and very well planned."

"Oh, please, Monie, don't give me that crap. I am so sick of secrets and hiding. Giving only the information you want others to have. This cloak and dagger bull is overrated and tiring. I am the aunt. Did you really want me to say no when I was asked point blank?"

I tisked, "How did the information get out in the first place for you to be asked point blank, Cassia?"

She raised her voice, "I don't know, Monet, but I wasn't going to lie."

I loved this woman with all my heart, but I also disliked her six out of seven days a week. She was always the pushover. That always infringed on my balls of steel, "How could you not tell me this information was out?"

"I was asked not to."

I was not going to explode. *Nope, Monet, you just calm your little self down because you love these people too much to kill them.* "Cassia, I am on my way to pick you up, cramps be damned!"

I hung up in her face, threw on some baggy jeans, an Obama t-shirt, and some sneaks. I threw a baseball cap on backwards over my jet black, angled bob cut. I applied some tinted gloss that complimented my caramel complexion and some mascara to accentuate my big brown eyes. Just because I was mad didn't mean I had to go out the door looking all plain and uneventful. I was Monet Grayson. I did not want to disappoint my public. I grabbed my keys, purse, and headed out the door.

I made it to Cassia's place in record time. She knew me so well that when my silver Navigator pulled up in her driveway, she was locking her front door and heading towards the truck. I didn't even have to come to a complete stop. She hopped in wearing a black velour suit and a baseball cap to match. Her tanned complexion made her green eyes stand out. The auburn hair was really fly on her, even though it wasn't her natural shade of brunette. She rocked it very well.

I put the car in park, "Cassia, talk!"

She rolled her eyes, "Monie, where are we going?"

"You know exactly where we are going. Now, spill."

I backed out and headed towards my destination. I heard her call me a heifa under her breath. That was cool 'cause I was about to be worthy of being called a lot worse.

She began talking. She used her hands to express every word as usual. "I was caught off guard. The questions just came out like rounds in a semi-automatic. With all the emotions and shock, I just caved. I said, yes, you have a brother, but that's it, I didn't give any details. I don't understand about all the manipulation and some girl being pregnant. It was just supposed to be a confirmation. I don't know how it was originally found out. The agreement was to wait until he made contact with you. We would all be one big happy family. I never heard anything else about it."

I was trying to focus on the traffic instead of my temper because someone was about to give me some answers. I said, "Well, how long ago did this little pow wow take place?"

She muttered, "Eight months ago."

I screamed, "Eight months? How could you keep this from me?"

She got sassy, "Oh, the Mighty Monet, wasn't able to see all and be all to everyone around her. What's the big deal? It's the same thing you were doing, so why should I deny his own blood from the information?"

"You know what, Cassia, don't even go there. The life we lived required me to be able to see all and to control the information that people received."

She was starting to get under my skin. It didn't matter 'cause I was about to take my frustrations out on one of my offspring."

I pulled up to the house and shot daggers at Cassia, "You know I should beat your behind for not letting me know this was in play."

She rolled her eyes, "Monie, please, don't go there. If you wanna settle this with hands, I'm down, but you know as well as I do, my bite is much bigger than my bark so we can deal with this like adults, or we can deal with this the way it comes natural."

I wanted to scream because we knew each other too well for threats to work. I still had a chance to hit somebody though, my son. Cassia and I would argue for days, but we would never raise a hand to the other though we have raised many hands to many others on many occasions. It did make me wonder, though, if we ever fought who would actually win, but that was irrelevant today.

I opened my door, "Let's go."

We got out and walked up the landscaped walkway to a two-story brick townhouse. I knew someone was home because the porch light wasn't on. I rang the bell. Then, I knocked mercilessly. I heard a man's voice, "Yo chill."

The door swung open. I looked into a face that looked just like Seth's. The look on my face must've told him I was about to put my foot in his behind because he backed up with his palms out and up, surprise was on his face as he said, "Ma, Auntie, what y'all doing here?"

I walked in and got in his face, "No, I'm asking the questions. So, where were you Martin Luther King, Jr. Weekend?"

He blinked twice, "Ma, I was in Miami, just like y'all was."

I smirked because so far he was right. We were there checking up on some graduates of the program. He was there just for fun. He really thought that, I, of all people, couldn't figure this out. It was absolutely insulting. "Yeah, you were. Where was your brother?"

He hesitated just for a moment. I saw the lie flash across his eyes. "He was there with us, don't you remember?"

This Negro just lied in my face. I punched him square in his chest like I could care less that my five-five frame couldn't match his six-two build. The look on my face dared him to react naturally. Cassia ran in between us, "Monie, stop, this isn't necessary."

"Stay the hell out of this, Cassia. This is my child."

"The hell I will. He's my child, too, so back off."

She bent down to check on him. He was trying to catch his breath. He better be glad all I did was knock the wind out of his lying, scheming behind. He coughed and said, "Ma, what the hell?"

Oh, so is he cussin' at me, now? Oh, no. I ran up and was about to clock him in his mouth, but Cassia jumped in between and threw my aim off. She caught most of my fury in her shoulder. She staggered, but didn't fall.

Cassia yelled, "Monie, if you don't calm the hell down, I'm gonna lay you out."

I bared my teeth, "Try it."

"I don't wanna hit you, Monie, but I will. Okay, let's just everybody calm down."

"You want me to calm down? This ingrate just looked me in my face and lied to me."

"Ma, I'm not lying. Both of us were there with you. Why are you acting crazy?"

It took everything in me not to slap him, "Boy, do you know who I am. You seriously didn't even have a better story to cover your behind when I found out. Yeah, I saw you and "your brother," but when I was forced to think about it, I never actually saw you both at the same time. Since you claimed you met some nice young ladies, I didn't think too much of it. So, while you were in Miami pretending to be you and your twin, your brother was down in Tallahassee pretending to be your triplet."

His face showed he was busted. He finally gave up his denial. "So, ma, you swinging on me over this cat you don't even know?"

"Oh, I know him. I've always known him, you just didn't."

I saw the shock and hurt on his face, but I was too mad to care at the moment. I asked, "Orlando, where is Dallas?"

He sucked his teeth and turned his head as if to say he wasn't gonna answer me. I was about to knock his teeth out, but Cassia knew me too well and stepped back in between.

She said in a tired voice, "Baby, answer your mama. No more secrets, okay."

He looked hesitant but she pleaded, "Do it for me, baby, please."

He cut his eyes. "He's not here, ma, he just went to the store right quick. We ain't got no tissue."

That was lame. I didn't buy it. I crouched down to get in his face because he was still on the floor. Barely short of a growl, I said, "Now, technically, no one can actually tell you two apart. Y'all made sure of that by getting identical tattoos, but you are going to tell me which one of you impersonated Seth and why. You're also going to tell me how in the hell you found out about him in the first place, and why y'all went behind my back." I tossed him my phone. "Call your brother and tell him to get his black behind home, and I mean now!"

Chapter 34:
True Lies

Cassia Reynolds

I had been dreading this moment for a couple of days. Dallas refused to come home the other day because Monie's crazy behind was threatening bodily harm. I had to manhandle her, but she eventually agreed that everyone should cool off and reconvene when we were capable of compartmentalizing our emotions, her asinine terminology, not mine. I swore that friend of mine could sometimes be a certifiable case, but you gotta love her.

I was on my way to Monie's house. I was as nervous as a weed head about to take a piss test. I just didn't feel right. I hadn't slept well in two days. Life, as we knew it, was about to change. Monie was right. I should have asked more questions. I was already predisposed to be soft on them. My long lost stepbrother had just recently reached out to me. I was making strides on repairing my once hopeless relationship with my moms. Life was crazy, but it was about to get a little crazier. I didn't mind the twins finding their brother, but impersonating and knocking some chick up wasn't even like them. How could they keep this from me? I'm the cool aunt. I get all the secrets. I always covered for the little ingrates, and this is the thanks I get.

I pulled up to Monie's place so we could have our come to Jesus meeting in the boardroom she put in when she had her house built. Her place was arrogant and sophisticated with just a hint of danger, just like its owner. It was one of five homes in an entire subdivision. She had the cul-de-sac. The first level was gray stone with floor-to-ceiling windows. The second level was glass, bullet proof of course. The woman was as paranoid as a schizophrenic in a padded white room with ambient noises.

I got out and walked up the long slate walkway to the towering glass doors. I was going to knock, but I decided not to mess with Monie and just use my key. When I walked in, the hardwood floors were immaculate as usual. Her purple suede couches were very inviting, but I turned left, and ran up the glass spiral staircase. I didn't want to scare her because knowing Monie she'd probably pull a gun on me. I opted for the safe plan and yelled for her as I walked into her mini version of our headquarters' board room, "Monie! I'm here."

She was on the phone, and she shushed me. She looked like she was not thrilled about the conversation she was having. I had to admit that I never saw Monie look as stressed as she did now. She usually handled everything life threw at her with a viciousness and steady hand that would make a crooked politician bow at her feet. I guess this was indeed a matter of the heart for her, which was way out of her element of things she could control. She had her hair barely pulled into a sad little ponytail. She had on a wrinkled plain white t-shirt, baggy jeans, and oh, my God, she was barefoot with her toes not freshly done. I seriously underestimated what this situation was doing to my friend.

I crossed the room wearing a green sweat suit and sneakers just in case I had to jump in between the fighting Grayson's. I just wanted to hug her and convince her it was going to be okay, but I couldn't say that with complete conviction. She finally ran into a situation she had no control over, or rather the control she had was gone. I took a seat at the rectangular slate table that was jagged on one end that seated eight. The soft gray high-backed swivel chairs were just what I needed to relax before we opened up the floodgates of our lives that started so many years ago. It was finally coming to a head.

Monie clicked off the phone and placed her head in both her hands. She took an audibly deep breath and scrubbed her hands over her face. As she looked at me with her red eyes she said, "That was the private investigator. I wanted him to check out the mother of my soon-to-be first-grandchild. I needed to know the circumstances behind all this drama and I needed to know her family history, and what kinda blood will be running through the veins of my grand."

I shook my head. Monie still had to be in control. "Monie, have you not learned anything from all this? You're still trying to control everything, enough with the secrets already. Enough with the spying, can we just be normal people for once?"

She glared at me. I didn't care. Her wrath didn't scare me, I had traveled that lone road to hell one too many times for a look to scare me. I changed the subject to keep the peace because it was sure to disappear the moment the twins came into the room. I said, "Monie, it's only been two days. How did he get the information so fast?"

She grinned, "Well, that's why he is on my payroll because he is indeed the best."

I rolled my eyes, "So, what did he find out?"

"Well, according to the church gossip, Ebony, who was so easily persuaded with a couple hundred, and according to the background checks, she has been crushing on Seth for a while. She claimed that Seth knocked her up one weekend when they were out of town together. He denied it, and she was livid. She got booted out of the choir. He had to be sat down from his ministerial post."

I gasped, "Oh, my God. No wonder he's angry!"

She nodded and said, "Yeah, I can't blame him. He must have been beside himself when the DNA test that his wife made him get came back a match. Get this, he was out of town, in the same city, on the same weekend the chick was."

I shook my head. Oh, the tangled web we had weaved. She went on, "Crazy, right? Looks like fate gave her a big screw you. Her name is Naomi. Apparently, Seth's wife has tried to lay her out a couple times."

She smiled and said, "Now, that's the type of daughter-in-law I can be down for. Anyways, it caused a big uproar in the church and put a great strain on Seth's marriage. As far as the one carting around my grandbaby, her mother is dead, and she was raised by her aunt, her mother's sister. She doesn't know who her father is. He is possibly of another race and is believed to not be native to the United States. That's about it. It really doesn't matter because I plan to get it straight from the horse's mouth."

I sighed, "Monie, please, tell me you are not going to confront this girl you don't even know."

She shot me a hard look, "Now, Cassia, how well do you know me? There is no way me and this child are not going to have a conversation. She is the mother of my first grandchild. I think it's pretty normal for us to have a chit chat, don't you?"

"I sure do, Monie. I think the two of you should have a chat about how she's going to decorate the baby's room. What is she going to name the baby and where she is registered?"

I could tell I struck a nerve. She was about to go off, but the twins stepped through the door. Orlando walked in looking like the computer engineer he was, wearing cargo khaki pants and a pale yellow polo shirt. His rectangular rimless eyeglasses made him look confident and sophisticated. You would never believe how much of a clown he could be. Dallas, in contrast, never looked like the intelligent architect he actually was. He had on baggy jeans, though they weren't hanging off his butt because Monie and I would both knock him silly for that. He had on an Enyce t-shirt and wore that smile that I'm sure so many women found irresistible. They both wore their hair in low-cut Caesars, much shorter than usual. Since Orlando looked solemn and Dallas had a mischievous grin on his face, I could pretty much tell who was father of this infamous grandchild. Dallas was the culprit, no doubt. Since no one could actually tell them apart though, only a confession from one of them would make it official.

Monie rolled her eyes at both of them as they greeted us. I waved but kept silent because I was too busy studying them for clues. Those two were as tight as twins could ever be, and they were loyal to a fault. When they were about thirteen, they began doing studies on twins because Monie was always urging them to read. In their studies, they found a criminal case against a set of identical twins. They could not pin the crime on either one. They couldn't prosecute identical twins because they could not be told apart via their DNA. Only an identifying mark and an eyewitness who saw the mark could point the finger. It was Dallas' bright idea for them to get matching tattoos so they could never be independently identified. When they were eighteen, they got it done. Thankfully, they had never committed a crime. Still, they could impersonate each other down to the mannerisms and no one would be the wiser.

After the boys were seated, Monie spoke. She looked at them intensely. "I want to know everything that happened from the beginning, starting with how you two found out that you were actually born as three." Her tone was very finite. They knew she was done playing games. I just sat back because I knew this was about to get interesting.

Orlando cleared his throat, "Ma, let me just say that we're sorry for any hurt that we caused anybody, especially our brother."

Dallas interrupted, "Speak for yourself. I ain't sorry for nothing." He pointed at Monie, "She's the one that should be explaining herself. She's the liar."

Ooooh, this boy had lost his rabid mind. I wasn't even going to stand in the way if Monie slapped him because we didn't tolerate disrespect. Right or wrong she was still his mother. Monie sat back and didn't react, which was unusual and very scary. One point goes to Monie for her self control. I prayed her many weapons were very far out of her reach. Orlando said, "Yo, man, chill wit all that. I'm sick of the secrets, like I told you last night, I am telling the whole story, the good, the bad, and the ugly."

Dallas sucked his teeth when he stood up and said, "Whatever. I'm out."

Monie shot him the most vicious look I had ever seen and told him to put his posterior back in the chair. However, her words were much more colorful and contained minimal letters. I gasped audibly. I had never heard Monie curse at her kids, ever. He must've been just as shocked because he quickly took his seat as he folded his arms across his chest. Three points to Monie for throwing the curve ball.

Orlando cleared his throat, "Ma, the short version is about nine months ago, I was at the Boulevard Mall when this cat walked up to me all happy and shocked to see me. He was reaching for my hand, smiling like he knew me. I ain't wit that gay mess so I told homeboy to step off. Then, he looked at me like I was crazy. He called me Seth and asked me why I was acting like I didn't know him. Then, I relaxed because I knew it was just a mistaken identity. Dude wasn't gay, he was just weird. I told him my name wasn't Seth. He laughed and told me to quit playing. He told me I was the music minister at the church he went to in Tallahassee when he was in college, and that he used to sing for me in the choir. He said he was shocked to see me in Vegas. I told him he had me confused with someone else. He started to get noticeably upset because he thought I was playing

Surviving Sunday   - 233 -

or lying I guess. This cat argued me down for like five minutes about what my name was. He finally walked away frustrated. In anger, he told me to have a chat with my parents because I had a twin in Florida."

All I could think was wow, God sure had a way of revealing all things now didn't he. Five points for fate. I smirked and looked over at Monie. I had been telling her for years to come clean with the twins. They had a right to know. Monie didn't speak, but her clear brown skin was starting to tint red with fury. She took a breath and gestured with her hand for him to continue.

I focused back on Orlando as he continued. "So this, of course, left me unsettled. I mean, I knew I had a twin. I also knew he was not in Florida, and his name was not Seth. So, I left the mall and hit Dallas up to tell him what went down. Seeing as how nothing about our childhood was ever normal, we figured there was no reason why we couldn't have a triplet. So, we figured we would find out."

Monie asked, "So, why didn't you just come to me then to get clarification?"

Dallas said, "How come you didn't just tell us that you popped out three of us instead of just us two?"

I smirked. Two points for the twins for the snappy come back. I could tell Dallas was angry and hurt so I was going to have to ignore the disrespect until we got through to the truth behind all this. He looked at me and said, "We asked Aunt Cassia. She confirmed but would give no particulars. She said that you were working to get in contact with him. She asked us to wait, and we agreed, but that was a lie. There is no integrity amongst liars, huh?"

It took everything in me not to snap at him because I didn't lie. Orlando said, "Chill, Dallas. We are all civilized adults."

He looked at Monie to make sure she was chilled as well. "Ma, we started looking to see if we could find anything. As you know, if you look for something hard enough, something is bound to turn up."

Dallas smirked and took over the story. "Yeah, you know, you raised us to put education at the top of our list of things to do. So, we used our educated minds to find out what that private investigator you had on tap had been up to. Because let's face it, if we did have another sibling, not only did you know where he was, you would know everything he was doing. We also know that there was only one private investigator you trusted to do your dirt."

Ooh, four points for the twins knowing Monie so well. I looked over at Monie. Her arms were now folded across her chest. Who knew her kids were just as sneaky as she was? Monie said, "There is no way that Lewis gave you my information. If he did, his downfall will be on your conscience because, you know, no one crosses me and survives to tell about it."

This time it was Orlando who cut her off. "Yo, chill with all that femme fatale nonsense, ma. We," he pointed to him and Dallas, "are not afraid of you, besides, give us more credit than that. We didn't get the information from Lewis."

Dallas chuckled, "We got it from his assistant."

With a straight face Orlando said, "Let's just say she became chatty during pillow talk."

Dallas said, "As you know, she's always had a thing for us."

Oh, that nasty slut! Her butt did not screw one of my babies! She was well past my age. I guess it was smart on their part. Monie never treated the woman well. She was probably dying to get back at her. Even though I was disturbed, I just had to ask, "So, whose pillow heard her talking?"

They both showed me the exact same smirk at the exact same time and Dallas said, "The world may never know." Well, five points for the twins for hitting her with the unexpected.

Monie had had enough. I got ready to jump in between them at any given moment. Just as quickly as she jumped up, she sat back down. She rubbed her hands over her face and screamed. The three of us just sat there and watched to see what she would do next. She removed her hands and looked at Dallas and said, "Please, continue."

Okay, she was starting to scare the crap out of me. This was not a woman who chose talking over violence. Dallas said, "She told us that we had a brother in Tallahassee who had been adopted by a white family. She said he was married and was a minister at Kingdom Builders Worship Center. So, naturally, we got curious and wanted to check him out."

Orlando said, "She gave us copies of all the files Lewis had collected over the years. She also told us how proud you were of

Seth and all the things you did to make sure he was well taken care of. She told us how you were behind his scholarship to school, how you sent money to the church he attends under another name, and how he has a trust fund that he gets when he turns thirty."

Dallas cut in, "Imagine our surprise that after thoroughly searching your financial records, there was no trust fund for Orlando and me."

Monie was livid. I know she had to be feeling awfully exposed. She said through clenched teeth, "I have my reasons. How exactly did you get a thorough look at my financials? I have great security."

They looked at each other and laughed. Orlando said, "Mama, you ain't raise no fools."

Monie got up, walked out the room, and slammed the door behind her for emphasis. Orlando sighed and leaned back in his chair. Dallas had a smirk on his face. I knew them as well as a mother could. He was hurting. I just wanted to hold him. I knew Monie was a hard woman to understand, but she loved her boys, all three of them, the same. She had her reasons. Now getting her to come clean with her sons was altogether another story.

I said, "Look, guys, I know this seems kind of shady, but if you could just give her time to calm down, I'm sure she will tell you everything. There's still so much you don't know."

Dallas backed away from the table and stood up, "Man, whateva. If she wanted us to know, she would have told us years ago."

Orlando asked, "Auntie, do you know the whole story? Can you tell us because ma obviously had no intention of telling us?"

I shook my head, "It's not my story to tell. I can't betray your mom's confidence like that. She is my best friend, my family. Though I don't always agree with her, I won't give you information that isn't mine to give. I'm sorry."

Both of them looked away from me, and my heart was breaking for them and Monie, but what was I to do? "Listen, I promise I will do my best to convince your mom to give you the whole truth and nothing but."

Dallas said, "Man, this is some bull for real. Everybody's in on the lie, huh?" I decided to change the subject. It was time for them to know what damage they had caused.

"Can you please tell me how this girl, Naomi, ended up pregnant and which one of you is the father of her child?"

They stared at me like I had three heads. They had finally lost the upper hand. I said sarcastically, "Oh, that's right. You two didn't know that in all your plotting and scheming on your mother, you knocked up one of Seth's choir members and almost ruined his marriage and his reputation as a minister." Shocked silence.

I stood up and put my hands on the table as I leaned forward to get in their faces. "Now, I will not take up for your mother and say she doesn't have some things to answer for, but you two have gone just a little too far. You don't know anything about Seth. Now because of your selfishness, you have caused him irreparable pain and suffering. What the hell were y'all thinking? I wanna know what happened, and I wanna know now."

Dallas cleared his throat, "Auntie, did she say Naomi was pregnant."

"Yes, that's right. She is, and one of you is about to be a father. I don't know how, but thank God, Seth found out it wasn't his before he lost everything." I sarcastically said, "Oh, that's right he's innocent, too. He doesn't know about the two of you, either. Your mom kept him in the dark as well. So, whatever beef you have with him, it ends now. Do y'all hear me?"

They looked away. I asked, "Do I make myself clear?"

They both said, "Yes, ma'am."

I sat back down, flipped my hair and said, "Now spill it."

Dallas scooted to the edge of his chair and said, "I went up to Tallahassee to check him out while Orlando stayed here to keep mom off our scent."

I asked, "How exactly did you check out a man that looks just like you without anyone noticing you."

He smiled, "Auntie, I am a man of many talents. I didn't look like him when I went to Tallahassee for a few days. Let's just say being Monet Grayson's son has its privileges."

I didn't know what that meant. I decided I didn't want to know either so I waved impatiently for him to continue.

"Anyways, I can't explain what it was like to see him looking like us and wondering if he had a clue. He wore his hair a little higher and thicker, but yeah, he had our exact face. The church service was actually pretty good for a Wednesday night. I mean, we didn't exactly get exposed to church growing up, just the principles of the Bible. After service, I heard people chatting about the new song he wrote and how much they liked it. The music was actually the best part for me. The message was cool, too. That pastor of his was a character. I got a glimpse of his wife. She was hot, and he seemed like a cool cat. I headed back to Jacksonville the next day because I was tired of wearing the disguise. That's why we took separate flights to Miami than you and ma. I actually had been gone days before y'all left. I hung out in Jacksonville. On Saturday, I went to one of the malls, I don't remember which one. This broad walked up to me and, basically, threw herself at me. Chick was bad as hell. She was acting like her and Seth had dealt with each other before. So, I figured Monet's little golden boy was not all he was cracked up to be. I took her up on her offer to prove it."

I threw my hands up. "Okay, let me get this straight. You knocked off some strange chick because she approached you as your brother in the mall. You did it because you wanted to prove he wasn't who he seemed to be?"

"Well, when you say it like that, it seems wrong, but dang, auntie, she was fine as hell. Under normal circumstances, I wouldn't need a reason to drop my seed off. After I knocked her off, she thought I was asleep, but I wasn't. I waited for her to fall asleep and that's when I went through her bag and found a journal. All I can say is that she was obsessed with Seth. She was plotting on trying to get him away from his wife, but he wasn't biting. Some Pastor told her that he was her husband or some bull like that. She was a whack job, and she was plotting on him something serious. The next morning, I tossed her silly behind as payback for what she was trying to do to Seth and caught my flight. Now, we did our thing, a few times actually, but I used protection. So, I'm going to want a blood test because that ain't my kid."

I rolled my eyes because men could be so stupid. "So, genius, did it ever occur to you she did it on purpose, and I'm pretty sure that it's yours because Seth's wife already got a blood test, and it tested positive for his kid. You can imagine how shocked he was seeing as how you were the one that had the pleasure of putting the bun in her oven! I guess you felt awfully stupid that in the end you wanted to protect him instead of prove him to be a phony?"

He shook his head, "Nah, not really. He was my blood, and she was just some crazy broad. Blood, whether you know about it or not, is thicker than molasses."

Orlando finally spoke up. "Auntie, we never meant for all this to happen. It was a mistake. We were upset and we were hurt. When Dallas told me what he did, I panicked because I knew that some kinda way this was going to end badly. After we thought about it, we just figured that since she was delusional, no one would believe her anyway. Besides, Seth would obviously have an alibi for the night in question. Now, I'm sorry for all that has happened, but the bottom line is some truths needed to be revealed. As soon as your precious Monie gets herself together, she can spill her guts, too."

I had a headache. I couldn't wait for all this to be over. I had to tell Mr. Know It All that he couldn't be more wrong. "Well, sweetheart, I would like to inform you that fate screwed your logic royally because Seth did not have a solid alibi. He was apparently in the same city as you were that night—giving him ample opportunity to be the one to knock her up." Shock resonated on both their faces. Just then, Monie walked back in. She looked calm, cool, and collected like the Monie I knew.

We all stared at her as she cleared her throat. "I just got off the phone with Seth. I have scheduled a family meeting."

I smirked. It looked like she was back to her old self, in control, and in command. She went on, "I asked him how he found out that he had a twin, and he gave me just two words, the tattoo. I couldn't help but chuckle at the irony because the very tattoo that you two decided to get to keep everyone from telling you apart is the one thing that separates and sets your triplet apart from you."

The twins shared a glance. I didn't say a word. She walked up to get in their faces, "So, who's the father of this child?"

Orlando cleared his throat, and Dallas sheepishly raised his hand. Monie narrowed her eyes and said sarcastically, "Now, there's a shocker. Make no mistake about it; you will handle your responsibilities. It's bad enough my first grandchild will be a bastard. I had hoped you two would take a more morally sound road than I did." Dallas shifted uncomfortably in his seat but didn't respond.

Monet continued, "Now, we will meet on neutral ground at a hotel conference room in Tallahassee so that I can finally clear my conscience. I am very disappointed in the two of you for going behind my back and concerning yourselves with things you have no clue about. I can't change the past, but I can give you the information you have so maliciously sought out. Hopefully, you'll find some peace with your personal demons. We leave in three days."

She walked out and closed the door behind her. I thought, *Ten points for Monie for getting the very last word!*

Chapter 35: Revelations

Lance and Darrow stood over Josiah and Darcy sleeping peacefully. Since their adversary was scrambling to mount forces after what had taken place during the last battle they had no resistance. It was time to reveal all that was behind this current attack. Lance glorified and laid his hand on Josiah's head. Darrow glorified and touched Darcy on the crown of her head. The room was washed in a brilliant emerald shimmer.

After a while Josiah woke up in a cold sweat. His heart was pounding. The dream he just had really had him out of his element. Josiah looked over at Darcy to see if he had awakened her. Just then, she popped up, too. Darcy grabbed her chest and started breathing deeply trying to calm herself. Her eyes met Josiah's, and they just stared in silence for a moment. Josiah swallowed and said, "I had a disturbing dream."

Darcy blinked twice and said, "I had a disturbing dream too."

A little calmer now Josiah said, "My dream had Naomi and Pastor Percy in it."

Darcy's eyes widened, "My dream had Kadijah and Pastor Percy in it."

Josiah looked at his beautiful wife wearing the expression of someone ripped from their sleep. They both said, "It's Percy."

They scrambled out of bed. Darcy walked to her closet where Orion was waiting to minister and reveal to her as he glorified. Josiah walked to his closet and Roman was there already glorified. The sapphire glow replaced the emerald shimmer. The couple was none the wiser. It was time for some spiritual warfare that could only be fought in one's secret closet. They were on a mission to protect their congregation and they relied on God to show them all they needed to know in order to stop it.

Chapter 36:
A Family Affair

The boardroom at the Double Tree Hotel in Tallahassee was about to witness a meeting the likes of which it had never seen before. The presence and the power of the matchless king of creation was about to unfold. Already in attendance for this family reunion was Seth at the head of the glossy oak wood table that sat twelve. To the left of him sat Sheridan, Emma Lee Ellis, Darcy Stone, and Seth's parents, Shayla and Reece Richards.

Pastor Josiah was pacing the room silently praying to set the atmosphere for God to reveal and heal. He was glad his wife was there. She was his rock. Darcy looked in her husband's eyes and knew exactly what he was up to. She slightly bowed her head and began to give God praise for working everything out. Also present in the room, but not seen, were all four ministering angels, Aidan, Gage, Orion, and Roman ready to minister to the needs of God's people.

Seth was a nervous wreck. He had no idea what was about to take place and how it would affect his life going forward. He looked at his wife, his constant, and she smiled as she reached for his hand. Their marriage was back on track these days. They both owned up to their faults and both decided to forgive and rebuild. He was so grateful to have her back in his corner with nothing but love and complete trust between them. His stomach was in knots. He looked at his parents for their reassurance and was pleased to see that they looked calm and ready for whatever the day brought on.

His mother was beautiful with wild strawberry blonde curls that complimented her deep blue eyes. She reached for her husband's calloused hand and smiled at his handsome face. Reece Richards was a strikingly handsome man with angular features and jet black hair that dramatically contrasted his light gray eyes, giving him a mysterious look. Sheridan's mother, Emma Lee, reached for her daughter's hand. She was honey brown with big black eyes. Her hair was a short texturized salt and pepper precisely cut coif that complimented her flawless slender face.

No one had yet to spark up a conversation. The silence was about to drive Reece insane. Just when he thought of something clever to break the tension in the room the door opened and in walked Naomi and Tameka as if someone had just yelled action! Immediately, Seth noticed something was different about Naomi. He couldn't quite put his finger on it because his mind was too preoccupied. They walked to the other side of the table. Before they sat, Tameka gave Naomi a light push in her back for her to come clean right then.

Sheridan came to the realization that Naomi's belly was indeed missing more than a few inches. The confusion made her head hurt. Naomi cleared her throat and tried to find the most sympathetic face in the room to make eye contact with. She couldn't find one so she looked down at her trembling hands. She knew she had to do it so she thought the best way to do it would be like ripping off a Band-Aid.

She cleared her throat and said, "There's something I need to tell everyone in this room." Sheridan tightened her grip on her husband's hand and Naomi uttered the words, "I lost the baby four weeks after the paternity test. I've been pretending like I was still pregnant because I thought it would help me get Seth. Then, the lie just snowballed. After I found about his brother, I knew it was time to tell the truth."

She took a long exhale. Shayla's gasp was loud, but she didn't say anything. Darcy shook her head as she thought, *that girl is going to hell on a scholarship if she does not get her little self together.*

Naomi looked sincerely defeated and said, "I'm so sorry. I wanted to let it go, but I kept hearing the words Pastor Percy said to me, that Seth was my husband, and I wanted to believe it so bad that I was willing to do anything to see it come to fruition."

Sheridan could literally feel her blood pressure rise and rush through her veins as she stood up. Seth, already anticipating this, had a firm grip on her elbow. Before he could tell her to sit or make sense of this new information, the strangers who were his family began to enter into the room.

In the hallway, outside the conference room stood two angelic beings guarding the doorway protecting what was to take place. Valter and Nero stood on either side of the door as the clan from

Nevada approached. With them, came a little imp named, Bitterness, walking with Dallas. The other military angels were on assignment due to their recent victory. They could not afford to leave any of their assigned saints unprotected. Ahiga had to return back to his post as one of the guardians of the gates at the church because they were expecting a new onslaught of demonic activity. They were the only two available until help arrived. Valter had not yet wanted his presence revealed, but this meeting could not take place without sufficient spiritual covering.

The imp wasn't likely to know him. They were dressed as ministering angels. The imp looked up with his beady yellow eyes that met those of Valter. He looked over toward Nero. He knew immediately that he was in trouble. He didn't think they were military, but you could never be sure when it came to the other side. Military or not, they still had significant power. He began to tremble in his black scales. As they approached, Nero drew his sword. As he placed it into the imp's neck, it became coated with a blue flame, the same blue flame that was now in his eyes.

Valter said, "You are not permitted to enter into this room, for this is holy ground."

Bitterness whined and said, "He is my host. He wants me with him. I have a right."

Nero said, "Not anymore. He has already been set free. The prayers of the righteous avail much."

Bitterness sneered and attempted to continue into the room.

Valter drew his sabre, but didn't let it flame, "Go now or die here."

Bitterness spat, "This means war. I will tell his highness that warriors are present."

Valter didn't respond. Bitterness was enraged that he wasn't able to keep his hold on his human. He also knew that he was no match for the two warriors. He sneered once for good measure before turning around to leave. Before he could complete the turn, Nero's sword sliced through him and limbs went flapping and flying. There was a muffled howl, and then there was nothing.

Valter looked at Nero. He just shrugged, "What? Nobody saw it. He was just annoying me. Now our adversary will never know that the Captain of the Host is present."

Valter shook his head, "He didn't know who I was."

Nero grinned and said, "Perhaps, but that one was for Ahiga." Valter smiled.

Cassia walked in first looking like a splash of beauty with her auburn hair pulled back into a classy chignon and not a hair out of place. Her make-up looked strategically placed to draw a second glance from any onlooker. She had on a royal blue sundress that managed to both hug her curves and flow freely at the same time.

Monet made her show stopping entrance just as Sheridan imagined she would, in an all white, a-line St. Johns suit. It screamed I am in control, and I look good doing it. It made all the others who were dressed in jeans and causal shirts feel under dressed for the apparent fashion show.

Just then, Orlando walked in wearing jeans and a white polo shirt. Seth thought he was looking at the nerdier version of himself. His second thought was he didn't look like the type of man to get Naomi pregnant. When Dallas walked in looking like the thugged out version of his self, before it dawned on him, he was three and not two. He thought he did look like the type to get her pregnant.

Then, it hit him, he literally heard his heart splash in the pit of his stomach as he blurted out what everyone in the room was thinking, "Oh, my God!"

Just then, the full meaning of Josiah's dream had hit him. He realized why the basketball game had been three-on-three. It also explained why he had it three times. He was just a little annoyed with his self that he didn't dig deeper for an explanation. Then, maybe it wasn't meant to be revealed until this very moment.

Monet had anticipated this reaction because after all, Seth only knew himself to be a twin, not a triplet. She seized the opportunity to take control over this little gathering. She walked right to the other head chair where she knew she belonged and stood behind it.

Her voice was strong and sultry. "I've waited almost thirty years for this moment. Seth, I realize this is a shock to you, but I told you there were many things I would wait to reveal. Since fate has forced my hand, I would like you to meet your mirror reflections, Orlando, and Dallas Grayson."

Naomi was having more trouble than all that attended as she looked at each of the triplets because at this moment, she had no idea which one she had slept with. That just did not sit well with her. Sheridan cleared her throat and slowly said, "Somebody better start talking and fast because my last nerve left the building when Naomi decided to tell us that she was faking her pregnancy for the last few months."

Sheridan had thrown a curve ball of her own. Dallas looked at Naomi and said, "Is she for real?"

Naomi felt unexpected shame for her transgressions and slowly nodded her head. Dallas fell into his chair like the wind had been knocked out of him. His emotions were already raw. This information had been the catalyst to make them explode. The knowledge he had a child on the way was a tough pill to swallow. The more he thought about his life and the lack of a father figure, the more he wanted to make it right for this child. The loss he felt at that moment was like no pain he had ever known. Pastor Josiah was not fazed by any of these revelations. He just kept right on pacing and praying for God to have his way.

Seth just stared at his mother. All he could think was how beautiful she was. Yet, at the same time, he loathed the very ground she walked on. She had controlled too much of his life, even though he had never laid eyes on her until this very moment.

Shayla despised the feelings of inferiority she began to feel the moment she saw Monet. The woman exuded beauty and grace with such effortless military precision it made her self-conscious. She resented the fact that she was jealous of this woman because she felt competitive for Seth's love. Reece knew his wife so well. He could sense everything she was going through. He whispered in her ear. "This isn't a competition, Shayla. Seth's love for you will never change. This is going to extend his family, not replace it. It's okay, sweetheart."

Shayla blinked back tears and realized her husband was right. She decided to work hard to let go of all her counterproductive emotions.

Tameka looked around and thought; *thank God, I am just an innocent bystander in all this mess. I can't believe there are three Seth's in one room. This has got to be the most bizarre thing I have ever seen.*

Orlando began to feel Dallas' pain. He could see why Naomi got his brother caught up. She was breathtaking. He also could see why Seth didn't want her because his wife was a knockout. He hadn't realized how sincere Dallas was about his child until his brother's pain shot through his heart. Had Seth not been so caught up in his own turmoil over seeing his mother for the first time, he too would realize that the deeper ache was Dallas' pain, not his own.

Monet was heated. She wanted to slap the little manipulative wench into the middle of the next decade. She stared hard at Naomi making her shrink down in her seat. "How exactly did you get the paternity of a pregnancy you faked?"

Naomi muttered, "I lost the baby a few weeks after the test was completed."

Monet could not believe her ears so she chose to temporarily block it out. She pointed at Tameka and asked, "And you are?"

Tameka cleared her throat and said quickly, "I'm Naomi's best friend. Just here for support."

Monet didn't like that her question had gone unanswered. She was trying to manifest her softer side these days so she smiled and asked, "And do you have a name?"

She said, "Yes, ma'am. I'm Tameka."

"Well, Tameka, this really only concerns family so I would ask you to please leave. You can take your little lying friend too since she is no longer incubating my family's DNA."

Cassia groaned deeply on the inside, silently begging Monet not to go there, but it was too late. She said, "Monie, chill. She should be in this room, too. She and Dallas definitely have some things that need to be cleared up."

Monet was pissed that Cassia just fronted her. She did not want all these random people in her business so she said, "Tameka, you can keep moving." Tameka had had it, but she didn't want to disrespect an elder. So had Darcy and it was time to let Ms. Monet know.

"Excuse me, Ms. Grayson. I understand you probably possess the most information to clear things up, but that doesn't give you the right to treat people like pawns on a chessboard. No one is in control of this meeting, least of all you. So, Tameka stays. Naomi needs a source of support, too. Didn't you bring your best friend with you to metaphorically hold your hand while you faced your demons?"

Monet was beyond shocked and pissed, but she was not a woman to be caught and stay off guard. Monet stared at her incredulously. Darcy met her stare and said, "I ain't always been a first lady so if you feeling froggy."

Josiah shot his wife a look that said please don't go there as he prayed for peace in the room.

Emma Lee thought her money would be best spent on Darcy, although she could see that Monet was nobody's pushover. However, if she thought she was going to just run up on her first lady, she had another thing coming.

Cassia vowed never to put her hands on a person of the cloth, but if this first lady took it to the streets, she would just have to meet her there. No matter what the situation, she had Monie's back.

Monet never thought she'd meet a first lady with that spine. She found herself strangely respecting the woman so she didn't give her the tongue lashing she normally have coming. With their eyes, they made a silent truce. Emma Lee and Cassia felt the tension ease so they too went back to being ladies. Monet cleared her throat and said, "Let's try this again."

She focused her attention on Reece and Shayla as she allowed the words that had marinated in her heart so long to see the light of day. "I didn't exactly know that I would have an audience of people when I finally revealed this information to my sons. Mr. and Mrs. Richards, I cannot even begin to thank you for what you did for my son. I want you to know that I don't have any judgment in my heart for how you two came to be my son's parents. I want to thank you for loving him and allowing him to grow up to be the strong man he was always purposed to be. Whether you know it or not, you were an answered prayer. I believe that God's hands were always at work in all of our lives. I also wish I had the opportunity to thank the Redding's because I know they were very instrumental in shaping the man he is today. Since they're gone now, Cassia and I would like to establish something in their names. Could you please find a project in your hometown that really needs support and will make the difference in a child's life?"

Shayla had unshed tears swimming in her eyes and she said, "Yes, I'm sure that won't be an issue." Reece held tight to his wife's hand to let her know he understood this was a difficult moment for her as he gave Monet an appreciative nod.

Josiah now stood stationary in the back of the room as he continued to pray for hearts to open and communication to freely flow. The Lord was revealing to him every burden and every hurt of those hearts that needed some pruning.

Emma Lee patted Sheridan's hands as she knew her daughter was getting antsy. Sheridan cleared her throat and looked at Monet to nicely suggest she get on with this. Her concern was for her husband. So far, none of this was getting him any closer to reconciliation.

Monet smirked and thought again, she was going to get along with Sheridan just fine. Cassia reached out and grabbed Seth's hand. Her eyes never left Monet. Somewhere inside, Seth already knew that he loved Cassia and that she was a very special woman with a beautiful spirit. He had some emotion for his mother, but he wasn't quite sure what it was.

Monet sat down and said, "To my sons, you need to know that I love you all very much. There are no words that can describe how much. You all need to know that I love you equally," she said as she looked at Dallas. She knew he was the one that felt the most betrayed because he was the closest one to her. They had always had a tight bond as Orlando did with Cassia. Orlando was just like her so they tended not to always see eye to eye.

She continued to look at him and said, "This was never meant to be a betrayal. I had my reasons. While you may never understand, I will not apologize for them. The bottom line is because my pregnancy was surrounded with nonstop drama, I didn't get much prenatal care. I didn't know I was having triplets until a week before y'all were due. I told Cassia's brother, but our deal was only for one baby. I told him not to even think about making me give up the other two. He had no intentions of doing so. Seth, you just happened to be the first one out. That's how you ended up in Shayla's arms instead of mine."

Seth had a strange feeling of protection for his two brothers now that he knew he was the oldest. He didn't know them, but now he was aware that there was an almost telepathic connection being felt. He couldn't explain why, but he knew Dallas was taking this the hardest. Somehow, he also knew Dallas was the baby, the last one out.

Dallas was struggling with the feeling that he had to unburden his heart. There was no way he was about to cry in front of all these people. There was no way he was about to let his big brother's second impression of him be of a crybaby. Because the spirit of bitterness had left him, he no longer had any reason to hold back.

Orlando, the analytical one, was just processing each piece of information as it came out. He also had the realization that Seth was now connected to his thoughts. He wasn't quite comfortable with it. After all, he had only known him about twenty minutes. It was unnerving to realize Seth could understand his thoughts. He did his best to keep them neutral and keep Seth out.

Cassia said, "Listen, guys, we had a hard strange life. Seth, there was just no need to bring you out of your normal one into our chaotic one. Twins, we did the best we could. I wanted you to be sheltered from the life of Vegas, but your mother felt like reality was reality. There was no use hiding it. Yes, it is true that your mom has a trust fund for Seth that he will receive when he turns thirty."

All in the room who hadn't known this information was understandably shocked. Seth said, "I don't want your money, Ms. Grayson. I wanted a mother who wanted me. I wanted the father that gave me life to love me."

Monet didn't even flinch. She honestly felt no guilt for killing their father because she had convinced herself of that fact for many years.

She said, "Seth, it's not a pay off. It's what is rightfully yours. I cannot bring your father back. I don't know how else to say that you weren't abandoned. You were just loved from a distance."

Cassia knew the twins felt betrayed by their mother's words. She quickly said, "Orlando and Dallas, you two also have trust funds that you will receive when you turn thirty because it is also what is rightfully yours. It was started from the money your father left behind." That got all of their attention.

Cassia continued, "It was all Monet had to give you from the man who gave you life. However, while y'all were busy snooping through your mom's financials, you obviously didn't look at mine because your trusts are in my name. She did this because if Seth ever found her and had her investigated, she still wanted to be the one to tell him about you two."

They both looked at her in shock. Their hearts no longer carried the pain of being second rate sons to their newly found brother. That was, however, only one issue that was resolved.

Dallas could no longer keep his feelings to himself. Though he had control of his tears, he didn't have control of his words. "It's not about that corrupted money, ma. You raised us in a whorehouse. Do you have any idea what that did to our minds? How that made us see you? You took our father from us. Yeah, he was a bastard, but that wasn't your choice to make! We will never get to meet him. Even if he was behind bars, we would still get to lay our eyes on him and let him explain himself to his sons. You took his life without a thought. You have yet to show one ounce of regret. You act like you deserve a parade for taking him out."

For the first time in twenty-seven years, Monet finally felt something for having pulled that trigger. She didn't know what it was, but she didn't like it. The pain in her baby's eyes and words were causing her usually unmovable poker face to waver.

He continued, "That wasn't cool, ma. You made the choice to give Seth a chance for a normal life, but you were too selfish to do it for us."

He pointed at himself and Orlando. He turned his attention to Seth. "Big bro, to be honest, I was bitter. When we found out about you and the life she chose to let you have, the way she kept us from you like we weren't good enough, I hated you. It didn't matter whether you knew about us or not. Really, when I checked up on you, I didn't think you really had the integrity you were portraying yourself to have. I mean, I know you were raised differently, but in my mind, having a pimped out woman beater for a father and a murdering whore turned madam for a moms, you was bound to be deeply flawed just like us."

Monet's resistance had faded. Her son's true opinion of her coming to light in front of a room full of strangers was breaking down every façade she ever had. Cassia said, "Now, you wait just a minute, Dallas Levon Grayson. I don't care what you feel or don't feel. That is your mother, and you should be grateful to her for no other reason than she gave you life. You will show her the respect she deserves. Your father was a lowdown bastard that raped and beat me like I was nothing since I was fifteen-years old. You didn't live through what we did so you don't get to say what should and should not have taken place. He was evil, and he deserved to be punished."

She caught herself because she didn't mean to let all of that out. The twins weren't privied to all those details, but it was too late. She hadn't even realized her past hurts were so close to the surface. Her eyes met Monet's. She apologized with her eyes, but went on. "She took his life to protect mine, hers, and yours. Now, you apologize. If you ever call her out of her name again, you're going to have more issues than you can handle. Do you understand me?"

They were stunned. The new information only served to add more confusion to how they should feel. Dallas couldn't help it. The floodgates had been opened. He couldn't turn it back now. The little boy inside him who wanted his father said, "Don't make us choose between loving you and loving the man whose blood we carry. We will never know if he could have changed."

Seth felt a deep sadness for the soul of the father he would never know. Not because of the type of man he was or because he was killed, but because he never knew God. Even when Seth made it to heaven, he would still never get to meet the man who's DNA he carried. That was a pain he would never remove from deep in his heart. This was in direct contrast to the feeling of being blessed about the choice his mother made for him. His heart was breaking for his brother. He wondered where Orlando stood on the emotional scale. As if Orlando could read his thoughts, he looked at him and stood up.

"Come on, Dallas; let's step out for some air." Orlando looked at his aunt who was about to put a halt to it. "Just for a few minutes auntie, he needs to calm down and so does mama." He looked over at Monet. He didn't think she even realized tears were running down her face. Dallas stood up and followed his brother out of the room.

At that moment, Emma Lee, Shayla, Reece, Sheridan, and Tameka all felt the prick of the Holy Spirit to begin praying for this family. They all obliged.

Josiah started pacing as he asked God to release angels to minister to the two brothers standing in the hall. Seth felt the pull on his spirit as he got up and walked out to be the tower of strength his brothers needed. Behind Seth went Aidan and Gage to minister to the brothers that finally found each other.

Josiah then focused his attention on Naomi as he went to her and placed his hand on her shoulder. He began to specifically intercede for her. Orion placed his hand on her other shoulder. As he began to minister to her, he glorified. In the spirit, there was a grandiose glistening blue sapphire light that cast sparkles all over the room and illuminated everything with a bold blue shimmer as he performed what he had been sent to do.

Cassia got up and went to Monet. She grabbed her friend and held her. In the comfort of her lifelong friend, Monet finally found the strength to be weak.

She released years of fear, regret, and anger on the thankfully, sturdy shoulders of her partner in crime. Monet suddenly realized her arrogance and controlling issues that caused her sons so much pain. She also realized the guilt she had buried long ago for playing God and taking a life. It's not that she didn't have the right to protect herself, but she didn't have the right to be so nonchalant and unapologetic about ending that life.

Darcy's heart prick led her to the two friends embracing. She went to them to cover them in prayer as the healing process began.

Roman went with her, laid his hands on Cassia and Monet and he glorified as the healing began. The blue sapphire shimmer was so bold it would have blinded the humans present if they could only behold it.

Naomi was being flooded with the realization of all her abandonment issues. Wounds she refused to deal with were being opened. She could feel the spirit of God pruning her heart as the tears of freedom began to fall incessantly from her pain-filled eyes.

Outside, in the hall, Seth saw Orlando with his hand on his brother's shoulder as Dallas gave in to his pain. He wasn't sure how to approach them as he silently asked God for guidance because he knew Orlando was fighting their connection. He was overwhelmed by the love and loyalty he felt to these two men who he had only known for a few moments. When he and Orlando made eye contact, Seth was taken aback that he knew exactly what he was thinking. At the same time, he could feel Dallas' hurt. Aidan touched Orlando and glorified as he began to minister to him.

Orlando had felt an inexplicable presence hit him that somehow made him understand that Seth could indeed be trusted. So, he let him in. Seth obliged his brother's silent request. He sat on the bench beside him. He reached for Orlando's hand as Orlando's other hand was still resting on Dallas' shoulder. Gage laid a hand on Seth's shoulder and glorified. He began to guide his prayer. The brilliance of their sapphire light coated everything within a mile of them. Valter and Nero marveled. It was such a beautiful sight to behold as the power of the Lord God Almighty shaped and changed lives. They rejoiced as they glorified with a blinding white light. Oblivious to all the grandeur around them, Seth began to silently pray. He knew both of his brother's could hear every word he was saying without him ever opening his mouth:

Dear Lord, thank you for finally bringing us all together and for giving us an opportunity to unburden our hearts. Lord, let this be a moment we always remember as a turning point in each of our lives. Let us remember this as the day you delivered us from all the issues that we have as a result of a past none of us had any control over. Father, help us to believe and accept that all things work together for our good whether we understand it or not. Help us to realize that your thoughts are higher than our thoughts and your ways are not our ways and because of this, we can trust you to bring about healing. Thank you for bringing my brothers and our beautiful mother into my life. Thank you for our Aunt Cassia who paid a high price to love us unconditionally. Help all of our families to be stronger because there is an abundance of love. Lord, show us the purpose that you have for us and guide our steps to reach it. Help us to forgive our father, our mother, and each other for all the things that have manifested. Father, please, forgive us of our sins and connect each of our hearts to each other and to our mother.

Please heal all the hurts and let your peace that surpasses understanding rest upon us right now. Give us the courage to be honest and open with each other and give us the strength to accept one another's feelings. Give us the wisdom to deal with it all in Jesus name I pray. Amen.

Dallas and Orlando both said, "Amen."

It served to shock Seth as well. He just couldn't get used to having his every thought known. The twins laughed at their brother's ignorance of their twin speak. They had several stories to tell him about their exploits but another time. As they stood, Orlando said, "I don't have as much anger as Dallas does, but I do pretty much feel the same way he does. I just happened to be the one to inherit Monet's ability to compartmentalize my emotions and not let them dictate my actions."

Seth said, "I had so much love in my life growing up, I really didn't have a complaint, but there was always this emptiness, this feeling like a part of me was missing. I assumed it was my birth parents because as you can tell, it was obvious that my parents were a little different."

Dallas had his composure back as he looked at Seth and said, "I am so sorry for everything I've put you through."

Seth said, "You know what? While I was going through it, I couldn't see the light at the end of the tunnel, but now that I have, I know God was in control the whole time. It was all worth it to be standing here with you two right now. Dallas, it doesn't matter who our parents were or are. We are who God says we are, and we are not constricted to be either one of our parents. You are fearfully and wonderfully made, and you are made in the image of God."

Dallas accepted the seed of wisdom and let it take root in his heart. The brothers embraced as their burdened hearts were freed. When they separated, Dallas asked Seth, "Who's Renet?"

Again, Seth was stunned at how much they could read each other's thoughts—talk about accountability. He said, "She's my little sister. I guess I was thinking about how she would feel knowing she had two more brothers?"

Dallas and Orlando were shocked to hear about a little sister. Each one began to make room in their hearts for yet another addition to this rapidly growing family.

Orlando smiled and said, "Well, we can't wait to meet her."

Seth responded, "Y'all are gonna love her. She's great. She is going to flip when she looks up and sees three of me?"

Dallas joked, "Well, how come it can't be three of me?" They all laughed.

Valter and Nero met eyes with Aidan and Gage. They all nodded and smiled, the way a proud parent would.

When they walked back in, Dallas walked straight to Naomi as Sheridan ran to hold her husband. Dallas squatted down to be eye level with Naomi and said, "I am so sorry for all the pain I have caused you. I only did what I did for selfish reasons without any regard to how it would affect your life. For that, I apologize. I'm also sorry for the loss of our child. I can't imagine what that must have been like for you to go through."

Naomi's heart was so overwhelmed with her visit from the presence of Jesus Christ. She reached for his hand and said, "I accept your apology and offer you one of my own because my intentions were just as wrong as yours. I'm so sorry. I'm sorry that I lost your son or daughter."

"I didn't think I cared, but there's a pain for that loss that I just didn't expect. Maybe we can have a memorial stone put up for the baby so we can properly say goodbye."

Naomi smiled because she knew that would finally help her put her child to rest. "I would like that very much." Neither one of them knew it, but the seed had just been planted for a very special friendship that both of them never knew they always needed.

Monet walked across the room to her sons as Dallas stood to his full height. It was breathtaking and did her heart good to see all three of her handsome sons standing side-by-side. For the first time, she could see how much they actually looked like their father instead of just each other. It was like them being together put a look on their face that was never quite complete until that moment.

She stood in front of them with genuine remorse and said, "I am sorry I took your father away from you. I was afraid. In my mind, not only was I protecting me and Cassia, I was protecting all of you.

I cannot give him back to you, but we can put our heads together and figure out how we move forward with that issue."

Seth asked, "What was his name?"

"His name was Parker Easton." They all nodded and had the same thought to consider taking on their father's last name. It just didn't seem right that his name hadn't lived on.

Seth didn't want to disrespect the man who raised him, but they all felt that somehow his name should live on. Maybe they could bring honor to it in this generation and erase the negative connotation from their bloodline. Ultimately, Seth decided to keep his last name to honor the man who raised him because he had no other son. Orlando kept their mother's. Dallas was the one to change his last name to their father's so that all of their legacies would live on.

Monet went to her baby, Dallas, and placed her hands on his cheeks as the silent tears flowed from his eyes. He whispered, "I didn't mean it, ma. I'm sorry."

She kissed his tears and said, "I know, baby. I'm sorry I couldn't see the pain sooner. Seems like the two of us need to have a heart-to-heart and put some things to rest."

He nodded and said, "I'm ready when you are."

Monet smiled as she moved to Orlando who had no emotion on his face. She knew she was looking at herself in the male form. He said, "I'm letting it go, ma. I forgive you, and I love you. I know we gon' be alright."

She let her tears fall as he kissed her forehead. Monet suddenly had a thought. While she had the attention of both Dallas and Orlando she asked, "Okay, since we are all spilling our guts, please, tell me whose pillow did the assistant talk to?"

Dallas burst out laughing really hard. Orlando smiled, and then blushed just for a moment as they both put back on their stoic faces. Technically, neither admitted anything but a mother knows. She thought that cougar better be glad she just got right with God otherwise, she would've caught a royal beat down on the house. She digressed. The much anticipated moment of holding her first born son was finally here.

She stepped over, looked him in his eyes as she grabbed his right hand, and looked to Sheridan to release the other so she could hold both of them. Sheridan gave her a no-nonsense look that she interpreted correctly as protective. She smiled because she knew she would enjoy getting to know her son's wife. They were both cut from two very similar cloths.

Sheridan reluctantly placed his hand in his mother's and whispered through her teeth, "Don't you dare cause him one more ounce of pain or we are going to have some problems."

Seth just shook his head and thought, *God I love that woman.*

He squeezed both his mother's hands as their eyes met. She said, "I love you, Seth. I want to always be a part of your life. I know that you have a mother. I don't want to take her place. I know I gave up that right years ago, but please find a place for me in your heart and in your life."

Seth grabbed his mother, held her tight, and finally let himself cry. After a few minutes, they released each other.

Cassia walked up to him all smiles and tears. She hugged him as she whispered, "I love you, baby. I've always loved you. I am so beyond ready to make up for all the years I didn't get to spoil you."

His heart warmed. He knew how truly blessed he was to be a part of this very unique family. He met Shayla's eyes. She was still holding his father's hands. They smiled to let him know they would be right there with him every step of this new journey.

Chapter 37:
Who Is Able to Stand before Jealousy

Pastor Josiah was sitting in the conference room at the church with his wife staring at that sniveling weasel, Pastor Percy. He used the term Pastor very loosely. They were seated at an eight-person conference table across from Percy. Also in attendance was a woman he had only talked to on the phone, Kadijah's mother or rather her stepmother, Margaret, who sat next to Darcy. Lastly, there was one of his own church members, Tiara, whom he recently found out had a connection to Kadijah that even she herself didn't know about. She was seated next to Percy. Orion and Roman were also in attendance. They were silently waiting for Kadijah to arrive.

He had purposely told her a later time because he wanted to observe these three people together. He wanted to see their reactions to Kadijah walking in. Margaret had already nearly had a stroke when she laid eyes on Tiara and then a heart attack when her eyes met Percy's. Because of his spiritual gifts of prophecy and the word of knowledge, Josiah could easily read their spirits. There was guilt and shame coming from Margaret. Confusion, resentment, and unforgiveness radiated from Tiara to the point it almost made her glow.

Percy wore anger and jealously like a second skin. All of those imps by the same names stood around the table with their human hosts. They weren't afraid of the angels present because they knew they were only there to minister. For her part, Darcy did what she knew she was supposed to do. She continued to pray in the spirit for truths to be revealed and for the healing of every hurting heart in the room.

Just then, there was a knock at the door. Kadijah heard Josiah's deep voice say, "Come in."

When she walked in, she was shocked to see her mother. Also with her were her protectors, Quan and Cheveyo. They did not conceal their identity. When they came in, the demons that were with the others all bared their fangs and hissed. They were the color of smoke, scaly skinned, and a few had wings. They resembled flying gremlins.

The one who had the strongest hold was Confusion. He knew he had a right to be there because Tiara had yet to rebuke him or to seek help for deliverance from him. However, the hosts were unfazed because they knew he was on borrowed time. The others that tormented her would not make it out of this room. Quan stood at the door and Cheveyo stood on the other side of the table against the wall to the right of Confusion. He drew his weapon and had it ready by his side to let the demon know his behavior would be controlled. There was plenty of prayer cover in the room and the demon knew it.

"Hey, ma," Kadijah said nervously. "What are you doing here?"

She caught sight of Tiara. Her spine stiffened, her palms went moist, and her throat went dry. Tiara stared back with such hatred that Darcy shivered. Kadijah didn't know for sure who Percy was though she vaguely remembered his face. Maybe she saw him in passing. Maybe he'd visited their church before. That probably wasn't the important issue at this point.

Josiah said, "Have a seat."

She obliged and sat next to her mother. He began again, "When you contacted me about a week ago with your disturbing story, I called a friend I have in law enforcement and began to do some digging. After I prayed, the Holy Spirit pointed me in the direction of your mother. Why don't you tell her who Tiara is Margaret?"

Margaret was a thick woman who had a pleasant oval face and inviting dark brown eyes, the same complexion as her skin. Today, however, those eyes were frantic with pain, guilt, and worry over the fact that her past was now back to take a bite out of the perfect little life she had carved out for herself. She licked her full red lips and began to stammer. Quan drew his weapon and cut down Guilt and Shame until they were nothing but vapors.

The other imps began to tremble as Margaret was finally able to confess. "She's, she's, she is my daughter."

Kadijah stared at her mother and blinked once, then twice. She stared so long her mother shrank down just a little in her seat.

"I had her about five years before I met your father. This is her father. She pointed at Percy. When I heard about her trying to take your life, I knew I could no longer run from my past. I haven't seen or talked to her since she was born. I had no idea her father even knew she existed."

Percy jumped in, "That's right you conniving wench. You told me you aborted our child. I didn't want you, but I definitely would have wanted to know I had a child walking on this earth. The only reason I got with you is because you were just there at a time I needed someone to be there. Imagine my surprise when I ran into a mutual friend of ours a year later who told me it was a good thing I got rid of you because they saw you knocked up and had I stayed with you a little longer, it could have been mine. Imagine my shock to hear you were pregnant. Then, you get rid of her, dump her off on somebody else while you go off and marry a man who already has a daughter and raise her like you were June freakin' Cleaver. You had all the love in the world to lavish on this man's child, but didn't even give your own a second thought, did you?"

At this point, Margaret was all but a puddle of tears. Kadijah was starting to put the pieces together, but it still didn't make her feel any better about this disturbing new revelation.

Percy went on, "You can keep your tears because I've been a presence in my daughter's life every since she was nine-years old. That's how long it took me to find her. When she asked me about you, I told her the whole ugly truth. I took her out of the horrible existence you left her in. I knew she had resentment. I don't blame her. While I can't condone the measures she took, I can definitely understand them. I saw no reason not to let her hate for you be felt, if that's what she wanted or needed."

He looked over and cut his eyes at Josiah, and then looked back at Kadijah. "So, are you going to press charges on her or not because if you are, I will have her bonded out within the hour and the best attorney money can buy. She will plead temporary insanity and no jury is going to see otherwise when they hear about what she had to endure. If anything, they'll lock her sorry excuse for a mother up. If you're not, we will be on our way. I have had my fill of you people for one day."

Josiah spoke up calmly, but yet in control. "Percy, what is your issue with me and this ministry? I know this isn't the only problem you were at the root of. You also had something to do with the drama that took place with a choir member and my minister of music."

Orion touched Percy and convicted him to tell the truth. Percy looked momentarily shocked and pissed that he had been found out. Then, he thought, there was no time like the present to unburden his soul. "Don't sit up there on your righteous high horse, Josiah. You ain't nothing but a country Negro who hooked up with the right woman, my woman, and that's the only reason you are where you are today. This ministry should have been mine. Darcy should have been mine, but no, you went behind my back and took her and took my life. You are just as conniving as this no good mother of my child. The only reason I was even with her is because you took Darcy."

Darcy said, "Say what? Percy, what in the heck are you talking about?"

His eyes held hers. Josiah saw genuine love for her in them, but he didn't even bother with jealously because Percy was obviously living in a fantasy world. "Don't act like you didn't know I was in love with you. Of course, we were going to end up together. Why wouldn't we? We had been friends since we were children. We went to prom together. We even went away to college together. Then, this country bumpkin came out of nowhere with his little prayer group, and you acted like I didn't exist anymore. I know he told you nothing but lies about me to get you to leave me. It broke my heart to know you fell for it."

Darcy just looked at him for a moment. She realized she had to be careful with what she would say because he was on that thin line between insanity and psychotic, dangling dangerously close to the latter. "Yes, we were childhood friends. Of course, I loved you, but only as a friend. We went to prom together because we both didn't have a date and decided at the last minute to even go. It was just the logical choice, Percy. We didn't go to college together. You gave up your scholarship to Howard to follow me to FAMU. How could you possibly think there was anything between us? Granted, we spent a lot of time together, but we were like best friends back then. Nothing beyond friendship ever happened between us. Not even a single kiss." She'd said that for Josiah's benefit.

She continued, "Josiah never said anything bad about you. He never even thought you were an issue because I told him we were just childhood friends. You never once told me you felt more for me than that. Besides, you did date other women."

Percy genuinely looked crushed to hear the words come from her mouth. He knew her well enough to know she wouldn't lie because her integrity was one of the things he adored most about her, especially since he so rarely had any these days. His face contorted with the pain of knowing she never loved him the way he had loved her. The embarrassment flushed over him with the realization that all this time, his own imagination had been fueling his life into this downward spiral.

Percy's voice was barely above a whisper, "I dated them only to make you jealous, to make you see that you didn't want him. You wanted me. Why do you think I always told you about my relationships?"

Percy could feel the tears wanting to surface, but he refused to cry. He stood up to step outside and get some air. Quan cut down Anger and Jealousy. They were also vapors. Resentment and Unforgiveness began to back away from Tiara, but Confusion stood its ground with no fear. He knew he was too deeply rooted. All Josiah could do was think, *Wow.*

He definitely didn't see that as the root issue. He faced Tiara and said, "Sweetheart, your dad has been projecting his latent issues on you. While your mom owes you some explanations, Kadijah has nothing to do with what happened in your life."

Confusion eased his razor sharp talons into Tiara's skull. She made a sound no one could quite comprehend. It stopped Percy dead in his tracks. No one recognized her as the sweet shy Tiara. Now, her whole demeanor changed, even her posture. She was cold, calculating, and the polar opposite of whom they knew Tiara to be.

Her eyes even became darker. She said, "You don't know me. You don't know a thing about me. You don't know what I've been through, what I had to endure as a child. All because this complete waste of skin," she pointed at her mother, "was too selfish to be a mother to her own flesh and blood."

Her eyes took on a far off look as she said, "All the beatings, all the missed meals, all the neglect. For what, so she could play Mary Poppins a million miles away? Kadijah's not even her own flesh and blood. At least that would have been more understandable, but no, I couldn't even get a second thought. No happy birthdays, no loving grandparents, no trips to the park, no new dress for Easter, nothing but hate, and disdain from the people you left to raise me. You know how many foster homes I was in and out of? You didn't even care enough to have me adopted. You just left me at the hospital. It's all good because I did what I had to do."

Tiara had a flash of that defining moment in her life, when she was only five-years old. The day that her foster mother kicked her and broke a rib, in that moment, she didn't only break her bones, she broke her mind. The pain was so great that she was blinded by it. Tiara retreated because she could no longer face the life that was before her. In that moment, Janet was born. Her foster mother had stopped hurting her long enough for her rib to heal. By the time she was six, Janet had decided Tiara would no longer be a victim. She made sure of it. One night when her foster mother was sleeping on the raggedy sofa, she took the biggest knife she could find and held it to her throat.

Janet said, "Wake up."

She didn't budge, so she pressed the knife into her flesh enough to draw blood.

The woman was startled, but quickly got her wits when she realized her life was in danger. Janet told her that if she ever touched her again, she would kill her in her sleep, and burn the remains. Six days later, she was sent to another home. Even though the abuse had ceased, she didn't exactly have happy childhoods in the next few foster homes she lived in until her dad found her. The damage, however, had already been done.

Margaret's sobs were even louder. Kadijah's face held her own tears of pain for her mother's daughter. She was starting to understand Tiara's wrath and starting to lose respect for the woman who had raised her, loved her, and helped shape her into the person she was today. Then, she felt something she had begun to realize in the past week as Holy Spirit conviction. She knew the right thing to do was to forgive her mother and Tiara, and to let God work it all out. That was easier said than done.

She asked, "Tiara, what happened to me?"

Janet smiled a smile so evil it made Kadijah's skin crawl. "My name is Janet. That wuss Tiara could never do what I did to you. I just slipped something into your drink that last time we hung out, and I took you to the club. My intention was to first ruin your reputation before I sent you away permanently. I was hoping someone would see us there. It didn't matter if they saw me because after I was done with you, I was leaving this dump anyway.

Through no fault of my own, you fell down the stairs at the club. You bruised your ribs, fell, and hit your face. You were lucky you left with all your teeth. Once I got your drunken butt in the car, I took you to this abandoned house I'd found. My intention was to set it on fire while you were still in it. I left you there because I had to leave to go take care of some other things. I knew no one would find you. When I got back about an hour or so later, I started to sprinkle the gasoline to make sure the whole place would be engulfed in the flames. However, every single time I tried to light it, the flame would go out."

She pounded her fist with every word to drive her anger home. The hosts exchanged a knowing smile. She couldn't light it because Quan kept blowing it out. She went on, "Then, I heard a car start. I knew it had to be you. It couldn't have been anyone else. When I went to get in my car, I couldn't get the door to open. It just wouldn't budge like it was stuck."

The angels were at fault there too as Cheveyo had stood against it to get Kadijah the head start she needed. The others in the room were frozen in shock and surprise. She continued, "I finally got it open. Your tire blowing out was pure luck. Finally, something was working out in my favor." Confusion smirked at the angelic hosts because he was the one to use his talons to slash the tire.

"I just don't know what happened with that gun. Someone somewhere must have really been praying for you. Once I realized you weren't going to shoot me, I figured I would just try again another way, another time. The only reason I am here is because my dad asked me to be." One angel had jammed the gun while the other told Kadijah what to do with it.

Kadijah was never really angry with Tiara so much as confused, but her mother, that was probably going to take some time. She felt such a peace flood over her as Orion touched her. She was shocked by the words that left her own mouth. She looked over at Tiara and said, "I forgive you. I won't be pressing charges. What do I have to fear? Obviously, no weapon formed against me shall prosper. My wounds are surface and will heal in no time. Yours are ingrained. That's where your energy should be focused. I'm so sorry about the things that happened to you."

Cheveyo raised his war scythe to Confusion's neck and told him to let Tiara speak. Confusion reluctantly removed his talons from her head. Just then, they all witnessed her once confident face fall to pieces and look like the shy Tiara they always knew. Even her eyes changed back to their original shade.

She was sobbing uncontrollably and begging, "Please, help me, please. I don't wanna do this anymore. Make her stop. Tell Janet to go away, I don't want to do this anymore. I'm tired of missing spaces of time, waking up, and not knowing what I've done. She's trying to take over. She doesn't want me here. Kadijah, I'm sorry. I tried to stop her. I swear to God, I tried. I'm just not strong enough."

Darcy was traumatized to say the least. She felt like she knew what she was witnessing, but she wasn't willing to accept it as reality. She asked, "Tiara, who is Janet."

Still sobbing, she said, "She's the one who protected me when I couldn't handle any more pain. Now I can't control her. I can't stop her. She has so much hatred in her. I can't fight anymore. I can't fight her."

Percy felt his knees weaken. He had to lean against the wall for support. Percy was a man with many faults, but there was one pure thing in him. That was his love for his daughter. He knew she had issues because of her initial upbringing, but he had no idea it was to this level. He could clearly see he played his part in this moment as well as her mother. He whimpered, "Dear God, please, no."

Roman began to minister to Percy, to convict his heart to make him see it was time he rededicated his life to Christ. Margaret finally got her voice and said, "Oh, God, what have I done?" Cheveyo quickly took out Resentment and Unforgiveness. At least they wouldn't torture that poor soul anymore. Quan moved to take out

Confusion, who hissed. Cheveyo said, "This kind comes only by fasting and praying." Quan could feel his indignation rising. He knew Cheveyo was right. Confusion had gained power over the near two decades he had been tormenting Tiara.

Darcy reached for Tiara's hand. "There is a psychologist here at our church. I think you should start seeing her. This will take some serious prayer, fasting, and I know Godly counsel. It may even take medication, but we will help you. God would not bring this issue to the front if he wasn't going to do anything about it. It is well with your soul. You are no longer in this alone."

Orion gently laid a hand on Darcy's shoulder and said, "It's time to remember."

A secret she had been keeping for decades rose up like bile in her throat. It began to transition from the recesses of her mind and burdened her heart. She knew it was time to tell Josiah the whole truth. This situation hit too close to home for it to be a coincidence.

Percy went to his daughter and held her close as Margaret reached for Kadijah's hand. Kadijah sweetly eased her hand from her mother's grasp. She didn't hate her, but there just hadn't been enough time to digest all of this. The respect she once had for her mother was rapidly fading.

Josiah was overwhelmed by all that transpired in his ministry. In all his years, he had never witnessed so much that hit on levels like this. He was a man of faith. Even though he knew this battle was far from over, he was willing to do what he had to do. As long as God gave him the strength, he would keep on doing what God called him to do.

He looked at Percy. Before he could say anything, Percy said, "Josiah, I am ashamed of the man I have been for the last few years, but there isn't anything I wouldn't do for my child. I have lost my wife, my ministry, and my reputation. I know God will probably never allow me back in another pulpit. That's okay. I do know God is real, and I do know he is able. I will serve him with all my heart until he calls me home, if he would just save my child."

Josiah nodded with the understanding from one father to another and said, "Let's pray."

As they prayed, Cree came in and whispered something to Quan who still stood by the door. Quan looked at Confusion and commanded him to leave. Tiara had made it clear that she no longer wanted him there. The saints had begun to pray over her. They knew he would be back, but not this moment. For this moment, Tiara would have peace in her mind. Cheveyo asked, "What was the message?"

Cree replied, "The next phase of the battle is on the horizon. The Almighty has sent a message to Josiah that this is inevitable. Josiah needs to train his saints for what's coming. They need to be discipled. They need to be rooted and grounded in the Word and their faith. They need to mature above the petty stuff, the gossiping, backbiting, complaining, and doubt. They need to stay in tune with the spirit. This ministry is destined for greatness to make changes in the earth, but there is an attack coming to stop it. He must be warned now! He must start preparing the saints now! The next battle has been set. Josiah's house will be tested. Lives hang in the balance so he must pass what is to come. There are great trials coming for the saints, but it is all for God's Glory. We must go and prepare our army for the battle ahead."

The warriors left the saints in the conference room praying with Orion and Roman to minister.

Chapter 38:
Chariots of Fire

In Josiah's prayer time, God told him to set his seven ordained ministers, three ministers in-training, plus all his deacons, and deaconesses on a seven-day fast. They were to send for help and for protection for what was to come. All of the leaders were on one accord. They were obedient to the call of their shepherd because they too, could feel something was indeed going on. As the week began to come to a close, they had fasted and prayed their hearts out. Unbeknownst to their sight, but not their faith, help did indeed arrive.

All throughout Tallahassee and the surrounding cities, military angels began dropping in. Hundreds of them descended like streaks of blue fire that only lasted for a tenth of a second. They began to conceal themselves in the woods by taking on the form of animals. Some hid in churches. Some took up residence in the homes of praying saints from every denomination. Others hid in plain sight as humans. They were there to stir up prayers and keep evil at bay, making sure the saints were ready to send for more of their kind. They would wait patiently for the shofar to blow when the Captain of the Host would lead them into war.

Epilogue:
Six Months Later

Sheridan

I heard the ring and walked over to pick up my cell. It was Mia. "Hey, Mia, how are you?"

"I'm fine. I was just calling to finish finalizing the plan for our bootleg family reunion."

I laughed, "Yeah, I guess it is kinda bootleg. You got white folk, black folk, blood relatives, fake cousins, Christians, sinners, and everyone in between."

She laughed, "Hush, nut. Anyways, so Jeremiah has worked out the menu. You know, he has a million siblings so he definitely knows how to cook for a multitude."

Seth walked over and kissed me on the forehead, and then he kissed my not yet visible baby bump.

I slapped him on his butt and said, "Well, anyways, Monet is staying with one of the twins. It's been interesting ever since they moved to Tallahassee. Seth's parents and sister will be staying here. Cassia won't get here until that Saturday because she will be on her honeymoon so she will be staying at a hotel."

"Oh, I'm so jealous she is going to be on a cruise. Though I doubt I'd be appealing to look at with my belly sticking out in between the bikini pieces."

That made me snort, "Girl, shut up. I am so happy for Cassia. Logan is going to walk her down the aisle. Her mom is going to be one of her attendants."

"Girl, God is too good."

"I know, right. Anyways, so Naomi and Tameka have confirmed their RSVP, and they will be here."

She asked, "And you're okay with that?"

"Yep, very much so. Besides, she and Dallas are like best buds or something. It's really funny how life turns out."

"Do you think something is going on between those two?"

"No because they both are dating other people. I suppose it's strictly platonic. Who woulda thunk it?"

"You better not let Grey hear you talking like that with that bad grammar."

"I know, right. She would fuss me out."

"Speaking of Grey, she and her new beau are coming so he can meet the fam. I'm sure her clan is coming, too."

"Oh, that's right. She did finally hook up with her neighbor's cousin."

"Yeah, I hope he don't run after he meet y'all n-words." I laughed because we were all trying to stop using the term that so easily slipped off the tongue.

She went on, "However, Kadijah doesn't know if she is up for all the family stuff just yet. She isn't exactly on great terms with her mom. Tiara and her mother have a long way to go. I told her not to wallow in all that stuff and to get on with her life before she gets caught up in stuff she really doesn't wanna be in."

"Girl, I know. Sometimes you have to let folk go and just pray for them. God is doing some great things though. I can't talk about it, but I have seen some progress in Tiara. I believe God is showing me something there. I'm still praying about it. I am confident she will be completely healed. It didn't happen overnight, and it won't go away overnight."

"Oh, in other news, Jeremiah has this coworker that I think would be perfect for Orlando."

"Oh, Lawd, Mia, you are not trying to play matchmaker at my family gathering are you?"

"Well, maybe, it depends on how you define matchmaker. I won't throw them right in each other's faces. I'll just drop little hints and plant opportunities for them to notice each other, that's all."

I laughed, "Any mess you make, you are cleaning up on your own."

"Uh, what happened to female solidarity?"

"The same thing that happened to your sanity, it flew right over the cuckoo's nest."

She laughed and said, "And on that note, I am hanging up the phone. I will be there Friday morning to help you decorate. Well, more like supervise the decorations because my hubby says I can't do any heavy lifting, so nah-nah-na-boo-boo."

I couldn't help but laugh, "Bye!"

Letter to the Reader

Hello Reader,

I hope you have enjoyed reading *Surviving Sunday* as much as I have enjoyed writing it. Spiritual warfare has always fascinated me in ways I cannot even express. We have all experienced some event in life that lets us know there is something greater out there working on a level we just can't comprehend.

Even though this is a fictitious account, I hope it offered some insight as to how prayer works in our lives and the importance of each of our destinies. I also hope, in addition to entertaining you, you realize that no matter who you are or where you come from, God loves you and He has a plan for your life.

If this book in any way, shape, or form made you want to know Jesus Christ as your personal Lord and Savior, then I want to extend to you the free gift of salvation. It doesn't matter who you are, where you are or what you've done. You can stop right now and ask Jesus to come into your heart. It's as easy as your ABC's.

A = Admit you are a sinner, ask for forgiveness
B = Believe in Jesus Christ, that he died and rose again
C = Confess, I accept Jesus as my personal Lord and Savior

Romans 10:9-10 (NASB) —That if you confess with your mouth Jesus as Lord, and believe in your heart that God raised Him from the dead, you will be saved; for with the heart a person believes, resulting in righteousness, and with the mouth he confesses, resulting in salvation.

Sincerely,

Melinda Michelle

Discussion Questions

1. Have you ever been a victim of someone trying to use the Bible against you because you didn't understand it?

2. Have you ever had an experience that you feel you may have encountered an angel or a demon? Explain.

3. Do you feel that Monet was justified in taking a life?

4. Do you feel that Naomi losing the baby was a punishment or just life?

5. Did you agree with Sheridan's behavior throughout the ordeal?

6. If you were Seth, how would you handle the facts versus the truth?

7. Have you ever felt a burden to pray for someone? Were you obedient?

8. If you were Grey, would you have walked away from your house or trusted God to save it?

9. Do you believe that mental illness can be healed through the power of prayer?

10. Even though Naomi's case was extreme, for entertainment value, have you ever had someone tell you a prophecy that you later found out just wasn't true? How did you handle it?

11. Has reading this book changed your perspective about your Christian faith?

Author Biography

Gwendolyn *Melinda Michelle* Evans (GMME) was born in Jacksonville, Florida. She was raised in Sanford, Florida and was introduced to reading at a young age. She has been a lover of reading since she could put two letters together to form a word. Growing up in a family of readers she was exposed to different genres of writing and developed an eclectic taste in books.

She is a graduate of Florida A&M University with a bachelor of science in accounting. She went on to pursue her MBA with a concentration in finance and accounting at American Intercontinental University. She has worked for financial institutions for the past nine years only recently stepping out to write full time in 2012. She is the owner and founder of Global Multi Media Enterprise (GMME) a free-lance writing, publishing and media company. She currently resides in Tallahassee, Florida.

Through the encouragement of family and close friends she turned her passion for reading into a passion for writing. She can always be found with a book somewhere within her reach. Once she realized it was a gift from God it was easy to see the purpose behind it. Being able to combine her faith and her passion to tell a good story is something she counts as a blessing.

It is her hope and desire that she can shed a positive image on the church, which she feels is viewed negatively by the world because of the actions of a small percentage of Christians. It is her desire to be able to tell a story that connects with Christians but also connects to people who just like to read. She tries to create a captivating story with powerful testimonies about the power of God.

Melinda Michelle's other published works include the short story "You Can Never Leave." It can be found on Amazon in e-book only. Her novel "Surviving Sunday" is the first of seven in a series. Book two, "Monday Madness" is due out in the summer of 2013.

Surviving Sunday

CPSIA information can be obtained
at www.ICGtesting.com
Printed in the USA
LVHW041504190219
608034LV00002B/289/P